IVORY TOWER

The Curious Cases of
Professor Colmes as told by his loyal assistant
William Hobson A.B.D.

IVORY TOWER

The Curious Cases of
Professor Colmes as told by his loyal assistant
William Hobson A.B.D.

BY
COLIN HESTON

READ-ME.ORG INC.
PUBLISHERS

Australia, New York & Philadelphia

Library of Congress Control Number: 2024932957

ISBN: 978-0-911577-70-9 (Paper)
ISBN: 978-0-911577-72-3 (Digital)

TABLE OF CONTENTS

Prologue

By William Hobson A.B.D.

Many friends and relatives or others who claim to know me have asked whether or not a particular novel or short story I wrote was "autobiographical." To this unavoidably prurient question I always answer, "all writing is autobiographical, and that includes nonfiction as well as fiction." To me the answer is obvious. I am a human. All of what I do is part of me, and thus logically is autobiographical.

Take any piece of writing no matter what topic or author. The syntax is often a dead giveaway, the choice of favorite or habitual words another. In nonfiction, the authors claim objectivity which is of course an impossibility (note that the words "author" and "autobiographical" begin with the same Greek syllable). You may doubt the truth of this claim, especially in respect to scientific writing. But just look closely at the issue or scientific topic that has been chosen. Will I experiment with frogs, chickens, or humans? Shall I study the mechanics of the brain? The eye? The anus? Shall I study atomic energy? Climate change? All such choices are value choices and it is values that form the basis of any human personality. So the case that nonfiction is unavoidably partly autobiographical is easy to make. I say "partly' with some caution, though many dedicated (note that value-added word) individuals devote their lives to their entire scientific field of study.

The question of embedded autobiographical traits in fiction is much more difficult to discern. The novelist or story writer is very much a play actor, magician, teaser, and most of all liar. The saying "oh what a tangled web we weave" (Sir Walter Scott—a creature of the courtroom where plots are invented and uncovered) sums it up nicely. Fiction writers of course write about themselves and inextricably about those they have met, some momentarily, others every day of their lives. The devilish fun of the fiction writer is to hide the habits, traits, peccadilloes, physical and other attributes, some of them sliced off the real life character so that they will not even be recognized in the characters that the fiction writer invents. Novelists bury all these small and large attributes in a thicket of plot, mystery, action, even physical surroundings such as furniture.

This book is essentially a collection of short stories, though they are loosely connected to a vague plot that remains in the background. In this sense I have adopted (some might say distorted) the style and structure of story writing from the works of Arthur Conan Doyle, though his books of collected short stories were published well after each of his stories had appeared in various weekly or monthly magazines. Faithful to his two central characters, Sherlock Holmes and Doctor Watson, the two main characters in this book are Professor Thomas Colmes, the Sherlock character, and William Hobson A.B.D. the Dr. Watson character. What A.B.D signifies will become clear as the stories unfold, though readers who have studied at the graduate level of a university will immediately recognize it. The setting for all the stories is not Victorian London, but a provincial university in a provincial town in upstate New York, late twentieth century to early 21st century. The university is called Schumaker University a state university named after the revered democratic senator of a similar name who reigned (that word chosen carefully) in New York for some decades and who laid its foundation stone in 1961.

The stories are written in the form of cases just like Conan Doyle, and they are recounted by myself, Colmes's trusted assistant and admirer. All cases are based on absolute fact, unless the reader discerns otherwise. To put it another way, the truth of the stories lies hidden behind the facts.

1. Colmes

The relationships among humans and the institutions in which they reside are mysterious and ephemeral, so insists Professor Thomas Colmes. They are fraught with unexpected events, unpredictable consequences of actions, yet driven by the hard choices people make every day of their lives. How humans act and react to each other remains the greatest question of life, according to the professor. If you can foresee, indeed, "understand" how others respond to each and every person they meet, you will know how to arrange their social and physical environment and thus solve the problems of human action that present themselves.

In the matter of "criminal action," most often the mistakes made in commission of a criminal act, combined with the mistakes made in uncovering and detecting such an act, if understood, will lead to a solution of the problem. I have never quite grasped this approach to human problems, but it is what Professor Colmes preaches to me and applies to the treatment of his clients daily.

His great skill, however, is the professor's ability to size up a quarry (that is, someone who comes to him for help) and to draw conclusions as to what they really think and plan to do. That is what he means by "truth" something that he insists is fleeting, exists only temporarily in time. All one can do is to make a calculated guess about any statement that a person makes, as to what it means, or more importantly, what it intends.

If this sounds rather academic, maybe full of fluff, indeed that is so. We inhabit, after all, academia. Any academic institution resides in a thick cerebral fog within the bricks and mortar of its building, filling its offices, oozing under the cracks of closed doors into hallways,

3

classrooms, even wafting in the breeze of courtyards and sports grounds (though the latter exist warily on the fringe of academic bounds as our later case of *The Student Body* suggests). It's a fog of words. I give you here only a small taste of Colmes's magic. His "method" if one may call it that, is far more complex, as becomes apparent when you see it at work in his cases.

*

I might say that Professor Colmes remains a mystery to me, even though I have known him, and have been his research assistant—the polite name of one who serves his master in academia— for almost all of my many years here in the land of the (almost) mighty dollar. I am quite sure that he was instrumental in my admission to the university, for I cannot understand how I would have qualified for admission otherwise. After all, my English was, and is, only passable, having come from Australia in 1975. He has always referred to me by my last name, Hobson, as he does to everyone else, student or faculty, which maybe belies his British origin, though his accent is very faint. Rather his American accent is more Bostonian if anything. In any event, his overall presentation is one of Victorian intellectual superiority and refined upbringing. But the scuttlebutt among the students is that his accent is put on, and that he really grew up in the slums of Chicago. Whatever!

Yet his role as a problem solver is embedded in the university administration. Whenever a particular problem arises, large or small, he is called in. I should say that this is not quite correct. I am never sure how he communicates or gets a case referred to him. But I always know that something is up when I hear the bang on the wall of my office that separates mine from his, "Hobson!" And sometimes if he is in a jolly mood "Hobs!" And off I trot, out of my office and into is.

***

We reside in Schumaker University just seven miles east of Albany, New York's capital city, across the other side of the Hudson as if to avoid interference from the New York State legislature. It is a magnificent edifice, laid out in rectangular pattern, four high rise dormitories at each corner of a huge square, built during the golden years in the 1960s during the reign of Governor Nelson Rockefeller. Our offices are located on a part of the campus that few would even know exists, with the exceptions of those who attend the submerged heating, cooling and other mechanical systems essential to keep the physical structures of the university up and running. That is, our offices are in a basement. Mine is a long narrow office, more like the end of a tunnel or narrow hallway, one side of it covered with cupboards and closets that house what is probably the communications system of the building, because it lets out a constant low hum. What building it resides under one can only guess, what with the high rise towers of some sixteen floors at each corner, connected to a quadrangle, not unlike the early design of an American penitentiary. All of this hovering over wide tunnels that form a basement, one of which houses our offices.

The professor's square-shaped office, is lined with books on all four of its walls, though strangely as I noticed the first time I entered, there were no filing cabinets, at least nothing to speak of. The exceptions are the drawers that make up the sides of his desk. Though I know that they too are almost empty. One would think that during the course of thirty years and counting, he would have accumulated many documents concerning his past cases. I almost said "problems that he has solved," but that would be an exaggeration, for Professor Colmes insists that no matter what the problem, it can rarely be completely solved. All one can do is to reach an agreeable conclusion with a decisive action that will solve the problem for that moment to the satisfaction of all parties, but in truth, the relationships between people are so complex and their desires so irascible, that relationships are constantly on the edge of dissolution. Thus he considers it a gross exaggeration to claim that one has completely solved a problem.

But back to the filing cabinets, or lack thereof. They instead line my office, along one wall, bookshelves above them, which means I have very little room to spare for anything else except my narrow desk and a small square stool that I stand on to reach the top shelves. The cabinets only exist because I started long ago to write up the cases we dealt with, collected the relevant documents, and stored them away in the filing cabinets. Colmes was amused at this, and I detected a kind of resentment that I took it on myself to do it. The reason I did so will become apparent as I describe his many fascinating cases, drawing on the notes I kept along the way in my time as his willing and doting assistant.

***

It is now almost sixteen years since I entered grad school. Good grief! You are understandably thinking. What a bludger! (Aussie slang describing one who lives off others and doesn't have a job). Professor Colmes, in his lighter moments, of which there are few, refers to me as the permanent fixture of the university, a little like a piece of furniture, a piece of furniture that evokes Andy Warhol's obsession with such—a wood filing cabinet with human features squashed into the top drawer its arms crossed in the second drawer, and legs, carved into the bottom.

I entered graduate school for all the wrong reasons, at least with no ambition to become any kind of scholar, or to study a particular subject in depth and eventually emerge as a "doctor" of something. Which is why I chose the new (at the time) criminal justice school, a school that nobody in academia had ever heard of before, a whole school devoted to criminal justice, at a university in the USA, and why, with my doubtful GRE scores—I never opened the envelope that contained my score, so I really do not know to this day what I got—the university chose me, for whatever reason. Actually, I know the reason but I am not telling you. For the purposes of these cases that I will describe, such information is irrelevant.

I am not a bludger! And worse, you probably and rightly do not think of grad school as being anything like work. As an aside, I acknowledge that being a professor in a grad school isn't much like real work either. And even if it were, you may think that sixteen years in grad school is way too long.

But I have my reasons. Simply put, it was, as is the case with the majority of students, a matter of money and with a minority of students, I could remain in the USA on my "F-1" visa, which was valid only while I was a student. This is why I have never graduated with my Ph.D. in criminal justice—that is, I studied criminal justice, wrote my dissertation, but never bothered to graduate. Instead, as soon as I had finished that course, I applied to the Philosophy department to do a doctorate in that field. I reached out to that field at the urging of Professor Colmes. But for the moment, that story can wait.

Criminal justice? At a university? Surely that field belonged at a technical college or community college of some kind, you may well ask. When I applied, I had no idea that there were universities, and there were *universities*. The real ones, you paid for if you had lots of money, the run-of-the-mill ones, were cheaper, almost affordable, and funding was more available. Either way, the School of Criminal Justice to which I applied, not only accepted my application, but also gave me a means of sustenance, a research assistantship funded by the U.S. Law Enforcement Assistance Administration (LEAA). Unfortunately, this turned out to be a bit of a fiasco, and my funding only lasted for my first semester. Someone in the U.S. Department of Justice noticed that I was not a U.S. Citizen, so therefore, the U.S. Government could not use American tax-payers' money to pay a non-citizen. It was the law, and nothing could be done about it.

The good part of this story (though it depends on what one means by "good") is that it was because of this crisis of money that I came to meet Professor Colmes. A slightly older fellow student, who always came to class dressed in collar and tie (ridiculous) and carrying a black briefcase, when he heard of my predicament, suggested that I seek out Professor Colmes, who, he said, was rumored to be a whiz at helping students in trouble. This mysterious professor was not a member of the department, or was it a school? I was confused even about this simple matter of nomenclature, coming from Australia I did not know the differences between a Department and a School. (I still don't).

I found my way to Professor Colmes's office (a challenge in itself), knocked timidly on his door, heard a muffled call, "enter!" I turned the large brass knob and pushed at the really heavy door that opened only just far enough for me to slip into the room. Professor Colmes sat at his desk reading the *New York Times*. (I discovered later that he never read it and got all his news, so it seemed, from the radio broadcasts and TV.) He looked up briefly, I saw a slight twitch at the corner of his tight-lipped mouth, a glimmer of amusement, I thought, dressed as I was in shorts, unshaven, long unkempt hair, scruffy shirt not tucked in.

I almost bowed in his presence, his demeanor was so overpowering, even though he made no attempt at all to stand or even stop what he was doing. In fact, he exclaimed "Ah yes!" picked up a pencil and filled in a word in the *Times* crossword puzzle.

"Sir, er Doctor, Professor Colmes" I mumbled, unsure how to address him.

"Yes, yes, take a seat. I've been expecting you. And for Heaven's sake, don't call me Doctor. I'm not a doctor, you understand?"

"Sorry sir!"

"And no sir either."

"Then what, sir, I mean..."

"Colmes, call me Colmes. Forget the rest."

And I have worked as his assistant ever since. I even had an office next to his! I had no idea where the money came from, but I received my meagre assistantship allowance every month, and it has been so now for all those many years.

If you have any acquaintance with university life, you may quickly ask, "how can Professor Colmes be your mentor in both departments, even different schools within the university?" You would have to ask him. I could venture a guess. It is because he occupies a unique position in the university, an official title of Professor of Interdisciplinary Studies, which allows him to serve in any department or school of his choosing, for any length of time.

The word "serve" of course does not really describe what he does. No doubt he carefully made sure of that. For, as far as I can remember, I have never seen him enter a classroom, unless he was investigating a particular case that required it. Nor do I know what his doctorate is in. He has always evaded it. In fact, he insists to everyone he meets that he be addressed as "Mister," his full name being Thomas Colmes, and he signs all his letters (of which there are very few) as simply "Colmes."

As for myself, my sixteen years have flown by much too quickly. As Colmes likes to say, and often, time is our worst enemy. One dare not stop to wonder why, or time will pass one by. And if one hurries, tries to cut corners, beat time maybe, time will surely trip you up. Colmes says, "there may be no time like the present, but if you pause to find it, it will already have passed."

But I digress. In fact I have found a quite comfortable means of living, now a supervisor of some years in the North West Dormitory high rise. No, I do not inhabit the top sixteenth floor. I inhabit a small (by grown-up standards) but comfortable apartment, self-contained, my own kitchen, a bedroom big enough that looks out over the courtyard through several long and narrow sealed windows that stretch up to the sixteenth floor. When I first acquired this space (a result of certain machinations of Colmes) I found it especially comforting, surrounded by what seemed to me then millions of tons of concrete that protected me from the evils of outside life. When I mentioned this to Colmes he looked down at me, his gaunt long face, pale and grey surrounding his penetrating dark greenish-grey eyes, sniffed and wrinkled his nose and said, "physical objects have their uses, but protecting you from yourself is not one of them."

"That's not what I meant," I countered defensively.

He ignored my remark, and turned back to his *Times* crossword puzzle, which he did every morning, as he feasted on his tea and toast that, until I was displaced by a live-in housekeeper, I dutifully picked up from the campus dining room as I crossed the campus from my dorm to his office.

Those of you who are old enough would already have surmised that the nine-eleven attack destroyed the idea that one could be protected by several million tons of concrete. For a few weeks after the attack, I took myself off to the Adirondacks with all my camping gear and camped in the cold, and even the snow. Colmes thought I was mad. In fact, he rarely stepped out of doors. His whitish, gray-lined sallow flesh showed it. The most he went outdoors was to emerge from his office to cross the podium and enter the gym where he worked out for at least one hour every day, and when dealing with a particularly difficult case, he might even stay there for several hours. His favorite workout: the punching bag. Actually, since you may have been wondering, his office also served as his apartment. There were doors, three in fact, that led out of his office, into a spacious apartment, large kitchen-dining room (the "open plan" as they call it in Australia), eating area and large bedroom with attached bathroom. It was several years after I became his assistant that I saw his apartment. And I saw it then only because of an incident that occurred in his office that required a quick exit.

But now you can see how difficult it is for me to remain on point. I started out telling you about my own situation, but inevitably ended up telling you more about my mentor. He is a dominating presence. No, I don't mean dominate as a tyrant or bully—though I have seen those characteristics, which he uses only as a technique to advance a solution to a case he is working on. I can attest that he is truly a passive person, taciturn to a degree, even shy and quiet, but behind that facade lies a person whose rational, even mathematical mind, causes him to lose touch with those around him, to be entirely enveloped in his own thoughts, driven by reason (his idea of it, to be clear) and an unquenchable thirst to solve problems, whether they be crossword puzzles, or grander puzzles that may affect the life and future of the institutions that comprise this university, or the life or lives of those whose problems have found their way to his office. Fittingly, in one corner of his office there is a small coffee table, upon which sits his chess set, a game always in play, and always against the same opponent, his Russian friend (Trotsky) who mails his move every few days, to which Colmes responds at about the same rate.

How he solves problems is the envy of all those who have benefited from his successes. And what sorts of problems does he tackle?

That question is impossible to answer. I have pondered on it for some years, in fact I once considered—many years ago when trying to come up with a topic for my criminal justice dissertation—doing one on problem solving. But in the end I gave up, for there seemed to be no clear structure to what Colmes did. In fact, there were many times when he made a spur of the moment decision based on no logic at all as far as I could see.

But now, I see him slowing down quite a bit, age catching up with him at long last, and he has begun to drink heavy amounts of red wine, even though alcohol is forbidden on campus (for the usual reasons). I have even entered his office to find him sitting back in his overstuffed leather chair in the far corner of his office, mumbling to himself, a glass of wine to his thin lips in between puffing a small cigarillo, his slightly graying hair ruffled (it is usually carefully groomed) locks of it creating a rough fringe on his still unlined forehead. Could this be a sign of his future demise? The end of Colmes? I hated myself for asking this of myself. It is why I have embarked on a quest to place in the official record, where all could see, his most memorable cases. And I will let those cases speak for themselves.

One final remark. An admission I suppose. Over the years I have actually written accounts of Colmes's cases, at least the most memorable and fascinating ones and sent them to the *Chronicle of Higher Education* so that the practitioners, administrators and teachers could learn of his accomplishments. But every single case I submitted was politely rejected with a simple form letter saying, "we do not publish memoirs, or other accounts of individuals whose privacy may be infringed by such cases.

2. The Snake

I have chosen this case to begin the collection of cases because it represents a case, the solution of which was essential if my position in the School of Justice were not to be terminated. [The omission of 'criminal' in the name of the school is not a mistake on my part. There occurred a name change in more recent times—as a matter of fact, the outcome of one of the few cases in which Colmes failed to prevail.]

I had just entered my office, having dropped off Colmes's tea and toast for his breakfast, when I heard the loud bang on my office wall signaling to me that my presence was required. "Hobson!" he called, the high-pitched sound of his voice easily penetrating the wall. I had planned on that morning at last to finish off a draft of my dissertation proposal. But yet again, it was not to be. I rarely answered his calls. Rather, simply walked out of my office and into his, without knocking.

Colmes looked up from his crossword and gulped down the last drop of tea from his daintily decorated English tea cup, having poured the tea into it, out of the much despised disposable cup in which it came.

"Hobson, we have a most interesting and pressing case before us. I will have to give it much careful thought before we proceed. I trust that you are not too busy? "

"I was just putting the finishing touches to the first draft of my dissertation proposal," I answered in my Australian monotone, trying to appear nonchalant.

"Well, I do not want to interfere with your studies," he said, still working on his crossword puzzle.

"It can wait," I answered. "You know me. I can only do a little at a time anyway, as you know it's so difficult for me."

"Your ADD ?" asked Colmes, still not looking up.

"I can manage it."

In fact, I had been diagnosed with Attention Deficit Disorder in Australia when I was eight years old. It was one of the reasons I ended up coming to the USA. In Australia they were good at diagnosing the disease, but hopeless at doing anything about it, especially in schools where teachers interpreted my inattention as a defect in discipline, and dealt with it accordingly. My ADD also interfered with my learning and memory. So at a very young age I developed a habit of recording everything, or just about everything, in a notebook or even on a scrap of paper if it were nearby. Hence, filing cabinets were the first piece of furniture I installed in my office.

Colmes finished his tea and returned the cup to its saucer. "This case has come to me directly from the President's office. You know he used to be the Dean of your school, right?"

"You mean criminal justice? I'm in the philosophy department now, you know."

"Yes, I am aware of that. But you have not yet defended your dissertation for criminal justice, is that not so?"

"Er, yes, that's right, but you know why that is."

"Indeed I do, Hobson," said Colmes with an amused smirk.

I decided to pick up where I left off. "Oh, yes, Dean O'Brien who was once the governor of Sing-Sing Prison, right?"

"Indeed. A most controlling sort of person. In fact he was once overheard to say in a meeting that he thought universities were not all that different from a prison to run. A good fit, wouldn't you say?"

I nodded, but refrained from responding. Colmes was used to this, and I can attest that he rarely, at least with me anyway, expected to get an answer when he asked a question, unless it was part of a direct interrogation of a suspect or witness. Otherwise his questions were almost always rhetorical.

Colmes continued. "It appears that our President-come-governor-come-Dean has decided on a cost-cutting operation and plans to disband your School."

This stirred me to ask, "you mean he's going to abolish the whole school, the doctoral program and all the faculty?"

"It's not altogether clear how far he intends to go. But my good friend who resides in the President's office—universities have spies and confidants hidden everywhere. Let's call my friend our "trusty" just like in a Mississippi prison. He has raised the alarm and asked me to devise a way to stop this terrible destruction of an essential part of the university."

I pulled up a wicker chair, one that was probably made by prison labor, and leaned my elbows on Colmes's desk. I detected the usual small twitch at the corner of his mouth, a sign that he found what he had just said amusing, almost a joke. Of course, one had to agree with the President. Whoever heard of a School of Criminal Justice anyway? Invented by some politician close to Governor Rockefeller, so I was told. Schumaker university was the first university to house such a school. Others followed, but remained very few. Judiciously, I remained silent.

Then he looked up from his crossword and stared at me intently, as only he could do. The twitch at the corner of his mouth remained. I knew I had to respond.

"If the School is abolished along with the faculty, I will not be able to defend my dissertation and anyway there will be no such thing as a Ph.D. in criminal justice. Criminal justice will be no more," I muttered.

Colmes stared back at me, his lips now pursed together tightly. I knew I had to speak again.

"And it will be the end of my assistantship. No money. No job." I muttered forlornly.

"Indeed. Indeed. That is so. An inevitable deduction, Hobson."

I sat back in my wicker chair and waited. Colmes would have a solution, I knew it.

"Now, now Hobson. Not so glum!" smiled Colmes. "With your assistance, we will fix this."

"I can put aside my dissertation draft. After all, there's no hurry to finish it, is there?" I answered with a touch of sarcam..

Colmes ignored my question. "Now here is what I want you to do."

"Dig up dirt on the President?" I asked eagerly.

"Hmmm. An obvious solution, but too direct and besides, I do not think that the main force behind this is the President. Or if he is, there is no easy way to get at him. Certainly, he cannot make such a big change without the assent of..."

I broke in, "The faculty senate!"

"Indeed not! Indeed not!" retorted Colmes. "It has little standing except a pretense that faculty are always 'consulted' by the administration. The senate is always consulted, but only after the decision has been made."

"Then what? Who?" I asked, perplexed.

"We will begin with the new Provost and Vice President for Academic Affairs."

"You will confront them?" I asked, with some happy anticipation.

"Confront? Indeed not! Confront creates resistance. And it's 'her' not 'them.' She has two titles, and so far she fits the Colmes basic rule of identification in academia. Her name is Doctor Catherine Dolittle"

I sat mute, awaiting his explication of the rule.

"The more the titles, the more the incompetence," pronounced Colmes his bottom lip dropping a little as though he had just said something disgusting.

"Very funny, sir," I said, inadvertently breaking another of his sacred rules: never address him as Sir.

Colmes stood and began to walk up and down in his office, hands behind his back, head and chin held high. He then stopped at my side, where I was still sitting on the wicker chair pulled up to the desk. "Hobson, you must stop and think. Everything revolves around the Provost. We must make her ours."

"But how?"

"Information, of course. Here's what you must do. Get a hold of her resume. Track down all the publications she lists and find any coauthors. Track her back to her undergraduate and high school academics. Get all of her grades. In short, find anything that could be a black mark against her."

"But how? I can't just go in and ask for all that stuff. What about the privacy rules?" I complained.

"Indeed. Indeed. But there are ways. Say that you are working for the Arcade Personnel Agency," Colmes handed me a business card, "and say that the Provost is applying for a top government position in Homeland Security and that you are gathering information to assist in her clearance."

"But will they believe me?"

"They will when you show them your badge," announced Colmes.

Struck speechless I mechanically put out my hand to receive the badge. It even had my photograph ID on it.

Colmes licked his top lip slightly as signal that he was most pleased with himself. "You will need money to get to Philadelphia."

"Philadelphia? You mean, that's where she got her doctorate?"

"Yes, at Drexel. In environmental studies, I believe." Colmes turned to the wall behind him that was lined with books from floor to ceiling.

It bears repeating that his entire office walls were lined with books. Not unusual for a professor. Professors either sported a large personal library, or instead piled up papers, books, folders, unread dissertations, ungraded papers all over the floor with barely a passage for any visitor to reach the professor's desk. This was their way of demonstrating to gullible students (graduate or undergraduate) their industry and total devotion to scholarship. But there was something out of place with Colmes's walls of books. None had been read, or at least one could not see any finger marks that had been left in the layers of dust that clung to the books.

Except for one that was shiny and well used. Colmes grabbed it, a heavy criminal law casebook. Immediately he lifted it from the shelf, it set in motion machinery that pushed back two rows of books, and in their place a safe appeared with two separate doors. He muttered something to himself, seemingly for a very long time, turned a knob, and the door on the left swung open. He reached in and pulled out a wad of $100 bills and counted out twenty of them.

"This should see you through. Bring back to me whatever is left over, if any. Take the train, it's the least stressful."

I was about to say thank you, and ask did I really need that much money, when he slammed the safe shut and closed up the bookshelf.

At the time—I did not know it—he had extremely sensitive hearing, supposedly a result of a birth defect, or should I say his inherited gift. Anyway, lucky for us, because right then the door to his office flew open, and there, standing right in the doorway was—there is no other way to describe her, his nemesis, Dr. Hannah Toekiarty, Vice President and Dean of Human Resources. In contrast to Colmes she had a way of showing up anywhere at any time. She obviously had a master key so could enter any room or office. And she was convinced that Colmes was not what or who he said he was. His personnel file lacked any information at all, except one folder within which was typed on a single legal size paper: NO CLEARANCE ALLOWED. She had taken this as high in the administration as she could go—to the President after all, supposedly a former prison governor (we know that was true) and should be a stickler for security, but he refused to do anything about it. Just shrugged it off and said to her, "there's nothing I can do. You know what they are like." And she would be ushered out of his office. Who "they" were she had no idea and not the courage to ask.

Colmes pushed back in his chair, placing his hands behind his head. "Good morning Dr. Toekiarty. You bring good news, I hope?"

Dr. Toekiarty answered only indirectly, which is to say she ignored him, instead she looked my way.

"Good morning. Mr. Hobson, isn't it?"

"That's right Doctor. I was just leaving," I answered in my most polite manner, conveying the fact that I recognized her power. She could make or break pretty much anyone on campus. Colmes had battled with her over many a case. But she did not step away from the doorway, so it was impossible for me to leave without bumping into her or nudging her aside, both options were sorely tempting. She just stood, hands on her protruding hips that seemed to hold up the weight of her balloon-like upper body, a scowl erupting all over her face, from chin over fatty bulging cheeks, a tiny flat sow-like nose, to eyes almost closed by the swelling of her cheeks and the deep frown of her forehead.

"Excuse me," I muttered meekly.

She turned back to Colmes who looked at me, enjoying every minute of this impossible encounter. His face, though, only gave the tiniest indication of his personal pleasure. I know him so well. He holds everything in. His stern grey face acts as a mirror, an aggressive mirror that turns any emotive behavior of anyone he meets, back on themselves. The result is that they invariably feel uncomfortable, and, in a different way, seriously inferior from this person, Colmes, a man of brilliance—as I attest that he in fact is.

Dr. Toekiarty made a small step forward. "The news is that your housekeeper position has been approved, though the money allocated is limited."

"Indeed! Indeed!" cried Colmes, breaking out all over in smiles, a rarity no less. "One Rose lost, another Rose found!"

Rose was the daughter of Colmes's former housekeeper, a kind of Victorian era housekeeper with a thick Russian accent, who would cook for him, clean his house (or office-apartment as one might call it), go food shopping or attend to any other tasks he required. The old Rose was in fact a graduate of the Department of Philosophy, the department with which I was now also enrolled doing my second Ph.D. Colmes had actually chaired her dissertation. The new housekeeper, her daughter Rose, had recently graduated with her Ph.D. in Criminal Justice, so I knew her somewhat from my studies there. In fact she looked exactly like her mother. Always dressed in rather ill-fitting knitted sweaters, shirts, and even leggings and dress. And when she was not tending to her chores, even when doing other things, such as defending a dissertation, she always found time to knit while someone asked her a question, or even while she answered.

I managed to step around Doctor Toekiarty, muttering an "excuse me." It was my first up-close encounter with her, and I was aghast at the smell, her tobacco breath blended with a strong whiff of excessive amounts of baby powder plastered all over her round, moonlike face. I quickly glanced over my shoulder at Colmes, and I am sure I saw him sniggering.

"And when will she start?" I heard Colmes as I made my way next door into the safety of my office, Toekiarty having stepped a little aside.

***

Upon returning to my office, I put away yet another rough draft of my dissertation proposal, and pottered around, placing books back on their shelves. As usual, I was not altogether sure what I was supposed to do. From Colmes, all I had was my pass as a headhunter. I retrieved as much information on Dolittle as I could from Google, it had only been going for a couple of years, but was already a great quick source of information. And the rest I scoured the *Chronicle of Higher Education* for any articles that might mention her. But obtained very little. I called the human resources office at Drexel and managed to confirm that she in fact did attend there, but they would give little else over the phone. A trip to Philadelphia was warranted. In all my time upstate New York I had never ventured south past New York City. A train trip was called for.

Meanwhile the scratchy, loud voice of Toekiarty seeped through the wall of my office, mixed with the steady high pitched mutterings of Colmes. I discovered later that Toekiarty had informed Colmes that she had launched an official investigation of him and that he would be required to answer some questions put to him by the university lawyer whose main function was to confront, warn and accuse individuals that Toekiarty fingered as having broken the equity and diversity rules of the university. This was not at all new. The Provost indulged in constant harassment of persons, whether student or faculty, whom she, for whatever reasons of her own, targeted for investigation and castigation. I even asked Colmes why he didn't go after her, but he responded that she was a known entity and that she had been a useful ploy on occasion, in fact helped solve a couple of cases. As I would find out in future cases.

*

Amazingly, the train from Rensselaer to New York was on time, and I managed without difficulty to change to the fast train to Philadelphia, out of 30th street station in New York, alighting in a little over an hour at Philadephia's 30th street station. Then it was an easy walk to Drexel university where I showed my badge and chatted with a human resources official. After the usual pleasantries and joking about my Aussie accent, I managed to get the entire file of Dolittle. It was huge, containing an amazing amount of irrelevant information, at least that is what I thought, concerning her personal life. She had had two abortions, it seems, was never married, failed her comprehensive exams for her doctorate in religious studies twice, and was saved only by the fact that her second abortion had affected her performance in the second attempt at her comprehensive exam, so she was given a conditional pass, taking into account her handicapped condition. While this was interesting scuttlebutt, I could not see how this would help Colmes to get Dolittle to desist from her attempt to destroy the School of Criminal Justice. There was little else in the thick file, most of it listing the various honors and awards she had received, especially a big one for being the diversity faculty of the year. This was a bit puzzling since she was, after all, a middle aged white woman from the main line of Philadelphia. There was also an award for her work with the Society for the Prevention of Cruelty to Animals. Apparently she also worked as a volunteer at the Philadelphia Zoo for many years. I phoned Colmes and informed him of my progress. He was most appreciative. I told him that I did have to pay a little money to get access to the file, $100 in all. He asked me to read out to him all the juicy bits of the file.

"Do you want copies of everything?" I asked. And to my surprise (at the time) he answered, "no need. Good job, Hobson. Get back as soon as you can. By the way, what was her dissertation topic?"

"Just a minute. I have it written down here... Ah yes. "The Inspiration of Species and the Discovery of Christian Purity.""

It was a long trip back as I missed the train connection in New York City. I found a Starbucks hidden away somewhere deep in the busy station, sipped coffee and wondered what Colmes was up to. I was puzzled that he did not want any copies of the Dolittle file. And it was then that I had realized that there were actually no file cabinets in Colmes's office. How could that be? When he must have dealt with many cases before I joined him? All the filing cabinets were in my office, but those were what I installed. There were no files of his, until I began to make them. And even then, he seemed a little annoyed that I had done so. Of course, I am so glad I did, because without them I could not be recounting to you our cases. And he would have been truly angry if he knew that I had submitted articles based on them to the *Chronicle of Higher Education.*

***

Of his many talents, Colmes was an outstanding photographer. He had, tucked away in the drawers of his desk and elsewhere in his apartment, a huge variety of cameras, old and new. They were hidden and operative all over his office. He had also installed them in various places around the university. To this day, I do not know where they are. I once asked him for a map or something so I could help keep track of them, but he scorned the idea. Besides, he insisted that he had what he called a ""photographic memory" and so knew exactly where every camera was installed. He could literally see the map inside his head. I had no idea what this meant, and certainly doubted that such a detailed map could be "seen" as though one had eyes inside one's head.

Correction. Of course eyes are physically located inside one's head. But in order to see something, there has to be a physical object outside the head (in this case a map) in order to see it inside one's head, right? Otherwise, if one sees something inside one's head without looking at something outside one's head, then you are having a "vision." Right? The sort of thing that the "prophet" Girolamo Savonarola in 15th century Florence insisted on seeing. But even there, the objects (sword, fire and brimstone etc.) had been seen prior to the vision. They could only take shape inside the head once their exterior shape previously had been seen and identified.

My apologies. There I go again, You can understand why I am doing my second Ph.D. in philosophy. It is a field that can make even the simplest of things very complicated.

***

The phone rang in my little dormitory apartment and woke me with a startle. I groped for the phone and mumbled, half asleep, "who is it?" After my long trip to Philadelphia, and missing the train connection back, I had arrived to the comfort of my Dorm apartment very late and so decided to sleep a little later than usual. I need not have asked who it was phoning me at this ungodly hour of eight a.m. It was Colmes of course.

"Hobson?"

"Colmes?" I retorted, annoyed.

"There, there, Hobson. The case is but solved, thanks to you!"

"What? Where? How?" I spluttered.

"Meet me in the environmental studies department in ten minutes."

"Colmes? Professor?" I called. But he had hung up.

I dashed out of bed, attended to my morning ablutions, rushed down to the small cafeteria that served our dormitory, grabbed a cup of coffee and a piece of bacon from one of the many plates of breakfast fast food, and was on my way, grabbing a napkin to wipe my greasy fingers as I went. What solution could he have come to—deduction as he called it—from the meager amount of information I gave him?

Fortunately, it was not too far to the environmental studies department, housed in a large section of the Science building, at one corner of the podium. It too, was a heavy concrete structure, though not a high-rise as were the dorms, instead a squat four story building with the characteristic ascending narrow windows. I no sooner entered the building via the heavy double doors at the entrance, and there was Colmes, pacing back and forth in the lobby.

"Ah Hobson, my boy! At last!"

I thought I had done very well getting there as soon as I did, and resented Colmes's impatience. And his calling me 'boy' of course I resented, though could not complain since I was, after all, his student. But I admit that I have carried such silly little resentments for many years. And I try not to take his frequent annoyances to heart. They are simply the symptoms of genius, unintended, and without malice.

"So, Provost Dolittle has moved to the department of environmental studies?" I asked.

"Not at all, though she does visit the department a lot," answered Colmes with a slight grin, more of a smirk. "But then, one can understand that, if she is continuing her devotion to the prevention of cruelty to animals."

"Sure, but how does this knowledge point to a solution to our case? And why was it so urgent that you had to call me so early in the morning?"

"All in good time, Hobson. Follow me!"

Colmes led the way down a narrow passage to the end, knocked then entered through the heavy door. We stepped into a large room, full of rows of benches populated with many cages and glass cases, all containing various kinds of animal life. A person, presumably a lab assistant (she was wearing a white lab coat) smiled as we approached.

"Doctor Colmes," she said extending her hand, "it's an honor to meet you, and I hope I can help in any way I can."

She was a small person, though seeming to have arms that were rather too long for the rest of her body. I realized that this impression was because she was stretching into a glass case in which there lay coiled up a very large snake, striped in yellow and dark brown.

"Is this what you had in mind?" she asked.

"Possibly" answered Colmes with a satisfied gleam in his eye.

"Just a minute," I intervened, "that's a tiger snake, isn't it?"

"It sure is," answered the lab assistant as she gently scooped up the snake and drew it out of the glass case. "I'm surprised that you recognized it."

"I'm Australian," I retorted proudly, "we're used to lots of snakes down there."

Colmes became a little agitated, and looked all around us. He was either annoyed that I had interrupted his mild interrogation or he was looking for something else. But I merrily continued on.

"But don't you have any rattle snakes? This is America after all," I said jokingly.

At this, Colmes quickly averted his penetrating gaze back to the tiger snake. The lab assistant noticed and held the snake out, now hanging loosely over her arm.

"Dr. Colmes, would you like to hold it?" she asked, smiling.

"I think not," growled Colmes with a frown, "but you did not answer my colleague's question."

This intervention pleased me greatly. I must have accidentally turned the interrogation into a direction that suited Colmes.

"Rattle snakes? Oh yes, we have a bunch of them in the annex along with a lot of other native varieties." She pointed out the window to a small wooden building that was obviously a temporary addition to the laboratory.

"And the Provost? She is satisfied that all your animals, snakes included are treated well?"

"Well of course, Dr. Colmes. We are very happy that she shows such interest and are well aware of her work with the Society. We work closely with her to make sure that all our species are well cared for. She even on occasion takes some of them home to mind, should we happen to be short staffed. And as I am sure you are well aware that in these times of austerity, we are often short staffed."

Colmes nodded his assent and smiled just a tiny bit, the corner of his mouth twitching. Of course, the university, as are all universities, was in a perpetual state of austerity, even in the best of times. Such a condition provided ready excuses for whatever criticism might be leveled at academia from time to time.

"And that includes the snakes?" he asked casually.

"Oh yes. They are quite safe if you know how to handle them. She comes by pretty much every week and takes a few home with her, and sometimes if she is too busy I will take an animal or two to her house."

"I see, said Colmes as he stood up straight and almost snapped his heels together. It was time for us to leave. "Come Hobson, I think our work here is done."

"Aren't we going to see the rattlers?" I asked in a silly schoolboy manner.

Colmes was already leaving as the lab assistant replied to my query. "Oh, I'm sorry, but there are none in the annex right now. They are with the Provost who is giving them special care this weekend. She feeds them a special diet. They have to be well fed or they become a little vicious and hard to handle."

I saw Colmes hesitate, a slight misstep perhaps, but he then called out over his shoulder. "Come, Hobson. We are done here!" And repeated, "come Hobson, we must now meet with the Provost and settle this problem once and for all."

I hurried to catch up with him. "Are we bringing the tiger snake?" I asked again with the relish of a mischievous schoolboy.

"No need!" cried Colmes who was already at the door to leave. "Thank you for your excellent help," he called over his shoulder to the lab assistant.

I also thanked the lab assistant, but then called out to Colmes, "Professor. Why don't we take the snake? Might get her to talk?"

Colmes was already at the door. He stopped and turned to face me.

"Ah, Hobson. You would enjoy that, now would you not?" he smiled, "but how would it look in the *Chronicle of Higher Education*, that Colmes and his assistant intentionally, with a venomous snake, scared the daylights out of the Provost, and they were both forcibly removed from the campus never again to return?"

"Oh, I suppose so," I answered with a snigger. This was one serious defect of Colmes, probably a symptom of his disability. He had a limited sense of humor.

"No, Hobson. We shall wait until we have all our evidence and then act," muttered Colmes.

We left the environmental studies building and Colmes led the way down to the tunnels, under the podium, and back to his office. I followed him into his office and took up my position on the old wicker chair at the front of his desk. I was itching to hear from Colmes what had led him to the snake, what on earth it could have to do with the Provost, and of course, how it would help us rescue the School of Criminal Justice. But as usual, Colmes more or less ignored me, which meant he discounted my ADD disability, but it also meant that he had solved the problem and would let me in on his piece of deductive brilliance when he was ready. If this sounds a little sarcastic, I admit that it is. I consider Colmes a great colleague and even friend, though the idea that one would be a devoted friend of one's professor is a little bit of a stretch. We could never be equals, not in a university setting, at least.

So now it was my usual turn to get up from my chair and walk to-and-fro in his office. In the meantime, Colmes had disappeared into one of the rooms in his apartment, Door One I called it, and I heard voices. I was about to leave and go to my own office when Colmes entered from Door Two.

"Rose is preparing morning tea for us. Would you like to stay, that is, unless you have pressing engagements elsewhere?" asked Colmes, seemingly oblivious to my fidgety condition. Of course, an affirmative answer was presumed. It was another of Colmes's questions that did not expect an answer, or at least to which there was only one presumed answer.

"Oh, sure. I'd love to," I quivered, embarrassed that I would now be in a position of having an equal, that is Rose, a fellow grad student, wait on me. Besides, I was hoping that Colmes would now inform me of how he planned to save the School of Criminal Justice from the Provost.

Rose entered carrying a large tray with embossed pewter handles, loaded with two ornate cups with saucers, a small matching plate with two scones, a teapot covered with a tea cozy, two small plates, and of course two tiny pots one with raspberry jam, the other with whipped cream. Colmes sat at his desk, while Rose struggled to place the contents of her tray on his desk. It was an amusing sight, one must agree. There she was stooping over the desk, trying not to spill the tea, all the time her knitting needles stuck in her thick hair bound loosely into a bun at the top, just like her mom.

"There you are, Professor Colmes, doesn't all that look lovely?" said Rose in her Russian voice, a light accent laced with inflections of upper class English vowels.

"Thank you Rose. You are a gem, and so was your mother," said Colmes, trying his best to sound nice and friendly. Trouble was, as I have already intimated, Colmes had trouble being friendly. He was a loner, through and through. It took me a long time to understand and accept that. We all have our own disabilities. Including Rose. Hers was her knitting, which she inherited from her mother.

But now Rose, having emptied the tray, stood back, drew the knitting needles from her hair, and tears came to her eyes. "Oh my dear mother," she cried "how will we ever survive without her?" She had also learned from Colmes. It was a question that did not expect an answer.

As for me, I just had to stand and walk around a little, until she had gone back to the kitchen through Door Two. "Thank you Rose," I whispered, not expecting that she would hear.

"Milk first?" asked Colmes with a grin.

"Whatever," I said, as Colmes poured a little milk in each cup, then poured the tea. This was a ritual with which I was well acquainted, being an Aussie and all. It was the kind of imperialism that I willingly bore. I sat on my wicker chair and looked across at Colmes as he devoured one scone with jam and cream with one huge mouthful. Nothing dainty about Colmes. This was surely Chicago style eating. Nothing English about that. But it was a good sign. I knew that once he had munched the scone and swallowed (you could see the bulge move down his neck) he would be ready to tell me what was going on.

"An excellent morning's work, Hobson, don't you think?"

"If you say so, Professor. But I don't know what the Aussie tiger snake has to do with getting the Provost to cancel the plans to do away with my former School."

"All in good time, young man," Colmes answered. That is, he once again, having taken the opportunity created by myself, put me in my place.

"Doctor Colmes," I said with a smirk, knowing how much this would get under his skin, though I could have added "it's Doctor Colmes, right?"

Colmes sipped his tea and looked past me at the open door of his office. Naturally, I turned to see who was there. But of course, there was no one.

"Hobson, close the door, if you don't mind," he said with a serious tone.

I carefully placed my cup on its saucer, got up to close the door, and returned quickly, now at the ready to receive his pearls of wisdom.

"When you mentioned that the Provost's dissertation was a combination of religion and environmental studies, it rang a bell," recited Colmes. "I often wonder what our unconscious mind is up to, when it seems to remember things that you do not know you have remembered until something triggers that memory. That is what happened when you mentioned religious studies."

I nodded in assent. It was the sign for him to continue.

"I suddenly remembered that she carries with her a small leather bound book, one of those that has a little ribbon that keeps one's place. Not only that. She carries it everywhere, meetings, even while giving a talk to a faculty meeting. I even saw her looking at it in the cafeteria when she was eating, even in the faculty dining room, though she kept it under her bottom on her seat."

Colmes paused. I knew not to interrupt. He gave a little cough, as if to warn me that something important was coming.

"At first I assumed that it was her daily diary, you know. These administrators have an awful lot of meetings to attend. They need a notebook of some kind. I understand that. Especially if those people have a poor memory, not like me. I have everything stored in my head."

Colmes looked at me frowning, not expecting me to say something in agreement, but simply assuming that I already knew that. Which I did. He had what lay people call a photographic memory, a characteristic of his dyslexia, and what, in my opinion contributed to his genius. I fidgeted a little with the pencils contained in an old honey jar that sat on the corner of his desk. It annoyed him, I knew. But then he gazed seeming vacantly over my shoulder, and again I turned to see if there was anyone there, but there was not. I turned back, and saw that tweak at the corner of his mouth. He was playing with me! Though I had worked for him for some sixteen years at this point, I was not always ready for his smart-ass tricks of what could only be described as broken social graces. Still, I knew to keep my mouth shut, and in time, he would reveal his plot or plan.

"Hobson, are you not curious at all? Do you not see where the snake fits into this puzzle?" teased Colmes.

"It's a puzzle of your making," I mumbled, "so I suppose you are the only one who knows its answer." There, I had taken him on, sort of.

"Quite right, Hobson! You are quite right! But mind you, it was your research that pointed the way to the solution."

I slumped back in my chair and looked at the pencil jar. I wasn't going to get dragged in to another "I told you so."

Colmes again looked over my shoulder to the door, but this time I heard footsteps followed by a light knock at the door.

"Enter!" called Colmes.

I turned and saw before me the most beautiful young thing ever. No doubt a young undergraduate, oozing with the sprightliness of youth, her African American hair pulled tightly to a bunch at the top of a tall slender body, her face gleaming with life. Good God, I thought to myself, how did Colmes find her?

"Ah, Cecilia," purred Colmes with much solicitude, "you got it."

"Yes, Professor. It was easy. Doctor Dolittle is such a lovely person. And she didn't mind one bit when I got up close to her. I think she likes people like me, if you see what I mean."

Did I see Cecilia wink just a little at Colmes? I admit that I was completely overwhelmed by her presence, not to mention Colmes's solicitude. Colmes reached out and Cecilia placed in his hand (their hands did not touch, I watched closely, I can tell you) what I guessed to be the Provost's diary.

Colmes got up from his chair and stood up straight; for a moment I thought he was going to click his heels and salute. But then he flipped through the diary as Cecilia turned to leave.

"No wait, my dear," called Colmes, "I need only a few minutes then you can take it back and put it in her handbag and she will never know it had been on a small journey without her."

He flipped through the pages, quickly taking in every important notation. I had known him long enough to recognize his incredible mental gift at work, he was memorizing the entire relevant contents of the book. And he even chatted as he did so.

"And how is granny, these days? Healthy and robust I hope?" asked Colmes.

"She's great, all thanks to you, Professor. She sends her love by the way."

I tried to catch Colmes's eye, but no luck. His eyes were fixed squarely on the book as the pages zipped by. This was a mystery remaining just out of sight, that I would for several years hope to find the answer. Were Cecilia's mother, or was it grandmother, and my boss once a couple? I ventured to ask myself, not game to ask Colmes of course.

"Excellent. This is exactly what I needed," announced Colmes as he handed back the book and with a very light bow, or nod of the head, hard to say which, he thanked her again, and asked to give her mother his love.

"So you want me to sneak the diary back to the Provost?" asked Cecilia, smiling broadly, obviously enjoying her undercover work.

"Indeed. Indeed. No doubt you can do that, I have no doubt at all," answered Colmes with a broad smile, one that I rarely saw.

"Bye, then," grinned Cecilia, and off she trotted, even giving me a little nod as she passed me, glued as I was to my wicker chair.

I turned back to Colmes who was now leaning back in his chair, rhythmically tapping the fingers of both hands against each other.

"I think we have it," he said with a look of satisfaction that seemed to be focused over my shoulder. "Yes, indeed. We have."

"The book? Or was it a diary?" I asked. I could not see what kind of book it was from where I was sitting.

"Interestingly, Hobson, it is something of both. A diary, I'd say, primarily, but it has a page from various passages of the bible—New Testament mostly,—one for every day."

"Good Lord!" I exclaimed, grinning at my own sort of joke, "how could so much be crammed into such a small sized book? The printing must be very small, and the pages very thin."

"Right again Hobson. Indeed. Indeed. It was a bit of a challenge for me to comprehend all those passages from the bible, lucky that my eyesight is as good as an eagle's."

"But, professor, what does the bible have to do with environmental studies? And the snake…" I asked, feeling so foolish that I had not been able to deduce from this meager amount of information what Colmes obviously had.

Colmes appeared to take pity on me, or perhaps it was the natural expression of his superiority that could not be hidden. Either way, I was well used to it and took it simply as a defect in his character caused by the disability of his genius. He leaned forward a little in his chair, still tapping his fingers together.

"First, there was no entry for her visiting the Department of Environmental Studies at any time of the day and we already know that she went there often. Second there is a series of entries for every Saturday afternoon that simply states 'Voorheesville' I think that might be what we are looking for."

I turned to Colmes in consternation. "Voorheesville. It's just a little country village a few miles from here. So what? She could be visiting a relative or something."

"Indeed, indeed. It is time we met with the Provost.

***

What I am about to tell you is based on my experience over several years working under the Provost, fair disclosure I think, and necessary because as years pass, and incidents occur that may be unrelated to the current case, nevertheless may make me vulnerable to exhibiting biases or grudges even (I don't think I have any, but one never knows what is going on in one's, should I say it, "unconscious" a Freudian word that is very much out of favor these days). Since I have never been ambitious in the academic sense, I have never had to undergo those awful procedures of getting a tenure track line, getting one's position renewed or going up for tenure. It is the esteemed Provost who, as the academic head, and on the "advice" of various faculty committees and Deans, pronounces, as does a judge in a large courtroom, or an Emperor in the Colosseum, a thumbs up or down decision.

In any case, here is what I now know about her (at the time of the case I here describe I knew very little as she was quite a new addition to the faculty and administrative staff), some of it quite strange but very interesting. First, there is her Asiatic look and composure. I say "Asiatic" because I have never been sure, and never found the right moment or person to ask, exactly where she came from. One can detect no special accent in her English, though I have heard that she speaks Chinese and possibly Japanese. But I have no personal knowledge of such. Keep in mind, though, at the time, not that long after the Vietnam war, persons of Asiatic extraction were relatively rare in the small cities and towns of the USA, especially upstate New York. For those of us whose experience with a person of Asiatic extraction was limited to the stories of Fu Manchu, or to comic books of the Korean war, of Americans fighting the "Gooks," Asians were a mysterious bunch, who ate weird foods and too much rice.

Dr. Dolittle was, therefore, an object of curiosity to me, though in her mannerisms and physique rather entertaining. She was tiny, by my standards (I'd say about five feet), yet a solid squat body, not skinny as were all Asians supposed to be. She wore always a tightly fitting dark gray women's suit, the top piece, as a male I would call it the "suitcoat" seemed to be too small for her, tightly buttoned giving the impression that her breasts were fighting to be released. And the shoulders of the jacket square and pointy, as though the jacket in that respect was a little too wide at the shoulders. And then, the most unappealing part, she wore no makeup as far as I could tell. And no perfume that I could tell. In fact if I happened to get close to her which was rare, she had the faint aroma of boiled cabbage, none too enticing. Her face was round, even broad, high cheeks of course, pushing up against her, yes, slit-like eyes by Caucasian standards, but a beautifully glistening darkish skin (not yellow as we all thought it should be), and a thin almost always tightly drawn mouth, out of which came, when she spoke, a deep and reson-ating voice. Again, not what one like me would have expected. All in all, this was a face and body that did not reveal to me, or anyone who was a "westerner" what she might be thinking, or reacting to whatever people or environment might be around her. I suppose, in retrospect, I am trying to say that she was kind of foreign, I hesitate to admit it, and not quite as human as we Anglo-Saxons.

In sum, she was someone to be reckoned with. Someone who could suddenly turn on you. Give snappy orders and commands. And when speaking in a meeting or conference or any other setting, she appeared not to look anyone in the eye. All of this taken as an indication of her ruthlessness, her lack of empathy. One might say, the perfect administrator, no doubt why she was hired as a Provost. So, given this admittedly jaundiced and cynical view I had of her, and maybe mixed with a little racism as well, I was not all that surprised that it was she who came up with the idea to demolish the School of Criminal Justice. After all, it was composed of just a little more than a dozen faculty and was founded upon the distinct policy of not offering a major in criminal justice to undergraduates. It was established and designed to be an elite graduate school.

If you are not familiar with academic institutions at all, the dozen faculty of the Criminal Justice school compares to the fifty or more faculty who inhabit the School of Education, for example, and similarly for the School of Arts and Sciences. So you can see why the School of Criminal Justice was an easy and logical target. Regardless of whether or not it was rated as number one by *U.S. News and World Report*.

But I bore you with these little details.

***

Provost Doctor Dolittle sat at her desk in a very large office, three times the size of a standard full professor's office, and one entered it through a large anteroom that contained three desks with a secretary or assistant at each desk, each banging away on the latest Dell computer. And although the sounds of their keyboard did not match the clacking of their forebears the IBM selectric typewriter, they gave the impression that a lot of work was being done, all were very busy.

Colmes ignored them and led the way into the Provost's office. And before she could welcome us, Colmes had already pulled up a chair for himself, and I followed suit as we sat across from her desk.

"Good morning," spoke the Provost, laced with sarcasm. "What trouble are you bringing me today, Mr. Colmes?" The Provost delighted in calling him "Mister" rather than any of the other academic terms that recognized one's status on the academic hierarchy. "And you, Mr. Hobson," she said looking at me with a peremptory glance then back to Colmes, "I see that the two of you are still together."

Colmes ignored the insinuation. Instead he pulled up a seat right beside the Provost's desk and leaned into her, his face so close to hers one would have thought they were about to kiss.

"I will not allow you to demolish the School of Criminal Justice," he growled. "I will not."

"Mister Colmes. This is really quite an act. You, who has no authority or even any statutory reason to exist on this campus, deigns to tell me what to do with my faculty."

I wanted to blurt out that we (or I should say they) are not *your* faculty, but had learned that my place as a permanent graduate student was to watch only and to shut up. And the days of student protest were long past.

"I am aware of your dealings with the Department of Environmental Studies, Madam Provost," announced Colmes as he leaned back, then stood up, raising himself to his lean six feet in height.

"And I am aware of your nosing about in faculty business," the Provost quickly interjected. "I will be submitting a report to the President to have you marched out of this place. Besides, it is well known in academic institutions all over the United States that I am at the forefront of charitable work to rid us of animal cruelty and save endangered species. And of course I visit the Department of Environmental studies often. And I repeat, it's none of your business. Now, get out of my office, both of you."

I quickly and robotically stood up from my chair and turned to leave. Colmes, however, stood as erect as he could, his hands on his hips, chest pushed forward, as though he had just finished a marathon run.

"Thank you, Madam Provost. You have been most helpful. You have told me all I need to know." He turned, slapped the top of her desk with his hand and said, "come Hobson. Our work here is done."

I followed my leader out and more or less had to trot to keep up with him.

***

Outside the Provost's door, the secretaries were slavishly tapping away on their Dell computers or the occasional IBM Selectric. None looked up. Colmes looked at his watch, a massive contraption that covered the entire width of his wrist.

"I have one more important stop to make. Shall we meet up in my office in, say, one hour?" he asked as he looked down his nose at me. Then irrelevantly added, "a most unpleasant person, Hobson, I'm sure you would agree."

"Who? I asked in feigned ignorance with a grin. "I don't mind accompanying you. It will save me having to sit in my office staring at a blank page trying to come up with a dissertation topic."

Colmes looked away. His mind was somewhere else. And typically, my joking around simply passed over his densely populated and rational brain.

"No need," he said, "just looking up an old friend of mine in the biochemistry department.

This was his code for "mind your own business." I shrugged and we each went our own ways. He to the biochemistry department, in a wing of the same department of environmental studies building. Me, well, back to my dorm apartment for a badly needed nap. I was naturally, well, I think so anyway, puzzled and annoyed that Colmes would share with me his thoughts and trial hypotheses of what line of attack we should take to save the School. Like a dog, I was forced simply to follow him around, at his heels in fact, never truly knowing why we were going in whatever direction. And, just as dogs get into a habit of behaviors, I too habitually followed Colmes around, though unlike a dog, it was not without question. A serious side effect of this animal habit was that, when my master was not there to lead me, I found myself often walking around in a kind of daze, not necessarily going in the original direction I intended. So at this moment, I suddenly found myself, not at my dorm apartment, indeed nowhere near it, but outside my office door right next to my master's. What other choice did I have at that moment but to sit at my desk and make another attempt at writing an outline for my dissertation proposal. I sat, pen in hand, intending to jot down ideas, but none came. It's possible I fell asleep, but in any case, I was much relieved when I heard the bang on my office wall and the professor calling, "Hobson!"

I quickly went to his office and pulled up the wicker chair to his desk.

Colmes looked at me with a slight glimmer of a smile. "Do you still have your little Mini Minor?" he asked.

"You mean my car?" I asked foolishly. After all, what else could it be?

Colmes did not answer, but just looked at me with an expression of amusement, perhaps even derision.

"I do," I said. "Don't know how much gas is in it though. Haven't used it in a couple of weeks."

"Then please get it ready. Tomorrow afternoon we are taking a trip to Voorheesville"

"Why there?" I asked perplexed as usual.

"Hobson, young man, you are so impatient."

"I wouldn't be if you would just keep me informed as to what you are up to. I'm only a research assistant, but surely I'm a bit more than that to you by now? I mean, we collaborate, I mean, I don't want to suggest that we are equals, of course that would be silly. But it's not fair that you keep me in the dark for so long. I do my best to help you, and have done so for some time now and hopefully will for long into the future…"

My voice trailed off, and I looked down, embarrassed. Colmes looked across his desk to me. I thought he was even going to put out his hand and hold mine to reassure me. But he did not. Silly of me to have thought so.

"Hobson, young man," said Colmes his grey-green eyes staring right in mine (dark brown I think). "You are irreplaceable to me. I could never manage without you. My apologies for holding back. But you also know me. I do not like to expose my thoughts until I have the entire problem solved in my head. Then I share them. And I am very close to that now."

I looked down, thankful for the apology. Then looked up again. "Why Voorheesville?" I asked meekly. "What did you find out from the Provost that I did not?"

"Ah! Hobson. There you are. At last you have realized that you missed something there. Did you not notice the necklace she was wearing?"

"Well come to think of it, I did see it. Silver, I think it was."

Colmes smiled. "Ah Hobson! Very good. And were you not surprised when I leaned forward so close to her I could have kissed her?"

"Well, yes, I did see that, I was very surprised," I answered.

Colmes continued. "The necklace held a kind of medallion that on first glance I thought was the Caduceus of the medical profession. You know? The snake curled around a staff topped with the wings of an eagle?"

I nodded. There was obviously more to come.

"Well, when I leaned forward into her to get a closer look at the necklace, I saw that it was not a Caduceus, but two snakes coiled around a human body arms spread out as though on a cross."

Colmes looked at me as though expecting me to ask what that stood for, but I just sat, my mind stuck as though covered tightly by a lid of some sort. I couldn't think of an answer. And Colmes did not continue. A tense silence had descended upon us.

This was too much for me. I could not sit in one place for long in the best of circumstances, but now this silence, I also could not take. I stood up abruptly and the wicker chair almost fell backwards behind me.

"But Voorheesville?" I persisted.

Colmes smiled with great satisfaction. "As soon as I saw that necklace I went back to Cecilia and asked her to check out whether the Provost has a frequent visit to any place off campus. But more important, to check out all the student clubs."

"And?" I asked, thoroughly involved.

"She goes often to the village of Voorheesville, and the repeated entries in her diary, as I now recollect say 'town meeting Vhs.' "

"So maybe she lives there," I said, unconvinced of its relevance. "But anyway, what does this have to do with her wanting to demolish the School of Criminal Justice?"

Colmes pursed his lips, his sign of impatience. And I admit, he needed to have plenty of patience, once I got attached to a line of thinking, I couldn't let go.

"She does not live there," said Colmes, almost sighing.

"And the student clubs? What could they possibly have to do with the Provost and the eradication of my School?" I persisted, now well aware that I had adopted a tone that was typical of my mentor: interrogation ad nauseam. But Colmes simply ignored me and continued with his own line of responses.

"She founded a student club called φίδι, which is Greek for 'snake'!" Colmes pushed back in his chair and stood.

"No kidding!" I exclaimed, jumping out of my chair. "What does a snake club do and how is it relevant to our case?" I asked with a stupid grin.

Colmes returned to his chair, and leaned back tapping the tips of his fingers together, indicating that he was finished with me and that I should stop with my impudence.

"Thank you Hobson. It will be a pleasant trip to the foothills of the Helderberg mountains and we can have a classic American lunch at the Voohreesville Diner on the way."

"I'll get the car ready and see you tomorrow," I said grumpily. "Let's hope it will start," I called out over my shoulder as a kind of parting jab.

***

I had planned at the time to rid myself of my old Morris Mini-minor. To be honest I could not justify the expense of owning and maintaining it, given that I used it so rarely. In any case, I had always preferred to walk wherever I needed to go on campus, and off campus sometimes a bicycle, weather permitting, to the shopping center for

occasional items for personal use. In fact, I kept it solely for Colmes's
use (he contributed to its upkeep) for those occasions when we needed
to travel to places that could not be reached easily by train or bus. Later
when Uber emerged we found it much more convenient, and certainly
more comfortable than two fully grown adults squeezing their bodies
into such a small space.

Owning a car on campus was, quite frankly, a nuisance. One had to
have a parking sticker, could only park in designated places which were
always a long way from the dormitories or offices, fine when the
weather was warm and the winds calm, but a version of Dante's hell
frozen over, in the depths of winter. Thanks to Colmes, though, I did
have a coveted special parking permit that allowed me to park the car in
many more spaces than were available to regular students. However, the
cars were naturally kept outside, there being no need of an underground
or covered garage since the campus grounds were extensive, having
been built, so I was told, on land that was previously a golf course. The
result was a campus, supposedly designed by Frank Lloyd Wright, that
took up pretty much the whole area of a few square miles, most of the
green of the former golf course transformed into concrete and bitumen,
though dotted with many young trees planted in rows all over, and as yet
too small to make much of a splash of green to compensate for the black
of the parking lots. As it happened, I was later to be relieved of the
nuisance of owning a car, but that is another story, indeed another case.

It was a beautiful day, late spring, when I reached my car, drove up
to the podium and parked in a special parking lot. I had taken a big risk
and not checked the day before that the car would actually start.
Normally I would have, but I think that I was still annoyed with
Colmes's refusal to reveal to me why we were going to Voorheesville.
But that's Colmes, I know. I should be used to it, but I was not, and still
am not.

I walked up the steps that led to the podium, the noise of its central
fountain echoing back and forth from the huge towers of concrete
dormitories at each corner of the campus that looked down from their

location. In spite of everything, the warmth of a spring day caused my feelings of resentment towards my mentor to subside and by the time I reached his office were transformed into excitement and anticipation.

Colmes met me at his office door. He nodded, a slight frown on his face, then we walked quickly together down the tunnel then up the steps to the spring day that awaited us.

"Ah, Hobson!" breathed my mentor, "at last a spring day that we can enjoy, though a pity it is so late in spring."

I wondered whether Colmes had been out of his office-come-apartment at all. His face was pale from not enough sunlight, I always thought.

We reached the car and I held open the door as Colmes struggled a little to get his long body curled up enough to squeeze into the passenger seat. I hurried to the other side, climbed in and pressed the starter button and to my great relief the little engine sprang to life. I drove out on to Western Avenue and we were away, on our route to Voorheesville. And once we got off the busy Western avenue into the bright green fields of small farms and deep greens of apple orchards, Colmes gave a little cough, and I knew that at last I was going to learn something of our case. Though it was not until we passed, on our way through the fringes of the little village of Voorheesville, a dilapidated old church, once bright white, now with paint peeling off, long grass and weeds growing all round it.

"Slow down a little," directed Colmes, "after we have had our brunch, that is where we shall find the solution to our case."

I slowed the car to a roll, quite a challenge with a stick shift, demanding a lot of manipulation of the clutch.

"It looks deserted to me," I said. "Are you sure that's it?"

"Do not doubt me, Hobson. It is indeed. According to the Provost's diary entry, they meet in this former old Methodist church every Saturday afternoon, 1.30 pm."

Colmes raised his hand and pointed. "Keep on going. The diner is just a few hundred yards ahead."

I drove on and sure enough there was the diner, a small village diner, one with only a few tables, most customers sitting up at the counter. And on entering, to my surprise, Colmes was greeted by the manager-come-waiter-come-cook as an old friend.

"Hello Professor. Here on a Saturday? You want the usual?" he asked with a friendly smile.

We took up our places at the counter and were quickly served a cup of coffee each in well-worn heavy mugs.

"Yes I'll have the usual, thanks Rudy," said Colmes, clearly very much at home.

"Could I have the menu?" I asked timidly.

The cook slid a sticky laminated menu across the counter.

"I recommend the hash browns," smiled Colmes.

"Is that what you're having?" I asked, trying to read the menu quickly.

"No, I'm having my usual lunch. Coffee and an order of fries."

"That's it?" I asked, querulously.

"Yes. Before I lived off campus, many years ago, I rented a little house in this township and came here for breakfast every morning," muttered Colmes, as though he did not actually want to answer me. This was quite a revelation. I had been working for him some years now, and never thought of him having a life outside the campus.

"I'll just have bacon and eggs," I said, trying to toss off this revelation as nothing special. I was about to ask him when that was, but the cook interrupted.

"Right you are," called the cook. "Eggs over easy or what?"

"Oh, er, easy will do," I said, then wished I had said hard.

"Coming right up."

I turned to Colmes. "Now," I said, twisting myself around at the counter so that I could look straight into his pallid face, "why are we here, exactly?"

"Now! Now! Hobson," Colmes grinned as his order of fries came sliding across the counter. He picked one up between thumb and forefinger and gobbled it down, his mouth open trying to cool the hot morsel as he chewed it. "You remember the snake we looked at in the department of environmental studies?"

"An Aussie tiger snake," I replied, "how could I forget that?"

"Well, I'm sure that there are other snakes involved. You remember the lab assistant said there were rattle snakes in the annex and in particular the Timber rattlesnake?"

"I don't understand. Involved in what?" I asked impatiently.

"Come! Come! Hobson. You can do better than that! The Provost, of course!"

"You mean…."

"The necklace, Hobson. Her necklace," pressed Colmes.

"You mean….she's a snake collector?"

"With a snake necklace like she has, don't you think it would be something more than a collector?" asked Colmes, impatiently. "The cross, Hobson! The cross!"

"Oh, now I see. She's a snake worshipper. But so what? What has this to do with her wanting to demolish the School of Criminal Justice?"

"My goodness, Hobson. It must be too early in the morning for you. The cross, Hobson, The cross tells us what she is up to, or, should I say, might be up to."

"So you're not sure yourself?" I asked, hoping in some way to bring my mentor down to my level.

"These are deductions I have made from what flimsy evidence we have so far. But as I have repeated to you often, Hobson, I only draw final conclusions as to the solution of a case once I have collected the evidence. We do not have sufficient evidence yet. But after today, hopefully I will have the evidence that will convince the Provost that destroying the School of Criminal Justice is not a wise thing for a person in her position to do."

Having reached a point at which I more or less knew as much about the case as did Colmes, we whiled away the time chatting with each other and the cook. I came to value this time very much, in retrospect.

Away from campus, away from the confines of Colmes's office, I felt a kind of personal freedom and one of almost true friendship with Colmes, the "true" part of it being that we were equals, perhaps not intellectually, though even there I began to feel at least his equal in many ways, that I could match him intellectually in other respects, especially when we were chatting without there being any "secret knowledge" that Colmes was holding back. From that time in the diner, I slowly came to realize that we were in fact friends, equals, respectful of the other's desires and outlook on life. We both had our disabilities and recognized them. His disability—his genius which I certainly did not have—was nevertheless matched by my ADD disability. We were, you might say, a "perfect couple," without the accoutrements that I am sure you have already imputed to us.

Colmes took care of the bill leaving a generous tip. We decided to leave the car at the diner, and walked the few hundred yards down the road to the old church. We could already see in the distance that there were now several cars pulled up outside the old church, including a small passenger van. I thought I could hear the sound of music or singing.

"You hear that?" asked Colmes, whose hearing as I have already noted, was amazingly acute as was his sense of smell. In fact all of his senses were way more acute than mine, or of most people.

"It is the half-chant-half singing style of the Pentecostal Charismatics sect, and if I am not mistaken, the Franciscan charismatics," observed Colmes, his anglicized accent standing out.

By now we had reached the old church and stood out front, listening intently. The voices were many. The singing high pitched, suggesting, observed Colmes, that there were many students in there as well as adults. Notice that. He did not consider students to be adults (and I admit I more or less agree with him).

"So are we going to stay outside or what?" I asked in my impatient manner that must annoy Colmes constantly.

"Indeed not! Indeed not!" exclaimed Colmes.

He led the way down the path overgrown with weeds, to the front entrance and when we got to the door, rickety and almost falling off its hinges, he reached into his tweed jacket and pulled out a small camera. The door creaked a little when opened, but the noise of the singing and chanting drowned it out. We stared down the aisle and saw one person dancing around, seemingly shuddering and shaking, as snakes hung precariously over each of her outstretched arms. Colmes looked across at me with a knowing stare. Yes, I acknowledged, she was aping the necklace, the cross and the snakes. And further, the 'she' was none other than the Provost, her dumpy little body writhing, twisting, bouncing and shaking all together, the snakes dangling, not doing much at all, and probably rattling, though if they were, the noise of the singing drowned it out. And once I took my eyes off the Provost, and scanned the cong-regation of some twenty or so, I observed that it was composed almost entirely of undergraduate students, more or less equally boys and girls, and in retrospect, for at the time I had taken no notice, diversities appropriately represented.

Now comes the fun part. Colmes handed his camera to me and nodded towards the Provost and whispered, "take as many pictures as possible, of everyone." Then he stepped into the aisle and began—I know it's hard to believe for such a tightly bound person as Colmes—to shake and wabble and dance in time with the Provost, gradually making his way up front. Some of the students recognized him, others did not, but were no doubt a little concerned, especially the girls, to have an aging male joining them in their, one might say, vulnerable condition, their bodies subject to the timeless gaze of the *other* (my apologies for lapsing into the current jargon of the social theorists of academia). In a kind of voyeur's delight, I snapped many pictures.

There was music somewhere, a portable keyboard. I searched for its source and found it away to the side in an alcove in which many years ago there was probably an organ or piano. At the keyboard was our acquaintance from the Environmental Studies department, and in a glass case on a stand at the side of the keyboard, was the tiger snake lying in a coil, its head probing this way and that, who knows what it was looking for, or whether it was the noise that was driving it a little crazy. For a moment the pianist looked up and caught a glimpse of Colmes or maybe me, no matter. The effect of it was that she suddenly stopped playing and quickly the singing faded out, the occasional voice lingering on. And with the music gone so was the dancing.

The Provost was aghast, to say the least. I sneaked around the side to the alcove and snapped a couple of photos of the pianist and then Colmes as he approached the front, still kind of jiggling, his arms out to the side, mimicking the dancers who stood staring, dumbfounded.

Still jiggling, Colmes turned his face up to the heavens, through the old oak beams of the roof rotting away, aged and weary as they were, some even broken, and cried, "Oh Saint Francis Keeper of God's precious animals! We offer you the venoms of our Timbers that you will know us when we meet thee!!"

The Provost, struck dumb for a brief moment, her arms outstretched to the sides, her entire body in the shape of a squat, though slightly corpulent cross, stood transfixed as Colmes danced towards her. The congregation of young students gawked and heaved great sighs of consternation, all wanting to laugh at the sight of a middle aged male dancing so ineptly, lacking grace, knees knocking each other, a wobbling eyesore, but a mockery of the deep religious joy that all had been promised by their fearless leader, the Provost. Anticipating some kind of calamity, the pianist turned back to her keyboard and began playing again, possibly a hymn that may have been 'Onward Christian Soldiers.'

"Stop it blasphemer!" yelled the Provost, "stop the music!" as she leaped forward, waving her arms, forgetting the snakes dangling over each of them. And Colmes, fearless, kept coming. A clash of the titans was inevitable. No matter. I was busy taking photographs as directed.

Then the most horrible thing happened. In fact many horrible things happened all at once. The students bolted out of their pews, shouting at Colmes, and chanted, "kill the sinner! Kill the sinner!" And the Provost stopped momentarily crying, "No! No! No violent protesting! Respect the University's protest guidelines!"

Then the worst came. I had dropped the camera after being shoved by a couple of students. I leaned down to retrieve it, and to my horror saw Colmes's head bang down on the floor right by my hand as I reached for the camera.

"Colmes!" I called. "Distinguished Professor Colmes!" I called foolishly thinking that calling him with his full title would garner more attention or whatever. I didn't know what I was doing. But I did snap many more pictures, and then a good shot of a rattler slithering out of the leg of Colmes's pants. "Colmes!" I called again.

I struggled to turn him on to his back. His eyes flickered. He tried to lift his head. "My hand!" he whispered. "Quick!"

I crawled across his body and reached for his right hand that was closed. His other hand I saw was open. I prized open his clenched hand and there fell out a small syringe. "Hurry!" called Colmes in a whisper that frightened me. "One minute left!"

I grabbed the syringe, flipped off the cap and plunged the needle into his neck. Why I chose his neck, I don't know. It just seemed to be the biggest bare piece of flesh available. I threw the syringe away and felt his neck for a pulse. I couldn't find it, though I probably didn't really know where to look. Then I was knocked forward and fell beside the comatose body of my mentor.

"You evil no-good-bully!" snarled the Provost who had pushed me over Colmes's body with her foot. "Perhaps now, you have at last found your proper place!"

Indeed. I thought. It seemed so. My mentor was dead! And, in my somber opinion. The Provost had killed him!

On the brink of collapse myself, I was about to cry, "someone call an ambulance." But remember, in those days, there were no mobile phones, so in order to call an ambulance someone would either have to drive to the nearest telephone box, or knock on a neighbor's door and ask them to call. I decided on the latter. I would run down to the diner.

But that was easier said than done. The student worshippers were running this way and that, the responsible ones trying to find the two snakes that had by now found comfortable places in the many nooks and crannies of the old wooden church. Others, though, if they were not howling and wailing on their knees (foolish if the snakes were still around) asking for mercy or whatever else, were pushing against the Provost who remained dumbstruck, leaning over Colmes's lifeless body, her shoulders pushing against my head as I tried still to feel for Colmes's pulse.

"For Christ sake, get back!" I cried, forgetting where I was. My call was greeted by angry voices of "blasphemer!" "go to hell where you belong" and I felt the crowd pressing down even more. Now I understood why first responders always said when they arrived at the scene of some incident, "get back please, give us room to breathe!"

I had now been crouching for some five minutes and my bent legs were beginning to cramp. I twisted my body around so that I could speak directly to the Provost, whose face now was inches from mine. Her breath smelled like boiled cabbage, no mistaking it. I took my hand off Colmes's neck and muttered, "please, you better get an ambulance," then added, "unless you want to call the cops."

The Provost at last came to her senses and managed to stand up, elbowing her way to an upright position. She looked around her wailing worshippers, then down at Colmes. Anger boiling up in me, I was about to yell, again, "for Christ sake call an ambulance," when I felt a tug on my arm, which quickly turned into a strong pull.

"Help me up," whispered Colmes, "I don't think an ambulance will be necessary."

I looked down, and there was Colmes now sitting up. I grasped his outstretched hand with both mine and he managed to stand, a little groggy, his face haggard and pale from want of blood. His apparent return from the dead had an immediate effect on the wailing congregation. Like wind in the willows, their collected gasps of awe spread throughout the old church. The Provost now stood, her hands on her hips.

"I think I'll call the police," she said, querulously.

"That won't be necessary, Madam Provost," muttered Colmes. He squeezed my hand, a silent and rarely offered communication of friendship. In response I grinned and nodded as I looked at him expectantly.

Colmes continued. "Yes, and thanks for administering the antidote. You are wondering where I got it." He smiled with smug satisfaction.

"Not only that, but why you knew ahead of time that you would need it," I said.

He smiled yet again, superior and much pleased with himself. "I will leave it to your fierce intellect to deduce that for yourself."

I stepped back. Annoyed of course. I had just saved his life and he was already treating me like some pathetic student. But then he tugged lightly on my sleeve. "You got lots of photos, I hope, especially of the snake biting me. But of everything."

"Indeed I did. All of it." I replied, though it was half a lie. I may have missed the snake biting him. It all happened so quickly.

In the meantime, the Provost had induced her congregation of students to quiet down and they sat cross-legged on the floor looking down, pondering the significance of this incredible demonstration of God's presence. Colmes approached her.

"And now a minute of silent prayer, after which we will sing a calm hymn, that we sing at the end of every meeting," announced the Provost as she looked over at the naturist-come-pianist at her keyboard, who nodded her assent.

The Provost approached Colmes warily. "So now, what is it you want, Mister Colmes?" she asked with a touch of belligerence, though nervously awaiting what she knew was to be his *coup de grâce*.

Colmes stood up as straight as he could, still a little weak at the knees. He turned first to me. "The camera, Hobson, please."

I fumbled in my pockets and finally produced it.

"The evidence is on this camera. Including my death, caused by your careless and foolish snake worshipping…"

The Provost interrupted. "We don't worship snakes, Mr. Colmes, we simply dance with them. In these troubled times, ruled by Marxist driven student protest, how else could I attract so many students to get close to Jesus Christ?"

"I need not enter into such a silly debate with you. The fact is that you almost killed me, and that you risk the lives of our students every time you meet, which I assume is every week. Your job is on the line, Madam Provost."

"What is it you want, Mister Colmes?" snarled the Provost.

"You know what I want. Leave the School of Criminal Justice alone. Cease and desist. If you do not. You will go down with it." He waved the camera in the air. "I have all the evidence I need."

The Provost's mouth, a small one at that, contorted into an awful look of a mixture of fear and disdain. For a moment I thought she was going to burst out into tears. But instead, she nodded a silent assent to Colmes, then turned to the pianist and cried in a shaky voice, "Our closing hymn, please."

The keyboard sprang to life, tuned to a sweet melodic cadence and the worshipers sang along:

"All things bright and beautiful,

all creatures great and small,

all things wise and wonderful:

the Lord God made them all."

I am not one hundred percent sure, but I would swear that I saw Colmes's lips moving, singing along with the congregation, as we quietly walked past them and out the rickety front door.

3. No Exit

Universities are dangerous places, where students are subjected to education unlike that of their previous schools of lower education. They are challenged to "think for themselves," not brainwashed, though there is a place for that, usually in small seminars where the favorite—usually fashionable—ideologies of professors assert their superiority. Such professors could not exist without the youthful exuberance of students who provide the mass approval of their radicalism. Thinking for themselves is often, perhaps inevitably, confused with questioning everything of the older generation. "Question everything" is fine except it becomes a tool to support an uprising or protest, in which the protesters instead of thinking for themselves behave without thinking as in an angry mob. Historically, dramatic changes in societies may develop or be fostered by such uprisings, protests, and demonstrations of university students. Probably, student protests helped end America's war in Vietnam.

In a later case I will report to you how Colmes dealt with an uprising that threatened the existence of the entire university. In the case that I am about to describe, the entire university was not under attack or threatened, although at times it appeared as though it might be, along with all universities everywhere. This case is also of great significance to me personally, because it was in this case that I first met Professor Colmes and was the case that brought the two of us together.

I came to the United States from Australia in the nineteen seventies. I prefer not to give specific dates because it would make it possible for some of my agile readers to track down the identities of some of the characters I mention in my stories. And while the people I describe are indeed real persons, I have of course reconstructed their features and habits to protect their privacy, in the true American spirit .

The seventies was the period in which the Weather Underground was in action throughout American universities. The members of that mildly communist organization, more a coming together of like minds, manage to build a loose network of members in many universities, and to pull off some successful violent attacks. If they were communists, of course, their organization would have been rigidly structured, each "cell" with its tough leader who ruled the cell with strict and merciless discipline. In that decade, discipline was the last consideration in any protest movement.

***

I was hard at work studying for my constitutional law exam, sitting in one of those cubicles they provide doctoral students in the maize of the main library that inhabited the entire west side of the university's square podium. There was no door to these cubicles, we students just sat at our desks that faced the wall, a shelf for books, a hard chair, the rest of the library at our backs. These cubicles were hard to come by and during periods of examinations, they were strictly let out only for limited periods, usually for two hours. There was a small slot attached to the cubicle entrance into which we had to place our library card and fill out our name and time of entry.

I was engrossed with my reading (a bit of an exaggeration, maybe I was dozing) when I heard a light tap on the side of my cubicle. I turned and there stood a strong looking man, medium height (tall compared to me), a long chiseled face, thin lips, a slight twitch at one corner, and a gleam in his blue-gray eyes.

"Mister Hobson, I presume?" he asked, his voice a slightly high pitched but most penetrating one, rather like the warble of an Australian magpie.

"G'day," I said in Australian, "and you are?"

"Interdisciplinary Professor Thomas Colmes, but you can call me just Colmes."

"OK. Colmes it is," I said with Aussie bluster, "and you can call me Bill. What's going on?"

"Hobson, if you don't mind, I never call students or anyone else for that matter, by their first name."

"No problem, mate," I replied a little put off. His accent was kind of English, as though there was a plumb in his mouth, like my Dad used to describe all pommies (English migrants to Australia). "You're a pom...I mean English?" I cheekily asked.

Colmes ignored the question. I would find out later that his particular origins were a bit of a mystery.

"I need a student I can trust who is unbiased, forthright, and down to earth." And then he added, unnecessarily I thought, "I see you are reading Tribe's *Constitutional Law*. I hope you have spied his deeply buried biases."

"Don't think so, Colmesy," I replied, "just learning it by rote for Professor Garcia's exam."

"Excellent!" he almost smiled. The bloke was too serious for my liking. "And it's Colmes, if you don't mind."

I ignored the correction and then asked the obvious, "so you wanted me specially for something or other?"

Colmes took a deep breath and looked around. "We cannot talk here. What I have to tell you is something that is of a very serious nature, and requires the utmost care and secrecy."

"Well I do have my comprehensive exam tomorrow," I kind of announced, like the information wasn't especially directed to him.

"I am aware of that," said Colmes, "and I also know that it is an open book examination, is it not?"

"Yair, but..."

"I need your help, Hobson, and I might add that it is a matter of life or death," he said firmly, his English accent exaggerated.

"Well, I suppose if you put it like that..." I mumbled submissively.

"I do indeed. I do indeed," spoke Colmes, a big frown on his forehead, his long ears slightly flinching.

I turned to my desk, shut the books I had open, placed them on the shelf above, grabbed my small canvas bag that contained my notebooks and lunch, and turned back to face this mysterious man called Colmes.

"Alright. Alright," I replied with a big grin, mimicking what I would later discover was his favourite expression "indeed."

Colmes had already turned and walked towards the library exit. I trotted along trying to catch him up

In other cases, I will describe for you Colmes's office, deep in the bowels of the underground tunnels that served the university. By my reckoning he led me down and through a maze of tunnels—as I thought at the time, now I know them like the back of my hand—to his office that I reckoned was somewhere under the main podium, maybe even under the big fountain that gushed next to the clock tower.

Colmes fiddled with his keys that were on a small chain hanging from his trouser pocket, not unlike the chain on a watch fob of older days. He led the way in, grabbed a wicker chair that sat just inside the door, and placed it at the front of his desk, across from his own desk chair. "This is your chair," he said all businesslike.

"The other one," I said jokingly pointing to the overstuffed leather chair in the corner, "looks more comfortable."

"The wicker chair," emphasized Colmes.

I was beginning to see that Colmes did not have much of a sense of humor, or at least showed it only rarely. On the other hand, we Aussies knew that the English had a pretty poor sense of humor compared to us Aussies. And they certainly couldn't take a joke. I was about to plonk myself down on the overstuffed chair, but held it back. Instead, I calmly sat on the wicker chair as directed.

"So what's up doc?" I said foolishly, indeed flippantly.

"If we are going to work together, it will be necessary for you to excise your Aussie superficialities. The business before us is very serious," lectured Colmes, a straight, now seeming gray to me, even sallow face. Did I really want to work for this bloke?

"Are you acquainted with a criminal justice student named Akira Tanaka?" asked Colmes seemingly unaware of my not well disguised doubts about working for him.

"Don't think so, Colmes," I said with a hint of belligerence, or that is how it seemed to me, calling an esteemed professor by his last name.

"I want you to find out as much as you can about his background, and especially as of now, what he is doing, what examinations he is lined up for, what courses he likes and dislikes. I would normally have Rose my Russian assistant do this for me, but I think that you would be less imposing or shall we say less scary than would Rose."

"Rose?" I asked with a grin. "The one with the knitting? Everyone knows Rose."

"Indeed, they do," answered Colmes. "She is a treasure, but not good for this particular job."

"So what do you want me to find out about this Akira guy?" I asked, and before he could reply I added, "what's the problem?"

"As you may have deduced, Hobson, he is Japanese. It has come to my attention, from a confidential source, that he is having suicidal thoughts."

"I leaned across his desk and muttered, "isn't that a Japanese thing? Like, Hara Kiri and all?"

"Perhaps one should not call it a Japanese thing," corrected Colmes.

"I thought you wanted me to be straight forward, no bull shit," I answered defensively.

"Indeed. Indeed. You are right Hobson. I thank you for being open and forthright. I doubt that in this case it is because he is Japanese, but simply a matter of his fear of failing his final comprehensive exam."

"I can attest to that," I said with a wry smile. "And you didn't say who gave you this information."

"Right again, Hobson. I did not..."

"And besides," I continued, "I'd say all grad students facing their finals suffer the same psychological trauma."

"Very good, Hobson. You have mastered the jargon of the psycho-therapist," said Colmes, and I thought I heard a quiet chortle, like a magpie.

I was about to add that I was a psychologist in my former life in Australia, but Colmes cut in first. "Yes, you worked for the Victorian education department. I hope it was not too Victorian?"

This was Colmes's idea of a joke.

"Probably not enough for you," I countered.

Colmes fingered his key chain. Then turned serious again and began to answer my original question. "The student counseling people have reached out to me. It seems he went to them saying that he was going to commit suicide, but would give no reason or hint of what it was that was driving him. Usually it is some form of depression, as you would no doubt know, Hobson, in your former role as psychologist.

"My cases were mainly younger children," I answered, "so I have no hands-on experience with teens or older. Nevertheless the fact that Akira went to the counseling department surely is an indicator that he is serious and is seeking help, a good thing."

"Indeed. Indeed. Now I want you to find out everything you can of him, his friends, any support group. Where and what he does every minute of the day. Rose had a brief poke around and reported to me that he is very secretive and does not mix much with the other students. Understandable, since according to Rose, he speaks very little English."

I was frankly flabbergasted. "No English and he's doing his comprehensive?" I gasped.

"Apparently it is all an open book written exam, an exam method that is all the rage these days."

"Seems to me that gives an advantage to students who can read and comprehend quickly," I mused.

"Perhaps. But it maybe works against a student who can memorize answers to anticipated questions, then write their answers down in the exam within the strict amount of time permitted. It's a matter of learning by wrote, as against reading, filtering, organizing and extracting information on the fly, as one would say, if it were open book."

I was considerably impressed by the way Colmes had succinctly summarized the situation. "So you think that this open book form of exam discriminates against those who come from an education system that emphasizes rote learning, as is common in some if not all, Asian countries?"

"Precisely. Indeed. Indeed. It is why I have taken on the case. In fact I informed the counseling department that I would take the case providing that they kept out of it and gave me complete control. They were only too happy to agree, They did not want a suicide on their hands."

"Neither do we," I said, making us a royal 'we' without thinking.

"Indeed. Hobson my boy. Indeed," endorsed Colmes, which much pleased me, except for the boy part.

I walked out of Colmes's office with a light step, pleased that this big deal professor had chosen me of all people, to assist him. I came away, though, only with the name of the student and nothing much more. Had I stayed in my position as president of the criminal justice students' association, I would have surely known Akira. But I had given up the students' association a couple of years back when student protests were running hot. I didn't mind the protests in themselves, but it was just mentally exhausting, and too much conflict for my liking. But I had best keep those things for another case, which pivoted around student protests.

Akira being Japanese made it a simple matter to find him. I looked up the class schedules that were pinned on the school noticeboard, and dropped by any that were meeting. It was the last week of classes, so I knew that I had to get on it right away. The final exams would be the following week. I saw that Professor Garcia's constitutional law class was on right then, so I hurried across the Podium to the lecture center. It was always a large class because his was a required course for all students, the Constitution after all, considered to be, the very core of criminal justice, and rightly so, in my opinion. I slipped in the door at the back of the lecture hall, way at the top, so I could look down at the rows of students, all sitting there, nervously waiting to be called on, by the professor, as I will describe in another case.

Looking down, though, only gave me a view of student heads, and since Akira was Japanese I assumed that his hair would be straight, copious, and black. I now realized that this was not a good idea, but now that I was in there, I would wait until class was dismissed and hopefully catch up with him as they all left. Eventually, not seeing any sign of him, I asked a student who looked Asian to point out Akira to me. I know, my doing this was tinged with a bit of racism, "they all look the same" mentality, but I did it anyway. And it paid off, to some degree. The student was most friendly, and said that Akira was in the class but he did not come to class because he was too afraid he would be called upon and couldn't speak much English. She then invited me to a meeting of the Asian students' association which Akira did attend, because it was a group that helped each other with studying and preparing for exams. And because Constitutional law class was by far the hardest and scary class, they all met after class in a small room that the school assistant dean had kindly put aside for them.

There were three others in the room, and I quickly recognized Akira. He was the only Japanese, the others were Chinese, I guessed. They all opened their notebooks, except Akira who sat with his notebook closed, staring blankly at the floor. One looked in my direction, then turned back to her books. I sat in the corner and watched them work, most industriously. They were studying the law on whether individuals could be committed to a prison or asylum without a trial, civil commitment they call it.

After fifteen minutes or so, Akira stirred, the other students turned to him, then he picked up his books and left, bowing nervously, backing out of the room until he hit the door, which I quickly opened for him and followed him out.

"Akira!" I called, "just one moment, please."

He stopped, and waited for me. He was a smallish person, of stocky stature, one could imagine him playing soccer, edging opponents out with his body, running fast up the field. "May I speak with you?" I asked.

He stopped and looked down. It was easy enough to see that he was not a happy person. "Speak English?" I asked.

"No," he said, shaking his head.

"I am Bill Hobson. Professor Colmes sent me to talk with you." I hoped that he had heard of this famous professor. Indeed, his eyes lit up a little, but then he looked down again. "I am here to help you," I said trying very hard to be kind and helpful.

"No one help me. Not can," he replied in a deep voice, unexpected from such a small person.

"I understand that the final Con Law exam is next week, a week from today, right?" He seemed to understand, nodded a little. "I am sure I can help you. Professor Colmes has found a Japanese translator who can sit with you in the exam. It's an open book exam, you understand what that is?"

Akira nodded, and he almost smiled, but there was a very deep frown on his face, his eyebrows forced down almost shutting his eyes. I started to gesticulate trying to convey what I assumed my English did not. "Come with me," I said pointing first to him then to me, "and we will meet with the translator and get everything sorted out."

I wanted to put my arm around him he seemed so forlorn, so deeply unhappy. But he appeared to have understood me and did follow me as I led us across the Podium to a small office buried in the labyrinth of the library. It was located in, of course, the Asian studies collection area, which heretofore I never knew existed. We entered the small office, not much bigger than a cubicle, three walls totally glass, one could see all the way down the library stacks. The translator, surprisingly, was not Asian at all, or did not appear so, though there was some hint of high cheek bones. She saw me gaping at her and said quickly, "I am a descendant of the Japanese who were locked away during World War Two," she said, then turned directly to Akira. "Please take a seat," she smiled. He complied, then to both our consternations, he broke down and cried. His head in his hands, his knees pulled up to his elbows, so that he sat precariously on the edge of the small chair.

The translator looked at me. "My name is Joan," she said. "Let's see what the problem is."

She leaned over and stroked Akira's head, as one would when consoling an unhappy dog, and out of her mouth I imagined came a stream of goodness, all in rapid Japanese. This seemed to have some effect, as Akira's sobbing gradually became less violent, and soon, just one small sob came every now and again, and Joan offered a tissue for him to wipe his eyes. He then responded with a stream of Japanese, gesticulating wildly, his face contorted with what looked to me was close to rage.

Joan sat back and looked across to me. "He is frightened he will fail the course because, he says, the open book exam makes it impossible for him to read the material quickly and then write an answer in English."

"Perhaps he could write it in Japanese and you, if you would be prepared, could translate it for the Professor to read?" I suggested.

Joan addressed this suggestion to Akira. His face became contorted again, as he replied at length to Joan, who frowned and said to me, "he says he tried that, even went to the Dean to request it, but Professor Garcia flatly refused. Seems that this professor once failed a student because of his illegible handwriting."

"I'm not at all surprised," I answered. "Then we will have to find another way."

Joan then spoke to Akira in a kind and motherly way, I thought, though I did not know what they were talking about. I assumed that she was reassuring him that a solution would be found. But when Joan spoke to me after her long conversation with Akira, she expressed much concern. It seems that the possibility of failure in Japanese culture, according to Joan who says she believes it to be so, for a family member to fail, especially he being the eldest of the three children in his family and the only male, is not unlike failing on the battlefield. The shame can only be eradicated by one thing, the only way out, suicide.

"Are you serious, I mean, is he serious?" I asked, aghast.

"Yes! Yes!" cried Akira. And he got up and departed. I was left wanting to speak more with Joan to see if there was anything we could do, but also wanting to chase after Akira to try to talk some sense into him. I rose from my seat, but as I did so, Joan grasped my arm.

"Leave him be. I think he is in the process of resolving the problem for himself. You may have noticed that he almost smiled."

I had noticed that, but had thought I imagined it. "What is he going to do?" I asked.

"He assured me that he will not commit suicide. At least not before the exam." She replied.

"That's not much of a reassurance," I said.

"No it's not. But at least it will give you a little more time to try to work something out with the professor, who sounds like an ogre, if you ask me," Joan said, raising her eyebrows.

"Indeed he is," I agreed, retreated to the door and expressed my deep appreciation for her help.

It was a week until the final exam.

I reported back to Professor Colmes, who praised me for my hard work, but was a little perturbed. "I am concerned that, after the emotional outburst that you describe, he miraculously, recovers and walks off saying he has a solution. We all know that the only viable solution is suicide. Unless..." Colmes mused.

"What?" I asked, "what?"

"I will speak with Garcia. Maybe he will listen to me, but I doubt it. I will suggest to him that he simply pass the student," said Colmes as though he were the Godfather who would make an offer that Garcia could not refuse.

"Really? You could get him to do that? And besides, is that not unfair to the other students who have worked hard to get their degrees. It cheapens their degree, don't you think?" I said in a most forthright manner, one that I regretted, only having just started to work for him.

"I appreciate your toughness, Hobson, Indeed I do. But really, what does it matter? One student, going back to Japan. Gets his degree in an unorthodox manner. His family are happy. So what? Is it worth losing one's life over an exam?" Colmes looked at me square in the face. It was a forceful, intellectual, or was it emotional, challenge?

"Whatever," I said dismissively. "Garcia will never go for it. He's heartless."

"We will see," said Colmes tapping the fingers of his outstretched hands together, communicating a kind of satisfied though pensive state of mind.

"Then we're done?" I asked Colmes, as I made to leave.

"Not quite. This case is not solved yet, we must keep at it. I will meet with Garcia and see what I can do. You should keep an eye on Akira to the extent that it is possible."

"You mean tail him? I mean, I'd have to live with him every minute of the day to stop him from trying to do himself in," I asserted.

"True. Just do what you can and let me know if anything happens."

"No problem," I replied, "and you will do the same, I take it?"

Colmes nodded and I took my leave.

As it turned out, from that day, Akira disappeared. I could not find him anywhere. If he had killed himself, surely the body would have been found, even if he jumped in the Hudson river. And Colmes insisted that we not report him as a missing person. That he would show up sooner or later.

***

The day of the constitutional law final exam came, and nervous students sat in their assigned seats chattering, arms full of books, waiting for Professor Garcia to show. Until now I have refrained from calling him by his nickname Ted the Red, because this was the very first case in which I was involved, and people except students did not refer to him by the nickname. But for this case, the nickname is pertinent, given that he earned his nickname from the demonstrations he had participated in downtown, protesting outside the legislature and capitol in Albany, against whatever issue it might be, for the most part the Vietnam war, death penalty abolition, homelessness, hunger, corruption, whatever the SDS or Weathermen or Black Power movements were pushing. All of these referred to by politicians and the popular press as communists of one kind or other. Hence Professor Theodore Garcia's nickname Ted the Red.

Now I sat at the back of the lecture hall and waited for Ted the Red to enter. He did so, carrying a stack of blue books, the traditional exam booklets in which all students were required to write their exam answers, and of course, the sheaf of legal size papers containing the exam questions. To my surprise, I spied Akira sitting in the front row. This being an exam, there were no assigned seats because the professor would not be calling on individuals by name.

I walked down to the lectern where Ted the Red was standing, checking over his list of students, counting them to see if all were present. He smiled at me as I passed Akira who seemed to be writing furiously and covered his work when he saw me. His round face seemed to be free of stress and anxiety that had overcome him during our meeting. What on earth could have happened, I wondered, and even suspected that it had all been an act. Ted waved at me with a sheet of paper in his hand. He looked amused, and looked down on me his face wrinkled with a mixture of amusement and superiority.

"Take a look at this," he said, handing me the paper. "Now you can see that I was right all along. The asshole was faking it."

I took one look and was struck speechless. It was a note typed in capitals in the middle of the paper that said:

PASS ALL CON LAW STUDENTS NOW OR SUFFER THE
CONSEQUENCES.
LONG LIVE THE WEATHER UNDERGROUND

"You have to dismiss the class," I proclaimed, "It's a bomb threat!"

"Bull shit! It's that little Japanese asshole trying to weasel his way out of the exam," he growled.

"But it *is* the Weather Underground. They've blown up several places over the past couple of years. You've got to dismiss the class!" I turned as if to address the class. "If you will not, I will!"

Ted grabbed me by the arm and roughly dragged me to the door of the lecture center and pushed me out. I tried to forced my way back in, but he was too strong and held the door closed. Thereupon I decided that my only alternative was to raise the alarm. I looked for a fire alarm, but could not find one. Then I realized that the bottom doors to the lecture centers opened into the tunnels. I would run to Colmes. He would have a solution, I hoped. I ran one way, then turned and ran the other. I had only been to his office that one time when he hired me. It was like a rabbit warren down there. Then I heard the clacking of a typewriter and followed the sound, which led me to a large office with one person, surrounded by TVs and other audio and video paraphernalia.

I rushed in and grabbed at the typist's phone that sat on her desk. This gave her a big fright and she was none too pleased.

"What are you doing?" she asked, "who are you?"

"I need to use the phone," I said.

"Put your quarter in the jar there and you can use it. Dial 7 to get an outside line."

"But I don't have a quarter. Besides this is an emergency," I cried.

"We have to mind our budget down here," said the typist as she grabbed my wrist in a very strong grip.

"Colmes! " I yelled. "Where's Professor Colmes's office?"

"Oh. Him? The one that never even says hello when you pass him in the tunnel," she said in a most disapproving manner.

"His office. Where is it?"

At this point she at last comprehended that there was something serious going on. She let go my wrist and pointed, "Go that way, first right, second on the left."

I rushed off and soon found Colmes's office and banged on his door. The lock quickly opened, and Colmes appeared, frowning. "What is it?" he asked.

"I went to Professor Garcia's exam in the off-chance that Akira might show, thinking that he would not be there of course, since he hasn't been seen for a couple of weeks."

"Indeed. Hobson. The situation is very serious. We must get to Garcia's class immediately. In fact I was about to go there when you banged on my door," said Colmes.

"It's just a few minutes down the tunnel," I said. "Akira showed up to the class and seemed to be writing his exam."

"I am sure that he was faking it. In fact, I have reliable information that he has been meeting with the Weather Underground and that they are, or have been, planning to plant a bomb in the examination classroom."

"That is what I was coming to tell you. Garcia received a bomb threat, here it is." I handed him the note but he pushed it away, saying that he could not read it. It was his dyslexia, of course, but at that time I did not know this. I simply put it down to his being easily annoyed and wanting to do his own thing. "I tried to get him to make an announcement and dismiss the class. But he would have none of it. Would not take the note seriously, even though it was signed by the Weather Underground."

"Yes," said Colmes as we got to the lecture center door, "that is to be expected. He has his reasons, I can tell you."

Breathless, I opened the lecture center door and we rushed in. All was quiet. Garcia walked back and forth in front of the blackboard of the lecture center. I spied Akira still apparently writing his exam.

"I've been waiting for your arrival," grinned Ted the Red, "you can see that we have not yet been blown up."

Colmes took a deep breath and walked up to the lectern. "Attention class!" he called. "Please close your examination booklets, make sure your name is written on the front and leave the classroom in an orderly fashion. Take all your things with you, and hand your exam booklet to Dr. Garcia, Mr. Hobson or myself as you leave. There has been a bomb threat and we have good reason to believe that it is the Weather

Underground."

Ted the Red was extremely angry. "Hold it! He screamed. "I will have no one vacate my class, or submit to threats by persons of violence and insurrection!" Some students stopped, others ignored him and kept going. Garcia continued and it was clear that he would not let up. "My father, his father and many of his relatives were murdered by the Nazis during world war two. It was only by the tenacity and bravery of my mother that she managed to escape with me out of Germany, and since none of the allies would take in Jewish refugees, we ended up in Cuba, and eventually the United States after the war was over..."

You can understand how strange, yet moving, this appeared. Here were scores of students scrambling to get out of a classroom to escape a bomb, and Ted the Red is reciting his personal history, banging the lectern to drive home his point, seemingly oblivious to the danger into which he had thrust his students.

Colmes gathered up Garcia's papers and wedged them under his arm, then gently, but nevertheless with some necessary force, guided Professor Garcia out of the classroom. I walked through the aisles collecting the exam blue books, as they called them (the covers were a light blue). I stayed until all had left, except Akira who remained, sitting silently, staring into space.

"You need to leave," I said softly.

Eventually, Akira did gather up his things and leave. I was the last one out, and there was, obviously, still no explosion. In the meantime, Colmes had called the authorities to report the threat. And as I exited, a couple of bomb specialists, dressed in their military-like uniforms, though they were New York State troopers, showed up to search for the bomb.

In fact a small bomb was found sitting in one of the cupboards that contained chalkboard materials just below the blackboard. According to the experts the bomb was poorly made, and they could find no indication of how it would be detonated, though there was a sizable amount of TNT sitting there. The days of remotely detonated bombs and suicide bombers were yet to come.

However, settling the dispute, and dispute it was, concerning the Con Law grades was no simple matter. There were two reasons for this. The first and obvious one was what is called, indeed revered, the principle of academic freedom. Supposedly the professor has total and complete authority to make all academic decisions including the content of their courses, grading of their students, and behavior in the classroom. So Ted the Red was completely within his rights to ignore the Weather Underground demands. The second was, how to assuage the inherent skepticism of the Weather Underground and their supporters that the professor's submission of the grades would in fact be recorded in the students' transcripts. The recording by a professor of a student's grade went through several layers of bureaucracy until it was finally entered into the student's official academic transcript. The process took weeks, if not months to be completed. Though the Weather Underground probably had no understanding of the lengthy process of recording a student's grade, they nevertheless were sufficiently distrustful of the people who were, derisively, over thirty years old, so effort would have to be made to assure them that indeed their demands had been met.

***

Of course, there is one final unfinished matter that I must now attend to. Did Akira commit suicide? And was he truly involved in the Weather Underground?

Colmes had the answers, although there was some controversy as to the true outcomes. Certainly, Akira did not commit suicide. Or at least not during the difficult negotiations with the Weather Underground whose representatives proved most cantankerous. But, according to Colmes, he was deeply involved in the Weather Underground planning and implementation of the bomb. He knew this from the intelligence he received from none other than his housekeeper Rose (later known as Rose the elder for reasons that will come clear in later cases) and permanent graduate student like myself, who had obtained the Weather

Underground's confidence by the simple fact that she was Russian and spoke English with a strong Russian accent. They assumed, wrongly, that she must be a communist, and therefore could be trusted even though she was probably over thirty.

Colmes, therefore, knew about the planting of the bomb, especially Akira's central part in it. Akira appears to have overcome his supposed deficit in the English language to convince the Weather Underground to attack Ted the Red, claiming that he was a CIA spy and only pretended to be a left wing extremist. Colmes claimed that this was a cunning trick on Akira's part, to get the Weather Underground to have Ted the Red pass all students regardless, the argument being that giving grades was just one more overbearing tactic of the professorial elite to keep the students in submission and stop them from seeing through the obvious hypocrisies of the academic ruling class. This was quite ahead of the times. There would be demonstrations throughout the United States and even Europe charging that assigning grades was a heartless act of authoritarianism and discriminated against those students who were not good at tests. Colmes leaked this information to the FBI and Akira was listed for deportation, which occurred soon after the faculty senate and university administration caved to the Weathermen demands and all Con Law students were given a passing grade. Needless to say, this created an uproar among all other students who immediately demanded automatic passing grades in all their courses.

Thus, concluded Colmes, a suicide had been averted, one life saved, at the cost of degrading the education of all other students from that time forward.

4. The Stalker

I began these the first case of the snakes because it demonstrated just how far Colmes would go in order to bring a case to its conclusion. He planned in quite some detail to construct a situation in which the Provost, bless her frozen heart, had no way out. The death of Colmes would have been easily pinned on her. And of course, the publicity of the snake worship would have destroyed her career. Police often use this technique to catch sex offenders. It is a trick of the law enforcement trade: install a red light camera at the bottom of a hill, catch speedsters by hiding in wait in a police car just around the corner and dart out to catch the once innocent driver. Install speed cameras in so many places, especially in areas that appear to be deserted, set up a 'sting' operation in which you advertise stolen goods for sale, or a very popular sting, engage anyone on social media pretending you are an underage girl, then set up a meeting for sex. One could go on.

The reasons stings are so popular with law enforcement is that (according to what I learned in my criminal law class) they have a very high conviction rate. Mind you, lawyers, especially defense lawyers, call these operations "entrapment." Their argument would seem to be insurmountable: police entrap an otherwise innocent suspect. By doing so, they create crime (they are supposed to prevent it, right?), because the innocent perpetrator would not have committed the crime had they not been offered the opportunity (or even enticement) to do so. Generally, so my law professor taught me, juries don't buy the entrapment defense, especially if there is video evidence.

There was no jury present in the case of Doctor Dolittle. But there was the threat of one. Colmes had risked his life by getting himself bitten by a rattle snake during a snake-worshiping charismatic meeting overseen by the University's Provost, arguably the person with the most authority and power in the whole university—in many cases more than the president himself, whose policy was to delegate authority to shield himself from responsibility in case of a scandal or something worse. That, no doubt, was why trusties were and are so popular in prisons as an enforcement arm of the prison administration. So I am told by the ex-convicts who now attend the university School of Justice as part of the out-reach program of the state of New York.

But it is also why an individual like Colmes existed on campus. He was an enforcer of sorts, though he would be most offended if I said this to him. He insisted that he simply responded to cries for help. He worked for no one. He was his own man. He was driven by a very strong sense—I would go so far as to say moral sense—of justice. If, when a case came before him, he perceived an injustice, or a situation that he thought would inevitably lead to injustice, he would take the case, and would not rest until it had been settled to his own satis-faction—not that of the justice system, I might add, to which he rarely forwarded a case.

I entreat my good readers to keep this fact about Colmes in mind. He and I had many heated debates over this matter. What (not who) gave him the right to decide on matters of what were fair and just and what were not? And so on. You get the point.

But now on to the present case that occurred well before the snake case. One in which there was no entrapment in the classic sense. There was no need of it, since we already knew who the alleged offender was.

***

I should begin by saying that the stalker was not the first and no doubt would not be the last stalker on campus. For it is a wonderful place for stalkers, so many people banded together in close proximity to each other, many young and beautiful people of all genders. And of the young, the vast majority of them wondering who they are and what will become of them? They are, thusly, ripe for the picking by someone who is, one might say more "mature" than they. (Though, the stereotype of stalkers is that they are immature, a judgment usually made after the stalker has been caught). But such predators, in our experience, are usually professors or those who are older and have established themselves or have given up on that life endeavor and simply live for the present. Indeed, the latter have unquenchable desires to consume as much of the present as they can. Given that outlook, they are, to some, if not many, the object of envy, for their crazed impossible quests for conquests return many more failures than successes, as Kierkegaard observed many years ago. He thought (or maybe not) that the small returns were worth the many failures.

But Colmes reckoned that our stalker fitted none of these categories. "Our stalker has tried," says Colmes, "these peripatetic endeavors. But unlike those he envies, he mortally fears failure. It takes only one, and that is enough to force him to climb back into his shell, a cloaked figure who sneaks around as though he were the hunchback of Notre Dame."

Perhaps I overstated it when I said we already knew who the stalker was. We did not, in fact. That is, we had no name, or any indication of who exactly they were. What I meant before was that we knew the kind of person that the stalker was. You may have noticed and it will become evident as I recount our most sustainable cases, that I do fall into a bit of exaggeration from time to time. It is all the result of my enthusiasm, which, as Colmes enjoys pointing out, spoils my otherwise ability to almost match him in rational thinking. It's getting it down on paper where I fall short. You might think that this must be a severe disappointment to Colmes who hired me to "keep intellectual house," as he called it, with the clear intention of utilizing my writing skills to make up for his dyslexia. However, as you have already gained an inkling, my writing is perfectly matched for recounting in an interesting manner the sustainable cases of Professor Colmes. It's just that it is not a proper style for writing a dissertation, which must be flat and boring, certainly with no climaxes, though, there are certain techniques, especially in the realm of statistics where exaggeration can be indulged in without penalty.

But now to our case.

Rose the elder had just brought us our afternoon tea of scones with jam and cream and a pot of hot tea, made with fast boiling water, left to sit and draw. And, of course, delivered on an ornate tray, teapot in a cozy, a tiny jug of milk (we both liked our tea strong with a small dash of milk). It was quite early in my new job as Colmes's assistant. I therefore found the English practice of afternoon teas and morning coffees, the whole ritual an amusing, silly after-birth of British Imperialism. But I kept all that to myself. After all, my relatives back in Australia indulged in this tea fetish, though without the fancy rituals.

This case explains a lot about Colmes, and maybe a little about me. You may wonder how Colmes came to have a housekeeper, in typical Victorian style, I might add. Perhaps I exaggerate a little (I have warned you!). But Rose, when she was an "older" graduate student (in her fifties, one never really knew) was well known around the university for her forthright manner, her often biting and raw criticisms of anything she observed around the campus and beyond. These observations and views she poured forth into the Student Newspaper, *The Flotsam*. And she never held back in the constitutional law class that I also took that same year (what year does not matter). In that class, the professor (that's right, Ted the Red, a man with an eye for any woman who would present herself) picked on individual students in the classic tradition. But Rose never waited to be picked upon, and, even though she did her knitting constantly, she thought nothing of butting into an interrogation between the professor and an intimidated student. Every time Rose intervened a titter flowed across the class like a swarm of locusts. As if that were not enough, though, she was always the student who approached the podium at the end of the class and peppered the professor with questions. Some students even remained after class to watch her in action. Knitting in hand, doing pearl stitch as she went, she would in her gruff Russian accented voice, point out to the professor (a most liberal one of course) that he had no idea what free speech was all about. The professor, a tall, heavily sun-tanned figure, an ex-basketball player one guessed, and a deep rolling voice would step up to her, looking down from his great height, she small and dumpy not looking up though. She had, after all, to watch her knitting. Instead, she prattled on as she knitted. The professor, nicknamed Ted the Red thought to be a communist because he led student protests downtown in front of the capitol building.

Colmes knew a lot of what went on in that professor's class because many students came to him to complain about the professor's bullying style. This, even when they knew that there was little Colmes could do, and besides he had no wish to cross this law professor. Why did the professor act in this way? The simple answer was that he was a bully. The complicated answer was that he considered it his responsibility to scare the hell out of students because that was what practicing the law was all about. Besides understanding the law required a lot of study and a lot of reading, something that many of the students in this (then) Criminal Justice Program were not used to doing. So, according to the professor, it was his duty to make them read the material. He was not there to entertain them. The students sniggered behind his back though. They knew of his failed and successful attempts with particular students of his fancy. And his quarries were not spurned by other students. Not at all. They were looked on in awe, especially by the male students who no doubt felt inferior because they were unable to conquer (a carefully chosen word) women the way the professor did.

It would come as no surprise then, that he and Colmes got along quite well. After all, Colmes was, as I have intimated, a bit of a bully himself. As I have noted, his interrogations were carefully targeted. So when students came to him to complain, he politely explained to them that he was not in a position to intervene in a professor's teaching style. It all had to do with the First Amendment in respect to free speech, did it not? And besides, he was not a school counsellor, he was the University Distinguished Professor of Interdisciplinary Studies.

***

I was tapping away on my little Olivetti portable typewriter, trying once more to write an outline for my dissertation. The title was going to be "Time and Place as a Life Course." And I was about to rip the sheet out of the typewriter in frustration, when I heard voices next door and Colmes banging on the wall between our offices to tell me my services were needed.

"Hobson!" came the shrill voice.

I grabbed my legal pad and pen and quickly ran in. Unfortunately, my wicker chair that was always drawn up to the front corner of Colmes's desk was already occupied by none other than Rose and her knitting. I stood uncomfortably next to her, as there was no other chair in the office except the overstuffed leather chair in the far corner, just behind the door through which I had just entered.

"Now what can I do for you, Rose?" Colmes asked warmly.

"I am being stalked," she growled in her gruff monotone, male-sounding Russian accent.

"Stalked?" asked Colmes trying to hide his surprise. "Are you sure?"

"I wouldn't come to you if I wasn't," snapped Rose.

"Tell me more," responded Colmes, almost smiling.

"Here. Look at this." Rose reached into her knitting bag and retrieved a handful of pieces of paper, that had clearly been screwed up and thrown away, then retrieved out of the waste bin.

"Good Heavens!" exclaimed Colmes with some exaggeration, "you have quite an admirer!"

Rose did not take kindly to this flippant remark, but continued in her monotone. "Also, I thought at first. But they kept coming. So I think something wrong."

"And rightly so," said Colmes trying to make up for his flippancy.

He took the papers and looked them over as he flattened each one then placed them carefully on his desk to examine them all together. "This is the lot, or are there more?" asked Colmes. "And when was the first one and where were they deposited?"

"In my student mailbox, ever since the beginning classes, which four weeks ago," said Rose, knitting away.

"Hmm. And on any particular days?" asked Colmes, leaning forward and scanning the notes."

"I think yes. Monday, Wednesday Friday. That is when I have my constitutional law class. I always check my mail box after class."

"Then we may deduce, perhaps that it is someone who is taking the same class?"

"Or maybe the stalker follows Rose to class but does not go in?" I offered.

"Do other students of that class also check their mailboxes at that time?" asked Colmes, ignoring my comment.

"Some do," said Rose, looking up from her knitting.

"I see that all the notes are handwritten. Do you recognize the writing by any chance?" continued Colmes.

"No," answered Rose. "And he's following me too. I feel like he's everywhere I go."

"Even now?" asked Colmes.

"Well, I don't know about now," said Rose, in the middle of a stitch.

I stepped up to look at the notes. Colmes sat back out of the way while I leaned forward. One thing immediately struck me, and Colmes noticed.

"What is it Hobson?"

"It's written by a left handed person with their right hand to try to cover it up. See how wobbly it is and the excessive slope?" I observed with satisfaction.

"Yes, I believe you are right, Hobson. Well done!"

"That not get us very far, does it?" put in Rose, looking up from her knitting.

"And we can hardly go over all the students in that class and ask who is left-handed. A violation of privacy or whatever." I observed sagely.

"And what else have you observed Hobson?" asked Colmes.

"The bits of paper. They are from a legal pad, I think." I said.

"Don't know how you figure that. Besides lots of people use them in the university. Pretty impossible to track it down, I'd say," observed Colmes.

"What I do?" asked Rose. "Dr. Colmes. Other student tell me you best person for this job."

"Indeed. Indeed," agreed Colmes. "I would suggest that one simple step be taken, and we will see what happens."

"Shouldn't we look over the notes and analyze what the stalker has written? They are all pretty adoring of you, Rose, I must say," I said a little condescendingly, unconsciously emulating my master.

"Is rubbish!" she growled.

"Rose, could you perhaps place them in order of when they appeared in your mail box?" asked Colmes. "Each one is different, you know."

This was a lot to ask of Rose. She would have to put down her knitting. But the fact that she did says a lot about the depths of her concern. She stood up, placed her knitting on my wicker chair, then stood beside Colmes and leaned over the notes. She juggled them around a bit, and finally ended up with an order that satisfied her. One could easily see the progression. They began with long, flowery expressions of love, affection, and adoration, laced with some lines of poetry of some English romantic poet. But they quickly degenerated into crass sexually explicit comments, then finally with lurid details as to what he would do once he had her in his arms, an all-encompassing embrace that she would never forget in a lifetime. The notes were written in such a way that the actual gender of the stalker was not clear. The immediate presumption was male, of course. What was clear was that the unknown stalker wanted Rose, and once he had her, she would be his slave. No wonder Rose was frightened.

[I should add that Colmes could not have read all the notes because of his dyslexia.]

"Yes, now. Indeed," muttered Colmes, "The notes have not told us much, except that we need to get you out of danger immediately," announced Colmes seriously. "There is a very simple first step, as I mentioned before."

"What that, Doctor?" asked Rose as she finished a line of knitting and switched over her needles.

"Remove your name from the mailboxes. The stalker will then be unable to deliver the notes and will have to try something else."

"But what if he keeps following me?" cried Rose. "If he leave notes, I put up with. But I know he stalk me!"

"I doubt it," said Colmes. "But don't worry, Rose. I have a spare bedroom here in my apartment. You can stay there until we solve this problem."

I tried not to show any surprise. Colmes, with a house mate? Hard to imagine. My having an office next to him is enough for me. Poor Rose!

Colmes looked at Rose expectantly. She looked directly at him and put down her knitting. "Oh! Dr. Colmes. I not impose like that," she said almost smiling, sounding a bit Victorian if you ask me.

"I consider it my duty and an honor to have you as my guest until we are sure you are safe," pronounced Colmes. "Either I or my excellent colleague Hobson here, will accompany you everywhere you go, twenty four hours a day. Won't we Hobson?"

I shifted uncomfortably. "Absolutely!" I said with a big smile.

And so the trap was set.

***

Rose's mailbox was removed from the student mailboxes. The administration of the school had agreed that she should call in at their office and collect her mail. It was left mostly to me to stay at her elbow, and when possible out of sight but watching closely for the stalker. I saw nothing.

Colmes happily took the night shift, and watched over her, presumably as she was sleeping in his spare bedroom. This went on for well over a week, after which time I was getting a little restless. I did attend the constitutional law classes with Rose and looked carefully at all the other students. None seemed to show any special interest in her, except for the obvious, her constantly interrupting the professor. Ted the Red, the law professor, seemingly did not notice my presence, since my name was not on his class list—I had taken his class a few years before. Of course I had made sure I was seated away from Rose, somewhere the back of the class so that I could spy anyone who might be paying her too much attention. And besides, the professor would have noticed me if I sat beside Rose, because she constantly peppered him with questions. And there was, of course, the professor's seat chart that he constantly checked.

Then on the tenth night, I had been out drinking with some friends and staggered back to my apartment, or thought I had, and by mistake I entered Colmes's apartment, to which of course I had a key in case of emergency (which this was not!). Realizing that I was in the wrong place I foolishly called out "Colmes! Never mind. It's just me!"

But there was no answer. I should have turned and left. But I did not. My eye caught the overstuffed chair in the corner, which beckoned my drunken body.

***

The relationship between Rose the elder and Colmes was rather complicated. She was I suppose fifteen years or more older than Colmes, whose age anyway was a mystery. But I was guessing somewhere in his forties. I could see from the beginning that Colmes enjoyed her abrupt manner, her refusal to put up with small talk, and persistence when demanding answers. This is what drove her professors mad in class, not just confined to Ted the Red. She was someone to be feared, that's what she was. And Colmes loved her for it. I don't mean "true love." I mean that he greatly approved of her behavior, so much so that he really, really liked her as a person. And at the time of the stalker case, that was about a far as it went, I thought.

However, when he suddenly announced that she could move in

with him until this stalker problem was solved surprised me, for he was also a man who greatly valued his privacy, rarely socialized with others beside myself, though I am not sure how much of our relationship was social in contrast to collegial. In any case, I am proud to state that we were and are very good friends as well as colleagues.

You may have noticed that I am avoiding getting to the point, beating about the bush as it is commonly called in Aussie talk. That is because I am embarrassed to described what happened next.

Curled up like a ball I snuggled into a corner of the overstuffed chair and let the alcohol take me into a deep slumber, or so I thought. Perhaps that is what happened. But from my viewpoint, I was just dropping into a deep slumber when I felt as though someone was stabbing me all over with some kind of sharp instrument. I tried to open my eyes but they would not open. This was a drunken nightmare of the likes I never had. Usually I went off like a light and knew nothing until morning when I woke up.

Then I felt two hands grab me by the ears and shake me. I cried in pain.

"I knew it!" growled Rose. "Can't hold your liquor, like all men!"

Barely conscious, I slid off the chair and on to the floor on my knees.

"Now I see why you not do the night shift to protect me," she said gruffly.

I shook my head and raised my arm hoping she would take it and help me stand. She did, which, had I been sober, I would have noticed. But all I could think of was to ask, "where's Colmes?"

"He come later. Say had important matter," answered Rose, looking back to the office door which was still open.

"Better close it," I mumbled and managed to stagger over and slam it shut. "Wasn't Colmes worried about leaving you alone?" I asked.

"Didn't seem like. But we only just in nearby faculty bar," replied Rose as she walked towards her bedroom. "I go to bed."

It didn't sound like Colmes to me. Surely he would not be that casual. Had I done the same he would no doubt have castigated me no end. It meant that Rose was alone for the five or so minutes it would take for her to walk from the faculty bar to Colmes' apartment. The overstuffed chair beckoned me again. It was too late to go to my own place. I settled down to another deep sleep. I was just dozing off when I thought I heard the light scratching of a key in Colmes's door. "That must be Colmes," I thought in my sleep or was I awake?

The door opened slowly and a dark, squat figure, its face only just visible inside a deep dark hood, the light bending its way from Rose's room through the various passages and into the eyes of the hooded creature. And creature it was. Pig-like flattened nose, one that surely snorted all the time. Eyes, placed wide apart on the face, each one almost touching its ear. As the dark figure turned to close the door quietly the light of the outside hallway revealed the big red rimmed pig-like eyes with thick, curly white eyelashes, above high piggy cheeks. In the gloom, I shook my head, straining to smother a gasp. The dark figure threw back the hood and for a moment, flashed open its cape, a witch's cape if you ask me, and I swear the figure was naked beneath, except for…

I remained breathless curled up in the black leather chair. I dared not move, for I had recognized who it was. The fright of its entry had sobered me up. I watched as the figure almost pranced forward out of Colmes's office and through door number 1, that led to both Colmes's and Rose's bedrooms. To this day, I wonder whether I should have done something then. For now I knew what was happening. This was all Colmes's doing. Or at least, he had set it up that way. This was the stalker! And how he knew it I still do not completely understand. But my recognition of who it was put me in an impossible position. No doubt Colmes had engineered this so that he could catch the stalker *in flagrante delitto*. But delaying would place Rose in danger of a dreadful attack by the obviously insane stalker. If I intervened right now, it would mess the sting up completely. The ungendered stalker would simply invent an excuse for having entered Colmes's apartment.

But perhaps Rose knew what Colmes was up to? In which case she would be ready for the stalker's momentous entry.

I need not have worried. The door to Colmes's office suddenly flew open. In walked Colmes, flicking on the light as he rushed past me. "Follow me Hobson!" he muttered. I staggered up and ran to catch up with Colmes who was already well down he passage. We both heard a deep guttural scream, Rose's voice to be sure.

"Get out! You filthy beast!" she cried.

But we heard nothing of the beast.

"Come Hobson, you are in for a treat!" yelled Colmes over his shoulder.

We then heard a faint voice, or kind of snivel. "I want you!" it cried. "Can you not want me? Look what I have to offer!"

Colmes and I arrived at the bedroom, both trying comically to fit through the doorway together. I stepped back of course to let my master through.

"So now! Toekiarty. Cease and desist!" Colmes ordered, "and cover that disgusting body."

It was only just dawning on me what was disgusting. I still had etched in my alcohol-poisoned mind the picture of the beast's entrance, the cape thrown open. I had not quite comprehended what it was I saw that frightened me. It was, ready for it, a huge red dildo attached to its body in exactly the place where ordinarily the appropriate piece of anatomy would be.

And now comes the cruel part. The whole scene looked to me like an 18th century Hogarth print. The lumpy unattractive figures of Rose hunched up at the head of the bed, reaching for her knitting, and Toekiarty standing over the bed, poised to fulfill the role of the Rake's progress, and Holmes and I representing the upright figures of morality. Colmes's usually tight lipped mouth opened just enough to allow a superior smile. But yours truly, lacking any sense of decency or decorum, let out a huge epithet, "Holy Shit!" and laughed until Colmes grabbed me tightly by the arm as if to say, "that's enough!"

Dear reader. Please understand. This occurred long before there was anything like LGBTQ etc.

Toekiarty sank to her knees, wrapping the cape around her disfigured body, pulling the hood back over her head. "All right. I am yours. Do as you wish," she sobbed. Tears streamed from her red-rimmed eyes, sticking to the piggy white lashes, then falling to the gray carpeted floor.

"You disgusting pervert!" snarled Rose the elder.

"There, there!" announced Colmes in his most steady, superior voice, the moral man in control. "This incident is very unfortunate," said Colmes, as though the whole incident was a kind of accident, even though I am sure he had engineered it all.

And then he said, as if it were not the 1990s but the 2020s, "all have the right to be who they are or want to be, so long as they do not trespass on the other."

And I wanted to add facetiously, "….so help me God!". But I did not of course.

Rose the elder had now recovered from her fright and returned to her abrupt manner, and to her knitting.

"Doctor Colmes. This filth must be removed from our sight," she demanded as only a Russian could.

"Indeed, indeed," agreed Colmes, but it was clear that he was thinking of other matters already. "Rose, my dear, you may pack up your things and Hobson here, my most dependable colleague, will accompany you to your apartment. It is off campus, I presume?"

"Yes professor, but what about *it*," she pointed at Toekiarty with her knitting needle,

"You can leave all that to me. Be assured that you will never be bothered again by this stalker," answered Colmes with authority. He then turned to me. "Hobson, young man, please conduct Rose to her apartment."

"Certainly, Sir. Come Rose, let me take your things," I replied reluctantly. All I wanted was to get to bed and sleep off the booze. "It's not too far I hope?"

Rose did not answer. She slid off the bed, gathered up her few overnight things and crammed them into an old leather bag. She was already dressed as she had not had time to change into her sleeping attire by the time Toekiarty showed up.

***

The next morning I arrived at Colmes's office as usual, carrying a tray of eggs on toast and tea that I collected from the cafeteria on my way. I was naturally curious to find out what Colmes did with Toekiarty, who would in years ahead become his nemesis, and how he had solved the case. The answer to the latter partially explained the former.

When I arrived Colmes was in good humor. He sat at his desk doing the NYT crossword puzzle, and avidly grabbed the tea when I arrived, poured it out of the paper cup into his little teapot, then into his decorative English tea cup.

"Come, Hobson," he smiled, that thin smile of his that projected both mystery and satisfaction.

"Colmes," I asked as I took up my place on the wicker chair, "do tell me what happened after I left!"

"You don't want to know how I solved the case?" asked Colmes, toying with me.

"Of course. That is most important, and I would have appreciated it if you had kept me informed from the beginning. But you always do this. Keep it all to yourself, and make me look foolish at the end by making the case look simple that any fool could have solved it."

"My goodness, Hobson. This is your hangover talking, no doubt," teased Colmes.

"Maybe. Sorry. Do tell," I replied sighing deeply.

"The solution was very simple," said Colmes leaning back in his chair, tapping his extended fingertips to each other. "It was in the fake handwriting on the notes. I recognized it immediately, the color of the ink, the thickness of the strokes, written with a cheap Bic ballpoint pen, and many more indications."

I remained silent. I was not going to give him the pleasure of my constantly having to ask him to explain and give more detail. So he continued:

"I have received many such notes on regular matters, usually containing threats—you have seen her threaten me on a regular basis in my office to which she has acquired a key—with the usual accusations, I am not qualified, I am an imposter and so on."

I continued my petulant silence.

"Though I had my suspicions, I was not entirely sure why she would have directed her repeated attack on Rose the elder. At first I thought it was because it was her way of getting at me, through someone she knew I considered a friend, and who, as you know, I have used as my housekeeper from time to time."

Silence again. I looked him right in the eye.

"Indeed. Indeed, Hobson. You are in a bad mood this morning," observed my master as he continued. "But then I asked myself to consider the, well, unlikely, possibility that Toekiarty was truly attracted to Rose, to her gruff, down to earth manner. And maybe, just maybe, behind all that knitting, the knitted clothing and so on, there lay a warm and inviting body. You get my drift, Hobson?"

This insight did catch my attention. I changed positions on my wicker chair and crossed my legs. "Ah, now I see…"

"Indeed. Indeed Hobson. Now I have your attention. We now have a solution that goes beyond the stereotype of the stalker being a ravishing male ready to pounce at any moment on his prey."

"So the 'he' of the stalker was a 'she' who was not really a 'he,' " I interrupted with grand enthusiasm.

"Or a he-want-to-be," responded Colmes, avoiding the common abbreviated expression..

I shifted in my chair again. "You could have shared this with me, Colmes, it's not fair that you purposely keep me in the dark. You withheld information from me. I would have reached similar conclusions as you did, had I known the details."

"Evidence, Hobson, evidence elucidated by deduction. You know me well, I think. I am always reticent to come out with a solution until I am absolutely sure that I am right. Sharing only half the truth is worse than sharing none," recounted Colmes. I of course, did—still do—know him well. And yes, this little lecture was his way of apologizing, but at the same time informing me that he was not likely to change his ways.

Thus, I remained silent.

Then, unusually for him, Colmes leaned across his desk and for a moment I thought he was going to reach out and clasp my hand. Oh, what an event that would be! All in my imagination, of course. Rather, he tapped on the desktop with his three middle fingers as though he were playing a trill on the piano. "Are you following me, Hobson my friend?"

He would usually have said "boy" or "young man." He was going to open up at last.

"The fact is, Hobson, that Toekiarty is my nemesis. She has badgered me and those above me incessantly since she came here four years ago. She is convinced that I am CIA or FBI or whatever else, and that I am not qualified in any way to be a university Professor. I am, you might say, a malignant obsessive object to her. Her constant harassment of me is a form of stalking. She has been through all my files and investigated my past (with no success I might add). And I have no doubt that she will continue to do so. But now, I have turned the tables on her. I have information that would destroy her career if it were made public."

"But there's only you, Rose and me to attest to it all," I countered.

"True. But you forget my cameras installed everywhere in here and all over campus as well. Believe me, I do have photographic evidence."

I looked at his fingers as he once again lightly drummed them on the desk, this time with a flourish.

"So are you going to tell me what you did with your nemesis after I left last night?"

"There's not a lot to tell," answered Colmes nonchalantly.

"Sure. Do tell," I said, implying that he was trying to hide information from me yet again.

"First of all, I could not allow her to remain with me dressed, or should I say undressed, the way she was. I went to my closet and found some trousers, a shirt and jacket. And told her to get dressed. I confiscated the dildo, which I will keep with her finger prints all over it, as evidence. She lived off campus so I phoned for a taxi to collect her from outside the cafeteria and accompanied her to that place. And as we waited for the cab, she began to compose herself muttering to me as the cab rolled up that nobody would believe me if I revealed all that had happened, especially about the dildo. I pointed out that I also had her stalker notes, and there would be Rose's testimony if needed. But I knew as she climbed into the cab that this was not the end of her dedication to my destruction. It had bought me time, that was all, and I would use the incident to force her into silence for as long as I could."

This explanation seemed to be enough for my report to end the case, though I had a nervous feeling that Toekiarty was here to stay and would not let up on Colmes. She was, if not anything else, an individual whose obsession would one day cause her to act in a way that would destroy herself, and possibly others that were within her range. This explains why she recklessly continued to harass Colmes about his past and lack of credentials long after this incident.

I asked Colmes why didn't he expose Toekiarty for what she was, a raving mad Lesbian, who stalked suitable targets and exposed herself at will. He looked at me, almost glaring.

"And who would replace her? You have not heard of the saying 'better the devil you know...' "

I nodded, yes I understood. Colmes was a master of social control. To make all public would be to lose control of both the narrative and all people involved, especially Toekiarty. The latter was a nuisance and would continue to snap at his heels, but for the foreseeable future (which one could never foresee anyway, according to Colmes) there was no point our making anything more of the incident. And what a field day the media would have if the story were made public.

I also learned a lesson from this incident. Don't get drunk on campus.

5. The Sit-In

The Vietnam War and its aftermath seeded a revolution in universities across America. Students, largely the product of the baby boom that followed World War II, spurned by adults as spoiled brats, suddenly saw through the hypocrisies of their adult forebears and refused to go to war. They instead began demonstrating in the streets against the injustices they claimed lay hidden behind the facade of suburban life, the "little boxes" as Pete Seeger sang, and of course racial discrimination. In response, politicians were moved to create the "great society" (probably a failure, but that is another story and one that not even Colmes could tackle), and students suddenly came to life *en masse*, especially after the great march on Washington demonstrating against the Vietnam War. Universities were exciting places, alive with all kinds of movements and demonstrations, though by the time of President Nixon's exit, the violence of student protests had died down.

An important part of that process was the "sit-in." Students copied the well-established non-violent form of protest pioneered by the African American students known as the "Greensboro Four" who in 1960 occupied "whites only" seats at the counter of an F.W. Woolworths store in North Carolina. When they were denied service they refused to leave. Gradually they were joined by many more students until the number reached over a thousand. Eventually, the civil rights act mandated desegregation in public accommodations.

These many protests had one thing in common, which was a list of demands. This case is about one such list. Well, I suppose I should admit that the case was not so much about the list of demands itself, but the ripple effect it had on some of its voluntary and involuntary participants. The case was more or less "solved" by Colmes, but that might depend on one's point of view.

One more caveat about universities. They are popularly looked upon by many, especially the media, as crucibles of change. This is probably false, at least a misleading generalization. Universities everywhere are and always have been places where the hierarchy of knowledge is religiously defended. I use that word intentionally, since most if not all modern universities had their beginnings as religious institutions of some kind or other. And the idea that universities add to the repository of knowledge is unshakeable. Dissertations are born and defended upon such a principle.

The hierarchy of knowledge is the foundation on which the classroom sits, solidly, though in subtle ways always vulnerable to attack. Questioning and doubt are rigidly controlled, allowed only as long as they do not undermine the tree of knowledge. The formal lectures are its colorful blossoms, in which the professor stands before the class in an auditorium of some kind, delivers a lecture, the gospel, students take notes and then are examined on their comprehension (that is, memory) of that knowledge.

This is the backbone of all education that begins in kindergarten. I provide you with this somewhat cynical view of education because it is that colossal structure that student sit-ins fight against. They are destined to lose. Or are they?

***

In the case of *No Exit*, I related how Akira Tanaka's suicide threat and the bomb scare set the stage for successful protest by students, taking advantage of the nervousness of the university administration, assuming that the administration would give in easily to a set of student demands. In the current case, the graduate student association called a meeting to discuss their grievances. Undergraduates were excluded from this meeting. They probably had their own grievances, and besides they were, and are, rather low on the maturity scale. Why such grievances became so severe that their resolution required an organized student protest I still do not quite understand. The matter seems to be full of contradictions.

Their opponents, university administrators and the academics who despise them, as I have noted, but it bears repeating, are bound by the belief in the hierarchy of knowledge, (sometimes called the cumulative theory of knowledge), is these days expressed by the popular caveat: "follow the science," for that field most clearly promotes the cumulative theory and practice of knowledge. Indeed, universities would collapse without it. And of course, it is the scientific method (the practice) that expresses most clearly the advantages of assuming this fortress of knowledge, the pieces of which we commonly refer to as facts.

My apologies as usual. I am here wandering off the path, unable to hide my preference for philosophical musings. At the time of this case I was, in fact, trying to write my dissertation for my criminal justice Ph.D., unable to shake off the fluff of thinking without boundaries, an admitted defect of mine, a symptom of my ADD, I insist.

But I do think that these ill-defined thoughts are surely related to explaining how the sit-in arose, or at least what started the demand for change. There are probably few acclaimed "liberal arts" universities in the USA and elsewhere where sit-ins of one kind or another have not taken place.

***

The sit-in and its resolution by Colmes had its start, I think, with what happened with Akira Tanaka, and the apparent solution that the faculty reached once the bomb was removed from the classroom and the issue of the grades for all students whose exam was interrupted by the bomb scare was resolved.

Note. I called it an "issue." The solution that was reached by a unanimous vote of the faculty student performance committee of the School of Criminal Justice, to accede to the demand of the bomber to pass all students who took the exam at that time. This was a momentous decision which, when it was taken before the full faculty, created much debate, not so much about issuing a pass for all students, but that Professor Garcia complained (an understatement) that his rights as a professor, his academic freedom, were recklessly disregarded. After a three hour faculty meeting, Ted the Red finally gave in and rather than vote against, was pressured by the Dean to simply abstain. It was essential that they have a unanimous faculty vote on such an important breaking of the rules of student grading. This decision would not become part of the University rules and procedures until it was approved by the faculty senate subcommittee on student grading, and then finally by a vote of the full faculty senate. And only after all that to be approved by the Provost then taken to the President for his signature.

***

A quiet sense of outrage simmered among the students that the faculty could simply decide who passed a particular exam, regardless of their performance. It seemed to suggest that examinations were not important any more if all students regardless of preparation, performance or whatever, were going to pass anyway. And this was worsened when a rumor circulated that the entire cause of this outrage was the threat by a student that he would kill himself if he did not receive a passing grade. On the other hand, many were pleased that his happened in the Constitutional law class, the professor of which, Ted the Red was a widely disliked individual by students, seen as a dictatorial bully, rigid and uncompromising. There was even the story that he had once failed a student because his writing was illegible, and would not budge from this decision, even though the student had it typed under careful supervision, so that no cheating would be possible. An exam is an exam, he insisted. You either do it properly or not at all. This and other stories of arbitrariness, especially of closed book timed exams, brought the students to formulate a bold statement demanding that all examination procedures and grading be reviewed and be changed to meet student needs, rather than those of the professors.

A meeting of the graduate student association was called. It had not met for some months, having apparently considered that there was no business to attend to. In fact, the main purpose that the graduate student association served was to organize the end of semester party. The position of president of the graduate student association was not elected, but simply fell on the student or students who took it upon themselves to organize the booze and goodies for the party. But now, with these rumors of protests and awful injustices being done to the students by their professor, there was cause for concern, and when serious issues arise, there must always be a committee established and chair of the committee elected.

Thus it was that a chain of events occurred to bring Colmes into a situation that would change his life—well, that's my look on it, I doubt he would agree and insist he was in control of all events into which he inserted himself. He proclaimed (boasted) that events never controlled him, he controlled them.

Professor Colmes had just been designated the university's Inter-disciplinary Professor, the sole such position in the entire university, rarity that struck awe and envy in other faculty, and wonder by students who bothered to find out who he was and what he did (a challenging task in itself). I was in my early stages with Colmes at this point. He had called me in on a few cases, the most recent the case I have just recounted of the threatened suicide. I now took it upon myself to attend the first student association meeting that was called by a lovely first year graduate student, Ruth Cardigan, a jolly, persistently happy person, whose constant big smile relaxed all in her presence. I took the unusual step for me, to propose Ruth for chair of the Graduate Student Association. As you may have already concluded I prefer on most occasions and certainly in social occasions, to remain in the background, observing, and speaking only when asked to do so. At the time I thought I did this on a whim, but later I realized that I did it because I thought that Colmes should be involved, but if I suggested it, I would end up having to take on being president of the association. Ruth was by far the most attractive person for that position, and I do not mean by her looks which were pleasant, but I would not say stunning or even beautiful. It was her happy and radiant smile coupled with what was obviously as soon as she spoke, someone who was very smart, or more accurately, sharp. I could see her sizing up those students present, eyeing them off one by one, smiling and joking.

Only four students showed up for the initial meeting, but I was sure that many more would join in once it got around that change was afoot, especially if it involved exams and grading. It would not be long before the students became very active, perceiving injustices in every corner and under every cushion.

I was about to recommend that we ask Professor Colmes to help us make our case, draw up a list of demands, when Rose the elder came into our meeting room, a small room buried in the catacombs of the library basement. I had met Rose a few times at various meetings, but did not really know much about her, except of course, her never ending knitting. Ruth's countenance lit up even more than ever when Rose entered.

"Oh Rose!" she smiled, "Come join us! We need your experience and no nonsense ways if we are to negotiate our demands with the faculty."

Rose plopped her rather weighty bottom on to the nearest chair and kept knitting. "Not let them bully you," she said calmly looking at her knitting.

"Rose, I knew you would say that! It's why we need you to be our spokeswoman. I can't do it, I'm too nice, so they say," said Ruth, giggling in an attractive self-effacing manner.

"No problem," answered Rose now furiously knitting, "is what you say?"

"Right on, Rose" I blurted with more enthusiasm than was called for.

Rose looked up from her knitting and directly at me, which made me cringe. "Him," she said pointing at me with a knitting needle, "go out. You should not be here."

Her Russian accent was solemn and deep, spoken with such harsh authority, I imagined being ordered around by a guard in the Gulag. Instead of speaking up for myself, I just sat staring at Ruth expecting her to ask why. But she just looked at me expecting me to answer, and when I did not, Rose continued.

"Colmes, your supervisor," Rose grumbled, "in this situation can't be trusted.

Ruth, still radiating goodness, looked at me raising her eyebrows, a pale brown. "Goodness!" she cried, "we can't have that, now, can we?" Spoken as though to a class of little children at Sunday school. Rose, though, wasn't fooling around.

"You stay until we have our list of demands. Then you take them to Colmes," she ordered, doing me the honor of looking up from her knitting.

I hesitated a little, which caused her to repeat, "otherwise you go now."

"But why to him?" I asked, "and who elected me as the messenger?" I added with not a little annoyance.

Ruth decided to speak up a little as the President elect. "From what I heard I thought Dr. Colmes was more on the side of students. I mean, he helped poor Akira, didn't he?"

"That's right," I added with too much enthusiasm.

"The faculty have already requested him to intercede," growled Rose.

"Are you sure? How do you know?" I asked, upset that Colmes might have told her something and not me.

Ruth then settled into her role as president elect. "I don't think those little things matter. Let's get down to making our list of demands."

"Only three, two if discount Mister Hobson," observed Rose.

"Maybe we three could draft a list of demands then put out a call for student input by leaving a note in their mail boxes inviting then to a meeting to discuss the list and any necessary changes," said Ruth calmly and sweetly. Rose grunted and nodded her assent.

***

Our problem was that we had to decide what complaint ailed us most. I will not bore you with the many twists and turns of our surprisingly calm discussion. We were, after all, in basic agreement that we were the good guys and the faculty the bad guys. That it would take some forceful action to get their attention in the first place. But we had to have some expression of our discontent made public and made forcefully.

After a few hours we came up with two demands.

1. General Complaint: Faculty should not make rules by fiat without student input. Solution: Students should have representation on all faculty governing committees and have equal voting rights.

2. Specific Complaint: The grading system is vague, rigid and arbitrary, and discriminates against those who for whatever reason are unable to pass them. Solution (a): A committee with equal numbers of faculty and students should meet and draft a new system of grading that is equitable and just, and does not discriminate against any person who is challenged by examinations. Solution (b) Abolish grading completely because of its labelling and stereotypical outcomes, dividing students into winners and losers.

Under pressure, I agreed to be the communications person and convey our demands to the faculty. This required the preparation of an additional document announcing our demands and calling for a sit-in. The document I designed looked something like this, only of course in much larger letters:

JOIN OUR SIT-IN
DEMAND EQUITY AND JUSTICE FOR ALL STUDENTS!
ABOLISH EXAMINATIONS
ABOLISH THE DICTATORSHIP OF THE FACULTY

Before I could finalize this document we had one more issue to decide. What place would we occupy?

This proved to be an especially difficult decision. I started by suggesting the library, since it was exams time and there would be a lot of students there. This was resoundingly rejected for the obvious reason that we were demonstrating against faculty not students. I could see that Ruth was a little hesitant about putting forward an alternative. Rose, of course, the heavyweight among us, said, "go for jugular, the President's office."

Ruth and I looked at each other. There was no option but to agree. It was a bold, and very scary move, but it followed the tactics of other successful sit-ins that had occurred at other universities. We wound up our meeting and agreed to meet again first thing in the morning outside the President's office. Ruth volunteered to bring as many supporters as she could find and a few sleeping bags. I would bring cups of coffee. Rose sat doing her knitting. She did not exactly say that she would join us. The rest of the time I spent crafting the notices, one listing the demands, the other announcing the sit-in. I gave a bunch to Ruth and we posted them on every noticeboard we could find. Ruth lived off-campus and I still lived in a dorm, a small room on the ground floor where I had the job of dorm supervisor. It was now late at night so I insisted on accompanying Ruth to her apartment off-campus that was maybe a ten minute walk down Eastern Avenue, one of the main roads that passed the university.

I won't deny it. I was very taken with Ruth. Her happy demeanor was so refreshing. She radiated love—both kinds. And when we reached her apartment we said our goodnights, I wistfully, she brightly, chirping that she would meet me at the President's office in the morning, "and don't you be late," she said laughing, wagging her finger.

***

Unfortunately, I was late getting to the President's office because I received an early morning phone call from my new mentor Colmes, requesting that I come by his office as soon as possible. It was urgent, he said. I hurriedly showered, though I was tempted not to, given that I faced the possibility of an all day and maybe night sit-in. I arrived at Colmes's office around eight-thirty. The door was ajar so I walked in, knocking lightly. Colmes sat at his desk, doing the NYT crossword.

"Ah, Hobson. There you are! At last," he said, not looking up.

"My apologies, sir," I said, "I was..." But Colmes cut me off.

"Never mind. We have a new and quite unusual case, Hobson."

"We? We're a team already?" I asked mischievously.

"For the moment, Hobson. Though I should add that it will depend on how this case ends up, given that you have already involved yourself in it."

"And what case is that?" I asked innocently, an awful feeling gripping my stomach.

"I believe you are involved with a very sweet young lady," said Colmes, raising his eyes from the crossword, and almost smiling, that twitch at the corner of his mouth.

"Sir, I can explain..." He cut me off again.

"Hobson, I told you when I first took you on that you must not call me 'sir.' Now, it's Colmes, or nothing. Right?"

"If you say so, Colmes," I said with a strong hint of defiance. It occurred to me that this might be the end of a very short relationship.

"Ruth, I think her name is," he said, and this time he did smile, well almost.

"I'm not really involved," I began, "I mean..."

"I know what you mean, Hobson. I do. And it's fine. And you were not to know."

"Know what?" I asked innocently.

"That I have been asked by the President and Provost to negotiate with the student representatives who have issued a list of demands, and are as we speak occupying the President's office."

I gulped, and bit my lip a little. Of course, I should have known. But then I followed up with a kind of recalcitrance that was to become a tendency of mine when working with Colmes. "I am just following your example with Rose," I said with a silly grin.

Colmes almost smiled again. "You Aussies. You must have your nettling jokes."

"If you say so, Colmes. And if you think you will be negotiating with me, you are wrong. Rose is our negotiator." I said this with a good deal of satisfaction. I had got one back at him.

"Yes indeed. Indeed. An interesting situation, don't you think Hobson?" He stared at me, but I did not flinch.

"Indeed," I said, "indeed."

***

Colmes had advised President O'Brien to get out of town for the day, as students would be taking over his office for a sit-in. It was a crisp day in early spring, so President O'Brien had taken off with wife Chi-Ling (and that is another story) for a day of skiing at Gore Mountain. He especially enjoyed demonstrating to everyone that even with his gammy leg, he could ski and without a walking stick, because he had poles of course. Chi-Ling had never skied before and although she took a lesson, decided it was not for her, so retired to read by the fire in the club house. She had heard of the sit-in and had urged him to be tough. Such lack of respect for their elders and particularly their teachers that these students showed was truly repulsive. If she were president she would punish them severely, suspend them for a semester, and for the most recalcitrant expel them for good. But Finneas was so kind, really too kind. And as she felt the warmth of the fire in her face, she moved away from it a little, and took a deep breath. 'You are in America' she reminded herself. 'Nobody respects authority here.'

***

I arrived at the President's office a little flustered. I had stopped by the cafeteria to buy some coffees and goodies to take to the sit-in but could only carry so much. And I was worried that I would be forced into some kind of confrontation with Colmes, and if that happened, I knew I would lose. When I arrived there, though, the place was deserted except for about ten students. All the outer office personnel, the organizers, secretaries, schedulers and the rest were gone. The President must have given them the day off. Many of the students already had drinks and munchies so I was most pleased to be able to offer something to Ruth who sat on the floor beside the President's desk, at the foot of Rose who sat in his chair, knitting what seemed to be a rather long scarf. I leaned down to offer her my last cup of coffee. She shook her head and almost smiled, raised her knitting as though to say how can I drink a cup of coffee while I am knitting?

Suddenly there was a blinding flash and I turned to see a photographer accompanied by a reporter approaching me. This was news! "Are you Colmes?" she asked, looking straight at me. Rose gave a big grunt and smiled a little, but kept looking at her knitting.

"Me? Colmes? Ha! That's a good one," I replied.

"Indeed it is," came a distant voice, you can guess whose it was.

"What's this sit-in all about?" asked the reporter addressing her remarks to no one in particular.

Rose put down her knitting. "Student needs ignored too long," she announced in her thick deep Russian voice. "We demand be heard!" then she returned to her knitting. I looked at Ruth who sat smiling and filling the room with her happiness.

Colmes approached the president's desk and leaned over to look very closely into Rose's face. She seemed a little shocked, dropped her knitting and leaned back as far as she could.

"Don't be frightened," said Colmes. "I won't bite you." His pompous manner was truly repulsive to us all. Murmurs of discontent spread among the students, and a few more students walked in, the President's office now beginning to feel a little cramped. Colmes did not appear to have noticed any of this. I was most surprised. I had thought that he would be an excellent manipulator of a large group. He seemed only to be interested in Rose.

"A very nice scarf," he observed, "the university colors too."

Rose ignored him. Ruth's innocent eyes were pleading with Colmes to back off. Instead he leaned further over and whispered to Rose. What he said was inaudible. But it had great effect. She dropped her knitting and leaned far forward. I swear their noses were almost touching.

"You leave us, come back when you have something sensible to say," she growled.

"What did he say?" asked Ruth.

"Yes, what?" cried other students. "Leave us! Leave us!" the students began to chant.

Colmes turned to face the small group. "I simply said..."

"Stop!" called Rose. "Stop!"

"Then you agree?" asked Colmes.

"Agree what?" asked the students frustrated.

Then Rose shocked us all. She threw down her knitting and stood up behind the desk. "He said that the university agrees to all our demands."

"Then that ends the sit-in," I naively muttered.

Loud cheers came from the students, the noise echoing off the walls of the president's office, a large office, but seeming very small when stuffed full of so many people.

Rose picked up her knitting and held it in one hand. "Is not to be believed. Is lies!"

The flash of the photographer added to the excitement, and the reporter rushed forward to Colmes. "Is that so? Is that what you said? You accede to all demands?" she asked, thrusting a microphone in his face.

Colmes raised his body into his very straight and upright position one that I would become most familiar with over the years. It reminded me of the soldiers who exaggerate their posture in the changing of the guard at Buckingham Palace. He addressed all those present.

"President O'Brien and the Provost have given me full rights to speak on their behalf. They accede to all the student demands. Of course, the demands are rather broad, and do not address the complexity or implications of what abolishing exams will mean. But in the name of peace on campus, I accept on their behalf and the university. It is for you, the students, to now present us with a detailed plan of what, if anything, will replace the exams. And, of course, it remains to be decided what kind of representation students may have on all university committees, that is what proportion. and how they will be selected. Will you, for example, have a place or places on promotion and tenure committees? On hiring? And so on."

All of this and more Colmes prattled on, seemingly for a very long time, and the students, their attention spans limited, especially when crammed in a small space, became very restless, and then, rather than start more chanting, began to slip away until there were only myself, Ruth, and Rose left. And Colmes finally stopped.

Rose had returned to her knitting, and it seemed that the world had returned to its former, recognizable self. Colmes appeared most pleased. It was as if he had won the battle, by losing. He looked down at Ruth and said in his most charming Victorian manner, "and with whom do I have the pleasure of meeting?"

Ruth scrambled to her feet and extended her hand. "I'm Ruth Cardigan," she said, "president of the graduate student association."

I stepped forward (I had never sat down) and stammered, "Oh, sorry, I should have introduced you."

Colmes looked at me with amusement, and then looked back at Rose. "Well Rose," he said, "I think we have much to talk about. Why don't we all retire to my office and apartment. This agreement calls for a small celebration, does it not? "

That celebration spawned something quite extraordinary, or at least I thought so. When we returned to his office he led us through what I would come to call Door Two, down to the kitchen. Ruth was all smiles and complimented him on his lovely kitchen while he dithered around making tea and retrieving some scones from a tin. Finally, Rose put down her knitting and elbowed him out of the way. "I make tea," she said. "You have jam and cream for scones?"

Indeed he did! And I watched in pleasant amusement as the two of them prepared tea and scones with jam and cream, pretty little floral tea cups, sauces and matching plates. And the tea left to draw in a teapot covered with a tea cozy, that I was sure had been knitted by Rose.

I edged my way across to Ruth and pulled out a chair from the table. "May I?" I asked displaying my excellent (for me) English manners.

As you could guess, the ensuing half-hearted attempts to abolish exams never produced results. The meetings among the students became abusive. They finally gave up on the idea of abolishing or even replacing exams with something else. But there was one small success, which was that one student representative was allowed to attend faculty meetings (little did they know what they were asking for), though, a new rule was introduced by the School of Criminal Justice, where after all, given the subject matter, authoritarian structures were always preferred, the student votes were counted separately, as were the assistant professors' and those of the untenured.

But from my point of view, the major outcome of this small student uprising was that Rose moved into Colmes's apartment and became his housekeeper, and Colmes offered me the office next to his should I become officially his research assistant. Of course, I could not decline such an offer, even though I was a little nervous about inhabiting an office so close to my supervisor, who I had concluded already was a bit of a bully. But my hesitancy was fueled more by my fantasy that I might move in with Ruth and live off campus.

6. The Cheat

Hou Wang's parents were so proud of him when he was born. He showed great intelligence immediately he was delivered. His eyes wide open, looking all around the room, and even cooing instead of crying. His gaze settled first on his father when he received him into his loving arms, then to his mother laying exhausted on the bed, head pushed back into the pillow. But there was no doubt about it. His eyes followed his mom or dad whoever was closer to his little body. He clearly absorbed everything around him. His dad loved to pick him up, raise him quickly above his head, and Hou Wang would scream with delight as his dad let go and caught him as gravity brought him down. Such a happy family!

They were certain that they had given birth to a genius. His mom double checked to make sure that his name was down for the very best English multi-lingual school in Beijing. It was not long before he was talking. His mom spoke to him in Chinese, his dad in English, not to mention some French and a little Spanish. They could hardly wait for him to start school.

There was, however, one troubling coincidence. The day Hou Wang was born was the day of the Tiananmen Square massacre. Of course, it was just a coincidence. But his mom was very concerned. Coincidences occurred for a reason, she insisted. But Dad told her not to be silly. They were both well educated, and serious devotees of Confucius so were not inclined to take much notice of the signs and symbols of everyday life. But they occasionally dropped by a Buddhist temple to say a little prayer and leave a frangipani petal just to let the great spirit know that they acknowledged a life beyond their own.

It so happened that on that infamous day, Dad, or about-to-be-Dad, sprinted across Tiananmen Square on his way to the hospital. He had received word that the baby would be born any time soon, and, remarkably, had received permission from his boss at the local post office to attend the birth. It was early in the morning and the demonstrators had not yet appeared at the Square. He noticed camera crews getting into place, arranging their cameras, but thought nothing much of it. There were often gatherings at the square. It was only much later when he arrived home with his wife and new baby that they heard from neighbors what had happened. None of it was, of course, shown on the TV. But there were other sources of information pouring in from the west via faxes, radio and so on. The Chinese Government had not caught up with the new communication technologies and was still working on controlling what the western media could have access to in Chinese territory.

But what the Chinese government did have well developed was a system of spies and some of their own technology, especially cameras installed in many places, particularly at Tiananmen Square, not to mention in the hospital where they monitored the one child policy.

The brief moment of joy that Hou Wang's mom and dad had when their one baby, and a boy at that, was born was soon shattered by an arrest of Dad and threats against Mom that the authorities would take away their one child, as it was clear to them that they were not responsible parents if the father was going to participate in an insurrection. In fact, a petty official pointed out to the father that the punishment for his appearance at Tiananmen square could have been death.

These were the origins of Hou Wang's life. How his parents eventually managed to escape to Brazil when Hou Wang was ten years old, where the family managed to scrape by running a tiny Chinese restaurant, the Confucian Grill, in Rio de Janeiro. But life was difficult for Chinese refugees for the usual reasons, racism, lack of opportunity, and constant fear of long tentacles of the Chinese security network. Finally, in search of a better life for Hou Wang, when he was sixteen years old, just graduated from high school, the family joined the thousands of refugees on the trek up through Mexico and the walk across the Rio Grande into the USA to enter God's promised land.

This wild adventure that almost killed his mom, Hou Wang had not told anyone at the School of Criminal Justice where he was accepted as a graduate student in 2005. His English by that time had developed greatly in its fluency, though his mother tongues remained Chinese and close seconds, Portuguese and Spanish. He zoomed through the School of Criminal Justice graduate program, and in fact I attended his dissertation defense, a brilliant performance and a dissertation written beautifully, the topic being a study of juvenile delinquency in New York City's Chinatown. It also happened that it was a dissertation that Colmes had helped supervise, though was not its chair. That position, was, believe it or not, occupied by the Provost, most unusual, since Provosts were supposed to be too busy with academic affairs to have the time to serve on dissertation committees. But it was her way, as Colmes pointed out to me later, of making herself look scholarly and very much one of the faculty, an academic first, and an administrator second. Hou Wang went on to pursue a career at John Jay college where he received early tenure in 2012. It was just after he received tenure that Colmes received the call.

***

I quickly stopped trying to draft my dissertation proposal and responded to Colmes's call and bang on the wall. No sooner had I taken up my place on the wicker chair than Colmes plunged into one of his favorite topics.

"Cheating," insisted Colmes, "is breaking a rule in order to gain unfair advantage."

We have had many a debate about this perennial problem that is endemic to academia, if not life in general, and Colmes went on as though this were the continuation of one of our debates. My retort has always been, yes, but rules are made to be broken, that without there being any rules, there would be no such thing as cheating. And therefore no villain to vilify. Colmes always made fun of my position, simply chuckling and saying what he thought was obvious, that rules are necessary to maintain order. What would happen if everyone did what they pleased, regardless of the rules? There would be chaos.

"Rules," pronounced Colmes in his Victorian manner, "maketh the man."

"Indeed, and you are their direct product," I would say with a grin.

"And I am proud of it," Colmes would retort in his most haughty manner. He would then go on to use the example of the game of cricket, a game above all games in his opinion, that could not be played without the detailed rules of the game put in place at its foundation, and the willingness of players to abide by those rules.

And again I would point out that there are many games, if not all, in which players will try to use the rules to their advantage, a typical technique being to trick an opponent into breaking a rule, such as in basketball, when one commonly tries to "draw a foul" from the opponent. (You will immediately see that this is yet another variation of "entrapment" as are described in other cases.)

"Ah yes, there you have me, Hobson, there you have me," Colmes would retort, sitting back in his chair, tapping his fingers together. "But this incontrovertible fact is a necessary evil, for without it there would be no game to play."

"True, so true," I would respond, "though maybe life would be better without competitive sport, which is basically what you are defending."

"The game of life, Hobson! Mutual aid is impossible, my boy! If only humans were made differently! You are, Hobson, an anarchist at heart," Colmes would say, signaling the end of our debate. For he had resorted to the trick of attacking the person rather than the issue. The first step to abuse.

But he always allowed himself the last word. There were, after all, no written rules for our discourse. Colmes would say that they were informally agreed upon. Which really meant that he made up the rules to suite himself.

"By the way, Hobson, you have surely noticed that all the Ivy

League universities have revered team sports since their very inception. They are a means of cementing students together, raising rules of the game to a sacred level."

"Colmes," I sighed. "Is this the only reason you summoned me? To make our past debates a kind of debating game? I am trying to write a dissertation, you know."

"I will withhold any comment on that," said Colmes with a wry smile.

I had left myself open on that, and deserved any sarcastic comment he might choose to make about my inability to get my dissertation done.

"Do you remember our student Hou Wang?" he asked as though we were starting our conversation afresh.

"I certainly do. A brilliant student."

"Indeed, indeed. I just received a frantic phone call from him asking for my help."

"What? Surely it's not something to do with our little cheating discussion?"

"It certainly is. He has been fired from his position. It seems that our dear Provost informed them that he in fact did not write his dissertation, that he paid someone else to ghost write it."

I was aghast and could not believe it.

***

The case of cheating that I will now relate to you is not especially unique or different from the many cases of cheating Colmes has had referred to him. One would think that, given cheating in academia is absolutely forbidden, there would be no necessity to refer any case of cheating to Colmes. The rules were clearly stated in the University's handbook, and professors were encouraged to include a statement something like "cheating is a serious matter and may result in expulsion of the student from the university" in their class syllabus.

But before we get to the case in hand, you should know—and if you have been a student yourself no doubt you have experienced cheating either as a participant or recipient of cheating and its outcomes—that there are many forms of cheating in academia. Here is just a short list of some of the ways students may gain unfair advantage:

- Submit a paper as your own that was written by someone else (a friend or foe, bought off the internet)
- In a formal written exam, short answer or multiple choice, copy answers from a person sitting next to you (perhaps the more traditional form of cheating, commonly practiced throughout one's life beginning in kindergarten).
- Copying chunks of text from a text book, stringing them together to make a paper, commonly called plagiarism (a very complex form of cheating as we will see in a later case).
- Feigning illness during a formal exam, thus gaining more time or even a chance of a do-over.
- Claiming a disability (e.g. dyslexia) in order to get more time to complete a formal exam.
- Students combining their efforts to complete a "take-home" exam. This is cheating unless assigned as a group effort by the teacher. The grading of these assignments is however fraught with difficulties, not the least being that there may be a freeloader in the group, who contributes little but still gets the group grade.
- Sneaking answers or forbidden materials such as books or notes into a formal exam.
- Requesting a bathroom break from a formal exam when it is not needed.
- Stealing a look at a formal exam paper ahead of time. This takes considerable effort and innovation on the part of the student or students.
- Bribing or other methods to get the answers to exam questions in advance.

- Asking a teacher to explain a particular multiple choice question in order to glean the correct answer.
- Sleeping with one's professor.

There are many more variations of the above. No doubt you are acquainted with many of them. The charge made against Hou Wang is one of the many types of cheating. This was unusual only because it was made a few years after the student had graduated and had a job elsewhere.

***

You will pardon me from indulging in a little, what one might say, racial or ethnic exegesis. I do this knowing that I may tread on a fine line and may perhaps fall off one side or the other. But it is necessary in order to understand the intricacies of this case.

Our Provost, as I have noted in other cases, is of Chinese origin, though I am not privy as to how much Chinese she is. I hasten to add that in my personal opinion the answer to that question is irrelevant to the actual substantive details of the case, that is, (1) whether or not employing a ghost writer is against the rules, and (2) does it make moral or ethical sense to retrospectively punish for the offense, the effects being catastrophic, loss of one's job, and in all likelihood, making it impossible for the likes of Hou Wang to work in academia ever again. Is it simply a matter of whether what Hou Wang did was cheating or not? Or does that irascible fact of time erase or soften the offense?

But let me take my observations further, further than is wise, I admit. It is my carefully considered observation that many whose background is similar to that of Hou Wang, educated in environments that place great emphasis on rote learning and recitation, especially the recitation of texts (often religious or political) are more likely to be charged with various forms of plagiarism. And yes, you see where I am going. Might this not also apply to the Provost who, if my guess is right, comes from a similar background as Hou Wang, has herself committed such acts of cheating?

I followed Colmes into the Provost's office. I was surprised that he had allowed this to happen. For being her "guests" we were surely placed on a somewhat lower platform, under her watchful eye.

"Please take a seat, gentlemen," said the Provost calmly, "I will be with you in a moment, just finishing off the official five year plan that the faculty senate has approved, ready President's signature."

Colmes took up a chair across from her desk and indicated for me to do the same. He had a serious look, though I was not sure whether this was put on for her benefit. I also of course, remembered the past incident of the snakes, so although the social setting in the Provost's office may have appeared that she had the upper hand, Colmes held, as always, the ace card. However, as he often reminded me. You only get to play the ace card once.

The Provost continued to write. Colmes glanced at me as if warning me that a red light was approaching. "Who made the call to John Jay and made this preposterous allegation against one of our finest alumni?" he asked in a demanding, pedantically controlled voice.

The Provost did not look up. "The letter came from me, but it was typed up by one of my secretaries," she replied in a monotone.

"I am aghast, Madam Provost, at your recklessness," Colmes pronounced in his best anglicized Chicago accent. This was enough for her to put down her pen and look across the desk, first at Colmes then at me.

"I don't know how you bear his hastiness," she addressed to me.

I shifted in my chair, but waited for Colmes to answer, since the question was really leveled at him.

"The revelation is all the more concerning should it become public knowledge. The media will have a field day with it," warned Colmes.

"So you don't deny that the allegation is true?" asked the Provost, herself the picture of moral righteousness.

"That is irrelevant. But tell me, why did you do this? Do you not understand what you have done? These issues are complicated as you well know. They are best left alone and kept within the bounds of the academic institution. Further, it is surely likely that similar activities go on at John Jay. It is not in their interest to have this revealed."

The Provost began writing again and did not look up. Now her endemic rudeness showed, a fact of which Colmes would take advantage. He continued. "It is puzzling to me, since I know that you are guilty of the same or similar offense, are you not?" Colmes had raised his voice at the end of the sentence, causing her to stop writing and stare at the paper upon which she wrote. "Are you not?" repeated Colmes aggressively.

I shifted on my chair and cleared my throat. The fact was, this was getting a bit too close to home. My own record was not unblemished. Who in academia could say they have not cheated in one way or another? Bearing in mind, of course, the huge array of actions that could fall under the general heading of "cheating."

The Provost finally stopped her writing put down her pen, pushed back in her chair and asked both of us, "What do you want of me? To take back the accusation?"

"Madam Provost. I think only of the reputation of our fine institution, but also of the life and livelihood of our outstanding alumnus. He is an outstanding individual, given where he came from, well on with a wonderful career, much of it thanks to us, but also recognizing all that he has overcome in his life, has achieved wonders..."

"I think Mr. Hobson should perhaps leave us for a moment," interrupted the Provost.

"Do not try to distract from the substance of this natter. My esteemed colleague and good friend is party to everything I do. He is completely trustworthy. At question here, Madam Provost, is your trust." Colmes was now at his bullying best. I thought I saw her cringe just slightly, hunching her shoulders a little. She gave me a quick look, then turned back to Colmes.

"So what are we to do?" she asked plaintively.

Colmes changed slightly his position, and placed one hand on her desk. "Who has dealt with this matter at John Jay?" Colmes asked now as though they were two friends plotting a course of action.

"Only my counterpart at John Jay."

"And have you spoken directly with Hou Wang?" asked Colmes.

"No. I left it all up to their Provost."

"Left what up to the Provost?"

"I did not make the first call. It was their Provost who called me. Someone had tipped him off. He would not tell me who."

"Indeed! Indeed!" cried Colmes. "Now I see what has happened. Our Hou Wang has an enemy. And most likely that enemy is someone working for the CCP."

"The who?" asked Provost Dolittle. I was glad she asked.

"The Chinese Communist Party. They never forget or forgive," pronounced Colmes with much affected authority. In any case, I believed it.

The room fell silent. Colmes looked across at me, as though expecting me to say something. Provost Dolittle returned to her writing. We were at an impasse.

For some reason, I was stirred to speak. I returned Colmes's look and made the plunge.

"If we are honest," I mused, as though speaking in a tutorial, "cheating is inevitable, indeed, cannot be avoided. Everyone does it. It's just the unlucky ones who get caught. And there are some who have suffered so much in life, they deserve a break…"

Madam Provost looked up from her writing and slowly and carefully put down her pen. But it was my boss Colmes who picked up the point, though not in a way I would have liked.

"Right you are, Hobson. But that does not solve our problem of how to repair the damage done."

I was about to respond when the Provost intervened. "Everyone does not cheat, and in any case, even if they did, it does not excuse Hou Wang's behavior. What would the roads be like if there were no punishments for traffic offenses, which everyone at some time in their lives commits?"

I stirred again. "It's not so much a matter of whether to punish, but how much. Hou Wang has been punished by having his entire career destroyed, this after a stellar performance. It is excessively destructive. What if people who committed speeding offenses lost their job for driving five miles per hour above he limit... their lives destroyed?"

At that moment there was a light knock at the door.

"Come!" called the Provost.

In walked a dapper, smartly dressed young man, thin, tall and standing stiffly upright like a staff, hands at his side, one hand holding a shiny new briefcase. For a moment I thought he was going to salute. It was Hou Wang. He looked younger than he did five years ago when he defended his dissertation.

"Come!" beckoned Colmes, "we were just finishing up."

The Provost glared at Colmes. We were neither finished, nor anywhere near a solution, as far as she was concerned.

Hou Wang stood nervously facing us all. There were no other chairs, and I quickly realized that Doctor Dolittle had no intention of calling for one. So I did. "Here, take my chair," I said as I made for the door and called for a chair. Hou Wang bowed slightly, his eastern habits still with him. But he remained standing. Colmes stood and shook his hand.

"Very nice to see you again after all these years," he said cordially.

"Thank you for inviting me," said Hou Wang, smiling nervously. Colmes could not help admiring his handsome eastern face, large brown eyes and beautifully smooth olive skin, a small nose and a thin mouth that lit up his entire face when he smiled.

"Do you have an appointment?" asked the Provost coldly. "Your name is not in my calendar."

By this time I had returned with another chair, but it was clear that Hou Wang wanted to stand. He opened his briefcase and retrieved a large stack of papers and placed them on the Provost's desk.

"What is this?" asked the Provost, as though he had dumped a rotten apple on her desk.

"It is his dissertation draft with corrections and additions, if I am not mistaken," intervened Colmes. "I remember it well."

"How come?" asked the Provost, clearly getting set for a fight.

"You forget that I was on his dissertation committee. In fact it was I who advised him to have a professional writer go over his work."

My jaw dropped, as did the Provost's. "You what?" she asked, like a dog following a scent.

"You heard me. I have done this with many of the doctoral students I have supervised over the years, especially those whose mother tongue is not English. I see no reason why they should be discriminated against simply because they cannot write flowing and fluent English as do those who are fortunate enough to have been born into the English speaking world." All of this Colmes had said with a wry smile. It was his turn to be righteous.

"I will need to speak with the President about this," mumbled Doctor Dolittle, indicating that she didn't really mean it.

"If I may," said Hou Wang nervously, "I simply took the advice of my supervisor. And besides all of my friends did the same, and it is standard practice at John Jay to help those whose mother tongue is not English."

The suggestion that John Jay was a step ahead of our school in reaching out to help foreign students, of which there was a rapidly growing number, and an important source of income to the university in times of budget freezes, was not lost on the Provost. She looked across to Colmes expecting him to speak up in support of his former student. But Colmes knew that this was a moment to let the Provost stew a little.

Seeing that he was making progress, Hou Wang then made a serious error. He took his argument a little further. "Some of my friends in grad school, and even some that I supervise at John Jay, pay professional statisticians to do complex statistical analyses if necessary. After all, that is what many seasoned academics do these days, as I understand it."

Dolittle sat dumbfounded. Colmes, sensing a pivotal moment, stood up and began in his characteristic fashion to walk back and forth in front of the Provost's desk. She looked at him with nothing less than scorn. "Times change," he waved his arm around to emphasize the point. We must change with them," he pronounced.

"Let me see your papers here," said the Provost as she reached for the dog-eared draft of his original dissertation. There were notes and comments scribbled all through it. Then Hou Wang produced a bound monograph from his briefcase, the finished submitted version of his dissertation. She quickly scanned a few pages and compared them to the original. They were obviously a distinct improvement, in fact excellent English. On the other hand, the original draft was written in grammatically correct English, but simply did not have the flow of proper English, and was not so easy to understand. Colmes watched her closely.

"If I may," said Hou Wang, "I think it is clear that I actually wrote the dissertation, but the professional polished it into a form that made the English more English, if you understand me."

"Indeed we do," intervened Colmes.

The Provost looked up, handed the copies of the dissertation back to Hou Wang, then said with a frown, "wait outside my office while we consider the matter."

I was expecting Colmes to say that he need not leave. But he did not. I found out why as soon as Hou Wang had left.

"Madam Provost," addressed Colmes, "you understand what is at stake here. I will, if necessary take the steps to exonerate this fine young man and get him re-instated in his position at John Jay. He has a wonderful career ahead of him, and has overcome many great challenges. He deserves nothing less. Besides, it is clear that in fact he has not cheated at all. Simply taken advantage of opportunities provided him, not to mention some of this at the recommendation of his adviser, that is, I. However, it is you who mistakenly jumped to the conclusion that he had cheated, and you who did him this terrible damage. Therefore it is you who must make this right." Colmes stood and raised his body straight so that he looked down upon what appeared to be the crunched up body of the Provost. I looked in awe as Colmes played the bully as he was want to do.

Doctor Dolittle sat, morose, looking down. Colmes laid it on a little more.

"I insist that you fix this," frowned Colmes.

The Provost remained silent. Then slowly, she looked up from her desk. "I will make the necessary calls to John Jay and get him reinstated. However, I will not do it until after I have cleared this with the President. In any case, any official business between this university administration and that of another university has to be approved by the President."

"That is your call," said Colmes, "though my advice to you, and actually to the President as well, is that the less he knows the better."

And there, I leave it. Another complex case solved by Colmes using nothing more than a little gentle persuasion. Of course, he did not need to mention anything of the snake. It lay there curled up. Always ready to strike.

7. In Gun We Trust

After the Fort Hood shooting in 2009 in which 14 people were killed and 32 injured, there was the usual call for gun control and its opponents' cry for the protection of the 2nd Amendment of the US constitution that states the right to bear arms for all citizens. People, including students, all over America protested in the streets demanding that the 2nd Amendment be abolished, or at least that "something be done."

The President of Schumaker University acted immediately and peremptorily. He announced to the press that the University's renowned School of Criminal Justice would respond to these student protests by scheduling a special seminar that would examine the 2nd Amendment in detail and consider whether or not it really did express the right for all citizens to carry or own assault weapons, and even consider whether it should be abolished all together. The obvious professor to teach such a seminar was, of course, the only lawyer on the Criminal Justice faculty, Professor Theodore Garcia (aka Ted the Red), currently demonstrating with the students, though also the most feared professor on campus.

This was a most remarkable and brash step of the university, especially as it garnered broad attention from the media. However, the edict came directly from the President's office, bypassing the faculty. That is, Provost Dolittle was not consulted, or if she was, she said she was not. You may remember that our university President was a former prison governor, so we should not be all that surprised that he would respond in this way. He had even once confided in Colmes (so Colmes once told me in one of his few lighter moments) that he had a collection of guns, and loved to go deer hunting every season. There was yet another concerning fact about this measure. The Dean of Criminal

117

Justice was not consulted either. Or more precisely, the Dean was informed by the President that he had asked Professor Garcia to teach the seminar on the 2nd Amendment. At the time, however, the President had not yet made contact with Ted the Red who was somewhere downtown demonstrating with students demanding more gun control.

Now, while one might understand the annoyance of the Dean of Criminal Justice for having this laid on her, the nuisance of having to adjust the class schedules to cope for this special class, there was a further issue that worried her. She was concerned that Ted the Red would not be capable of teaching such a small class, and further, he was so feared by the students that she doubted that anyone would sign up for a small class conducted by Ted the Red. It was one thing to sit in a class of maybe eighty or more students with Ted the Red haranguing them and calling on students to answer a question. In a large class there was a reasonable chance that one would not be called upon. But in a seminar of maybe a dozen students, the situation was, to say the least, frightening.

One might add that the Dean of Justice was a formidable force in her own right. She was a tall, upright woman in her late fifties, a copious head of gray hair, coifed in a way that a shock of hair hung down over her slightly drooping left eyelid. People joked that she could be Lady Justice, if given a set of scales to hold. And she would need to be formidable to cope with the likes of Ted the Red. In fact, the way that she dealt with this submerged possibility of some kind of abrasion between them, was to avoid him. So the President had, maybe by accident or maybe through cunning, communicated directly with Ted the Red to teach the seminar on the 2nd Amendment, thus saving the Dean from having to speak with Ted the Red herself. She was much relieved at this, so was almost happy to put up with the nuisance of rearranging the class schedules, though she knew that Ted the Red would demand a price for taking on the course. Probably, he would ask for a semester off teaching, which she would refuse, and he would then go directly to the President.

But Ted the Red had his own concerns.

***

According to Colmes's prodigious memory, Professor Theodore Garcia, aka Ted the Red, was born somewhere in Washington Heights, NYC, not far from the Dominican enclave that extended all the way uptown where it merged with Harlem. His biological parents, though, were unknown, because he was apparently abandoned and found wandering around the Holyrood Episcopal Church and was taken in by a Dominican Republic couple. To his adoptive parents' surprise, Ted grew at a rapid rate and by the time he was finishing high school he was well over six feet tall, lean and thin, surely a budding professional basketball player, which was of course his dream. The theory was, actually I think it was the Colmes theory, that Ted's aggressive persona that glowed from every point of his stringy body originated and was even encouraged by his high school basketball coach. His Dominican parents watched all of this in awe and consternation. Neither of them was tall, though they were not short either. Yet they felt small every time they found themselves near him or talking to him, because he did, as do many who are naturally very tall, look down at others, I mean eyes naturally lowered, while others, of course, had to look up to him.

A few headhunters sniffed around and watched Theodore play for his local high school, but eventually shrugged, and said that while he was obviously very tall, he could not play pro basketball because he was too thin and could not hold his own against the better built and musclebound opponents from Harlem and elsewhere. But Ted refused to give up on his dream and, thanks again to his parents' hard work and string-pulling (he was white after all, and they were not), received a basketball scholarship to enter college at NYU. Maybe College basketball was the place for him, said his parents.

So Ted's story was that he would have been a pro basketball player, if only his parents had encouraged him and fed him more so that he could muscle up. But his parents, although they could not afford it from the income they made in their tiny restaurant, fed him enormous amounts, but he remained skinny. And when his well-meaning parents saw that he was not going to get any bigger, and likely never would be a pro basketball player, they began to harp on him that he must study more and go to graduate school. Then as luck would have it (or bad luck however one chooses to look at it), when he was a senior in the final game of the College playoffs, he fell as he came down from the highest leap he had ever managed, and his left leg crumpled beneath him. He had thrown the winning goal, but his knee was severely damaged, and his ankle broken in several places. He would never play competitive basketball again.

His parents were greatly relieved and gave thanks to Jesus and Mary in their favorite Church of the Incarnation. And Ted reluctantly agreed that he would apply to law school. Again, his parents pulled out all the stops, and managed to get him accepted into NYU law school on a disability scholarship, the argument being that he was handicapped by having non-white parents. Though, as the admissions director pointed out to him, because he was born in Washington Heights there was a good chance that he was actually Jewish. "And what did that have to do with it?" Ted asked belligerently, though in retrospect, he realized (I am guessing here), that he was really asking that question of himself.

I needed to tell you all of this because what happened next could not have been anticipated. Ted did not especially excel at law school though he did well enough. There were many reasons for this. First, he felt out of place at the law school. He came from the Dominican Republic (the NYC version that is) and just did not fit in with the mostly all white students, even though he was white himself. The majority of his class mates were focused on one thing: graduating into a top law firm and making lots of money. And most of them would need to, of course, given the debts they ran up to pay for their law school fees. But more importantly, because of his outsider complex, it slowly dawned on him what his parents had done for him. Against all odds, they had so many hurdles to overcome to get him through high school and then to college. They had sacrificed a large portion of their lives. All for him.

And they continued to slave away in their little restaurant, dealing with rude government officials, cops who would expect a free lunch and the rest.

Please understand that I am only speculating here. Maybe there was some other reason. In any case, out of the blue as his last year in law school was coming to an end, and he had put up with the awful periods as an intern at various law firms, and had concluded, telling his parents, "I love the law, but I hate law firms," he received an offer from the Dean of the new School of Criminal Justice at upstate Schumaker University. As a professor in this great new experiment in higher education, he would be the only lawyer in the new school, the other professors would be from various kinds of social sciences and public administration.

***

Theodore Garcia accepted the generous offer for a position as Associate Professor with tenure, not realizing how incredibly unusual this was. Every beginning professor would traditionally in the American system receive a three year term as an assistant professor, then go up for renewal, then go up for tenure in their fifth or sixth year. Whether Professor Garcia knew how amazing this was, or whether he simply accepted it as his due, one cannot tell. I am inclined toward the latter for reasons that will become clear shortly. In any case, this matter of his teaching a special seminar on the 2nd amendment coincided with his having just received promotion to full professor. This, mind you, after barely five years as an associate. But during those five years he had established a reputation of being fiercely stern, a severe disciplinarian, and demanding of very high standards. I can attest to one case of the student whom he failed in a final exam outright with no possibility of appeal, because, Professor Garcia said, his handwriting was illegible.

So, bypassing the Dean, the President sent an emissary to Professor Garcia who was, as was his proud custom, demonstrating his solidarity with a small bunch of students, in front of the Capitol building in downtown Albany, demanding the re-hiring of a university gardener whom the President of the university had fired because he trimmed the hedge in front of his university residence too low.

When he felt the tug on his arm, Ted the Red raised that arm ready to slap whoever it was, assuming it was some kind of government official, maybe even a cop. It was, however, a pretty young woman, who might even have been a graduate student.

"May I have a word?" she asked, "the President sent me to give you this." She held out a brown New York State envelope.

"Can't you see I'm busy?" answered Ted curtly. Of course, like most of his professorial colleagues, he derided administration officials, regardless of rank.

"I am the President's secretary," she shouted trying to overcome the noise of the protesters.

"What, then?" called Ted, pulling up straight, reaching his full height, looking down on this puny but beautiful secretary.

"He wants you to teach a select seminar on the second amendment, starting next week. Twelve students, mixed graduate and undergraduate," she instructed with great satisfaction.

"Fuck off!" shouted Ted.

The plucky secretary held her own. She pushed the official memo from the President into Ted's hand and left hurriedly. Professor Garcia didn't scare her, but she was frightened that she may get scooped up by riot police and end up in jail with Ted the Red, a horrible thought!

***

Over severe protestations by Ted the Red at having to drop everything and teach a special seminar to just twelve students, the seminar was inserted into the official calendar of the School of Criminal Justice and twelve students, six seniors and six graduate students signed up for it, after some cajoling from the Dean but also the agreement that the seminar would be for six credits, and would be free. Professor Garcia could hardly have refused to teach the seminar. After all he had been downtown on several occasions protesting with students demanding that the 2nd amendment be abolished.

However Ted the Red had other concerns, in retrospect quite understandable, and had shared these concerns with none other than my mentor, Professor Colmes. I had heard Ted's gravelly rolling voice come through the wall from Colmes's office. So was none too surprised that I received the familiar bang on the wall and cry of "Hobson!"

I entered Colmes's office and found Professor Garcia sitting back in the old overstuffed leather chair in the corner, his long legs protruding well into the rest of the office. I took up my place on the wicker chair across from my mentor.

"The two of you have met?" asked Colmes directing the question to me. Ted showed no inclination to respond.

"We have, though maybe the professor does not remember. I took his constitutional law class some years ago," I said looking across at the professor.

"I expect that you have heard of the seminar on the 2nd amendment that Professor Garcia has kindly offered to teach," said Colmes with a wry smile.

"Sure. But what is the problem? I take it there *is* a problem or we would not be meeting like this," I said trying to convey a confidence of my own.

"The professor here is concerned that there may be some, shall we say, potential for violence, in the class," observed Colmes.

"With only a class of twelve? Surely that can be controlled easily enough," I said grandly, forgetting who was sitting, steaming, in the corner. I looked sideways and saw Ted cross and uncross his long legs.

"What we say stays in this room, right?" demanded Professor Garcia.

"Indeed. Indeed," assured Colmes. "Is that not right Hobson?"

"Of course, Colmes. Of course," I said assuming that the more I repeated myself the more likely I was to be believed.

Garcia sat forward on the edge of the old stuffed chair, doubling up his legs. "The fact is, that if I was teaching it in a regular class of my usual seventy or eighty students, that is easier to control than a small group that sits in a small room, where we are all on the same level, within touching distance of each other," explained the professor.

"How so?" I asked cheekily. I admit that I have never liked this pompous bully. A typical lawyer.

"Since you have taken my course, you know that I use the Socratic method," he informed me as though he were beginning a lecture.

Of course, I was well acquainted with it. It was the bastardization of the Socratic method as used in all law school teaching. The professor has a seat plan and every student is assigned a seat where they must sit in every lecture. This meant that the professor could call on someone at random by name and demand an answer in response to his question. It meant that in fact, the professor would rarely get to know anyone in his large class, never really relate to any of them person to person, even though it looked like that on the surface. The real Socrates engaged his students man-to-man, so to speak. "I do," I replied, biting my tongue.

Colmes intervened. "The professor is concerned that in any disc-ussion on such a heated topic, a fight might break out in the seminar, since people are basically sitting on top of one another, and ever so close to the professor, whom,—correct me if I am wrong about this, Professor—they may resent anyway, and maybe even direct their aggression towards whoever they see as the aggressor which may well be him, the professor."

"You mean," I offered, turning to face Garcia, "that up close in a small group you are not as scary a figure, as you are facing a large faceless crowd?" I asked a little cheekily.

"I would say so," answered Garcia, bristling a little.

"Isn't the answer, then," I said confidently, "to offer a series of lectures to a large crowd rather than to a small seminar?"

Colmes leaned forward. "I agree. But both the Provost and the President, neither of whom have much experience as teachers, will accept it. In their view they are doing Professor Garcia a favor. Much less preparation they point out, no long lectures to prepare. Simply assigned reading and serious discussion in an intimate setting. A highly personal experience for the students."

Garcia stood and looked down on us. "What really pisses me off is that if I were teaching in a law school, I would be paid twice the money I'm getting here," he said, to us, plaintively and pathetically, obviously a totally irrelevant observation.

I was about to say something that would be insulting, but Colmes intervened. "Indeed. Indeed. But I think that it is a different matter that you should take up with the Provost. For now, let me suggest that my excellent colleague here, Hobson, sit in on your seminar and act as a kind of rudder, should the discussion get out of hand."

"But you will not attend?" pleaded Garcia. "That is precisely why I came to you."

"For me to remain available to intervene when necessary, all my work must be behind the scenes. Besides I will appear like some intruder or something, as I am too old to be a student. Hobson here actually is technically still a student," insisted Colmes.

Ted the Red looked down to each of us in turn. He walked towards the door, then returned. "You understand, that it will be on you if something happens," he warned.

"Indeed. Indeed," repeated Colmes.

***

The seminar was scheduled in a small meeting room that sported rows of empty bookshelves around the walls, a small window at one end, the entire space of the room filled with one long polished rosewood table with lean-back chairs that seated twelve people comfortably. Rather like a small boardroom, as I imagined it to be, since I had never been in one. I purposely arrived a little late, planning to seat myself away from the table, but as it happened, I ended up sitting at one end, facing Garcia who, as he was unable to think otherwise, took up what he thought was his natural place at the head of the table.

Now, as an observer of the classroom of considerable experience, mostly as a full time student, but also on and off as a teaching assistant to various professors, I could see that by placing himself at the head of the table, Garcia assumed that he would be the natural supreme authority. He was, after all, a bully, and thought that it was his natural right to "lay down the law." As far as I could tell, the students were self-selected on a first come first served basis. There were half a dozen undergraduates who had no idea what to expect, cowed by the presence of half a dozen graduate students, all of them as far as I could see, doing their doctorate, except for one older male. One is tempted to characterize this class as a kind of academic version of the movie "Twelve Angry Men." There was in fact just one black student and she was female. The rest were an assortment of young students, except for one male who I guessed was one of the NYPD cops having a great time with a year off with pay to attend grad school and get his Masters. All the students leaned forward in their chairs expectantly. The cop pushed back in his seat as did I, to survey the scene before him.

Ted the Red, as he handed out a sheet of paper that contained a half dozen questions, introduced himself and the seminar. "Welcome to this our first seminar on the 2nd Amendment of the Constitution concerning citizen right to bear arms. Let us get to know each other. Starting on my left, please tell us who you are and a little of why you are here…"

I need not go into the niceties of the start of a class. But I can say that I already saw that the black female and the cop were both equally aggressive and opinionated. They would dominate the discussion.

Ted continued, "in case you have not read it, there is a brief summary of the 2nd amendment on the back of the question sheet. Let us begin with the first question. What are arms?"

Silence.

To a professor who is used to lecturing in class, or calling on a petrified student from a seating plan, silence is the most feared non-event in the classroom, like "dead air" in a radio broadcast. There is the assumption that nothing is happening. This may be so on the radio. But in the classroom there is a lot going on, especially during uncalled-for silence. I watched the cop, whose name was Ben, and the black female who told everyone to call her Peggy, the slave name of her grandmother.

For only a few seconds, that I undoubtedly seemed to Ted like many minutes, all students squirmed and shifted in their seats. Who would be first to break the silence?

The professor could not wait. The silence already informed him that he was not in control. Students were resisting his request. He wanted to call on someone as he would do in a class of fifty with a seating plan. He had no idea who these students were and had already forgotten their names. And so he broke the silence.

"Let's begin with the collective rights theory," he pronounced with his usual lawyerly authority.

The cop, Ben, immediately responded, tapping himself on a place near his left breast.

"I knew it. This is bullshit. Why not start with the individual right theory? You're biased like all the rest of the commie students and faculty at this place!"

"Please mind your language," growled Ted, staring down at the table, unable to believe that a student spoke like this, to a professor no less.

"Apologies. It's just that I'm sick of the obvious bias against guns without any understanding of why we must have them," responded Ben with an air of considerable confidence.

Ted was tempted to take up the argument, but managed not to get caught. Instead he continued with his professorial lawyerly style, and addressing Ben directly saying, "if you turn over the question sheet you will see the exact language of the 2nd amendment. Read it out for us, if you would please... Ben, is it?"

Ben's face went a little red. He was not going to do it. He sat looking sullenly at the table. Another dreaded silence descended on the room. It was more than Professor Garcia could stand, so, without thinking, he stood up and started to walk about the small room, reverting to his usual lecturing manner, reading the text of the 2nd Amendment. "A well regulated Militia, being necessary to the security of a free State, the right of the people to keep and bear Arms, shall not be...."

Suddenly, Ben again tapped the bulge near his left breast and said, "I'm a cop packing a gun right now. So what? Are you going to disarm me?"

"You racist son-of-a-bitch," blurted Peggy, the grand-daughter of a slave.

"Decorum please," pleaded Ted, who now had returned to his seat. The rest of the class looked down and shuffled nervously. "I hope this is just talk, Ben. Guns are not allowed on campus," lectured Ted. The necessity of the moment that he address students by their first name irked him. He preferred the formal last name, even though there was some difficulty these days concerning gender and marital status.

Ben was not going to let it go. "Who says? Where's the rule? Off-duty cops are allowed to carry their gun in New York."

Peggy would not remain quiet either. "You racist pigs are all the same. You think that shooting someone solves every problem!" she exclaimed, looking around the room trying to catch the eyes of everyone, but all were looking down at the table, the most useful piece of furniture in a seminar room.

"Please refrain from *ad hominem* dialogue," lectured Ted.

"Ad who?" mocked Peggy, "why not *ad feminem*?" Peggy grinned broadly. She had at least provoked a small titter from the other students, especially the women. Except for Ben, the male students in the room sat quiet, sullen.

Another dreaded silence descended.

Ben slowly and carefully reached for his gun and placed it carefully on the table in front of him. He looked around the room. All stared at it, shocked. Ted stared at it too. He was very tempted to reach out with his long arms and take it. Instead, he sat back and crossed his arms, as would a teacher who was about to make a wise and serious comment about his students' behavior.

At this point, I chose to excuse myself making certain movements to convey the fact that I needed to go to the bathroom. A few students looked sideways at me, but most kept their heads down, waiting for the next potentially explosive event. I had decided that things had already gone too far. I planned to find a phone and call Colmes who had asked me to keep him informed. However as soon as I exited, I almost tripped over Colmes's protruding leg where he sat just outside the door, cross legged.

"Trouble?" asked Colmes.

"You wouldn't believe it," I muttered. "One of the students who is a cop has produced his gun and placed it on the table."

"Was he provoked?" Colmes asked calmly.

"Maybe. The only black student in the class called him a racist pig."

"Indeed! Indeed!" exclaimed Colmes. Get back in there and tell Professor Garcia to dismiss the class. This is dangerous!"

"OK!" I turned to go back in.

"On second thoughts, I had better do it," said Colmes.

"OK again."

I went to open the door when it was suddenly thrust open and Peggy rushed out followed by all the other students who then dispersed in different directions, chattering loudly to each other.

"What happened?" I asked Peggy, as I hurried to keep up with her.

"Ask the asshole cop. I'm going home," she growled.

Colmes had already entered the seminar room and was quizzing Professor Garcia. Ben the cop sat, his gun no longer on the table, presumably he had put it away.

"I tried to inform them," said Ted, "that in a university differences are resolved by civilized discussion, that the presence of a gun undermines rational thought and action. That is why if they are not banned on campus, they should be."

Colmes turned to Ben. "I am Colmes," he announced quietly, "one of the university's security officers." He reached for his ID, but Ben immediately got up to leave.

"No need. I know who you are. I'm leaving," said Ben. "I can see that cops are unwelcome on a university campus. They will learn their lesson next time there is a campus mass shooting." He stalked out of the room, in a great hurry.

Colmes bowed ever so slightly in eastern style to Ted, and extended his hand.

"Sorry this has fallen on your shoulders," said Colmes.

"Does this mean that the seminar is off?" asked Ted, with an expectant grin.

"Who knows?" quipped Colmes. "We faculty are always the last to be consulted.

Ted eyed Colmes with a mixture of amusement and puzzlement. "Oh, I didn't realize you were one of us," by which he meant that he thought Colmes was not a professor but one of the diffuse administration.

"I teach every day," pronounced Colmes, "it never stops, does it Hobson?"

Taken by surprise, I quickly replied, "Oh right!" and then added, "you know, I think we should follow up on this disaster."

"There has been a disaster?" asked Colmes, "I was under the impression that it was just a fiery disagreement between a couple of prickly students."

Ted looked down at Colmes and growled, "true, but there was a gun involved."

Colmes appeared to ignore Ted and asked me, "follow up where or when?"

"The carpark. They both walked towards the carpark."

"Indeed! Indeed! Why did you not mention this before? Cars are just as dangerous as guns!" cried Colmes. "Hurry, there's no time to waste."

We both ran off, leaving Ted, who could not join us because of his knee injury. We arrived just in time to see Ben walking slowly to his car, preoccupied no doubt and wondering what the consequences of his confrontation with the African American woman in class would be. He had foolishly produced a gun in class. All the other cops who attended class carried their concealed weapons on campus. Now there would be an inquiry. And he would be blamed.

He looked across the car park and saw me and Colmes running towards him. Then he looked behind him and saw an old blue 1980s Dodge K-car bearing down on him. Peggy screamed "take this you fucking pig," as she drove straight at him. His head told him "pull out your gun! Your gun!" But his body had already responded and he reflexively jumped sideways enough for the K-car to just graze his backside and send him sprawling away from the speeding car.

"Racist shit! That will teach you!" yelled Peggy as she turned out of the car park and looking in her rear vision mirror, drove away, singing, "Go Down! Moses!" at the top of her voice.

I was about to wave to Peggy, but Colmes grabbed my arm. "Now, now! Dear boy! Don't reveal your colors," whatever that meant. "Let us tend to our policeman and make sure he is not harmed. It is a good idea to be on the right—I emphasize right—side of the law, don't you think Hobson?"

8. The Plagiarizer

During times of a budget crisis which, in respect to a public university is constant, the easiest way to save money is to fire teaching faculty who, by and large, are very expensive to maintain. Besides, even though they have cushy jobs in comparison to pretty much any nine-to-five job, professors are well known whiners, rarely happy in their jobs, habitually blaming the faceless ill-defined "administration" for all their woes. Academics, please forgive me for making this outlandishly exaggerated characterization. I know that many would retort, saying that it is true that their jobs are generally not nine to five, but in fact their working hours, most often self-inflicted, are much longer than 9 to 5. They work as much at home as they do in their offices, sometimes even more. And, while there is constant bickering over "teaching load" at elite colleges and schools, some teach maybe just two classes a week, compared to public universities and community colleges that are commonly eight or more. The *Chronicle of Higher Education* occasionally encourages this debate.

This bleak, admittedly incomplete and rough picture of the culture of academia sits brooding at the back of every university budget crisis. Indeed, it may even be the cause of budget crises. In any case, the immediate effect of a budget crisis is for an administration to survey its campus academic programs and look for any school or department that is not bringing in its fair share of money (that is, does not attract enough fee-paying students) to justify its continued existence. In any union controlled university, the usual caveat is that a tenured professor cannot be fired unless the an entire school or department is abolished. The logic of this policy or union rule is not altogether clear, except that it does have a significant effect on morale, incites fear in large numbers of faculty and even their administrators if they think that they are to be targeted. The outcome is that these conditions set professors against each other, school against school, administrator against administrator. One common indication of this internecine horror is to level a charge at a professor in a small department that has few students, for having violated the sacred prohibitions of academic research: having fudged one's data or plagiarized another's work.

Such was the case that spawned some of the most nasty, backbiting and infighting that I have ever seen. It was also probably the most irrational administrative decision: to eradicate the Classics Department. Irrational because it was the smallest department on campus with so few faculty that not a lot of savings would be made by getting rid of them. Although, "some was better than none," answered the bean counter in the budget office when I confronted him, and he also pointed out that if you added up the several years over which the department had taught maybe only a half dozen students, at the cost of five faculty, salary and benefits etc. per year, it worked out at a ridiculous amount spent on each student. I won't bore you with the arithmetic, but take it from me, it comes to a considerable sum. There were, however, other departments that were just as small, though admittedly they had maybe a few more students than the classics department. I pointed this out to Colmes who had called me in to discuss the issue. The President had asked him to fix the problem because various faculty and union operatives were threatening a law suit. The President had even received an anonymous death threat.

***

Colmes sat back in his chair, tapped his fingers together and I detected a twinkle in his eye. This usually meant that he already had solved the case, or at least was ready with a plan of action that he knew would solve it. Expectantly, I leaned forward from my wicker chair.

"Ah yes! Hobson I know what's going on. And indeed, some in this university have come to me complaining that if the Department of Classics is closed it will be the end of Western civilization—and I agree with them—the classics are the foundation of all Western thought, the profound basis of every university in the West. Eradicate the classics, they say, and you plant the seeds of destruction of our great university system."

Colmes sat back awaiting my response. I could tell he was very pleased with his little discourse.

"It's true, our universities were built on the ideas of classical times, but..." I mumbled.

Colmes interrupted.

"Yes, Hobson, I know. It's a bit of a stretch, a sign of panic maybe. Though, if one ignores history, events have a way of biting back, don't you think, Hobson?"

"Indeed. Indeed," I mused, imitating Colmes.

"Hobson, would you be surprised if I told you that there is another simpler reason for targeting the Classics Department?" asked Colmes, teasing me a little, that slight smile twitching at the edge of his mouth.

"You surprise me every time we meet," I quipped. "What is it then?"

"There is a feud going on between our Vice president for Community Outreach, John Porridge, who as you know is something of a linguist, and the Chair of the Classics Department, whose name I have for the moment forgotten."

"Cicero?" I asked, jokingly.

"Ha Ha, Hobson. We'll call him that for now. This is indeed a laughing matter!" retorted Colmes with satisfaction.

"There are only four faculty in the Department of Classics, if I am not mistaken, and that includes the chair," I opined.

"Correct," answered Colmes, "and they are all tenured, so can't be fired."

"And what does the Vice President for Community Outreach, whatever that is, have to do with the classics department?" I asked.

"Nothing, at least not now," answered Colmes with a friendly frown, "except that he appears to be a sworn enemy of the Classics

Department and once in fact threatened the chair that he would one day destroy the whole department."

"But what's his beef?"

"His beef, as you so rudely call it, is that some years ago he was an assistant professor in the Classics Department, taught Latin and Greek, and because he had only four students over three years, and was untenured, Cicero told him that he should look for another job," answered Colmes.

And I continued the discourse. "Being untenured, of course, he was fair game to the administration."

"Yes," said Colmes, "And Provost Dolittle informed the chair of her decision to move the faculty line elsewhere."

[For non-academics, a "line" is a position that is 'tenure track" in contrast to a temporary or limited period contract position.]

"And don't tell me. The Vice President for Community Outreach is John Porridge!"

"Indeed. Indeed. Excellent deduction, Hobson!" bellowed Colmes with enthusiasm.

"OK. But that can't be his actual beef. I mean, how is he working to get the Classics Department abolished?"

"He has launched a formal complaint against Cicero that he plagiarized a translation of Cicero's *De Divinatione*, claiming it was his, when in fact it is clear, so says the VP, that it was copied word for word from another translation."

"That's a very serious allegation. Enough to place the whole department in a very precarious position. Plagiarism can never be forgiven!" I exclaimed.

"Indeed. Indeed, Hobson. Though, as I will point out to the Provost, it is in fact a very complex issue in all fields of academia, a kind of occupational hazard, one might call it." Colmes closed his eyes for a moment, and took a deep breath.

"Really?' I asked, "I would have thought it was pretty straight forward. Either you wrote it yourself, or you didn't. It's as simple as that, isn't it Colmes?"

"Not at all, my dear Hobson. Not at all," answered Colmes opening his eyes and fixing his gaze directly on me. He retrieved a page of notes from a pile of papers on his desk. "Take a look at this," he said.

I took the paper and saw that Colmes (or more likely someone else, a secretary, given his dyslexia) had typed a page that had several sentences each separated by blank lines. They appeared to be repetitions of the same statement, except for the first, which was written in Latin. I stared blankly at the paper, then handed it back to Colmes.

"You appear puzzled," said Colmes. You did not take Latin when you were at school?"

I blushed a little and was quite annoyed with myself for doing so. These days, nobody took Latin unless they were made to, or went to some fancy private or religious college. It was no longer required for entry into a university, though maybe it was never required in American universities. I struggled with it so as to get accepted into Melbourne University in Australia, never mind the date.

Colmes drew himself up in his chair and sat up very straight. "These are quotations from Cicero's famous *De Divinatione*, roughly translated as *The Art of Telling the Future* —my translation of course," said Colmes showing off as was his want.

"OK. I can see that. I do remember that book, but why all the translations? They all look much the same with just a few details here and there a little different," I observed sagely.

Dear Reader, for your interest and fascination here is the original Latin followed by the several translations as typed on the page that Colmes gave me:

Sed nescio quo modo nihil tam absurde dici potest quod non dicatur ab aliquo philosphorum

- There is nothing so absurd but some philosopher has said it.
- Nothing so absurd can be said that some philosopher had not

said it.

- But somehow there is nothing that can be said so absurdly that it would not be said by some philosopher.

- One cannot conceive anything so strange and so implausible that it has not already been said by one philosopher or another.

"Very good, Hobson. You have a keen eye. But tell me, which one, if any, is plagiarized from another?" asked Colmes raising his right eyebrow a little for emphasis.

"Well, I don't know. They are all different, yet they are all very similar, except for the last one which is rather embellished," I observed, frowning, then continued, "oh, but I see what you are getting at. If you had a translation at hand, you would not even have to be able to translate Latin. Just copy the translation and change a couple of words here and there."

"Precisely," said Colmes with considerable satisfaction.

I now warmed to the subject and felt quite an enthusiasm building up. "And maybe whoever did the last translation, embellished it to make it look as though it was an original translation, when it most likely is not."

"Indeed. Indeed, Hobson," exclaimed Colmes, "very good! Very good indeed!" then immediately frowned at me and added, "but when is a translation not a translation? You can see that whoever made these translations, some were eager to stick very close to what we call a "literal" translation, whereas others, especially the last translation you have pointed out, want to adapt the translation and make it look more like every day English, or one might call it popular vernacular."

"So you're saying that all the translations on the page are legitimate translations and are not plagiarized," I said, a little defensively.

Colmes leaned back in his chair and tapped his fingers. "I think that to accuse someone of plagiarism you would need a lot of evidence, especially if it came to a translation. But even so, have you not had students write a term paper by copying various sections out of textbooks, and stringing them together?" challenged Colmes.

"Oh yes. A lot do that. But my rule of thumb is so long as the student gives the proper citation, then it's probably OK, though of course not as good as writing the paper in your own words," I said, expecting Colmes to tell me I was wrong. And he did.

"But they haven't actually written the paper if it is ninety percent quotations from a text book or books, even if they do cite their sources," is that not so Hobson?

"Yes, but.."

Colmes smiled wryly. "Perhaps we should stop there. For if we took the argument to its logical conclusion we would have to eventually conclude that just about all academic writing is a reproduction of what has been written before."

Again, my face flushed. "You're talking about my dissertation writing aren't you?" I asked again, defensively.

"Not in particular, but the fact that you see it as relevant to our case, demonstrates that we in academia are all guilty of habitually committing plagiarism every time we write something supposedly new." Colmes leaned forward expecting my immediate response.

We were getting rather close to home. "Now I see it. This is the reason I have so much trouble first coming up with a dissertation topic, and second once I settle on the topic, to write something about it that is original or new."

"Indeed. Indeed. The demand that every dissertation produce something new and adds to the aggregated pile of knowledge is prep-osterous," said Colmes with much vigor.

"If I were to follow your logic to its end I would have to conclude that most of academia is a fraud. It pretends to do the impossible," I said, quite troubled.

"I think you are having trouble with the truth," quipped Colmes, with, for him, a broad smile.

Fortunately, there was a knock at the door, so our thoroughly depressing conversation was thankfully halted. Though it would hover in the background of our coming attempts to sweep whatever plagiarisms there were away—or more precisely, under the rug.

***

Porridge the Vice President for Community Outreach, agreed to meet with Professor Colmes concerning the plagiarism charge that he had leveled against Cicero. However, being a cautious person, he decided to pay a short visit to the Director of Human Resources, Dr. Toekiarty, who, he had heard on the academic rumor mill, was out to get Colmes and had threatened to expose him as a fraud and imposter. His first inclination had been to decline the request for a meeting in Colmes's office, since Colmes was surely well below him on the administrator pecking order. However, after a brief phone call with Toekiarty, he realized that it would be a good idea to take her along. That way, he could leave it to her to throw whatever dirt was necessary to make Colmes desist from defending Cicero and the department of classics. He would appear at the meeting as the mediator, rather than the progenitor.

However, there was an unforeseen problem meeting with Colmes in his office, which was that there was not enough room for four adults to meet, nor were there enough chairs.

"Come!" called Colmes when he heard a key in his office door. He knew it had to be Toekiarty using her key, because of course, at this time of day the door was always unlocked when Colmes was present.

Toekiarty entered, almost running, followed by a cautious Porridge. She rapidly reached Colmes's desk, then glared down at me seated on my wicker chair as usual. I glared back. Colmes made a very slight nod and looked across to the overstuffed chair in the corner. I rose, pushing against her as she stood so close towering above me, until I was able to stand tall.

"Oh take my seat, Dr. Toekiarty," I said with exaggerated polite-ness, "or maybe you would prefer the more comfortable one over there?" I pointed at the overstuffed chair.

"Thank you, but I'll stand. This will not take long," she said smiling way too much, almost snarling.

I turned to Porridge. "Dr. Porridge?" I said, gesturing to my chair.

"Good day to you, Dr. Porridge, welcome to my humble office," said Colmes, trying not to smile.

Porridge nodded, I thought also grunted, and sat on the wicker chair, my usual seat. That left me with the overstuffed chair which I did not mind at all.

"Let's get on with it," demanded Toekiarty, "I am told that you are actually defending a renowned and well proven plagiarizer."

Colmes, I could tell, was in his rational emotive suppression mode.

"Not quite," he said, frowning.

"Not quite what?" pressed Toekiarty in her naturally belligerent manner. "Either the fellow is a plagiarizer or he isn't."

Colmes looked across to me. "Hobson, be a good fellow and show our defenders of the truth the page of translations I shared with you.

I had carried the copies with me to the old chair, so had to pull myself up out of it in order to hand out the translations. Toekiarty hardly looked at them. Porridge, of course, since it was in his field of expertise, looked at them very closely.

"What is your professional opinion?" asked Toekiarty turning to Porridge.

"They are all remarkably similar," he mused, hesitating, clearly not wanting to commit himself at this stage.

"Indeed. Indeed," added Colmes. "You do of course, recognize one of the translations to be your own?"

Porridge looked down, straining his eyes as though the words were difficult to read. "Well I'm not sure. It was quite some time ago when I did my translation of Cicero," he stammered.

Toekiarty stepped forward, pressing against Colmes's chair, trying to tower over him, hands on her hips. "Enough of this!" she almost shouted. "Porridge is not on trial here! The Classics Department and its proven plagiarizer chair are."

Colmes frowned and looked at his watch. And as if on cue, there was a light knock at his door, and in walked the Provost, looking as tiny as usual, even more so, her shoulders crunched up, head almost disappearing into them.

"My apologies if I am late," she said.

"Not at all, Dr. Dolittle. You are just in time," smiled Colmes who rose from his chair and beckoned to her to take it, which she did. Toekiarty's face reddened. She was now absolutely outranked, administratively that is. She nodded slightly and forced a polite smile, then backed away and stood towering above me in my overstuffed chair. Colmes walked to the door and closed it quietly. The Provost looked around the room. I had moved across to the other side of the office and pretended to examine some of the books on the shelves next to me. I wondered where this was all going.

Colmes looked over at Toekiarty. "Before you leave," Colmes said to her, "could you share with us how much money will be saved and where it will likely be spent if the Classics Department is dissolved?"

"I understand that there are four lines, all tenured, all full professors, so a lot of money will be saved," she said, "though I would have to work out the details, and of course, there are the salary benefits that have to be factored in." Toekiarty looked nervously at the Provost.

Colmes turned to the Provost. "And to what department will these lines be moved?" he asked.

"That has not yet been decided. In fact there is a good chance that the money will be put back into general revenue," said the Provost regretting her sharing of information.

Colmes looked at me, then around the room, making eye contact with each person in turn. "Then I think we all know that the true answer is that no money, that is no lines, will be saved at all. They will be lost forever into the abyss of general revenue," he announced with considerable confidence.

"Pardon, but I do not think that your expertise lies with budgeting," said the Provost, delivering to Colmes a small informational slap on the wrist.

"Indeed not," answered Colmes. "But it does reveal the charge of plagiarism against the classics department *vis a vis* its Chair, to be irrelevant."

"Crap! Utter crap!" cried Toekiarty.

Colmes ignored her. "You will need to find another excuse for abolishing the Classics Department, Dr. Dolittle," he urged.

"I do not need an excuse," as you so rudely call it. "My responsibility is to make sure our academic excellence is not sullied in any way. In fact the money saved by closing the classics department will be spent on upgrading the gymnasium and sports fields that are in very serious disrepair."

There, she had said it. I looked at Colmes who I could see was most gratified with this admission, which is what it was, and confirmed the usual suspicions of faculty generally in this university and truly universities everywhere: Academics came third. Administration was number one, sports number two.

Toekiarty harrumphed and scrunched up her shoulders. "This is unbelievable," she announced, and walked to the door.

"Don't go just yet," called Colmes, there is more, lots more."

Toekiarty turned, unable to leave without hearing more of what she hoped would be gossip or dirt, foolishly forgetting that Colmes was unrelenting and had vast hidden tentacles of information sources and resources, how and why a mystery to herself and other administrators.

Colmes continued. "Could I please ask you to look again at the list of translations. The last translation was made by Porridge. It is highly embellished and is a far cry from the first literal translation. I put it to you, Dr. Porridge, that you consulted all other translations and used them to inform your own translation. Am I right?"

"I do not really need to answer to you, Mr. Colmes," said Porridge sarcastically, "but for what it is worth, of course I consulted them. And in so doing I was able to show that my translation was much more relevant to the modern audience of today."

"Indeed. Indeed. I totally agree," responded Colmes. "What you did was not plagiarism. Nor was the translation of Cesare Beccaria's work *On Crimes and Punishments* done by your former department chair. He did the same as you, is that not so?"

Porridge remained silent. To disagree would be to extend the debate and there was no way around it that did not also imply that he too was a plagiarizer.

Colmes persisted. "I can produce a list of translations of Beccaria that will demonstrate the same as I have shown you of the Cicero translations."

"I think we will stop right there," announced Dr. Dolittle. "This has gone far enough."

Another light knock at the door. "May I come in?" called a light sweet voice.

"Enter!' called Colmes.

And in came Cecilia, her bright black radiance lighting up the entire office. She glided past Dr. Dolittle who smiled, though appeared a little irritated.

"Ah, thank you my dear. Just in time," said Colmes.

Cecilia handed Colmes a handful of papers. "I hope this is what you wanted. It was delivered at the convocation of 2003 University of Michigan," smiled Cecilia.

"Excellent Cecilia my dear. And my very best regards to your Mom, assuming she is in good spirits?" gleamed Colmes.

"She is fine thank you and sends you her love," said Cecilia whose entire presence emanated love. She brushed past the Provost, gave a quick glance to Toekiarty who remained impatiently at the door, as though Cecilia was taking too long to leave.

"Allow me to share with you all Exhibit A," said Colmes as he began in his characteristic style to walk back and forth across his office. "Perhaps it might be better for all present if Toekiarty and Porridge left us at this point. This is strictly an issue between Dr. Dolittle and myself. And certainly not Toekiarty."

Colmes passed the document to the Provost who took one quick

look at it and said, "Toekiarty, leave us please." Toekiarty left grum-
bling to herself and slammed the door behind her. The Provost
continued. "However, I think that Porridge should stay, given that he is
directly involved in this plagiarism mess."

"As a matter of fact," said Colmes, I do have a small document,
actually just one page of translations for Dr. Porridge to examine." He
handed the document to Porridge whose hand shook as he received it.

"Oh. So I see that you found my new translation of the famous
criminologist Cesare Beccaria'e treatise *On Crimes and Punishments,*"
he said proudly.

"Yes. My excellent colleague Hobson here did," answered Colmes.

"Then I am sure you have seen that my translation is easily the
best," bragged Porridge.

"I am not especially qualified to make such a determination," said
Colmes, "but my colleague Hobson who almost has a PhD. in Criminal
Justice, surely does."

At this point I should perhaps make a small apology to you, the
reader. I admit to a little resentment on my part. Colmes had in fact
asked Cecilia to find these translations, but it seems that she had suggested that I do it. I am not sure of the reason, but I admit that I would
have been a little annoyed had she done it since the topic obviously fell
within my realm, that of criminal justice. In fact, I could easily have
looked up the Cicero translations. In any case, after this case was
completed, I resolved to speak with Colmes about this matter. I
suspected that Colmes, as usual, was keeping information from me, that
something was going on between him and Cecilia, perhaps? But no,
Cecilia was not his type. His type was Rose the elder.

Now back to this fascinating case. Just by the way, though. I
wondered why someone who was formerly in the classics department
was translating Italian. Admittedly Italian probably owes much of its
syntax and vocabulary to Latin, but after all so do many western
languages, including English. So I could not resist asking Porridge,
"how come you chose Beccaria of all authors to translate?" He had a

ready answer.

"I believe that administrators should keep up their scholarship. Forced out of the classics department, I felt free to pursue other languages besides the classics. Italian, which I had studied as an undergraduate, was a logical choice."

Dear Reader, here is the list of three different translations of Beccaria's famous last sentence.

- "In order that every punishment not be an act of violence, committed by one man or by many against a single individual, it ought to be above all things public, speedy, necessary, the least possible in the given circumstances, proportioned to the crime, dictated by the laws." (1880)

- "So that any punishment be not an act of violence of one or of many against another, it is essential that it be public, prompt, necessary, minimal in severity as possible under given circumstances, proportional to the crime, and prescribed by the laws." (1950s)

- "So that every punishment should not be an act of violence of one or many against a private citizen, it must be essentially public, prompt, necessary, the minimum possible in the given circumstances, proportionate to the crimes, and dictated by the laws. (2012)

Porridge looked up. "Mine is the last, of course," he said. "I am impressed that you did not include the translations from the French editions of the Treatise that were bastardized by the translator who rearranged the text from its original and even added some of his own text," observed Porridge with an air of scholarly superiority.

"I studied Beccaria in my criminal justice courses," I responded quietly, though I thought that I perhaps need not have answered him.

"Excellent, " said Colmes.

The Provost, who had remained uncharacteristically quiet during these small interactions of scholarship, intervened. "I do not see what any of this has to do with closing the Classics Department," she asserted

Colmes responded. "Let me summarize it all for you, my dear Provost. It has been a demonstration of how very difficult it is, especially when it comes to translations of famous texts, to discern what is plagiarized and what is not. It would be entirely possible for a scholar to translate any text from whatever language into English, using an already done translation. Porridge's translation here, is very similar to those before it. And so it should be. After all, the actual content of the Treatise is the same, if you follow me."

The Provost did not respond. Colmes continued.

"My dear Provost, I have one more item to share with you, which then may help you change our mind. I thank my young assistant Cecilia for digging this up for me. I knew it existed somewhere, just a matter of sniffing it out, if I may say so."

Colmes passed another sheet of paper on which was written the following:

Provost Paul N. Courant's Remarks at the 80th Annual Honors Convocation "Responsible Citizenship" March 16, 2003

"One often hears of the community of scholars—a community of which all who we honor today are citizens. It is a community that cherishes disagreement and that supports the risk of failure that is inherent in the possibility of success. At its best, the University is a place where people can learn from each other easily, and teach each other easily, even though learning and teaching are invariably hard work. The more different are our initial points of view, the more different our backgrounds and expertise, the harder is the work, and the more there is to learn from each other. As citizens of this community, we create the environment—individually and collectively—that allows us to succeed. This is exactly the lesson that we take the broader world."

Colmes started to read it aloud to all present. But the Provost, her face red with anger and embarrassment screwed up the paper and threw it back at Colmes who impressively caught it and almost grinned with satisfaction. "You do recognize that speech, do you not, Madam Provost?"

Not only was it the speech of Provost Courant, but it was also part of Dr. Dolittle's recent speech to our own graduating class of 2012.

Colmes continued. "Indeed, there is great similarity between the text of your recent speech and that of Courant on 2003. It would be acceptable if it were taken from a translation, but, word for word..."

"Enough!" cried the Provost. "Colmes! I tell you. This prying into my entire life is atrocious behavior. I will one day see to it that you receive your due for this outrageous invasion of my privacy."

"Madam Provost. This is not prying, The information, in this wonderful age of the Internet is there for anyone to use, if they know where to find it," lectured Colmes.

Porridge could see where things were going. "I don't think my presence is needed here anymore, so I will say good-bye," he said and made for the door. Colmes gave me a quick look and I knew immediately to get to the door in time to collect all the papers we had distributed.

"What we have disseminated in this room stays here," ordered Colmes solemnly. He got up from his chair and approached the Provost. "Dr. Dolittle?" he said, "perhaps you can find savings elsewhere on campus. Let us keep the Department of Classics. It is all a modern university has to shield itself from the crass superficialities that daily bombard universities everywhere, and that will, I fear, one day destroy our great Western Civilization."

The Provost left without a word, and the question of the eradication of the Classics Department quietly slipped away.

9 Justice

The plagiarism case disturbed me quite a lot. Not so much the extreme difficulty of pinning down what was plagiarism and what was not, what was "new" knowledge and what was old knowledge. Rather, the setting in which it raised its ugly head. It was unknowingly provoked by the Provost in her attempt to eradicate a department. But Colmes was at the center of it. He had beaten the Provost this time, but he knew that she would return. And return she did, though under a different guise and leveling her supposed budget concerns at another small department, that actually was not a department but a school unto its self. The School of Criminal Justice, established no less by an act of the New York State Assembly. The canny understanding of academia of the then Governor of New York State Nelson Rockefeller had anticipated that the university may one day try to abolish this ground-breaking school. He fully recognized, informed by his several shrewd assistants, that the only way to protect it was to have it established by an act of the New York State Assembly. That way, the University could not touch it, should it want to.

The School of Criminal Justice was thus established, first with a Dean of its own, then stoked with five of the most famous professors whose work had shown direct relevance to that general topic of criminal justice. The idea of such a school was, to say the least, revolutionary at the time. Until then, universities were expected to be composed of roughly three schools: Arts, Sciences and one of Law or Medicine. These formed the basic backbone of the university. The School of Criminal Justice was, right from the start, defined as interdisciplinary, that is, it was not a discipline at all and so, from a conservative point of view, had no reason to exist, since its knowledge base could be covered by the already established main line disciplines.

It was a perfect time to establish such a school. It was when New York State's governor Rockefeller was rapidly expanding the New York State university system, which would become and continues to be the largest university system in the USA. It was therefore relatively easy to establish the School of Criminal Justice as a bold venture into the academic unknown. The name "criminal justice" was purely an invention to get the law passed to establish it. It had to be called something, and the founders did not want it to be characterized as a law school, which would without doubt swallow it up if the school appeared to be anything like a law school. Today, of course, the term "criminal justice" is a household term. Everybody thinks they know what it is.

And one final, but important point concerned the founders. They were very specific that the new school would be an *academic* school, by which they meant that it was not to be confused with a police training school or the like. It was to conduct its research and teaching according to the canons of the traditional arts and sciences. It would be assessed according to those academic canons, scientific research, and publication of findings in respected academic journals.

I apologize for this necessarily discursive review of the School's foundation. But it is very important if one is to understand what Colmes did when the school was attacked by the Provost and her hench-people, Toekiarty and the ever eager John Porridge. It also, I think shows why, in the long run, this turned out to be a case that was not settled to Colmes's satisfaction. In fact it was a rare case that he would one day eventually lose.

***

Neutralized by Colmes in her effort to close down the department of classics, Dr. Dolittle, at the instigation, I personally think, of the evil Toekiarty, turned her attention to what was always the most vulnerable school in the university, the School of Criminal Justice. She knew, from its legislative history that there was no way that she could abolish the school itself. It would take an act of the New York State Assembly to do that, and that was a non-starter. It was John Porridge, the former classics professor, now administrator, VP of Community Outreach who gave her the most cunning solution. It was so simple. Just remove the word Criminal from its title. The school would become "The School of Justice" and to any liberal arts academic that would immediately conjure up many classic texts, Plato's Republic, Socrates and so on. Over time, surely it would become apparent that a School of Justice was an unnecessary school since the idea of Justice was perhaps the most worshipped and studied topic in all of the departments in any Arts curriculum: literature, history, philosophy, social sciences and the rest. By changing the name, it would put into motion the gradual blurring and blending of the current School of Criminal Justice curriculum into the traditional arts and sciences.

***

The Provost was enamored when the College of Arts and Sciences reported to her that by far the most popular undergraduate courses in the college were those of criminal justice. If the School of Justice were moved inside the college of arts and sciences, its large number of students would boost the student numbers for the School of Liberal Arts. It could remain a department, if they insisted, but would be administratively attached to the department of sociology, or whatever department they wished. The best way to look at it, Dr. Dolittle observed in our first meeting with her, was to think of this administrative change as a sincere effort to ensure the long term survival of the School. In an agile twist of history, she would "save" it as she did the classics department.

***

Late one evening, a terrible winter's evening snowing outside most likely, dreadful winds blowing wildly between the tall towers of the dormitories, I grew very frustrated trying to write a one page draft of my dissertation proposal that my dissertation chair (Colmes of course) had demanded. You would think that writing a one-page summary is easy. Well, I can assure you it is not, at least it was not for me. The winter winds howled outside above me, creating a whining sound the likes of which I had never heard before from my office in the tunnels beneath the university. Usually, we were oblivious to the world above us. In winter I welcomed the gentle hum of machinery that heated the university and filtered the air. Annoyed with myself that I could not finish my one-page draft, I decided to subject myself to the freezing temperatures above, and would walk across the campus to my apartment in the East dormitory. It was possible to do this by taking a rather complicated route within the tunnel system, but I needed a sudden awakening that I hoped the ice-cold sub-zero winds would bring me.

I had donned my winter jacket, folded up the one-page non-draft, and just pulled my office door shut, when I heard the bang on the wall of my office and the unwelcome call of my mentor, "Hobson!"

I removed my coat, but as my office door was now shut, I decided to bring my coat with me into Colmes's office. Colmes was sitting back in his chair, his hands clasped behind his head.

"You're going out?" he asked, "in this blizzard?"

"Well, I need a little fresh air," I answered.

"Ah!" sighed Colmes, "trouble with your dissertation?"

"The usual," I said.

"I can put this off for another time if you wish," offered Colmes.

"No. It's fine. I'd rather have something else to think about," I sighed and removed my heavy coat and threw it down on the over-stuffed chair, then took my usual place on the wicker chair.

"Dr. Dolittle is up to her tricks again," said Colmes with his usual twitch at the corner of his mouth. "This time a cunning move to virtually abolish the School of Criminal Justice."

"Again? Virtually? What does that mean?"

"She has changed the name of the school. It seems that she can do that by fiat and has apparently already cleared it with the president and plans to move the school into the College of Arts and Sciences."

I was once again aghast. "But can she just do that, by fiat?" I asked, already thinking of what this would mean for my Ph.D. in criminal justice. For reasons that I have explained elsewhere, I had purposely delayed officially taking out my Ph.D. in criminal justice even though I had successfully defended my dissertation back in 2000. I was now hard at work trying to write my second dissertation, this time in philosophy and Colmes was my chair.

"I have researched the University Bylaws and found nothing there to stop her. These administrators. They have a lot of power, you know," observed Colmes.

Having recovered a little from my aberrant dissertation woes, I asked, "and what is the new name?"

"Justice. The School of Justice." Colmes leaned forward. "This is only the beginning," he said. "Once the name is changed she will move the school inside the College of Arts and Sciences, and there it will be gradually swallowed up by one or another school or department. I am totally against the name change."

"Can't you stop it?" I almost pleaded.

"If you want. I can give it a try, but to be honest my heart isn't quite in it. I can see the organizational logic and frankly, I think it's not a bad idea, except, that is, for the name change."

My heart sank. "But what about my criminal justice Ph.D.? You know that I completed everything, but have not officially filed it with the administration. My U.S. Visa, you know that, don't you?" I cried. "And besides it is the number one rated criminal justice program in the USA according to *U.S. News and World Report.*"

"My boy. You know as well as I do that it has nothing to do with your dissertation. I have no doubt that you will be able to claim your doctorate. The only difference will be that the Ph.D. will be in one of the major disciplines, such as sociology, rather than the non-existent discipline criminal justice. And quite frankly, I think that would be preferable."

"But it would not be from a number one rated school," I complained.

"Not if we insist that the name not be changed. Anyway, who believes the ratings of the *U.S. News and World Report?*"

Colmes's cold rationality hit me like the winds that were whirling around above us.

"I'd say a lot of the school's competitors," I swiftly responded.

"You have a point there," said Colmes pensively.

"So you will not stop the Provost from moving forward?" I pleaded.

"I will strongly object to the name change. You are right about that. But organizationally, would you not prefer a Ph.D. in, say, sociology, rather than criminal justice, a non-existent academic discipline?."

"You will not object to the move into the College of Arts and Sciences?" I persisted.

"Let's wait and see how she reacts when we meet with her. She is coming to my office tomorrow to discuss it."

"You invited her, or she invited herself?" I asked, belligerently. I was upset that Colmes was not showing his assertive, independent and tough self.

"As a matter of fact, she informed me that she would drop by to-morrow morning and talk about the change of name. She called me today, as she does from time to time, just to 'catch up' as she terms it. She has been doing that ever since the snake episode. So you see that our success with the snake episode has had quite a far reaching effect."

Colmes sat back in his chair and gave me one of his piercing looks. I looked down, somewhat dejected. I realized that my assessment of Colmes had to be revised. His outlook on his mission was not doggedly "one against all, solidarity no matter what," as I had so foolishly assumed. His approach was always driven by his number one talent for rationality. It was not a matter of choosing sides. There was, I now realized, no such thing with Colmes. He was moved only by a rational assessment of situations and circumstances that rarely involved any human characteristic that might not suggest rationality: feelings, empathy, duty, solidarity, friendship, kindness, and the rest. I shuddered as these thoughts descended upon me, feeling the chill of the winds above. The fact is, I was in shock and I did my best not to show it.

***

I spent the night in my office, unable to brave the cold winds and snow above to make my way back to my dorm apartment. I may have overslept, not having an alarm clock to wake me. Of course, there was no bathroom in my office, not like Colmes's office-apartment, so I sneaked out of my office and saw that the door to his office was open. This surprised me, so I went in and called for Colmes. I guessed on this occasion that Colmes had left the door open to convey the message that the Provost was welcome. I heard the clanking of dishes, then Rose the Elder appeared from door number three. She was dressed in a dark yellow robe, knitted with thick wool that reached to the floor.

"Tea in the kitchen," she said without any expression at all, though for once she was not knitting. "And he said use bathroom if you want." She turned and went back to what I supposed was her bedroom.

I passed through the kitchen, nodding good morning to Colmes who sat sipping his tea and munching on a bagel. I did my best to wash up and comb my hair, noting unfortunately a few gray streaks, and by that time Colmes had moved himself to his office. Unable to face anything to eat so early and only just awakened, I poured myself a strong cup of tea and brought it with me to the office where Colmes sat with the *Times* doing his crossword puzzle.

"What time is she coming?" I asked.

"On her way," said Colmes without looking up. And sure enough in a minute came a slight knock on the door and there she was, standing, all smiles, her piggy nostrils most pronounced this morning, her head nestled into her shoulders, and her ever present women's dark gray suit.

"Good morning Colmes," she said. He nodded but did not look up from his crossword. I vacated my wicker chair and took to the overstuffed chair in the corner.

"Good morning Dr. Doolittle," I said, and she nodded back.

"Colmes, I am not going to shift on this one. You are surely aware that the President is adamant about changing the name, and definitely moving the school into the College of Arts and Sciences."

"He agrees with the name change?" asked Colmes looking up from his crossword.

"Immovable," said the Provost, "and even I am surprised at that, given that he is one of the founding faculty of the School of Criminal Justice."

"Indeed. Indeed. I think it tells us a lot about our President and former prison warden," observed Colmes with what was almost a smile.

"Then why am I here?" asked the Provost, looking comfortable and even confident as she addressed, possibly, her worst enemy on campus, and she had a lot of them.

"I wanted to assure you that you have my partial support on this matter. The organizational move is logical. But the change of name is not. I am totally against the name change. The school will lose its unique identity of being the first school of its kind in the world."

The Provost looked him in the eye. "That is not possible. The move into the College of Arts and Sciences will come probably next year. The President wants the name change immediately. You know what he is like. As soon as he has made a decision, he wants it implemented yesterday."

"Yes. Indeed. Indeed," mused Colmes. "However I spoke with him last night and he has agreed to hold off on the name change. I warned him that there would be a revolt of the faculty in the School of Criminal Justice if the name were changed. I would make sure of it. They view themselves as pioneers in the new field., and I agree with them."

The Provost was clearly annoyed. "Must you do this?" she asked.

"Do what?" retorted Colmes with a grin.

"Go over my head? You are such an asshole!"

At this point I could not hold my tongue, and besides Colmes had looked at me as if expecting me to say something. "Don't the criminal justice faculty bring in a lot of research money? And they do teach one undergraduate course, if I am not mistaken," I said from my low position in the corner. The Provost answered me, or more accurately ignored me, and directed her answer to Colmes.

"The decision has been made. There is no going back. Trouble is that the School of Criminal Justice has too high opinion of itself. Many resent its special treatment, and all suspect that the President favors them because he was a founder of the school."

"And you agree with that?" asked Colmes.

"With what? The resentment or its special treatment?" retorted the Provost.

"Both," said Colmes, now impatient.

The Provost continued. "I do think it has received special treatment over the years., though possibly deserved. However I think that we have a case here of the President, as a former member of that school, wanting to show that there is no favoritism, that he is treating all schools and departments equally."

I saw that twinkle in Colmes's eye. Dr. Dolittle had just said something that he wanted to hear. "Interesting, most interesting," observed Colmes.

The Provost saw that Colmes was compliant and took the opportunity of driving a deal. "So you will not oppose the merger of the School of Criminal Justice into the College of Arts and Sciences?"

"Stated like that I most certainly disapprove. The word merger is poorly chosen, it implies that the school will disappear into a larger entity," answered Colmes. "How about, the School will be organizationally placed within the College of Arts and Sciences?"

I squirmed a little on the overstuffed chair, but said nothing. Colmes looked at me and I knew he wanted me to shut up. He was in fact giving her a thumbs up.

Dr. Dolittle stood smiling, clearly satisfied that she had accomplished something great. "I will use that terminology and will convey your support to the President," she said with much satisfaction.

"Pardon, Madam Provost. But that is inaccurate. I have not said that I support it. Things are fine the way they are and should be left alone. What I have said is that I will not oppose it."

"Of course, my apologies. But under the current circumstances, it amounts to the same thing," answered the Provost as she made a quick exit and closed the door behind her.

**

My consternation and rising anger was of course obvious to Colmes. He had just agreed to the eventual demolition of the School of Criminal Justice, the school in which I was a graduate student and in which I had completed and defended my dissertation. I could not hold back.

"You are going to let them get away with this? The demolition of a number one rated program?" I cried.

"My good fellow. Sometimes one must allow history to take its course. There are matters that go well beyond your dissertation. By the way, have you done that one page summary of your proposal yet?"

He turned back to his crossword.

I was so angry, I got up and walked out, scared I would lose my temper and yell at him or even quit. I needed to go back to my dorm apartment and have a shower.

And while under the shower, a great place to think of all good things, I wondered whether it was not time for me to look for a job back home, that is Australia. And I resolved to get my dissertation proposal done, finish the dissertation and at last get a job. It would have to be in Australia because my visa would run out here as soon as I graduated. And then I asked myself, "what greater good must Colmes be thinking of if he would sacrifice a whole number one rated school to get it?"

**

The next day I found out what he had done. Or at least I thought so. There at the bottom of the second page of the university newspaper the Flotsam, was a small article reporting that the School of Criminal Justice would be moved inside the College of Arts and Sciences for reasons of administrative efficiency. There was no statement on the name change, so I assumed, correctly as it turned out, that the name of the school would remain.

And then I wondered to myself, having just finished my one page draft of my dissertation proposal for my second Ph.D. in Philosophy, what would I prefer? A doctorate in criminal justice, or a doctorate in sociology or psychology, or social sciences? What's in a name? Did it matter?

Taking the *Flotsam* with me, I decided to ask Colmes. After all, he was a stickler for words, using the right ones, precision in everything. What would be his answer?

"Good morning, Hobson, "muttered Colmes as I entered. "Worried about what discipline your Ph.D. will be in?"

I tossed the *Flotsam* on his desk and said in a disrespectful tone, "well I can thank you for that."

Colmes looked up from his crossword and brushed *Flotsam* aside.

"My good Hobson. It is all in the name, I assure you! Forget your criminal justice Ph.D. Indeed, I sometimes wonder why you speak of such a so-called discipline when by your own choice you are in a school of criminal justice."

"Well, was, I suppose I still am, until I take the last step of lodging my dissertation with the administration. But, they have, no you have, moved the school into the College of Arts and Sciences. It will lose its identity and my defended dissertation will be lost."

"Stop Hobson, stop with this self-indulgent academic nonsense," said Colmes crossly. "When you take out your Ph.D. in criminal justice I assure you that when you apply for a job somewhere, you will have far fewer applicants competing with you, than say, if you were applying for a job in a department of sociology somewhere. There you will encounter thousands of competing applicants. In criminal justice, because the field is so new, unique even, you will have far fewer competitors. That is the advantage of a criminal justice Ph.D. in comparison to, say, a sociology Ph.D."

"Then you're saying that the field of criminal justice is narrow?" I asked, feeling a little stupid for asking.

"My dear Hobson. You are such a worrier. Of course it is narrow, that is the point of it. It's all in the words. And the word criminal narrows the field down considerably. One might argue far too much.

But for now, it offers you considerable academic advantage. Would you prefer a Ph.D. in "Justice"?

"Well, I…"

"Indeed, in the future it may become that, especially as the field of criminal justice begins to turn in on itself and question the narrowness of the word 'criminal'. Do not be surprised that one day academics will be asking "are we all criminals now?"

"You mean criminality is a matter of luck?" I asked

"Not luck. Word."

.

10. Consensual Rape

This amazing case, so typical of universities, eventually found its way to Colmes who, of course, relished its complexities. Severe repercussions might have followed had it not been for his ingenuity and his magical influence that reached far beyond the university campus.

Universities, large or small, are inhabited by young people most of whom are powered by excessive amounts of hormones, and those hormones press relentlessly to find their quarries in the cosmos of life and thereby justify their existence. Unavoidably, Colmes and me being males, sex is constantly on our minds, or should I say, constantly hammering at our minds. Though, I hesitate to apply this principle—which I call my number one rule of life—to Colmes whose sexuality is very much male, but definitely of the Victorian type. But let's put aside the special case of Colmes for the moment.

It is surely to be expected, indeed I can see no other way around it, that sex will completely dominate the lives of every single individual attending a university, especially those who are forced to live on top of each other (excuse the pun) in dormitories —the latter in most universities forced on all first year undergraduates (formerly called freshmen or freshettes). From my own experience as dorm supervisor of the South East Tower (once called the Columbus Tower but the name was recently woked out), I can attest that the majority of altercations, complaints or other unseemly events were at bottom (excuse the pun again) caused or driven by sex. Of course, as Sigmund Freud demonstrated over a century ago, civilization (the prime beacons of which are our universities) does much to suppress and caress this bubbling cauldron with learning, thinking, and doing (i.e. sport, which we will visit in a later case).

160

Now add an extra layer of young assistant professors, overlaid with a select bunch of full professors tenured and installed in the safety of their positions of authority and power, and the place is rife for the conflict (sex if you like) of hormones as they compete to find their places of Darwinian fitness. The university provides the perfect place for the natural use of power and authority of one over another. One graciously "gives" (authority), the other gratefully receives (the subordinated). I define the teacher-student relationship in which the rules of life are unconsciously implemented, and consciously overridden by learning.

The story I am about to tell exhibits all the elements of my admittedly somewhat abstract exposition here of university life. I am guessing that something like it happens every day over and over again on campuses all over America, indeed all over the human world where there are universities. (I am tempted to include the animal world here, but that would unnecessarily complicate my current exposition, given that animals appear to have sex "without thinking" and they do not have universities).

***

But first, it is necessary to tell you a little about the protagonist of this story who, no doubt you have already guessed, is the President of Schumaker university, Finneas O'Brien. Yes, very much of Irish extraction, supposedly his great grandparents came over from Ireland late in the 19th century with the many Irish migrants of that period. His father was a police officer in New York City, a den of Irish politicians and graft, and his grandfather before him was a police officer of some kind. So the idea of authority and power was, though little acknowledged, embedded in the family tradition. Little wonder that young Finneas became a guard at the infamous Rikers Island jail, while he attended part time at the City College of New York. He volunteered to serve in World War 2, and for a time served as adjutant to General Patton. Unfortunately, when assisting General Patton to exit from his vehicle, the general, in a rage because someone had misconstrued his orders, slammed the door of the jeep and broke O'Brien's leg. The injury never healed properly and he has walked with the aid of a cane ever since. He ended up supervising the Manzanar concentration camp for Japanese American citizens who were taken from their homes because of the war. The sorry story of those camps today is now well known, but at the time, there was not a great deal of concern. His experience in that camp made him a perfectly qualified candidate for the position of Warden of Sing Sing prison where he remained for ten years until his appointment in 1968 to the founding faculty of the new School of Criminal Justice at the brand new Rockefeller inspired, Schumaker University. After six years as a full professor (he was in fact initially appointed as a full professor with tenure, rare indeed) he became Dean of that school, and in 1985, he was appointed President of the university. You may well ask, as did many members of the small faculty at the university, how it was that Finneas O'Brien became president of one of the largest public universities in New York, indeed, the United States, when his only academic qualification was an AB from City College of New York? Today, one cannot get a lowly assistant professor position without a Ph.D.

***

As my introductory exposition makes clear, this story is about sex, though it is taking me a long time to get around to telling it. But then, the sex is better if you have to wait for it, is that not so?

To work with O'Brien was to meet a consummate bureaucrat-come-politician, one who reeked of devotion to manipulation, circuitous talk, inferences, interspersed with commands, requests, and deliverance of praise and solicitations. When he spoke, which was a lot and continuously, one had no choice but to listen, or at least appear to be listening to him. He looked around the room and stared each person right in the face, so you got the impression that he was watching you. His favorite expression when someone did not agree with him was "you're not hearing me..." To use the popular academic jargon of today, one could not escape his gaze. People sat in awe of him. Well, that is the flattering way to say it. The other way is that people sat in fear of him.

And worse, out of that unhealthy withered frame of his, skinny from the head down (I mean it), balding gray head and round forehead above colorless eyes (probably gray) sitting behind rimless glasses, came a kind of depressed roar, shaped by lips that had surely never kissed, a voice that seemed to come from his nose, a monotonous but penetrating sound that could be heard two rooms away. It was one of those voices that was not a loud voice, but a penetrating voice that could be heard even in a noisy crowd.

And now you have it. Overstated perhaps, but I ask you, who could be attracted to such a person as this President?

***

The way I have described university life so far sounds like a perfect place for sex everywhere. Yet we know that finding the "right" partner can be very difficult, especially if one does not know what one is looking for (except sex, which is a given, rather like a bicycle or car), or worse, if one does not know who or what to look for, and worse yet, one is hoping that someone is looking for one's self (that is, the perennial identity crisis that is supposed to be settled by the time one graduates from university). But one can see that under this very unsettled condition is an earthquake waiting to erupt, buried in every university, covered up by curricula, many rules of behavior, deadlines, homework, term papers, exams, team sports, clubs, and what one might politely term, social events. The popular forms of these are school picnics, welcome parties, all officially condoned under strict compliance with rules of behavior. We will not mention hazing, which is a product of this condition, its origin intended to impose some kind of order, but becomes hijacked by other facts of life such as tyranny of one or more over a few, or the tyranny of many over one.

A serious social event is a very special event when professors invite their students to their homes officially to promote friendly and even close relationships among students and faculty. One of the most common complaints expressed in routine student evaluations of their professors is that they do not get a chance to talk one-on-one with their professor. That the teaching is too distant. The professor stands apart, and lectures to the audience of students below (literally and figuratively). Social events are intended to overcome this gap between teacher and student.

And this, at last, is where our story begins. Ted the Red, the hero of the riveting case of *In Gun We Trust*, announced his annual hot tub party at his plush residence in Bethlehem, NY. At the time, hot tubs were not all that common, but they seemed a good extension of the summer picnics put on by the School in the Adirondacks where skinny dipping was unofficially required. Hot tub parties were always offered at the end of fall semester. This particular party was scheduled at the end of the semester which happened to be Finneas O'Brien's first semester as President of the university. However, in order to show that his rapid rise to power had not gone to his head, and that he still had a soft spot for his old School of Criminal Justice, he showed up at Ted the Red's house. Ted, of course, was most flattered and pleased. Especially as he would press the President on his perennial complaint that he was under paid and that lawyers on a law school faculty get twice as much as he does. Though essentially true, no one took this seriously, including O'Brien.

It was an especially cold night and snow was predicted. As usual, the majority of students who came were female (excessively so).

***

The President had declined to enter Ted's hot tub naked. His thin skeleton was too ugly for fine young women to see. Ted understood of course, though his own protruding belly against his otherwise slim tall body did not stop him from stepping into the hot water. What better scene than Ted the Male sitting in his hot tub surrounded by giggling naked graduate students all but one, at least by the look of them female, and one male, young, small, squat, but by and large a younger fitter and smoother looking body compared to Ted's.

Among the giggling guests was a Chinese girl, who had just arrived from Taiwan. There, she had risen to the level of Taipei Precinct chief one of the first female police officers to do so. A tiny, shy, and excessively well-mannered person, one would never have pegged her as the boss of an entire precinct. Though she did not look it, she was quite a bit older than the other students, who were young graduate students, and a couple still undergraduates. There is no other word to describe her than that she was simply a very nice person, with an infectious smile, and a lovely manner, one who made those around her feel most comfortable. And her looks were captured by her name, Chi-Ling, an excellent and beautiful young lady. Ted had invited her when he found himself sitting next to her at a committee meeting that he chaired, the faculty senate committee on human rights. The President had chosen him to chair the committee because he taught constitutional law.

Chi-Ling declined to enter the hot tub. She smiled broadly at Ted, then withdrew to the kitchen where she helped herself to a cup of English breakfast tea, which she found a little too tart, for her liking. President O'Brien followed her to the kitchen. He felt uncomfortable surrounded by naked girls frolicking in the hot tub entertaining his colleague, whom he had known for many years and certainly knew what he was about (it wasn't anything to do with Red). And there were no specific rules of the university, as far as he knew, that forbade skinny dipping or hot tub bathing with one's students. Besides, they were off campus, so most likely if there were any rules they would not apply.

Chi-Ling heard the President's walking stick hit the floor and turned to face him. "Cup of tea?" she asked, all smiles.

It seemed to the President that her entire body smiled. He screwed up his eyes as if he were looking at some kind of mirage. Her beauty was overwhelming. The end of the walking stick slipped a little, most likely on something that had been dropped on the kitchen floor, and he staggered trying to keep his balance.

"Oh! Doctor O'Brien, please let me help!" said Chi-Ling cocking her head as though she were a dog that heard a noise.

"No! No! I'm fine," rattled the President. "And please call me Finn."

"Finn? What name is that? Would you like a cup of tea?" asked Chi-Ling again.

"Short for Finneas, my Christian name. And yes, I would like a cup of tea," stammered the President, totally enthralled.

She passed her own cup of tea to him, and poured another for herself.

Then the President blurted out, "are you living on campus?"

"Campus? Oh, the university you mean?" replied Chi-Ling in her best mousey voice.

The sound of her voice blinded him. He was so taken with her that he almost dropped the cup of tea as he took it from her dainty, perfectly proportioned hand. And he had not heard her respond, though perhaps she had and he was so stupefied that he did not hear it.

The solution to this strange impasse, an event of indefinable inter-course, was a silence, that feared non-event of all human interaction, whether virtual or real.

It was Chi-Ling who had the courage to break it. "Finn. Such an unusual English name," she said sweetly, cocking her head a little, her thick black hair, just brushing her shoulders, her fringe dropping a little over her forehead. Her eyes bright, brown eyes fixed on his thin and sickly drawn face.

"Irish," responded Finneas, thankful to have something to say.

"Oh, that's nice. I have never met an Irishman before," she said smiling, shaking her head again.

Then the President remembered his initial question that awaited an answer. "Campus, he repeated, do you live on campus?"

"Of yes. It's much cheaper for me, I am a dorm supervisor." She sipped her tea, as did the President.

"Ah, that is very good. I am glad you are settling into our campus," smiled Finneas.

"You live on campus too?" she asked innocently.

The President chuckled a little then replied, "well not exactly. I live in the President's mansion that is technically off campus.

Another silence.

"Alone in a big house?" asked Chi-Ling, slightly cheeky.

"With my wife and two daughters," he replied. "And you, how come a student like yourself is already a dorm supervisor?"

"Oh. I am not a student. I am a visiting professor in the new department of Chinese and South Asian studies," replied Chi-Ling coyly.

"Yes of course! Now I remember. The Provost and I worked to establish that department some years ago and at last it has come to fruition. I trust all is going well there?"

Chi-Ling looked up at Finneas who now had inched closer to her and towered above her. He raised his cup of tea as in a toast. "Let's drink to the thriving Chinese studies department," he announced with the confident charm that came naturally to a President.

Laughter, giggling and splashing noises came from the hot tub in the other room.

"Does Professor Garcia have a wife and family also?" asked Chi-Ling with an air of false innocence.

"You mean Ted the Red? Oh Yes," answered the President with a similar smile. "I have known him and his family for many years. We met in my prison when I was Warden of Sing Sing. He came to visit a client, and we struck up a friendship."

Finneas looked down at Chi-Ling, trying hard to fix his gaze on her twinkling eyes through his glasses. "And you? I take it you are single if you are a dorm supervisor?"

"Oh, yes. I do not plan to marry. Not yet at least. There is too much life to enjoy with a freedom that may one day suddenly be taken from us. At least that is the way we look at things in Taiwan, living as close as we do to China."

This lapse into serious conversation brought another silence, eventually broken by Finneas. "Can I give you a ride back to campus?"

"Oh, thank you…"

"It's nothing…"

"I mean you don't need to. Professor Garcia said he would…"

"I wouldn't count on it. He's not getting out of that hot tub any time soon, or if he does, well, he won't be driving anywhere, if you see what I mean." Finneas gave his Presidential look to Chi-Ling who understood immediately.

"All right. It is very kind of you," she said with a very bright smile.

Finneas and Chi-Ling did not bother to thank their host or to say their good-byes. It would have interrupted what was obviously a very happy and joyous scene. Instead they slipped out the back door and walked to the President's car, such as it was. Finneas saw no reason to buy an expensive car, since he was mostly driven around by the university driver and campus car both of which, in those days, were a perk that came with every presidential university job. No such luxury these days.

Finneas held open the passenger door of his 1978 Toyota Tercel, and ushered Chi-Ling into the front seat. He went round to the driver side and pushed the seat forward so he could get his walking stick into the back seat. It had snowed during the day, but now a warm front had moved in and a light rain thankfully washed away the ice from the car windshield, and more importantly, the ice that had collected on the roads. He drove with some difficulty because of his disabled leg, and Chi-Ling was tempted to offer to drive, but thought better of it. In any case, it was only a ten minute drive to the campus.

***

It was very dark, the drizzle causing a mist to settle over the campus, the four dorm towers hardly visible, and the headlights of the car reflecting back from the mist making it difficult to see the road ahead. They drove in silence, Chi-Ling preferring to leave it to her new friend to navigate the roads. The President had only one thought in mind. Actually it was not a thought. It was something else.

"We're about there," he said, breaking the silence. "The north east tower, I think you said?"

"Yes, thank you. It's so kind of you." Chi-Ling leaned into him and placed her tiny hand on the thigh of his disabled leg.

The campus roads had been cleared, so there would be no snow ploughs to bother them. The lighting was almost non-existent around the campus, it being the heart of winter, and the university on an energy saving plan. Finneas pulled off to the side of the road that approached the rear of the dormitory.

"This will do fine," crooned Chi-Ling. She leaned forward and turned to face his withered and drawn face. "It is so very kind of you," she said, and gave him a light kiss on his balding forehead, mimicking a quick kiss good-bye. Yet it was a kiss, and could quite easily be taken for something other than a good-bye and thank you.

Finneas, mindful of his Catholic upbringing that was easily neutered by his Irish temperament, placed the car in Park with a sweaty hand, then placed his hand behind her head and returned her kiss with the biggest one he could manage, given his tight thin lips, placed squarely on her open mouth.

To quote someone. This was the start of something great.

The car engine appeared to rev itself up of its own accord, as did its occupants. The warmth of the car's little heater was enough to bring the two together as the seats of the car made way for their passions. The outside world stopped, as the inside world filled with the scent of sex and the steam of exertion.

"Ó qīn'ài de! [Oh dear!]" cried out Chi-Ling, chirping like a canary.

***

I have reconstructed these events to prepare you for what came to be known as one of the most memorable cases of Colmes, *The Case of Consensual Rape*. Of course, I do apologize for leaving my descriptions of the events in a sort of limbo-climax. At exactly what point of that climax it occurred remains to be discovered, probably it never will be, the mundane reason being that at the point of consensual contact between the two lovers, shall we say with some charity, there was a tap of metal on the driver side window door. And a distant, heavy voice called, "Open up!" Open up!"

All action stopped in mid climax. Steam turned to water trickling

down the window. And through that window the President made out the
dark shape of a campus police officer. It was the newly appointed
campus security officer, a cop retired from the local police force,
obediently doing his rounds of the campus. Cars had to be parked in the
car park, not on the side of campus roads. For a moment he was
tempted to simply drive off. But thought better of it. The President
lowered the window and looked at the officer who immediately
recognized him.

"Oh! Sorry sir!" called the officer, highly embarrassed and amused.
But he did have the foolish presence of mind to shine his very bright
flashlight into the car and thus light up the beautiful Chi-Ling, who
quickly covered her eyes and chest, squinting under the sudden light.

"I'm on my way home, officer, Larry, I think, isn't it? Larry
Cordner?"

"That's right sir. Thank you sir. Sorry to bother you sir."

"And thank you officer for doing your duty in such a mature
manner," said the President, "I'll be on my way."

Without thinking Chi-Ling went to get out of the car, which promp-
ted the officer to offer his services. "I can see you into the dorm, miss. I
have a big umbrella."

The president swallowed, an attempt to stop himself from telling
the cop to get the hell out of it. Instead, he said, "thank you Larry that's
very kind of you." He gave Chi-Ling a little prod and she obeyed.

"Not a word of this to anyone, including your superiors, you
understand?" commanded the President to his inferiors.

Larry certainly understood. His time as a cop had taught him that
you obey your seniors without question.

"Of course," he answered with a little salute to drive home his
obedience.

***

A couple of weeks after the great tub party, I received a light knock
on the wall of my office, but no call of "Hobs" that usually accompanied
the knock. Over the past few days I had heard dull noises of what

sounded like serious talk coming from Colmes's office, but I knew better than to go in and ask him what was going on. Anyway, I was reasonably sure I knew what might be happening. Being still a graduate student, beyond my duties as Colmes's research assistant, I was privy to the rumors and scuttlebutt that floated around among the students. It was all fun fare which I enjoyed passing on, though usually not to Colmes unless he asked me directly. And when I caught a glimpse of the campus cop Larry coming out of Colmes's office, I thought there must be something afoot. Then again, I knew that Colmes received a weekly report from campus security of any incidents, crimes or delinquencies, security breaks and the like. Usually petty stuff. Colmes went out of his way to have close ties with the campus security people, given that they had certain powers sometimes of persuasion, that he could make use of. Generally speaking, I knew from my criminal justice studies that police had trouble making friends outside the policing fraternity. Colmes was a perfect friend for a cop. He was sometimes mistakenly identified as some kind of cop, an investigator, the latter of which is fair enough. But on the other hand his official title on campus was academic, an inter-disciplinary Professor. So, he was able to move comfortably within both circles.

On the third soft knock, I walked out of my office and through the already open door to find Colmes walking around his office, pushing at the overstuffed chair, grabbing my wicker chair and putting it down in different places.

"No, it won't do," said Colmes.

"What's up?" I asked in a chirping manner, then realizing that I had not comprehended the seriousness of Colmes's demeanor.

"The next few days will be extremely nerve-racking, Hobson. No doubt you have already absorbed the biggest rumor of the week from your licentious student friends," he frowned, though I could see that there was an element of amusement in his twitching mouth.

"You mean Ted the Red's hot tub party?" I asked with a big grin.

"Tell me, Hobson. Tell me all, and I will set you right if I get the slightest whiff of exaggeration or outright fantasy," proclaimed Colmes.

"Nothing much really, at least nothing that we, or you, should or could be involved in. Just one of the girls, an undergrad I think, has lodged a complaint with human resources, I suppose that's Toekiarty's office, complaining that Ted forced her to get naked and get into the hot tub."

"Did she mean physical force?" probed Colmes.

"Not clear. Might have been. But then it seems that President O'Brien was also there, along with someone they all said was his sweetheart, Chi-Ling. And he didn't do anything about it. How does that sound? About right?"

"His sweetheart?" asked Colmes, of course knowing that he need not mention that O'Brien was married with two daughters in high school. "Based on what?"

"It seems that he and Chi-Ling didn't bother with the hot tub and hung out in the kitchen and then left together. So…"

"Go on, Hobson, give it to me," pressed Colmes.

"Well, nothing really. All fantasy and speculation of what they would look like, you know, together…you know her?"

"Chi-Ling? Maybe. Just appointed as visiting assistant professor in the new Chinese studies department, right?" asked Colmes as he walked round and round the office, moving my chair this way and that, trying to push the overstuffed chair further into the corner.

I continued my previous train of thought. "She wouldn't even be half his size, if you see what I mean," I said with an admittedly smirky grin.

"Hmm. Very interesting and fascinating to conjecture, eh Hobson?" quipped Colmes.

"Indeed. Indeed," I answered this time with a bigger grin.

"Hobson I need a few more chairs in here like yours, and the overstuffed chair removed temporarily," instructed Colmes. "Lend me a hand to lift it. Maybe put it in your office for the moment? There may be just enough room there."

And to my amazement, Colmes marched up to the chair, lifted it up from the front end and dragged it effortlessly out of his office and into mine.

"You have at least three chairs in your kitchen, don't you?" I asked him. Not waiting for an answer, I hurried through door two down the narrow passage to the kitchen where there were four old chrome kitchen chairs. "Are you sure you want to use these? They're a bit old," I noted. "How many are coming, anyway? And why crammed into your office? Oh, and by the way, who is it that is coming?"

"You are most inquisitive. It may be that you will not be able to attend, unless you stand in a corner and say nothing," answered Colmes hastily.

"And when are they coming?" I persisted, annoyed as usual with my mentor's teasing.

"Initially, just the President and Chi-Ling. Indeed, I am hoping it will be only them. I made it clear that none of the other persons of interest was welcome. You know my rule. Two is about right for an interrogation, more than that is a crowd as they say."

I looked at my impossible mentor, puzzled. "If it's just the President and Chi-Ling, why aren't you meeting in his office?"

Colmes sighed. "Hobson, young man, surely you can see that the President has gotten wind from the rumor-mill of his suspected dalliance with Chi-Ling. They don't to be seen together. There is no way Chi-Ling could go to his office without many people noticing. It would stoke the scandal mongering ever so more."

"Then why the four chairs, removal of the overstuffed chair, and actually, why are you involved at all?" I asked almost insolently.

"Because there is one other small piece of information that you apparently have not heard from your student gossips. Larry, the campus cop, is involved. I have been meeting with him on and off over the past few days. It's, shall I say, sensitive."

"Now this is beginning to sound like fun," I exclaimed with a boyish laugh.

"Indeed. Indeed," grunted Colmes as he placed all four kitchen chairs plus my wicker chair in a slightly curved row facing his desk.

"It looks like five against one," I observed caustically.

"One against five would be more accurate," Colmes corrected.

I was about to express my agreement wholeheartedly when the office door swung open and Larry the campus cop walked in.

"The door was open," he said apologetically.

"No matter. You have more to tell me?" asked Colmes, obviously concerned.

"Only that there was something that Chi-Ling whispered to me, or I think she did when I helped her out of the car and walked her to the back door of the dorm."

"Do tell us, my good man," said Colmes in his most friendly manner.

Larry looked across to me then back at Colmes.

"Don't worry. I was just leaving," I said.

But Colmes insisted. "No stay. It is time that you learned some of the background to this evolving crisis. And I assure you, officer, that my outstanding colleague here can be trusted without the slightest doubt."

Larry cleared his throat a little, then mumbled, "she said something to the effect that she was not raped and even if she was, she would deny it."

"You are sure about this?" pressed Colmes.

"Not really. As I said, I do not remember the exact words she said, but what I just told you is the gist of it." Larry fidgeted, then stepped back as if to leave. But just as he turned, President O'Brien entered, limping worse than usual, thumping the end of his walking stick heavily on the concrete floor as he took each uncertain step.

Colmes hurried forward but stopped half way. He did not want to insult the President by offering to help him walk, something he had done unaided for some two decades now. "Here, Mr. President, take my chair," he said as he gestured to the chair behind his desk.

The President did not hesitate and took the offer as his due. He was used to this treatment, and by golly, he expected it.

Larry, clearly uncomfortable, made to leave again, but just as he reached the open door, Chi-Ling appeared, her sweet smile and beautiful dark eyes riveting him to the spot. The President stayed seated and extended his hand. "Come my love, take a seat," he almost purred, his nasal voice as soft as he could make it. Chi-Ling bowed a little to him, then turned to each of us in turn and nodded slightly as if to bow. Now it was my turn to try and leave, but again Colmes intervened. He walked over to me and muttered, "stay, but I want you to take copious notes of the meeting as it goes forward." I nodded, then took my leave to return to my office to collect notepad and pen. Because of his dyslexia, pens and notebooks did not exist in Colmes's office at the time. The pencil and the *Times* crossword puzzle were all for show.

I carefully closed the door on my return, and took my place on the wicker chair that Colmes had left in its usual place at the corner of his desk, to the President's left. Colmes then placed himself on the kitchen chair to the President's far right. Chi-Ling sat immediately opposite her darling Finneas. Larry, even more agitated, stood where the overstuffed chair used to be.

"Now then," said the President, "Chi-Ling has a little something to say, but before she does, Professor Colmes, I want to thank you for making yourself and your pleasant office available to us."

Colmes nodded, his face expressionless, "you are most welcome," he said.

Chi-Ling then looked round the room and said, "I want to thank dear Mr. Policeman..."

"Call me Larry..."

"...Larry for having helped me out of Finneas's car and into my dorm apartment during that awful freezing rain and ice and snow," she said in her tweety voice."

Larry nodded. "Just doing my duty, Ma'am."

Colmes looked straight at the President who smiled approvingly.

Chi-Ling continued. "I have been upset and insulted by the rumors that have swept through the campus like a storm of its own. I was not raped, or if I was, it was at my request," she said calmly. "We fell in love at first sight, and will be married as soon as, ..."

"I arrange my divorce which is already in motion," added Finneas.

"My congratulations!" proclaimed Colmes as though he were the preacher marrying them, "but why have you come to me to tell me this?"

A very good question, I thought to myself. Why on earth? What does it have to do with Colmes?

"Mr. Colmes, I know from my experience as a precinct commander of police in Taipei that one must seek out and identify persons of interest who you know wield much power. I have determined that you are such a person," said Chi-Ling in a steady and certainly stronger voice. She was no longer a canary.

"I am flattered, Chi-Ling, indeed I am. But what is it that I must do for you? Even I cannot stop or prevent rumors and scandal from moving through the campus like an infectious disease," said Colmes in his most serious tone. He looked to Finneas for an answer, but quickly saw that this was all up to Chi-Ling. I gave Colmes a knowing look. We both suspected that she was doing this against the President's wishes.

Chi-Ling was about to explain when the noise of a key unlocked Colmes's door and in walked Toekiarty, followed by an assistant, an African American, probably from Ethiopia, thought Colmes, who had to bow his head slightly to get through the doorway, he was so tall. He looked like, and probably was, a basketball player. Toekiarty barged forward and plonked herself down beside Colmes and beckoned her assistant to sit next to her.

Toekiarty wasted no time. "I am informing you officially right now, she said to the President, that I am filing a formal charge of rape against you, on behalf of Miss Chi-Ling Chen."

The president remained in Colmes's chair, unmoved, sullen.

"On what evidence?" asked Colmes, the authority in his voice bouncing off the walls of his office.

"I will answer that," offered the basketball player in a deep voice.

"It's what we call structural rape."

"What?" asked Colmes incredulous.

Toekiarty interdicted. "My apologies, I should have introduced my colleague who is director of our department of critical race theory."

The room fell silent. The basketball player spoke up. "My name is Washington Bates."

Colmes was about to take over, when none other than Professor Theodore Garcia walked through the open door. "Sorry I'm late," he said, "traffic on the Northway."

"Have a seat," invited Colmes, pointing to the one vacant chair next to me.

Feeling overwhelmed by excessive height, I decamped to the corner with my wicker chair.

Professor Garcia took his place next to Mr. Bates. They were about the same height. "I'll say right out now," he said aggressively, "that nothing untoward happened at my hot tub party. All the rumors you hear are just that, the product of the rich imagination driven by wishful thinking that is typical of students."

Toekiarty twisted around in her seat so that she could confront Garcia. After Colmes, he was her biggest enemy whom she also had promised that she would "get" some day. "Professor Garcia," she pronounced. "the whole hot tub party tradition should be erased from our university. It is an insult and serious threat to the welfare of innocent students. Bates here is looking into it, and you can expect a summons any day now."

Ted the Red laughed. "Summons? What a laugh. You have no idea what you are doing, and you sure are not a prosecutor or whatever. You have no legal standing at all."

To any normal person, that would have been enough to put them in place. But not Toekiarty. She handed Ted a paper. "Maybe this will shut you up. It is my formal complaint in my capacity as Schumaker University Human Resources Director, to be laid before the Schumaker County District Attorney today."

This created a buzz of excitement. "Give me that," demanded the President, and Ted quickly handed it to him, at which The President tore it up, and threw the pieces in Colmes's bin.

The room fell silent again. It was time for Colmes to take over.

"The theory is the evidence," said Bates out of nowhere. "Gender is the same as race," he announced as though it were a law unto itself. "It is structured into capitalist, that is, slave society. In my position as owner of slave or like today owner of the means of production, anything I ask my slave to do, they have no choice but to do it. Unavoidably it is an abuse of power, exploitation of the weak, no matter whether I treat them with kindness of pay high wages."

"If that is so," said Colmes, "then it is not possible for a man and a woman to have sex without one raping the other," insisted Colmes. "Because it is the male who penetrates he female, it is the female who takes it in, no matter the aggression of either party. God or Darwin have made it so," Colmes announced in a quasi-religious tone. "The physiology of humans is such that it is not possible for a male and a female to be equals. The one must dominate the other at some point if they are to make children, or if they have decided, simply to enjoy its pleasure. It is a battle of ups and downs."

"Thank you for the sermon," said Toekiarty sarcastically. "It does not change a thing. A rape has occurred. Chi-Ling's innocence has been exploited by the most powerful person on campus. If she says she "wanted it" or however she describes the experience, no matter. If they had sex, then it is a simple matter of rape by the powerful man over the powerless woman."

"And I would add," said Bates, "that even if they did not have sex, the simple fact that The President drove the defenseless Chi-Ling home in his car late at night is enough evidence to support a charge of attempted rape."

All present wriggled uncomfortably. Larry had inched his way closer and closer to the door. He wanted to get out of this oven of madness. But it was my indefatigable mentor Thomas Colmes who settled the matter.

Colmes leaned across his desk and whispered something to the President. I now of course know what he whispered, but at the time I was thoroughly bamboozled. Anyway, his whisper had the effect of bringing on a great ear-to-ear smile on the President's otherwise drawn and haggard looking face. His eyes glowed with excitement and satisfaction. I did my best to look sideways to see if Chi-Ling had reacted in any way. But she was still smiling and sweet. Then Colmes disturbed everything by standing, and then asking everyone else to stand and to please move their chairs away from the desk and place them against the side wall. He reached out to Chi-Ling who pulled out a small rather tattered book from her handbag. At first I thought it was a bible, but then on closer inspection it appeared to be a Chinese book. Perhaps a Chinese version of the bible. I later discovered that it was the I-Ching.

She gave it to Colmes who held it in his hand as though he were a presbyterian minister.

Bates thought he knew what was going on. "You can swear on any book you like that you were not raped, it makes no difference. Swearing on ten bibles will not change the facts. And the facts are that you are female and he is male, and more importantly, he is your boss and you are his servant, or let's just sum it up by saying you are his voluntary slave."

All in the room stared at Bates as though he were a mad extremist, that is except Toekiarty. "Isn't he wonderful?" she said proudly. "And to think I hired him."

I was poised to ask her whether that made him her slave. But thought better of it. In any case, Colmes started to move about the room. His movement had loosened up the attendees and a little casual talk started to emerge. Ted leaned over to the President and said, "thanks for coming the other night, even if you didn't try the water."

"Too hot for me!" said Finneas, "but only too happy to take advantage of the opportunity to give Chi-Ling a good time and to introduce her to American academia."

"And I hear that she did have a good time," grinned Ted.

Finneas had already moved on to chat informally with others who were in the room. Colmes passed by me and pushed a note into my hand. "Larry can help you," he said nodding in Larry's direction.

The note said, "bring flowers from office." At first I thought this was one of Colmes's coded messages. But when I got to the door of my office, the door was open and there before me was the biggest bouquet of flowers I had ever seen. Too much for one person to carry, so now I knew why he suggested that Larry would help.

We returned from my office laden with flowers which, on Colmes's direction, we placed on his desk, and they completely covered it. Ted quickly stepped out of the way as did Bates and they naturally started to chat about basketball. Chi-Ling stood, smiling sweetly, her eyes following Finneas as he made his way to the front of the desk on Colmes's direction.

Toekiarty was astonished at how quickly the dreadful charges of rape that were laid just a few minutes ago, appeared to have disappeared over the horizon. She sat there, stubbornly refusing to move, convinced that the whole meeting had been carefully engineered by Colmes to push the charge, actually even the idea, of rape away. To bury it. "Flowers," she mocked, "you think you can soften us with flowers? Typical male sexism at its worst!" she pronounced a she huffed, and finally stood away from the desk. Actually she was kind of nudged away by Colmes who was arranging the flowers on the desk so that they completely covered it.

Satisfied with the flowers, Colmes took Chi-Ling by the hand, and brought her together with Finneas so that they stood before the flower laden desk. He then gave them the book for each to hold and announced:

"I bring before you all here today, the loving couple, Finneas and Chi-Ling who are joined by the wisdom of the I Ching that says:

When two people are at one:
in their inmost hearts,
they shatter even the strength of iron or bronze.

And when two people understand each other
in their inmost hearts,
their words are sweet and strong,
like the fragrance of orchids.

Colmes then placed his hand on theirs and the I Ching.

"Do you, Finneas O'Brien and Chi-Ling Chen take each other as your lawfully wedded mate, to have and to hold until death do you part?"

"We do," they answered softly, Chi-Ling looking up at her President, he looking down, whispering, his lips barely moving.

Colmes stood back and faced the tiny, puzzled audience, and announced, "as the official celebrant at this divine moment, according to the power invested in me by the State of New York, I pronounce you a married couple brought together by biology and love for each other. You may now kiss!"

"What happened to man and wife?" whispered Ted in my ear. I answered only with a grin.

"This changes nothing," proclaimed Toekiarty, aware a little too late that the brief, poignant ceremony had softened the onlookers' hearts.

Ted whispered into my ear again. "I thought he was married with two kids?"

I shrugged." I guess he's divorced," I said saying the obvious.

Then Toekiarty approached us with caution. "This doesn't change anything, you know."

Ted couldn't resist the bait and took up the necessary cudgel. "And when she has a baby, it will be the direct product of a rape?"

"Can't argue with nature," she said defensively.

Ted's lawyerly logic came to the fore. "So we are all the direct products of rape?" he said with a gotcha smirk.

Colmes, with his incredible hearing, from the other side of the room intervened. "Nature doesn't know what rape is. In fact nature doesn't know anything. Nature just does."

Larry gave me a look as if to say, "these eggheads are too much for me," and slipped away, waving to Colmes as he went. Colmes nodded his assent.

Then Bates had to have his say. "I'm black, you know."

"You don't say?" offered Ted laced with a heavy dose of sarcasm, "and I'm a white basketball player, you know the kind, the ones that can't jump."

Bates screwed up his face not knowing whether to laugh at what may have been a self-effacing joke, or more likely was an example of language violence, as he was taught last year in his graduate Justice and Equity seminar. "I was just making the point that gender is the same as race, or is that too difficult for a lawyer to understand?" said Bates, aggressively.

"You should come to my next hot tub party then you will learn that gender trumps race any day." And with that parting shot, Ted shook hands with his old mate Finneas, gave Chi-Ling a kiss on her flushed cheek, nodded to Colmes and left.

Toekiarty had watched and heard all that happened between her young assistant director Bates and that disgusting excuse for a lawyer, Garcia. Now the next thing was truly incredible to me. Maybe there's something about marriage ceremonies that softens even the hardest of hearts. She put her arm around Bates, to the extent that she, small and stocky, could, her head reaching not that far above his navel, and said, "don't take any notice of him, the taller they are the harder they fall, you know," then frowned to herself realizing too late that Bates was taller than O'Brien.

Bates was fortunately not listening to his boss. He was eyeing off Chi-Ling and was smitten by her Asian beauty. "May I kiss the bride?" he asked no one in particular.

"Don't ask me," said the President with a big smile, "ask Chi-Ling herself."

Chi-Ling stood on tippy toes and raised her head as high as she could. Bates leaned down and managed to place a kiss where her glistening dark hair met the top of her forehead. Toekiarty looked on with considerable displeasure. Then departed without a word. She knew that her job inevitably made enemies for her. And she also knew that if she tried to do something about Colmes and this latest cheap trick of his, to right the terrible wrong done to Chi-Ling by the President himself, she would lose her job and nobody on campus would give a damn. What she had not foreseen, and should have, was that the loving couple were not done yet. Not by a long way. Right now there were just the happy couple, a bright future ahead, Phineas would make sure of that.

***

Colmes and myself were now alone in his office. Colmes looked most satisfied. He had transformed what could have been the worst scandal of the year on campus, into a pleasant and happy circumstance. He was not quite done yet, for door one opened and in came Rose the Younger carrying a large tray of cupcakes made to look like mini wedding cakes, a large floral teapot of tea, matching cups and saucers, and of course, her knitting tucked under her arm.

"Thank you Rose," smiled Colmes as he took the tray and placed it on his desk beneath the flower arrangements. Colmes took it upon himself to pour the tea. "Who takes milk?" he asked.

The story might well end happily there. But there was much more happiness to come for the loving couple. You may wonder why the Provost was not invited to the wedding ceremony. In fact she was, but declined, because of her anger with the President. He had, this very day, informed her that the department of Chinese and South Asian studies was to be upgraded to a new School of its own, and Chi-Ling would be appointed its Dean.

I often wondered whether Colmes really did have a celebrant's license. He did produce the necessary marriage forms that Rose the Younger and I signed as witnesses over our cups of tea. And he once remarked to me, when someone questioned whether he was a real detective or not, that indeed he had a New York License to practice as a private detective and that it was nowhere near as difficult to qualify for, compared to becomng a New York State approved Celebrant.

11. Murder Not

Numbers don't lie, so they say (that is, politicians and scientists who are counting COVID deaths). There's no doubt about it, though, the scientists and their statisticians (who for the most part serve their bureaucratic masters) own numbers, totally. And look at what they have achieved with them. The wonders of modern civilization. But just to forewarn you, I have a foot in both camps. And currently, that foot is in the philosophy camp (which once owned the elements of criminal justice) where the truth of numbers is not at all self-evident. Just to give you a small but well known example. Numbers were around, I think, before the discovery of zero, which I am told is not exactly a number because it does not attach itself to anything (because it's zero or nothing of course). Furthermore, zero was not "discovered" rather it was invented by a human somewhere around the fourth century AD or before (OK, CE if you insist). It is a fiction just like any other, including the case that I am writing up right now. I should add that I have never been able to understand what I was taught in high school, or maybe primary school that two negatives equal a plus. Further, how is it possible to buy, say, negative 2 apples? The only solution I can figure out is to pay the grocer for two apples and not take them. But they would say that I automatically have a credit of two apples, if I do not return to pick up the apples before they go rotten. And the so-called "credit" goes away with them. And if I paid say, $1, for the apples then I have a credit with the grocer for $1 next time I come back to purchase something, assuming they sold the two apples to someone else. But wait. Is the dollar real? I mean who said that it is worth two apples, or two something else? And what's this I heard that "the government" actually "prints" its own money? Rather than go into debt? Only recently did the west give up its attachment to the concrete, touchable basis of money which was, before President Nixon got rid of it by fiat, the gold standard.   We end up in times of inflation and market fluctuations having to put up with the worrying fact that one dollar may not be worth one at all, but maybe only a fraction of one, say, 50 cents! You see what I mean? Even when a number looks real, it can be divided into an infinite number of parts. It is no wonder that numbers can be manipulated, when in actual fact, we philosophers understand—as do advanced mathematics professors, who are really a type of philosopher—that numbers are malleable and reformable and manipulatable. I could go on, but I know I should stop or my lack of mathematical training and understanding will be starkly exposed.

What I am trying to say is that there is a point where one is forced to accept certain abstractions that appear as concrete facts of everyday life. One must have faith in knowledge. Doubts are for dreamers. Faith is for doers. Too much faith is dangerous. Too little is self-destructive.

I admit that all of this is banter, a typical gambit, for me at least, to begin the telling of this case, probably the most painful case that I was exposed to as Colmes's assistant and colleague. But numbers, especially rare numbers, are not all that irrelevant to this case as I will now try to demonstrate.

The statistical composition of a run-of-the-mill university like Schumaker university in New York State is of about 12,000 students, and about 1,000 faculty of which maybe ten percent of the latter would be full professors, so probably over 50. This is truly a startling statistics if one thinks about it. I have harped on this in other cases, how the composition of youth and genders make for a preoccupation with the unavoidable force of the hormonal behaviors of university students.

But the statistics also tell another story. In a university the young greatly outnumber the old, so that when someone dies it is more likely to be a professor, but since there are so few of them, and many retire before they die (though many try to hang on for understandable reasons), deaths if they occur on campus are indeed newsworthy.

Especially if that death is of a young and vibrant student. And as a final piece of unnecessary detail, we know from the criminal justice statistics collected in the United States and pretty much everywhere, (excluding war-torn places) murder is an extremely rare event. Statistically, that is. Of course, mass shootings which are currently the rage, are amplified extensively by the media. They do not generally, report the number of deaths resulting from car accidents, which are, as you would probably guess, equivalent to fighting a war in Vietnam every year.

Indeed, I digress, or seemingly so. But the start of this case is one in which the gradual fading of faith appears in the enthusiasm of universal worship, as shown by a fading number of students, including myself.

***

The vivacious, lovely, happy Ruth was a bright star in my life from the very day I met her in those days of the sit-ins. I was so taken with her that I admit I became a sort of stalker, though not the kind that is obnoxious or dangerous. I became very active in the student association just so I could be in the same room as her. I cannot recollect any occasion in which she was not smiling and happy. I never saw even the slightest hint of a frown on her face. I occasionally managed to accompany her to the cafeteria so I could sit and chat with her, but she was most elusive, would not allow me to buy her a cup of coffee, and anyway, she was so popular and social, that it was impossible to be alone with her. She seemed to know everyone on campus, and everyone seemed to know her. I did manage once to show off my old mini-minor that sat rusting away in the student car park. The park was adjacent to the cafeteria, so I was able to point it out. "We must go for a drive one day," I imagined myself saying.

When I was in my late teens, an old uncle of mine had once advised me, in response to my sordid question of how to get, well, you know what I mean, advised me thus:

"It's simple. Just get control of her time."

Well I found that in many cases, this seemed to work, but in Ruth's case, it was an impossibility. She was never on her own, or at least she was never in a space where she was not surrounded by other people. Yet, as I observed closely, while she was so ebullient, so happy, so outgoing, smiling and laughing and chatting, she was in fact, not talking seriously or closely to any one person. She related to many people at once. She did not, would not, or maybe could not, relate to any single person and have a chat one-on-one. So it seemed. And perhaps through my admittedly hormonal gaze, I could not find a way in, through the wall of sociability.

I remained frustrated for some time. And I admit it. I was obsessed with her. And surely she must have realized this. I showed up everywhere she was that seemed "natural." It was a period in my life when I became an incredibly social being, a persona that I had always denied. Since working with Colmes, I had always thought of myself as being a little like him, introverted and frankly antisocial. This is what a wonderful girl like Ruth had done to me. And that's right, I thought of her as a girl, not a woman. She would always be a happy girl. That I was sure of. Oh how she would brighten up my life!

On the rare occasions on which I spent a non-working social time with Colmes, I was tempted to ask him for his advice, or at least just confide my feelings and longings to him. But I managed not to do so, for it was clear to me, so I thought, that he had no idea of social relationships anyway. I could not imagine him loving anyone.

Then as life would have it, I found myself in a place where Ruth appeared, one place that I had never imagined I would find her, indeed, was not even looking for her, or at least, I was looking for something else, solace, perhaps, being a student of philosophy, looking for meaning somewhere other than in myself. I had found the university's place of universal worship. A church that was not a church, a squat building, still with the university signature vertical slits of windows embedded in concrete, nestling among the few natural trees that had been left over from the old golf course upon which the modern university had been built.

***

As I approached the building, a dull day, I would like to remember it as spring, but I think it may have been the early days of the Fall. I heard the sound, unmistakable sound, of chanting. A low, monotonal hum, a sound I had never heard before. In fact, I was used to the sound of rousing hymns coming from a church, that I had foolishly assumed this place of worship was.

I peeked in the door and there before me were rows, neatly formed, of students and maybe others as well, sitting cross-legged on the hard concrete floor, all in what I was told later, was the lotus position. I could see only the backs, except for one individual dressed in bright yellow robes of a Tibetan, maybe, monk. I really had no idea. But this monk walked up and down the rows, every now and again prodding someone if it looked as though they were going to sleep—or at least, that is what I presumed.

The door closed behind me and I stared, then suddenly found myself trying to sit in the lotus position, but with great difficulty. The monk came up behind me and pinched my hair at the short at my neck. It hurt. I looked up angrily, and the monk tapped the back of my head, signaling to me to look straight ahead, eyes closed, as were all the others. But before I closed my eyes I saw ahead of me, I am absolutely sure, the back of Ruth, in whom even from her back, I could be sure she was happily smiling (in this place forbidden).

The pain of cramping became unbearable. I squeezed my eyes closed as if to relieve the pain. I yearned for the chanting to stop. But I was not going to stand up and leave, not until I affirmed that it was Ruth who was right in front of me.

I was in a trancelike state, I admit it. Brought on by the combination of the excruciating pain of cramping, and my crazy vision of Ruth and me walking together hand in hand through a beautiful Japanese garden, everything clipped finely, everything in its place. Until I suddenly felt a hand on my shoulder, someone saying, "William!! William! Are your there?" Cramped, and unused to sitting in such a position, I fell backwards, sprawled on the floor, opened my eyes and there looking down at me was that unbelievable vision, the happy vivacious face of my dreams, Ruth. I stretched out my hand, kind of expecting her to reach down and help pull me up. And I am sure she would have done so, except that the yellow robed monk stepped in and pulled me up.

"Welcome to our small group of Zen," he said, with an immediately recognizable fake Russian accent.

I struggled up and kind of shook myself like a dog after it has rolled in the grass. "And you are?" I ask, not at all friendly.

"This is our Zen leader for this week," answered Ruth, all smiles. "We're not really Zen, are we?" she said, almost with a giggle, looking up at the Zen leader.

"And I'm not really a Buddhist monk," said the monk. "This is a universal place of worship. We just try out every means of worship each week. This week it is Zen. Next week it is Old Russian orthodox. And Ruth here will play the leader."

Now, admittedly, given what I have already told you of my desires on Ruth, when the monk looked at her, I was immediately seized with a horrible urge to push him away (actually to be honest, punch him on the nose). "Oh, is that right?" I said with an approving smile.

"Yes, I'll be leading the group in worship as an old Balkan nun," chirped Ruth.

"I'll definitely be here for that," I said with too big a grin. The monk stared at me and I sensed hatred. It was mutual.

"Oh, do come. I'll be all dressed for the part, gowns, prayer rope, the works. And why not invite your boss's friend Rose? She's Russian, right? She probably knows lots about Orthodox."

"I will definitely invite them both," I lied.

The monk grunted, then took Ruth's hand which she (I thought) reluctantly gave to him. "Come on Ruth, I will show you the paraphernalia we have for the Russian Orthodox. A lot has accumulated over the years."

He tugged at her a little and I could not help but think that she was reluctant. Yet her smile stayed bright. I grabbed the monk's yellow robe and said, "I don't think she wants to go." He looked at me with what had to be a snarl, his nostrils expanding with each breath.

"I don't think it's any of your business," he said, feigning a smile.

"Hey guys," chirped Ruth, "let's just all go over to the cafeteria. I'm famished after all that chanting.

***

I spent the rest of the week reading up on the Russian Orthodox church. It was fascinating, though obviously, a sign of mental illness on my part. My obsession with Ruth was becoming overwhelming. I was unable to do much else but think of her day and night. I even went next door and asked Colmes's advice. Imagine that. Getting advice from an old Victorian gentleman, who had even less ability to approach women than did I. Or so I thought.

But I found Colmes most understanding, even comforting. I sat on my wicker chair and told him of my obsession. He had met Ruth once at the sit-in and remembered her well. Who would not? Colmes smiled, yes, really a smile, as he looked up from his crossword puzzle. I also asked him about Russian Orthodox and would he mention it to Rose? He looked at me with a slight frown, and asked, "Of course, I will do so, but why don't you ask her yourself?"

Colmes got up from his chair and I thought that he did so with a slight wabble, it was an effort. I wondered whether he had been drinking. But this early in the morning? I knew he liked his booze, but had not seen him under the weather, so he kept it well hidden, if he was really on the bottle.

"Are you OK Colmes?" I asked.

Colmes did not answer. Instead he called out, "tea and scones for two, Rose my dear. And you are welcome to join us!"

It was on this day that I began to worry about him, and though I would not find out the reason for his slow but steady deterioration. We had an enjoyable repast of tea and scones and a most stimulating discussion with Rose and her knitting, all about Russian Orthodox beliefs and practices, and its very long history. Most of the time, though, I spent imagining Ruth dressed up as a Balkan nun, looking down on us as if from heaven.

***

We finished our tea and scones and I helped Rose gather up the dishes. Carrying my cup and saucer, I followed her through door two to the kitchen where I intended to continue our conversation about Russian Orthodoxy and to invite her to attend the next worship at the University Inter Faith center. We had almost reached the kitchen when I heard Colmes's phone ring, and almost immediately, Colmes was calling for me. There was a quiver in his usually strong and penetrating voice. I knew then that there must be something very wrong.

"Coming Colmes," I called.

I left Rose with the dishes and ran back to the office.

"It seems that there has been a very bad car accident in which one of our students was killed."

Now you would think that since this occurred off campus that it was not within the University's jurisdiction to get involved. But this was a death, an extremely rare event, as I have already told you, so when something like this happened, on or off campus, the university was sure to be involved, and apparently there was some kind of reciprocal agreement between the campus police and local police to keep each other informed.

"Do we know who it was?" I asked.

"Not yet," answered Colmes. "But the whole thing sounds most strange. Apparently the driver crashed his or her car into the front of the Cathedral of Immaculate Conception."

There was a knock at the door, which was already open. The campus police chief waddled in, all 250 pounds of him. A former pro football player turned cop, he approached us with a mixture of urgency and excitement. Nothing like this ever happened on campus.

Colmes rose from his chair and shook hands. "Hobson," he said looking at me, "meet Chief Irving Masterson, the best cop on campus."

The chief nodded my way, then helped himself to the overstuffed chair in the corner.

"It's very bad. A sweet young thing she was. All banged up. Didn't make it. Died at the scene," puffed the chief.

"One of ours?" asked Colmes.

"Yeh. Lovely little thing. Don't know what she was doing. Must have been on something. You know these students. They'll try anything."

"You mean she drove that car up those steps into the cathedral?" I asked in disbelief.

"Just about. But looked like she hit her head on the steering wheel or something like that. Those little cars, you know. They shouldn't be allowed," said the Chief.

Colmes was getting down to business. "You said she died at the scene? Was anyone with her?"

"You mean when she died? Yeh. Some neighbor. It was around one in the morning, so they say. Woke up the neighbor who ran across the street and tried to get her out of the car, but she was out to it."

"They called 911, of course," observed Colmes.

"Yeh. They were there in minutes, so the neighbor said. But it was too late. She had died at the scene."

"Well, thank you for letting me know. Is there anything more I can do to help?" asked Colmes.

"Not much right now. But you could save me a bit of time, I suppose. The car. Its campus parking sticker is registered in the name of one of our students. It's actually the reason I came straight to you. William Hobson is the name."

The chief gave me a devilish look, then looked back at Colmes. I stood up from my wicker chair so quickly that it capsized behind me. "Wha-at?!" I stammered.

Colmes sat forward on his chair. "I take it you know nothing about this?" he asked me calmly.

"Nothing, I answered. You know yourself I rarely use it, in fact have been considering selling it."

"You better get yourself in order," advised the chief trying to be helpful. "Won't be long until the local police show up. Leaving the scene of an accident, maybe? I take it you were driving it?"

I cannot express how deeply disturbed I became. I picked up my wicker chair and sat down on it, trying to come to my senses. I mumbled something about being on campus all night. And the worst part was that I wondered out loud, "who would be handy enough to steal my car, start it without the keys?"

Colmes coughed a little to get the chief's attention. "Irving," he said in his more formal voice. "You have not told us the name of the student who was killed. I assume that's the real reason you are here?"

"Oh yeh. Forgot. A sweet looking kid, as I said. Her driving license said she was Ruth Cardigan. She was one of our students all right. You want me to tell President O'Brien, or will you? I know the president likes you to handle messy things, and I'm guessing by the looks of things…" the chief looked at me intently "…this is a messy thing."

He struggled to get up from the overstuffed chair when there was a loud bang on the office door, which was already open, and a uniformed police officer barged in holding handcuffs in one hand, followed by a shabbily dressed man in his mid-forties, a crumpled ill-fitting dark gray suit, off-white shirt collar unbuttoned, tie tied in an ugly loose knot. It was detective Conrad Summers of whom I was to see quite a lot over the next few weeks.

Chief Masterson fell back in his chair, trying not to show his amusement. Detective Summers, his long and wavy blonde hair partly covering one of his eyes as he looked this way and that, first to Chief Masterson, then to Colmes.

"It seems that the rarity of numbers has caught up with us," mumbled Colmes to me, such that the others did not hear.

I shrugged and looked down. I had an awful feeling, an empty feeling, indeed, as though I were on the edge of a precipice.

***

Now, before I continue to explain what happened to yours truly I should pause once again and explain to you something more of the rarity of numbers as they relate to campus life. Although it is not so much numbers, but of boundaries, perimeters if you like. This case, more than any other demonstrates why Colmes was essential to the university. As I have described already, the campus is a relatively small space into which are tucked away some twelve thousand young people and a tiny number of adults.

There are some 30,000 deaths on road accidents every year in the United States. The chances of one being a university student are miniscule. But when it occurs, even if not on campus as it appeared that this one was not, the regents of the university and others of high standing, in this case President O'Brien, become very anxious and must take rapid steps to prevent the news of this travelling too far, and certainly must take steps to control what news leaks beyond the campus boundary. There are several matters that are best contained within the campus community. But the most important is that of crime or untoward death for which the university might be blamed.

Why is this such a serious matter? You guessed it! Money and reputation. Parents do not want their children to attend an unsafe university. Thus, any bad news that reaches beyond the campus perimeter concerning any of its students is assumed to be potentially very bad, and it is the role of Colmes to control such events and make sure that their repercussions are kept to a minimum. In sum, should a crime occur on, or even off the campus, in which students are involved, it is Colmes's job to take care of them. This is why, for many years, until 1990 when the Clery Act of Congress required it, universities routinely never reported any campus crime incidents to police or anywhere else.

Colmes has always resisted the suggestion that he was a private detective on campus. He insists that he is more of a crisis manager. Whatever he was, he certainly was not a campus cop. There is no way he could work the way he does within the confines of a police department with its many rules of procedures and forms to fill in. And of course, as no doubt you have already concluded, Colmes is his own boss. He could never be beholden to anyone, even his close friend, President O'Brien.

***

Detective Summers knew everyone in the room, except yours truly. He looked directly at me, and I knew that I was in for it. "And who are you?" he asked rudely.

I answered, foolishly, but I wasn't thinking straight, indeed unable to think at all, "what's it to you?"

Colmes stared at me, and then said calmly, "Detective, this is William Hobson my very valuable assistant."

"You're harboring a fugitive," snarled Summers. "Officer, cuff this killer."

"Wait a minute now!" Colmes said firmly. I can attest for this young man's whereabouts last night."

Summers ignored Colmes and almost spat at his officer who had stopped in his tracks when Colmes had intervened. "Well, go on then, cuff him, I told you," commanded Summers.

"Right you are sir," answered the officer who was obviously eager to do it all along. He reached out to me, the cuffs jingling as he ordered, "put out your hands." Dizziness took over, I had no control over my thoughts or actions, felt my knees sagging, then found myself staggering behind Colmes's desk, and fell down on my knees. The officer leaned down. "Come on, your hands! Or I'll do more than cuff you," he threatened. I stretched out my hands, helpless, feeling such despair, I didn't care what would happen to me. My whole body shook with uncontrollable sobbing.

Colmes stood up. "Officer, I can attest to this young man's whereabouts. He has not been off campus for weeks, let alone last night. He worked for me until very late last night as we wrote up a case report. Or should I say that he wrote it up. Then I accompanied him back to his dormitory. It is surely obvious that someone stole the car."

"You mean the young lady found dead in the car?" retorted Summers. "That she stole it? And how would she start it without the keys? Unless, of course the owner had left the keys in the car, or even loaned her the car?"

Colmes looked down at me. I winced as the officer roughly hand-cuffed me and pulled me up so that I was standing once more. Not thinking, I tried to put my hand in my pocket, but of course, the cuffs prevented me from doing so. "My pocket," I mumbled in between sobs, "the keys are in my pocket."

The officer roughly felt in my pocket, and withdrew the keys. "Looks like that's settled it then," he said to his boss and went to un-cuff me.

"Not so fast," ordered Summers. "There might be two sets of keys."

"Or, Hobson here drove the car up the steps with the young lady in it, then somehow got back here without the car," said Colmes.

"But you just said he was with you until late at night," said Summers, impatiently.

"I did. Which means that there is someone else out there who stole the car," observed Colmes calmly.

Then Chief Masterson stirred in his comfortable chair and said quietly, "pardon just a poor campus cop, but isn't it a bit sexist to assume that because she is a she, she would not know how to start an old car without the keys?"

By this time I felt so weak, I sagged once again and sat on the floor. No one seemed to care, including Colmes. Instead, he began a line of questioning of the detective.

"Who was first at the scene?" asked Colmes.

"The neighbor who called it in," answered Summers.

"And did you interview her or whoever?"

"We did. She said that the noise of the crash woke her up. About two a.m., she said. She immediately called 911, then ran over to the crash. She saw the young lady moaning. The driver side door had popped open and she tried to grab her and pull her out of the car. But could not. Her foot was stuck under the brake pedal."

"And the young lady was dead or at least not conscious?" probed Colmes.

"It seems that she was alive, barely. Mumbled something about 'not-murder-not.' "

Colmes looked down at me, then back up to the detective. "Say that again, detective. Are you sure that is what the dying girl said?"

"I'm only repeating what the neighbor told me. 'Not murder not' is what the poor young girl mumbled. I pressed the neighbor on it a number of times. But she was certain that was what the poor little thing said."

Colmes shifted to a different line of inquiry. "Was she girl badly smashed up? Blood? "

"She had a bad laceration to her forehead where we suppose she must have banged it when the car hit the steps and stopped abruptly. You know, these little cars. They're dangerous," answered Summers, trying to be helpful.

"And no other marks that you could see?" Colmes pressed.

"There appeared to be some scratches or blotches, don't know what, around parts of her neck. But we will not know what they had to do with it, if anything, until we get the coroner's report," replied Summers.

"Indeed. Indeed," said Colmes. "I would like to examine the body, if you can arrange it? Were any photographs taken of the scene, by the way?"

"No photos. Didn't look like a crime scene to us. Just assumed that someone had a bit too much to drink and ran the car up the steps. And that's probably what happened. These students, you know. They can't hold their liquor."

"She had been drinking?" pressed Colmes.

"Of course. You could smell it."

"And the car?" asked Colmes.

"Towed to the junk yard. It's a write-off."

Colmes looked a little startled. "You didn't impound it?" he asked.

"As I said, it looked like an ordinary accident caused by someone having too much to drink. We get these cases often, close to one a week."

"Then I take it you are not going to arrest my esteemed colleague here?" Colmes asked as he looked down on my pathetic self.

"You may not take it. We still do not know how the car got there. If she drove it, as seems likely, someone gave her the keys, or maybe accompanied her then ran off as soon as the accident occurred." Detective Summers looked Colmes squarely in his long drawn face.

"But I have vouched for his whereabouts," complained Colmes.

"He could have loaned her the car. Most people have two sets of keys." Summers turned to me. "I don't suppose you keep one set of keys hidden somewhere in the car?" he asked.

But I did not answer. I was still sobbing and whimpering over the loss of the only girl I had ever loved, or would ever love.

The fact was that Colmes knew full well the modus operandi of these detectives. They routinely cited the Miranda rule, suspects' rights and so on, and then proceeded to do what they liked. Their tricks, authoritarian manner, intrusive and abusive interrogation techniques would, he well knew, force me to say something incriminating, and would distort the facts of what actually happened, and so make it even more difficult than it already was, to get at the truth. Worse, from the university's point of view, "facts" would leak out to the media, and do damage to the university's ever fragile reputation.

"Tell you what," said Colmes. I will retain Hobson here with me, in my own lock-up, until you get the coroner's report, and you can come here to interrogate him further should the report deem that necessary."

Chief Masterson stirred a little. It was clear that he was uncomfortable with this arrangement. If it got out that the university had its own jail, and that's what it was, the media would have a field day with it. Besides, it was not Colmes's lock-up, it was the campus police lock-up.

"You mean the university has its own jail on its campus?" asked Summers in disbelief.

"No, no, of course not," said Colmes with a devilish frown, "though it would be appropriate given that our President was formerly a prison warden as I'm sure you know."

"Then what do you mean, professor?" demanded Summers not hiding his resentment and perhaps with a little hostility.

"I mean that I, and Chief Masterson here, will watch over Hobson who in any case works in his office right next door to me, and there is, if I am not mistaken even a bed in it that he uses when he does an all-nighter. That right Hobson?" Colmes gave me a slight wink and even a bit of a smirky smile.

"Yes, sir, Professor," I whimpered in between sobs. "I'm not going anywhere."

Summers took a deep breath and his old gray suit seemed to sag more when he breathed out. "I shouldn't do his," he said. "But in the interests of our close relationship with the campus community, I'll allow it. But he must not leave his office, you understand me?"

"Or my office," added Colmes, since his office and apartment had a toilet. He raised an eyebrow as if to translate the meaning of his comment to Summers, who immediately understood.

"Un-cuff him," ordered Summers, and the officer leaned down and unlocked my wrists. I took this as a sign to stand and get a hold of myself. Which I did.

Colmes stood also, which was a sign to all the cops present to take their leave. Which they did, without another word. Except that Colmes called to Masterson.

"Chief, a word before you go?" he asked.

"Yes professor?"

"I would like to speak with the neighbor. Those last words. We must get to the bottom of them. They must surely be a clue."

"And you want me to take you there?" smiled the Chief. "That's all we cops on campus are these days. Glorified taxi drivers."

Colmes ignored the complaint. "I have a few matters to attend to here, then I will come to your office. Oh as well, I want to examine the car, what's left of it. Do you know what they did with it? Summers said they had not impounded it."

"It will be in one of the two junk yards in town. We can check them out after we look over the   body. I take it you still want to do that, right?" said the Chief.

Colmes was already at his desk perusing his crossword puzzle. I thought I heard him grunt, which I assume the Chief took as a 'yes' as he struggled out of the overstuffed chair and waddled to the door.

***

Rose had been listening to all of this, pottering around in the kitchen and of course attending to her knitting. She had, in fact, been hanging around just behind door one. I caught a quick glimpse of her when I dropped to my knees. What I did not know was that Rose had met with Ruth just a couple of days before the car accident.

Colmes had also noticed her. "Rose?" he called. "Do you have something you want to say?"

"Ruth? She is gone to Heaven, then?" asked Rose in a shaky voice, clasping her knitting close to her breast.

"I'm very sorry to say, that it is so," said Colmes in a low voice.

"Not sorry," muttered Rose, "is Heaven. Ruth talk about that."

"You mean Ruth knew something was going to happen?" asked Colmes quickly, surprised.

"No, no. Just talked about Russian orthodox beliefs. She ask many questions."

Now it was my turn. "Yes, Colmes. She was going to host a session on Russian Orthodox at the Universal Church on campus. I was there a couple of weeks ago when they did one on Zen." The memory of that disturbed me. I looked down, sick in my stomach. Colmes noticed. He notices everything.

"You had better go lie down," he said.

" Those puzzling last words," I groaned. "I must accompany you to interview the neighbor."

Colmes looked down at me. "You are in no state to go anywhere. In any case, you are in my charge, as we agreed with Summers. Rose will take care of you."

I struggled across to the overstuffed chair and collapsed into it.

"You all right, mister William?" I heard Rose faintly.

I was under house arrest.

***

What I will recount now is second hand, you understand. Since I could not accompany Colmes, what I write now is based on my conversations with Colmes soon after he returned. By that time, I had more or less come to my senses, though of course, I did not relish hearing the details of Colmes's examination of the body.

The campus police office was a tiny precinct buried in the basement at the other end of the central campus building. Colmes followed the Chief along the winding tunnels, large in themselves, but filled with the huge pipes that were plastered with insulation, carrying whatever necessities, hot air and water, to their many destinations. Colmes, of course, knew his way there quite well, not only because he liked to keep up to date with all events that came to the attention of Masterson and his two subordinates, but also it was right next to the campus hairdresser to whom Colmes paid a visit every couple of weeks. This also to keep abreast of any rumors or scandals that might be circulating.

They soon sighted the police car, an inconspicuous dark gray souped up Chev Malibu, a small crest painted on each side, depicting a police shield on which was inscribed PROTECT AND SERVE. Because of the contours of the campus, a previous golf course as I have described elsewhere, there were slight hills and dips in the location into which the huge concrete structure of the campus was embedded. So the end at which the campus police precinct was built, opened out directly to the surface, whereas my office and that of Colmes at the other end were sunk two levels underground.

The hairdresser, everyone called him Harry, a short and stout fellow with a large round chin, came to the door. "Everything all right?" he called loudly, his voice absorbed by the insulation of the enormous pipes. Of course, bad news travels fast, and no doubt the hairdresser had heard much of what had happened.

"We're on it," answered the Chief, also a regular customer.

Colmes nodded to Harry, and continued on, his head down, deep in thought no doubt. Ruth's last words would not let up. "Not murder." It made no sense.

Chief Masterson squeezed into the aging Malibu, its age signaling the level of importance it held on the ladder of university expenditures. Colmes remained silent as they drove down Madison Avenue, across Washington Park and eventually pulled up outside the great cathedral of the Immaculate Conception. There was not much to see at the crash site, a few scuffs and scratches on the stone steps, but little else. Masterson led the way across the street to a small row house. "This one, " he mumbled, "let's hope she's home."

In contrast to his soft mumble, he thumped loudly on the door, which was quickly opened by a tiny, shriveled lady, her small face lined like a squashed paper bag, her nose hardly apparent, but her bright active eyes conveying a person of sharp intellect. "I thought it might be you," she said, clasping her hands together.

"Thank you, Mrs…?"

"Johnson," she quickly replied, "my husband passed away two years ago."

"I am Chief Masterson and this is my colleague from the university, Professor Colmes. May we have a few words with you?"

"There's not much to say. I told the other officers everything. How I called 911 and…"

"Yes, Mrs. Johnson, thank you we do already know about that," interrupted the ever impatient Colmes. "We are however interested in what you think you heard the poor girl gasp in her last words to you."

"I don't *think* I heard," answered Mrs. Johnson abruptly, "I *know* what I heard. She said 'not,' gasped for breath and rubbed her neck and then said 'murder' and possibly 'not' again."

"Her neck, you say, "she grabbed at her neck?" pressed Colmes.

"I'll say she did, and I could see it was all red and splotchy, like."

"And did you notice anything else? Did she try to say anything else?" asked Colmes.

"No, nothing," answered Mrs. Johnson. "Mind you I think from her gasps she was trying to say something else, but she just could not get it out, and she gave a big kind of sigh, and then she died, I'd say."

"Thank you, Mrs. Johnson, you are being most helpful. Did you see any sign of another person who might have been in the car, or at the scene of the accident?" probed Colmes.

"No, it was such a big noise so late at night. I looked out the window and saw the car on the steps and ran back to the kitchen to call 911 immediately," replied Mrs. Johnson.

"One last question, Mrs. Johnson. Did she have her seat belt on?" asked Colmes.

"No. She didn't. I was surprised at that. But I suppose that someone who would drive a little car like that up those big steps in front of a big church wouldn't bother much with seat belts," said Mrs. Johnson with a grim smile.

"Indeed. Indeed, Mrs. Johnson. I am most appreciative of your help." Colmes stepped back and left, calling out over his shoulder, "you are a marvel Mrs. Johnson!"

Chief Masterson nodded his head in agreement, then struggled to catch up with Colmes. "Where next?" he called in between puffs.

"The car, Masterson. The car."

***

A phone call to detective Summers at the Albany PD was necessary in order to locate the car, which had been towed to a random junk yard. When Colmes told me this, I expressed my surprise, as I could not see how a car could be deemed a write-off when it was run up some stone steps. There might be some damage underneath, but the rest of the car would not be at all dinted or smashed, was I not right?

Colmes replied that I was mostly right, although being a tiny car, a Mini-Minor he reminded me, the front end of the car was bent where the low fender hit the stone steps as it bounced up. In any case, the inside of the car appeared to be undamaged, reported Colmes. However, Colmes had come to the conclusion that Ruth was not driving the car and that there must, therefore, have been another occupant. Furthermore, there were no dents or signs of blood inside the car, especially on the dashboard where you would expect someone to have banged themselves when the car stopped and shuddered as it bounced up the steps. Mind you, of course, the age of the car was well before airbags existed. It was the positioning of the seat belts that attracted Colmes's attention. It seemed as though they had been either straightened after the smash or not used at all.

Colmes turned to Masterson. "We must return to Mrs. Johnson," he said.

The Chief knew Colmes well and did not bother to ask why. He simply performed his role as Colmes's driver and retuned him to Mrs. Johnson's doorstep. And when she answered, Colmes gave her his best Victorian smile.

"Mrs. Johnson, one more question, if I may?" he asked.

"Oh it's so nice to see you again already. Won't you come in for a cup of coffee?"

"Thank you, my dear, but I cannot. The caffeine is too much for me. May I ask, could you describe to me in as much detail as you can, the position of the girl's body when you spoke to her? I take it that the door window was down, or the door itself was open? Otherwise you would not have heard her speak."

"You are quite right Mr. Colmes. The door was open and her hand was stuck in the handle, so she could not push the door any more. It was open just enough so I could stick my head in and I reached out to take her hand. Although, Mr. Colmes I was a bit worried about pulling her out of the car, because I thought I might make any injuries she had even worse."

"Indeed. Mrs. Johnson. You did well. Where was the rest of her body? Was she sitting in the driver's seat, her feet on or near the peddles, or ..."

"You're right, Mr. Colmes. She was kind of slumped sideways. One of her legs was stuck on the passenger side of the car. But she was all slumped, you know what I mean? Kind of like someone is when they were drunk."

"Are you suggesting that she was drunk?" asked Colmes with a frown.

"Oh No. I don't think so. I would have smelled it, especially when I got real close to her mouth when she was trying to speak."

Colmes smiled again. "Mrs. Johnson, you have been most helpful. Oh and by the way, were the seat belts jumbled around at all? Or were they in their unused position?"

"I'd say, never used, Mr. Colmes. These young people, they think they are invulnerable," announced Mrs. Johnson wisely.

"Indeed. Indeed," Mrs. Johnson. Thank you again.

***

I awakened from my dizzy unconsciousness—I would not call it sleep—to find Rose leaning over me.

"I have made you a nice cup of tea. Is young man here see you. Russian Orthodox Priest."

"What?" I asked rudely.

"Priest, says he Russian Orthodox. But he not. Just dressed like one. Though he has his *chotki.*"

I took the cup of tea, and tried to look past Rose's round silhouetted figure, her bunched up hair and knitting getting in the way. I rubbed my eyes, but everything seemed blurred. Perhaps I was not awake at all.

"Tell him to go," I said and fell back into the chair, Rose grabbing my hand with the cup of tea just in time.

Rose, as only she could, told the visitor to go, and he promptly left. I managed to sip a little of the tea, and slowly came to my senses, such as they were.

"Rose," I called in a pathetic, feeble voice.

"You like more tea? Special Russian tea. Good, strong," answered Rose.

"What did you and Ruth talk about?" I asked.

***

The body lay waiting for Colmes and the Chief in the Saint Peters Hospital. Detective Summers met them and showed the way, past security down to the morgue. The body was laid out awaiting the coroner's assistant to begin the autopsy. As soon as Colmes saw it, the once happy face no more, Colmes was overtaken by a sense of relief and grief, relieved that I was not there to see that awful sight, sad because this was a beautiful young girl who once had such a bright and happy future.

Summers and Masterson stood back as Colmes stepped up, a magnifying glass in hand, to examine the body. He would start at the head and work down. There was a slight cut and bruising on her forehead where, Colmes assumed, she must have come in contact with the car's dashboard. But his attention was quickly drawn to the contusions around her neck. There were red marks that were, he was convinced, caused by something rough, maybe rope or cord, that had been tied around her neck. There were pronounced red blotches all around, suggesting something that had beads on it, or a rope that was twisted in some way. He continued his examination all the way down to her feet, and there saw the only other mark on her body, a bloody contusion around her ankle and other cuts on her left foot, suggesting that it had been caught on something, maybe the underneath of the car seat.

He turned to the lab assistant. "Do you have the clothes that she wore?" he asked.

The attendant checked the number that was on the tag tied to

Ruth's left big toe, went to a bank of lockers and withdrew a plastic bag in which were all of Ruth's clothes and meagre belongings. Colmes directed that they be laid out on a table. The left shoe was missing.

He turned to Detective Summers, who had been watching Colmes with some amusement. He considered him to be, of course, an amateur.

"Was the left shoe found in the car?" Colmes asked.

"Probably. But quite frankly, the car was bare. Nothing in it," said Summers impatiently, "except a yellow robe of some kind. Looked like someone had been sleeping in it."

Colmes turned to the lab assistant. "Thank you. We are done here." Then he turned to Summers and to Masterson who held back, not enjoying this visit to the morgue. "In my opinion Ruth was not driving the car. She was strangled either in the car or before, placed in the passenger seat, then driven by the killer to the church and up the steps. He then pulled her out of the passenger seat and on to the driver's seat to make it look like she was the driver. If you look closely in her hair, you will see contusions where the killer grabbed her head and banged it as many times as he could, against the steering wheel of the dashboard of the car. Her left shoe will be under the passenger seat.

Summers stepped forward and looked closely at the marks on Ruth's head. "But the contusions are not serious enough to kill her, are they?" He turned to the lab assistant for corroboration.

The lab assistant shrugged. "You'd have to ask the boss. I'm still an apprentice. But I'd agree with you if I had to give an opinion."

***

I was still snoozing on the overstuffed chair when Colmes returned. Rose had taken to playing nurse to me, and sat in Colmes's chair knitting away. Colmes stood in front of me, his hands on his hips, a sign that he was impatient, and eager to solve this case. I stirred a little, and squinted up at him.

"Colmes?" I asked.

Colmes did not respond. Instead he turned to Rose and asked, "how is our patient?"

Rose stood up and gathered her knitting from his desk. "Had nice talk. Russian orthodox church," answered Rose, no sign of a smile or anything else.

I managed to lean forward and rubbed my eyes. "Yes, we had a good talk. Some strange character showed up in your office saying he was a Greek orthodox priest and wanted to talk to Rose."

"Bad person. Mad person," said Rose as she made way for Colmes to take back his chair.

"So he was not a genuine Russian Orthodox Priest?" asked Colmes. "And if not, why was he dressed like one? And what did he want?"

I had now recovered fully my senses, and thought only of Ruth. "Ruth, did you see Ruth?" I asked plaintively.

Colmes ignored me and continued with Rose. "My dear Rose, please tell me more about this strange person. Did you not suspect that there was perhaps something wrong? That he might be a mad killer? The mad killer of Ruth?"

"You mean it was not an accident?" asked Rose crossly. "Why not tell before?"

"Yes," I cried, "why didn't you tell us?"

"I am telling you now," answered Colmes calmly. "Although before I saw the body I had my suspicions, but once I saw it, I was convinced it was no an accident."

"Do tell," I said not even trying to hide my resentment.

"She was strangled," announced Colmes. "Probably in your car, then the killer drove the car up the church steps, pulled her into the driver's seat, and fled."

"She wasn't dead when the killer left?" I asked.

"That's right. Dear Ruth managed to say her last words to the nice old lady who called 911," replied Colmes with satisfaction.

I hesitated, then asked in a thin voice, "how was she killed, then?"

"Strangled, probably with a rope, or something like a rope, rough, as though it had knots tied all along it," said Colmes.

Rose stopped her knitting, even dropped a knitting needle. "The *chotki*," she exclaimed.

"What?" asked Colmes, "*chotki*? Don't tell me..."

"Yes, it Russian Orthodox prayer rope tied in 100 knots. The killer! He was here!" cried Rose.

And with excitement I added, "and when Ruth said 'not murder' she meant the knots in the prayer rope."

"Would you recognize this madman, Rose?" asked Comes.

"Well, not. He dressed in robes, big long gray beard," answered Rose, picking up her knitting again. Then she added as if an afterthought, "but I think she knew him."

"That is a good start, Rose. Most murders are by people who already knew the victim."

I stirred from my slumbered state and jumped up from the overstuffed chair. "I know who it is! Well, I don't know exactly who it is, but I have met him, I am sure."

"Universal Church club," said Rose. "Ruth told me all about and how you hated that Buddhist priest ..."

"I wouldn't say it quite like that, but now I certainly hate him. Bet it was him. He couldn't take his eyes off Ruth, and I got really annoyed. A sneaky, greasy character." I wanted to stamp my feet and yell "let's get him!"

"And your car?" asked Colmes. "How did the killer know it was your car? And how was he able to steal it?"

I looked away. Guilty. My face went red, much against my wishes. "I gave Ruth the keys," I mumbled, looking down as though I was about to be admonished by my teacher.

"Do tell," said Colmes.

"She wanted to buy some things for our next Universal Church meeting. The last meeting was Zen Buddhism, and the next meeting was to be Russian Orthodox. I only attended one meeting which was the Zen meeting. They dress up as priests, worshippers and so on." I looked down, for some reason feeling embarrassed.

How that crazy guy dressed as a Zen priest managed to con Ruth into taking him in the car, I could not imagine. Actually I did not want to imagine because I would have hoped that she would ask me to take her. Once we caught the bastard I would find out. Or maybe it would be best not to know.

"When is the next Universal Church club meeting?" asked Colmes.

I shrugged. Frankly, I did not want to know. But Rose spoke up. She had joined us with morning tea. Colmes actually carried a kitchen chair to his office so that the three of us could sit together. By now, I had realized that Colmes had a soft spot for Rose, *indeed*, as he would say. And Rose in her gruff manner, returned the favor. We were about to sip our tea, perfectly drawn and poured, when Colmes got up abruptly and hurried down to the kitchen. We heard him coughing. He quickly returned and we resumed our tea. Rose had leaned over to me and touched my upper arm. "Has some little asthma," she said. "It has only just come on but insists he had it since was boy."

I had noticed his wheezing for some time, and had urged him to quit smoking. That was some years ago now, and he eventually did, along with many others on campus when president O'Brien banned all smoking on campus. At first inside, but eventually outside no matter where.

Colmes placed his empty cup on its saucer, then sat back and said in his typically determined voice that told me he had a plan. "You will attend the next Universal Church club meeting tonight. Rose has put together some typical Russian Orthodox clothing and other things, prayer ropes, beads and so on. I will rely on Rose and you, Hobson to identify the killer. Presumably, he will be dressed as he was when he paid that strange visit to our office, the long beard, the Russian Orthodox priest. You will both have to agree that it is our killer. And if you do, we will act accordingly.

"Not come to meeting?" asked Rose.

"I have other important things to do with this case, which requires that Chief Masterson and I pay a visit to detective Summers and again to the morgue, depending on what Summers tells us."

"But what if Rose and I do not agree who it is?" I asked.

"Then we will have to take the suspect into custody and I will inter-rogate him," answered Colmes. "Once I am satisfied that we have our man, I will take the appropriate action."

"And what might that be?" I asked in my usual combative way.

"Hobson, it is in your best interest not to know," ordered Colmes. "However, for her own safety, once the killer has been identified, I want you, Rose, to leave. I do not want you to risk your life. You already have done a great deal for us. We cannot manage without you. Besides, you have your growing daughter to attend to."

"Not need help. Is in grad school now," replied Rose, showing a rare smile.

"You mean here, this campus?" exclaimed Colmes, very much surprised. "And don't tell me. She's doing a Ph.D., let me see, in philosophy."

Rose started knitting furiously. "Is not doctorate in philosophy program any more. Now it's changed name to Human Culture program."

"My goodness!" cried Colmes. "You mean she will get a Ph.D. in Human Culture?"

Rose sighed. "Yes. Different words, but same thing."

What happened next, I can only affirm in general terms. Colmes forbade me to write notes on this case for my rapidly growing file of cases, so I have had to rely on my memory, many of the details of which are most likely exaggerated, and as you know, that is one of my disabilities, or more honestly, defects. The fact is, we three were certain that it was that Buddha—the one that ordered me about at the last club meeting, I did not even know his name—that strangled our Ruth in my car, or possibly somewhere else then put her in the car. There appeared to have been no alcohol involved, though the coroners had yet to confirm that assumption, so we guessed, well, Colmes deduced that the killer had strangled the victim inside the car, late at night, where no noise would be heard and little would be seen. There were plenty of places where the car could have been driven, either on campus or somewhere else, although the campus was the ideal place away from the local cops. With just a couple of security guys, not that well trained, patrolling the campus, it would be easy to avoid them. In fact, Masterson had reported to Colmes that his men had seen nothing untoward.

I have mentioned to you that this university was built on a golf course and that the architects retained a little of its contours. This included a large pond that, amazingly, the planners and builders left largely untouched. It was, and still is the happy home of a large flock of Canadian geese, tortoises, turtles, gophers and lots of fish (though I would not be inclined to eat them, given the effluent that flows out of the university pipes and gutters and probably eventually ends up in the pond). And while there are signs up forbidding entry of motor vehicles on to the walking paths, many do, and it is not policed. Security turns a blind eye. They know that young people like to hang out in such places. And my mini minor could easily find its way among the trees and narrow paths. More likely, though, is my conjecture that the Buddha drove my car with Ruth down to the edge of the trees surrounding the pond, convinced her or dragged her into the trees, raped her and strangled her then carried her back to the car and drove off. I'm only guessing here. There was no evidence reported of rape, but then that is because the incident was classified by the cops as an accident, so the coroner or their assistant would not go looking for anything like that. I suggested that to Colmes, but he shrugged it off. I surmised that he did not want this incident to be turned into a big media event, and if evidence of rape were found, it certainly would become one. From Colmes's point of view, a big media event highlighting the murder and rape of one of the university's students would be a disaster. His very job, in fact, was to cover up this tragedy and any others that might affect the University's good standing in the community. I am not altogether proud of my position on this "duty" of Colmes to cover up the facts of certain crimes. Over the years I have come to accept it as an occupational hazard, and certainly it could be a serious hazard. And as I describe next what Colmes did, you will begin to understand the complicated shenanigans that lie just beneath the surface of university life. In fact I often think it a great irony, and maybe Colmes intended it this way, that his office is located beneath the university in its tunnels. The tunnels are its bowels, without them operating efficiently, the university would grind to a stop. Nothing would work. And without someone like Colmes, to make sure the university is protected from outside interference, that all inside runs smoothly, there would be bedlam and the university would collapse in on itself.

You may think I am exaggerating. But at this university with its president, a former prison warden it is perfectly understood. The very first thing President O'Brien did when he was appointed President was to name Colmes as the Distinguished Multi-disciplinary Professor. The two of them had been great friends for some years, ever since Colmes helped him avoid a very serious prison riot. O'Brien saw his primary role as warden of the prison, first, to protect those inside from each other, and second, to avoid any interference from the outside, that justice reigned inside where all wrongs were made right. He viewed the university in the same way, as did Colmes.

You may think that once again I am putting off what I must tell you. But I have expended this energy in explaining to you Colmes's mindset so that you will more easily understand what happened next.

***

Colmes left Rose and me to wash the dishes and then to put together a costume that would give us the look of a Russian Orthodox worshipper. For Rose it was rather easy. She tied one of her knitted scarves over her head, squashing her usually high bundle of hair underneath. For me, there was not much I could do. Rose rummaged around in Colmes's closet. I was just a little surprised that she knew his closet so well. Then again I had suspected for some time that maybe, just maybe they were a couple. And maybe, just maybe, Rose's daughter was a product of their relationship. If that were the case, Colmes had feigned ignorance of Rose the younger's attendance at grad school. Unless they had had a tryst and that was all. I could see Colmes doing that. He was an incredibly independent, withdrawn individual. An island unto himself, one might say. Anyway, I ended up wearing an old pair of dark gray pants, baggy, and a long sleeved shirt also too big for me. But I looked the part. A shabbily dressed Russian worshipper.

That evening, as expected, the small group of worshippers, mostly males, showed up at the Universal Church. Rose and I had timed it so that we would get there just at the beginning of the service, and we were most surprised to see leading the service a tall, gaunt man with sparkling eyes, leading the service. An actual Russian Orthodox priest! The service, such as it was, began with continuous chanting, the priest starting out, reciting in Russian. Then after a couple of verses, he switched to English. I could tell that Rose was already quite perturbed, and then understood why when I heard the chant, from somewhere in Psalms. I am not what one would call a bible reader. Had enough of that in Sunday School:

He sitteth in the lurking places of the villages
In the secret places doth he murder the innocent
His eyes are privily set against the poor.
His eyes watch in secret for his victims
He preys on the innocent.

I looked at Rose, but she had joined in the chanting, as though in some kind of trance. Being Russian, perhaps she had lapsed into some kind of reverie, seeing her past life come before her. I stared at the priest trying to convince myself that he was the killer. Otherwise why choose this particular psalm? The few verses that seemed to be God's approval of murder and mayhem?

But then the answer quickly came to me. It was all Colmes's doing. He wanted to spice up the meeting, make sure that our suspect knew he was a suspect, tempt him into some kind of uncontrolled error, to reveal himself.

I searched the congregation, even quietly walked around the

worshippers, only some twenty of them I guessed, looking for our quarry. Rose stood, looking down, her knitting tucked under her arm. I returned to my place beside her, but found that it was taken by a Russian Orthodox priest with a very large beard. He had come between us.

***

Colmes walked down to the far end of the tunnels on his way to the campus police precinct. He dropped by the hairdresser to say hello.

The hairdresser was reading the student newspaper, *Flotsam*. "Hello Professor. Need a clip?" he asked as he looked up from the paper. "Awful that poor student getting killed in a car accident," he said.

"Yes, terrible, and no clip today, thanks Harry," answered Colmes.

The hairdresser also specialized in theatrical make-up and often worked with the university's performing arts center.

"Did a student come by and get made up as a Russian Orthodox priest, by any chance?" asked Colmes.

"Yes, yesterday. Insisted on a big gray beard. Weird guy." Harry grimaced.

"Don't suppose you gave him a coke or something like you often do for your customers?" queried Colmes.

"Well, not a Coke, though I offered it to him. He said he was very thirsty and could he have a glass of water."

Colmes had been standing at the door, and now walked in right up to the chair. "Don't suppose you still have the glass?"

"Gees, professor. I apologize. Been busy and never got around to washing it. It's right there." Harry pointed to the ledge where he kept all his hairdressing tools and paraphernalia.

"May I borrow it?" asked Colmes, much pleased.

"Here," said Harry, "I'll get it for you and clean it up."

Colmes hurried to the glass. "No! No! Harry, I need it just as it is. Don't touch it. Don't suppose you have a plastic bag? I'd like to borrow the glass for a few days."

He bagged the glass, said his good-bye along with a nice tip, and proceeded to Chief Masterson who impatiently awaited him.

"What have you there?" demanded the Chief.

"I'm hoping that you are still a qualified finger printing expert," said Colmes.

"Of course! I'm the best, though in this job I don't get a lot of work. I mainly do any extra stuff the local PD needs doing."

Colmes showed him the glass. "I want you to lift the prints off this glass and compare them to the prints I hope you can take off the steering wheel of Hobson's car. His of course, will be on them, and maybe Ruth's. But there should be another set of prints that match this glass."

"So you're going ahead with this?" asked the Chief, showing considerable doubt.

"It's a complicated case and I need your expert help and, as usual, understanding," said Colmes.

"I thought you were going to bury it and leave it as an accident," said Masterson as he took the plastic bag that held the glass and locked it inside a small safe in his office.

"I do want to bury it, but Summers insisted that Hobson caused it. As you know he's under house arrest in my office," said Colmes. "We need to get Summers off our backs."

"Understood," replied Masterson.

***

They arrived at the wreckers and Masterson lifted several sets of prints from the car steering wheel and a few other places. While Masterson did his work, Colmes looked over the rest of the car once again. He did find Ruth's left shoe under the passenger seat. But nothing else of importance. The shoe suggested to Colmes that his theory was correct. That Ruth had been drugged or otherwise made unconscious, through strangling, most likely. This occurred either inside the car, or outside and she was carried to the car. Either way. This was no accident. Nor was it Hobson's doing, he certainly hoped. Besides Hobson had an alibi. He was with him all the time the car was taken. If the real suspect's finger prints showed up on the steering wheel, it would confirm his theory beyond reasonable doubt. I say "reasonable doubt" because that is how Colmes talked, purposely parroting the legal terminology of a trial. And there wasn't going to be a trial.

Chief Masterson's expert analysis of the finger prints did indeed return three sets of prints. He was able to confirm that one set of prints definitely matched those from the hairdresser's glass. The other two sets probably belonged to Hobson and Ruth. They could test those later. For now, Colmes was satisfied that he could go to Summers and convince him to drop the silly accusation against Hobson, and classify the disaster as an unfortunate accident.

Detective Summers was no fool, not by a long way, confided Colmes to Masterson as they drove to the Albany police precinct. Now Colmes, and by default the Chief, had to go much further than simply clearing Hobson. They had to convince Summers to treat the whole thing as an accident, and leave them, the campus police and Colmes, to deal with the prime suspect, another university student, it seemed. They were asking Summers to turn a blind eye. To let the university deal with its own homicide. In other words, bypass the legitimate criminal justice system. Prevent the outside from interfering with the inside.

Perhaps you can now see where this is going? It is why I have been most uncomfortable relating this case. A case in which I was deeply involved, though did not actively take part in what must be called a cover-up. What worried me even more was that Colmes saw no particular difficulty in this arrangement. In fact, he was an ardent defender of avoiding the "corrupt, moribund and biased" criminal justice system, as he saw it. If the case went through the official system many, many people's lives would be affected and likely ruined; not only the lives of accused and accuser, but of their families and friends, of witnesses and their families, of juries and their families, the list is endless. The problem was that there was too much obsession with juries, finding of guilt (rarely innocence) and a preoccupation with some kind of abstract notion of "due process." Colmes loved to quote a saying of an old Italian friend of his who said, of the inquisitorial system of justice: "We do everything we can to ensure that no innocent person is brought to trial." Colmes essentially operated according to that principle.

"Do we have a name?" asked Masterson as they pulled into the University police department car park.

"Name?" answered Colmes, startled.

"Yeh. You know. The perp. Or these days they say person of interest," said the Chief.

"Hopefully, Hobson and Rose are working on it. In fact I was hoping Hobson would show up here after their contact with the perp, as you call it," said Colmes amused.

"How would he get here?" asked Masterson. "He hasn't got a car."

"There's a university bus that passes right by here. I told him to get it, if he and Rose were successful in nailing the suspect."

The Chief responded with considerable concern. "Nailing? What does that mean?"

"Whatever Hobson takes it to mean."

Colmes never liked to be questioned.

***

The Russian Orthodox meeting ended and the priest sauntered down to us, along with our suspect.

"That's a wonderfully authentic costume you are wearing, Nicholas, if I am not mistaken?" said the priest.

Our suspect did not acknowledge his name. But simply raised his *chotki* in both hands and stretched up to Heaven.

"And a truly authentic 100 knot prayer rope, if I am not mistaken?" continued the priest.

"I am Nicholas," stated our quarry, still looking up. "God has given me power over life and death. I am his doer of all that is good, I bring sinners to Heaven."

Nicholas lowered his arms and turned to look at Rose and me. "Take these, and I will show you the way," commanded Nicholas in a preachily tone.

"And what way is that?" I asked with as much belligerence as I could muster.

Rose took the *chotki* in one hand, and in the other produced her knitting. "One day I make a *chotki* with my knitting," she said, inspecting the *chotki* closely. "May I borrow it so I can see how I can make it?"

Nicholas went to take the *chotki* back, but the priest took both his hands in his and pulled them to his breast. "May you do God's work in kindness, to love the poor and spurn the wicked," he announced as if giving Nicholas an order.

And in an instant, I realized that Rose had left, taking the *chotki* with her. I was left standing, dumbfounded, wanting to run after her, but knowing that I must stay and try to keep our suspect engaged. "Don't worry," I said, "I will bring it to you this evening or first thing in the morning. Where's your dorm?"

Nicholas looked embarrassed. The priest and I looked at each other. "So you live off campus?" I pressed.

"Not exactly.."

"You are a student, right?" I persisted.

The priest felt it his duty to insert good will. "It matters not. You are one of God's children, one of our students or not."

"Indeed," I said. "Father why not let him have your prayer rope? I can see that he is a little nervous, perhaps needs some spiritual support."

Then Nicholas blurted out, "I'm a freshman and I live in whatever car is left overnight on campus."

The priest smiled with approval, but I had to hide my consternation. It meant that there was an additional explanation should his finger prints be found in my car. And before I knew what I was saying, I blurted out, "that's nothing. Why don't you come stay in my dorm until we get this sorted out. I have a good friend who will work with the university bureaucracy and will have you in your own dorm room in no time. There might even be a spare dorm in my building. Where I'm supervisor."

"But I have no money!" cried Nicholas.

"Don't worry about that," offered the priest, "we will find a way to help you over your crisis."

Nicholas dropped on a chair and continued to sob. "Come, come!" continued the priest, "is there some other awful thing that has happened to you? Being homeless is no big deal."

"It's not that," cried Nicholas. "I just can't…"

The priest looked at me in a most severe way, and then looked down at Nicholas, his big beard coming detached from his face. "I think," he said cautiously, that I had better bring you to the small rooms I keep at the back of this church. Dr. Colmes, who I think is your mentor," he looked at me earnestly, "arranged for this place just in case of such emergencies. You can stay here over night and I, with God's help, will watch over you."

That left me on my own. I was glad to be relieved of our suspect, did not relish the thought of babysitting the murderer of my heart throb. Who knows what I would have done. But it all worked out a bit too smoothly. I began to suspect that Colmes was somehow behind this. In cahoots with the priest. His network of influence was tremendous.

I decided to go back to my office and see what Rose was up to. She had pocketed Nicholas's prayer rope. It looked well used and fingered. I was guessing that she was going to have it checked for blood. Ruth's blood. Or Ruth's saliva. Or maybe DNA. I don't know much about such things, even though Colmes was always talking up the promise of science and technology to eradicate crime. Fat chance. I doubt he believed it either.

***

I returned to my office to find Colmes's door ajar, and Rose sitting at his desk. She was knitting at full pace.

"Any luck with the knots?" I asked.

"Wait Colmes's friend in environmental studies lab. Has all the latest equipment. But needs something of Ruth's to compare findings. Have anything?"

"Colmes said he retrieved her shoe from the car. But I don't have it. Maybe it's in his desk or something?"

I rummaged around in his desk, but found nothing. And then the phone rang. And to my surprise, Rose reached over and picked it up.

"Doctor Colmes office," she said, then her face brightened. "Oh! Colmes. Yes. He's here. Yes. Albany PD. Yes. Bus."

"What? Ask him where the shoe is," I mumbled. I had sunk down in the overstuffed chair and was ready for a nap. Rose ignored me and listened while Colmes apparently was issuing instructions. Soon, she hung up and continued with her knitting. I waited expectantly. Until she finally said, not looking up, "you take bus now. He has shoe."

I reached the Schumaker Police Department maybe an hour later. I had to wait for a while for the bus, and I admit, I was in no hurry. I was supposed to be under house arrest. I fully expected to be interrogated and thrown into their lockup.

The bus stopped right at the entrance to the police station and I alighted. Colmes and Masterson stood out front. Colmes looked serious. Masterson amused.

"Summers will be here shortly," he said, I have informed him of our findings."

"What findings, exactly?" I snapped.

"That our suspect drove your car, and crashed it with Ruth inside it, then pulled her across to the driver side to make it look like she drove it."

"And you can place the suspect in the car? By the way his name is Nicholas," I said.

"Yes, I know. Father Sokolov called me. The fellow is apparently in a sorry state and in the father's care at the Universal Church."

"I know that too. And Rose managed to get Nicholas's *chotka*, the prayer rope with 100 knots. She left it with your pal at the environmental studies lab."

A police car pulled up at the curb and Detective Summers stepped out. "Good afternoon, gentlemen," he said, his baggy pants and suit jacket blotting out the rest of him. "My apologies for keeping you waiting. I was held up at the morgue. The coroner's lab assistant has finished her report. Actually, I had thought you were going to meet me there again?"

"We were," said Masterson, " but then we decided there was no need with you taking care of all those details. We just need the report for our records at the university, then the body can be released to her parents, I take it?"

"What does it say?" asked Colmes, warily.

"Accidental death caused by trauma to the head contacting the dashboard and steering wheel, when the car hit the concrete steps of the church," said Summers putting on his official sounding voice.

Colmes looked at Summers, and that tiny twitch at the corner of his mouth appeared. Summers returned a frown, his face peeping out from behind his baggy pants and jacket. It was a curious communication and I understood it, having worked for Colmes for some years now. They had a "gentleman's agreement." Nothing needed to be said. The cover up had been agreed to.

I shifted uneasily on my feet, then said to Summers, "then I am free to go, no longer under house arrest?" Summers ignored me and walked away briskly to his office. Colmes lightly touched my arm. "Now we can go to the morgue and look more carefully at poor Ruth."

"What? I'm not going there! You heard Summers. It's all wrapped up," I cried shaking at the knees.

"As far as the Albany PD is concerned, that is so," answered Colmes in a voice that I thought was a little condescending. "It is now a university case, not an Albany PD case."

I looked at Masterson hoping to get some kind of support, or I don't know what. But he simply shrugged and said, "the master has spoken," his face full of detached amusement.

I looked, no I stared, right at Colmes. Turned to him and got up way too close. He stepped back, upset that I had invaded his space. "Now that's enough, Hobson. I see I have misjudged you. I had thought you had recovered from the trauma of imagining Ruth in that terrible state. In some ways it's worse than actually seeing her. Take my advice and come with us. You can always turn around and not venture in."

I pursed my lips and frowned. I made a huge effort to hold back sobs and tears. And he was right. The imagination can do far more damage than can reality. And he was right again. We did still have a case, call it a university case or whatever. It was a murder we knew that. And the perpetrator had to be punished for it. And if the Albany PD would not do so, then it was up to the university to do it. I could faintly hear Colmes and Masterson chatting away, serious smiles on their faces. They were seasoned university investigators. I was not; at least, not in this case. I trailed along behind them to Masterson's car and we went to the morgue.

***

To this day, I still do not know whether I should have viewed the corpse of my beloved—unconsummated I might add and maybe that complicates things even more—or stayed away. Colmes and Masterson walked quickly down the hallway of the hospital—all hospitals have long hallways in their basements—then entered the morgue, Masterson showing his badge as they passed through the heavy swinging door. I held back, uncertain and shaking. It was not until several minutes, maybe longer, maybe shorter, that Colmes came back through the doors. I reflexively withdrew from his approach, my arms crossed over my chest. Colmes looked at me with what I hope was pity. And I was in a pitiful state. I admit it. And I see no reason to be embarrassed by it.

"Are you sure you will not join us?" asked Colmes. "It is the only way that you will get any closure. If you do not, her death will live with you forever, and pop up at inconvenient times."

This angered me. Ruth lies there dead and Colmes is telling me that I need to avoid the inconvenience of her memory. I was about to blurt out something like "you cold-hearted asshole, how would you know?" when I realized that my anger had shaken me into an acute conscious-ness. And of course, Colmes had no doubt seen much more of the awful side of peoples' lives compared to me. But I said nothing. Just allowed myself to be ushered through the swinging doors, Colmes gently touching my elbow as we approached the body together.

When I saw Ruth, naked, laid out on the gurney, I had to turn away. I had never seen her naked and had many times dreamed of doing so. I loved her, after all. And then, unwanted, a thought, like a bolt of lightning striking me behind the eyes, "was she raped?"

Colmes observed the swift movement of my eyes. He well knew what I was thinking. I wanted to strike him for putting me through this. All surely unnecessary. His hand was still gently at my elbow. I brushed it away. And he responded, "look closely at her neck. You can see where the skin has been broken at regular intervals, most likely caused by the knots of the *chotki*. She was strangled with it I have no doubt."

I forced myself to lean forward to examine the contusions. "The poor sweet little thing," I whispered to myself. I nodded in agreement with Colmes. And Masterson came up beside us. "So it was murder by strangulation, then," he said in his official policeman's voice.

"Indeed. Indeed," answered Colmes, "we need not look any further," by which I guessed Colmes meant that they need not examine the body any further, making me much relieved. Though now opening the wide door of revenge.

"The killer must be identified and punished!" I cried as I led the way out of the morgue.

"Hold on!" cried Colmes. "Get a hold of yourself!" he ordered.

But I was already in the front seat of Masterson's police car. As Colmes climbed into the back seat I turned and cried, "So where's the killer?" in an admittedly accusatory way, as if I were blaming Colmes for having let the killer get away with murder. Which of course was ridiculous. In point of fact, it was Colmes who was methodically leading the way to a just outcome.

"Well now," replied Colmes calmly, "of the three of us, you are the one who saw the killer last."

"Oh! You mean the church?" I asked apologetically.

"Indeed, Hobson. Indeed. Father Sokolov will be waiting for us.

Let us hope he has managed to keep our quarry safe and secure."

***

Chief Masterson pulled into the church drive and dropped us off at the Universal Church door. I got out quickly and opened the door for Colmes. He nodded his thanks and seemed a little slow and stiff getting out. I reached out and he took my hand.

"Thank you, Hobson," he said, the corner of his mouth doing its little twitch, "age is catching up to me."

"You're not coming?" I called to Masterson as I leaned into the police car.

"You don't need me. The three of you should be enough to extract a confession," he answered. His usual slight look of amusement had faded. I looked to Colmes. I would have thought that having an official police presence, even if only a campus cop, would be essential to make the confession official. Or something like that. I clearly did not quite understand what was going on. But I was eager to get on with it, slammed the car door, the Chief took off, and in big strides I caught up to Colmes as he was entering the church. He also was eager, walking in big strides down the side aisle and into the adjoining small apartment adjoining the church. We entered the kitchen, and I was surprised to see Father Sokolov sitting at the large kitchen table, a large teapot in its cozy, standard issue prison-like mugs.

"Cup of tea?" he asked. "I just boiled the kettle." I quickly declined. Colmes felt under the cozy.

"Indeed, it is very hot," he observed, "but I will not partake for the moment. He had slipped into his Victorian mode, and leaned across the table to the suspect, stretched out his hand and said, "Colmes, Professor Colmes, and you are?"

The killer, as I preferred to call him, sat crumpled over the table, his head in his hands, looking down, a cup of tea in front of him. Incredibly, the long gray beard was still roughly attached to his face. He appeared old, but I knew from our first meeting when he played the part of a Zen monk, that he was much younger than me, probably a freshman.

"I know I did it," mumbled the killer. I know, I know, I know."

"Your name, young man, your name?" persisted Colmes, unmoved.

"Come on, out with it!" I snarled, and sat down on the chair right next to him. Colmes gave me a very critical look. So much so that I stood up and walked away and stood with my arms folded, as a spectator looking on. It was how Colmes wanted it.

Then Father Sokolov spoke. "His name is John Rivers, he says."

"But you called him Nicholas," I spoke in an accusing manner.

"Yes, that was to calm him," answered Sokolov.

"A student?" asked Colmes.

"Apparently not, according to the student records people, and by his own admission," said Sokolov.

"Hmm. That changes things a lot," mused Colmes.

I could not see why. The bastard was a killer, so what if he was not a student? I ran over to the killer and ripped off his beard. "Let's see who you really are!" I cried in a quivering, threatening voice. The priest placed his gentle hand on the killer who was now sobbing. I brushed his hand away. "Let him die!" I screamed, "let him die!"

Colmes looked at me in consternation. The disapproving look was enough for me to stop my foolish outburst, and I retreated to the kitchen refrigerator.

"Now Mr. Rivers," said Colmes as he took a chair and placed it right next to the killer. "Suppose you tell as exactly what happened, starting with the car and how Ruth came to be in it, and how it ended half way up the steps of the cathedral of the Immaculate Conception. By the way, my colleague has your *chotki*. The lab found traces of your DNA and that of Ruth all over it. That is what you used to strangle her, was it not?"

The killer looked up briefly and sniffed. Father Sokolov offered him a couple of tissues which he took to wipe his eyes and sniveling nose. I looked the other way. I found everything about him disgusting.

"Mr. Rivers?" pressed Colmes. He now tightened his grip on the killer's lower arm, but the killer did not respond, just sniffed some more. Colmes slowly but forcefully, pulled the killer's hand away from his face and in doing so forced the killer to sit back, his elbows no longer on the table. Except for the killer's intermittent sobs, the room fell silent. Colmes seemed satisfied with this. And there we all remained for several minutes, maybe longer. It was to me an unbearable silence. I wanted to beat the truth out of the bastard. That's what I wanted.

And then he spoke. "There was this black kid in my class...."

We all shuffled uncomfortably.

"...our grades were about the same, maybe his were a little better. We both came from poor families. We played basketball together. He was a lot taller than me, not quite six feet. I admit, though that he was a better player. He got accepted at some fancy school with a full scholarship. I got accepted here but no money."

"But if you were accepted, how come you are not listed as a student here?" asked Father Sokolov.

"I got accepted but I didn't enroll. I mean, how could I? I couldn't pay for it." The killer looked down, more sobs.

"And?" probed Colmes.

"I don't know. I just sort of came here and went to some classes and pretended I was a student and no one seemed to notice. Only thing was I didn't have a place to stay, so I started using a car each night. There's hundreds of cars parked here, so it's not hard to find one that's left open."

"Go on," said Colmes, most satisfied.

"Well, I accumulated a few things, like that yellow robe the Father has, and some other stuff and kept it all in a locker at the gym that came to be my kind of home. "

Tears again formed in his eyes, and dribbled down his pale cheeks. A tall, thin young man, frail looking, so thin, skin and bones.

"And the Zen monk act?" asked Colmes.

"It just kind of happened. I found I liked the chanting, I heard it when I was scouting around looking for a car for the night, so I went in and then started going regularly to their meetings, and learned all their chants. I really like their chants." The killer's eyes wandered beyond the room, trance-like.

"The yellow robe was found in Mr. Hobson's car, as you probably guessed. How did it get there?" asked Colmes, now beginning to sound a little more like an interrogator.

"I, I'm not sure. I was in the car, I had no idea whose it was. It was open so that was all that mattered, though admittedly it was a bit small for my lanky body. But when you're destitute, you know. Beggars can't…"

"…be choosers. Yes we know that," interrupted Colmes, "continue."

"Well I was wrapped up in my robe and trying to move the seats around so I had more room to stretch out my legs, those Mini-minors, you know, too small, and this gorgeous girl with such a happy face peeped in and asked me what was I doing?" The killer sobbed some more.

"Go on!" I demanded, and in return got a snappy look from Colmes. The killer continued.

"I climbed out of the car and looked down at her beautiful face that radiated love and kindness. Such a meek little thing, I wanted to take her in my arms and let her warm me and tell me everything was going to be all right. And then I remembered that I had seen her once before, when I was leading the Buddhists at the church in my favorite chant. And she remembered me, which made me so, don't know how to say it, joyful. 'You're the Zen monk,' she said with a big smile, her eyes so full of life."

I looked to Colmes, annoyed that he was not pressing the killer harder. But Colmes pursed his lips and stared back at me. I had to shut up. And the killer continued his story:

" 'Well, I'm not really,' I answered, so embarrassed, and then all of a sudden I heard myself saying, 'it's a lovely evening. Like a walk around the pond?' Her face lit up as if it were possible for it to become even happier. 'Sure, why not?' She says, 'as you say, it's a lovely evening.' "

I gave Colmes a knowing look, as I did some quick calculations. I usually parked my car in the parking lot that was up a slight hill some five minutes' walk from the woods that surrounded the pond. As I have mentioned in my other cases, it is a marvel that his piece of land was left by the architects and designers of the university untouched and roughly in its original state of nature.

"Go on, Mr. Rivers." ordered Colmes.

"Well, I er.. We entered the main path that circled the pond, but I was well acquainted with all the woods as I had spent some time there camping out, until I got sick of it and decided to spend the nights in the car of my choice. So I led her off the regular path, trying to impress her, I suppose, with my knowledge of the woods that nobody else on campus would know about. She had allowed me, much to my amazement, allowed me to hold her hand and lead her into the woods. She was so loving. So trusting."

"Get on with it!" I snapped, and received yet another dreadfully glaring look from Colmes.

The killer buried his head in his hands and continued, though his voice was naturally smothered. Colmes gave me another glaring look as if to say that it was my fault.

"Please sit up, Mr. Rivers and speak so we can hear you," requested Colmes in a much too friendly voice.

"There's not much more I can tell you, because it's not clear. Everything goes blank when I try to remember it. I know I was overtaken by her love, took her in my arms, and she let me kiss her, and I was shocked by that. And then all the confusion, dizziness, I am so dizzy even now trying to think about it. The next thing I knew I looked down and she was lying on the ground, a soft grassy patch, and gasping for air. I lifted her up, she was so light, and she remained unconscious. I placed her down again on the soft grass. I had to get her to a hospital. The car. I would get that car. And I knew that the keys had been left on the sun visor. So I ran to the car and drove it into the woods as far as I could, and then found that I could actually drive it along the regular walking path, the car was so small. And I grabbed her up in my arms, and put her into the car. She groaned a bit, then went unconscious again. I drove out of the campus to the hospital, or so I thought. But I got confused. Wasn't used to driving in Albany. Took a wrong turn and found myself driving down the street to the great cathedral. At this point Ruth woke up and blinked her eyes and I was so elated, but then she slumped back into unconsciousness and I turned to her to see if she was breathing, but then felt a huge thump and found the car bounding up the steps of the cathedral. The two of us were thrown all over the front, especially Ruth whose limp body just went smashing wherever the force of gravity sent her. I felt her pulse, and she still had one, but panic took over and I tumbled out of the car and ran straight into the cathedral that was empty, then found my way out of a back entrance, then walked back to campus."

The killer raised his head and took a deep breath as though he were replenishing a body that was spent. He sat up, his arms hanging over the back of the chair pulling his shoulders back, his neck exposed, his Adam's apple reverberating as he swallowed excessive saliva. It was all I could do to resist grabbing his bare neck and doing to him what he had done to my love...

"You raped her then strangled her with your *chotki*, you know that, don't you?" I yelled, placing my angry mouth right in his ear. I expected a disapproving mental slap from Colmes. But he remained passive. So I kept on it. "Come on. Stop the bullshit. You raped her, strangled her then crashed my car to make it all look like an accident."

The killer turned his head and now our faces were just some few inches apart. "I would gladly admit it if I could remember it, but I can't! It's all a blank, confused dizzy mess!" he cried, a spray of spittle hitting my face.

I stepped back. "Father Sokolov," I said quietly, "do you have the *chotki*?"

He handed it to me. I waved it in front of the killer's face, even made it hit his nose and mouth. "You remember this, right?" I asked, full of sarcasm.

"Yes, I do. It's mine. I can tell by the way the knots are tied."

This seemed to me to indicate a confession of guilt. "So you admit it? You raped her, strangled her, carried her to my car, then smashed it into the cathedral steps to make it all look like an accident. Correct?"

The killer looked down, then up, then to Colmes in a kind of pleading way, then back to me. I responded with a glaring look that could kill, literally.

He leaned back over his chair again and took a deep breath, his head dropped well over the back of the chair, his arms and shoulders forced to follow. He then sat up straight, squinted as though the light was too bright, and said, "I did everything as you say. Do with me what you will."

I did not say it out loud, but to myself. "Be assured, you will get what you deserve." Then I pushed a sheet of paper to him and presented him with a pen. "Please write the following as I dictate it, then sign it with your full name."

The killer picked up the pen. But instantly, Colmes intervened.

"I think that will not be necessary," he announced in a most officious tone.

"But," I complained, " we need a confession."

"Indeed, we do, or should I say, we did," answered Colmes calmly. "He has confessed in the most colorful and detailed way one could ask for." Colmes looked at me and then to Father Sokolov. "The three of us are agreed and find the confession of Mr. John Rivers acceptable and authentic?"

I nodded as did the father, though not as enthusiastically as did I. Colmes then continued. "Excellent. Then I think we can reasonably move on to the final stage of our inquiry and close out our case. What is to be done? What sentence must we deliver and administer for such a heinous crime?"

I looked a Colmes in a most puzzled way. I had assumed that the next step would be to hand the killer over to law enforcement to be arraigned, tried and convicted. I looked at father Sokolov and he looked back at me, an expression that I could not fathom. I suppose he was used to people around him doing the strangest things, and, coming from Russia after all, he was well used to peoples' lives being upended and punished for complex reasons, but almost always based on an open confession. And when I looked at him more closely, he averted his gaze from mine, so I concluded that his look was one of complicity.

"Father Sokolov," said Colmes, "if you would be so kind as to take Mr. Rivers in in your charge, make him comfortable, and pray with him should he request it. Perhaps you could join him in some of his chanting."

He then turned to the killer and asked, "young man, have you been baptized in the Russian Orthodox Church? Perhaps Father Sokolov you may want to discuss this with him? In the meantime, I must work on closing out this case with my esteemed colleague here. Our eyes met. He was referring to me!

***

Perhaps I have not been as direct as I could have been in informing you of the actual principles that lay behind the sense of justice that drove Colmes in this case, and in fact all his cases. Justice had to be done, every serious offence matched to its deserved outcome. A careful, impartial collection and examination of the facts of the case was necessary before justice could be served. Actually, it was the procedure that was, in effect, according to Colmes, justice itself. The final verdict, that is the punishment that followed logically from the careful weighing of the evidence was the clear indication to all involved that justice had been done. However, unlike a prison, where only the inmates, that is those inside, had to be satisfied that justice had been done, there were many outside a university who had to be considered. These were of two kinds: the parents of the offender, if a student, and the parents of the victim, if a student.

The status of the killer in this case was somewhat ambiguous since

he was not a student, so technically an outsider. However, he masquer-
aded as a student, and as far as outsiders were concerned, since the
victim was a student, it was important that the "accident" be imported
into the university's realm. Besides, the actual murder was perpetrated
on campus grounds, according to the killer. If I seem to be going around
in circles, I apologize and acknowledge that it depicts my true state of
mind in this matter. Having studied criminal justice I am well aware of
the acclaimed morality and equity offered by "due process" that
backbone of American criminal justice. But I am also well aware of its
many faults, especially the lopsided power that lies with both the police,
who, having "caught" the criminal, are eager to see that he is found
guilty (of anything) that justifies their unavoidable bullying of citizens
involved in the case, and prosecutors who look upon the prosecution and
trial as a kind of football game in which winning far outweighs the
discovery of what actually happened. But here again, I digress.

What would we have without the formal procedures and worship of
American ("civilized") criminal justice? We would have a system that
my mentor Colmes has constructed inside the university. Criminal
justice scholars call it "informal criminal justice" and in those parts of
the world where it is practiced it is called "customary" justice, where an
honored tribal leader hears each side of a case then pronounces guilt or
innocence, and if guilty pronounces the punishment. Obviously, the
"tribal" leader in this case (the judge) has a tremendous amount of
power, and it is that power that the "civilized" concept of due process—
arrest, charge, finding of guilt, punishment—supposedly mitigates that
power. It does not of course. It simply distributes the power over several
criminal justice actors, and in that sense, increases its likely abuse,
simply because there are more than one person exerting it. And the
responsibility for any shocking outcome, indeed in cases where obvious
miscarriages have occurred, can be laid on the jury or the major
contestants, the prosecutor or defense counsel. The judge simply shrugs
and blames it all on the participants, as though the judge were not a
participant at all.

Which finally brings me to the question of why Summers washed his hands of the case, and you may have noticed that the campus chief Masterson essentially stayed on the sidelines. Detective Summers, responsible to his own chief of police, was well aware of the importance of the university with its 12,000 students, the size of a small town, to the city he worked for. So, he worked closely with Masterson and indirectly with Colmes, whose role had always puzzled him, but whose authority he knew was unquestioned in the university. Because they wield so much power every day, police, the higher up the ladder they climb, the more sensitive they are to the power and authority of others. So over the years he, Masterson and Colmes had worked out a way to live with each other, rarely having direct disagreements over who had what authority. This is why there was no jurisdictional bickering. Each knew his part and allowed events to unfold. Thus, the official announcement by Summers was that Ruth's death was an accident. In their unofficial role of Colmes as the tribal leader, the Shaman, and Masterson as his parallel assistant one might say, they planned and guided the case to the end solution that would be approved and accepted by all those inside the university.

Then, there was me. Colmes had deftly used my anger to his advantage. He had allowed me to cajole the killer, impute to him the evil that was necessary to justify the punishment that would follow. Except that there was yet another layer of complexity that Colmes was quietly engineering. After all, if we were wielding customary justice, a severe punishment would follow and be inflicted on the killer. If we were, say, to hang him, or otherwise punish him it would cause outrage once the outside got wind of it, and they certainly would. And obviously the university did not have an appropriate prison into which Colmes could sentence him for the rest of his life. (Of course, all of us were already in a prison, in the mind of President O'Brien).

So what was Colmes's solution? It was staring me in the face, as was often the case with Colmes. It lay with Father Sokolov.

***

Father Sokolov was a worldly man, when it came to faith. He enjoyed and truly loved all the sacred trappings of the Russian Orthodox Church, its prayer knots, gowns, hats, altars of piety, gaudy (some would say) decorations of the church, gold leaf or its equivalent applied everywhere, the rich sky blues. But his worship of such faith did not stop there. He reveled in the faith of others in the world, those of different faiths, Islam, Buddhism, Roman Catholicism and even Protestantism (though a little less so since they had shaken off much of their accoutrements of worship).

So it was that he had managed to sneak into the university and after some years eventually take over the Universal Church. It used to be called the "Interfaith Meeting House," but he thought that it sounded too much like the Quakers and besides Interfaith sounded as though the faiths were separate from each other. And of course appeared to exclude those without faith. His view was that all faiths were one, and as well people who said they were without faith were welcome to join the Universal Church where, since it was attended by people of all faiths, the faithless might perhaps find a faith that suited them. Thus, he changed the name to Universal Church. One of the unintended consequences of this view of Church was that it attracted people who were lost. That is, people who were in fact faithless. Such was the case with the killer, John Rivers. And from now on I will refer to him by name. It will please Colmes who several times has lectured me that I should "get over it," and let it go. Rivers would be punished for his crime, he assured me. If I had any faith at all, I should trust him, my mentor. That's what Colmes said. Imagine that! He thought of himself as a kind of God. What else could it be when he asks me to have faith in him?

But I went along with him. Did what I was told, grudgingly. He had returned to his office to attend to another emergency, so he said, something to do with the University's pond, that wonderful sanctuary of forest and water right in the middle of the university. I was to remain with Rivers and Father Sokolov.

I tried very hard to think of the killer (there I go again) as a person just like anyone else. He wasn't like anyone else, he was a murderer. It was not an accident, any of it. Yet he had claimed that he did not intend to hurt Ruth in any way. He seemed not even to remember doing any of it. He was as tortured as I was over her death. On whose side was faith? I asked myself. And as I watched Father Sokolov begin his chant, place his hand on Rivers' bowed head, I stupidly felt left out, why wasn't the Father putting his hand on my head? Well, I hadn't kneeled down before him, I suppose that was a good reason why. Then why not do it? Kneel before him?

So I did. And I started muttering in time and tune with the chant, though I had no idea what it was saying. It didn't seem to matter. I closed my eyes. I then discovered faith. That is, I think my mind went blank, maybe I fell asleep. Eventually, the chanting stopped. I opened my eyes and there I was, kneeling in front of the altar, alone. I heard a distant voice saying, "Mister Hobson, you will be the witness. According to church rules, there must be a witness to the baptism."

I shook my head and struggled to my feet. Father Sokolov was attending to Rivers. He had kept the yellow robe and was draping it around Rivers' body. Rivers seemed to be in some kind of trance. Then Father Sokolov placed both his hands on Rivers' head and pronounced, "In the name of One God, I ask that you repent of your sins and ask forgiveness."

Rivers looked up. I was already feeling anger and resentment. How does one forgive the murder of the only woman I ever loved? What kind of god forgives murder?

Father Sokolov sensed my thirst for vengeance. He took his hands off Rivers and turned to me. "Young man," he said, "please allow God time to do his justice. It will be done."

He turned back to Rivers. "And now, my son. It is time for your Triple Immersion Baptism."

Rivers meekly looked up to Sokolov, as a compliant dog looks up at its master. The priest continued.

"Do you wish to seek forgiveness by triple immersion, each immersion to wash away your sins?"

"I do," mumbled Rivers.

"You must look to the sky of Heaven and shout your answer clearly so that it can be heard throughout the universe of faith," commanded Sokolov, "stand and cry out!"

Rivers struggled to stand, then shouted, "I do!" he shouted "I do!"

"Let us proceed to the pond where we will baptize you, and you will begin a new and sinless life," said Father Sokolov.

The killer, I will not call him by his name if he is going to get out of this murder with just a dunking, followed Father Sokolov and I followed on, mumbling to myself, disgusted, feeling let down and quite frankly double-crossed by Colmes. This was no solution. It was abrogation.

It was late in the afternoon, the sun was setting. The animals were quiet, and I heard a few squeaks from chipmunks getting ready for bed. No birds chirping. I imagined them sitting in the trees looking down, also disgusted.

We reached the edge of the pond. The water was still and dark. Father Sokolov stood at the edge, pulling up his robe so it would not get wet. He gesticulated to the killer to wade in until the water came to his chest. "The church rules say that I am not to touch you as you have sinned so badly. You must immerse yourself totally, three times. After that, I will approach you and pronounce you free of sin, and ready to begin life's journey all over again."

Father Sokolov then turned to me and warned, "stay back from the water, my son. You do not want any of his sin to soil you."

The killer entered the water, pulling his yellow robe around his body as though to protect it from the chill of the water. As I watched, my mind was overcome with competing words, phrases, images, scenes from the past. And I remembered one that came into focus. It was a sign board of all things. A sign that I could not read, it jumped around in my head. Then I heard Sokolov call out, "My son! Cleanse thyself!"

And the killer dropped down beneath the water. Then pushed

himself up again, his hands now tangled in his robe.

"Once more!" cried the Priest.

The killer obeyed, and dropped below the water, then he must have pushed himself up with his legs, as he burst out of the water like a dolphin. And he cried, "third and last!" and dropped well below the surface, I reckoned. It was not all that deep in this area of the pond.

And now, all was silent. The killer remained under. Had he escaped or something? Was he playing games? I looked at Father Sokolov. He stood, expressionless.

"You think there's something wrong?" I asked. Should I go in and see if he's OK?"

Sokolov quickly answered. "Do not enter! It's dangerous! Sin all around us!"

And then there was a great churning of the water, I am sure I saw a flash of lightning, and the killer's body appeared on the surface, quivering and shaking, steam coming off his body, his yellow robe twisted and charred.

It was then that I remembered the sign I had seen. It was in this pond just twenty feet away. I had given it no mind. It said :

WARNING!

SUBMERGED CABLES!

NO SWIMMING!

And above the writing was a lightning sign, warning of electricity.

Justice had been done. An accidental death was repaid by an accidental death. Colmes had fulfilled his promise. My mentor had once again given me a lesson on justice, that no case can be solved without.

12. Circle of Truth

You may have noticed in your own working lives that some people are driven by whatever it is, to rise to the top, or at least to move "up" in the perceived hierarchy of one's employment line. Or, if you have not yet entered the work place and are still a student somewhere, that there are always those in the class who are, as counsellors and teachers observe, "motivated." This is a view of work as some kind of race to the "top" though usually those who are ambitious enough to persist in such a race, are often surprised to find that when they get there, somehow, it is not enough. And along the way, such ambitious persons, most likely, and unavoidably, may have purposely, or even rashly, and with little regard or even knowledge of, how they may have affected those perceived to be the competition, whether or not such persons saw themselves as in the same race. This is, as experts call it, a zero-sum game. My promotion means that someone else did not get a promotion. And of course, in a given organization there can only be a certain number of persons at the "top of the ladder." Otherwise we can't all be at the top, because if we were, what would be the point of struggling to rise above another?

I have thought about this a good deal because as I have already demonstrated in my descriptions of my mentor's cases, I have been quite comfortable staying where I am, still an adult who is essentially a permanent student. My critics might call this immature, lazy or something like it, or would put it bluntly as a lack of ambition. And it's true that with Colmes, I am in a kind of servitude, serving my master happily (for the most part), with no wish to take his place or become his boss by some other devious means (e.g., become president of this university, which of course is a ridiculous thought). And it is true, as some of my older relatives in Australia tell my other relatives, that I am probably immature, that I should get married and "settle down" and have kids, all of which they are certain would hasten my maturity. Actually, what they are saying is that it's time I grew up.

These are all vague generalizations that apply to any workplace, not just academia, a mysterious place to those who have never been to unicersity—about two-thirds of Americans and a greater number of Australians, the latter referring to Australian born, not the eager and industrious immigrants from various parts of Asia and Middle East.

That said, the case that I will shortly describe reveals some of the special attributes of the academic workplace that affect how one who is ambitious enough (that is driven) to claw one's way up the professorial ladder. I must also point out that this story occurs in an American university academic setting. The hierarchies of other university systems may be structured quite differently. For example, I was told when I once applied for an academic job in Australia (it was in a moment of weakness on my part) that there was not much difference in salary between senior lecturers (roughly equivalent to an American associate professor level) and a full professor, so why bother to go up for promotion to full professor? In fact, the salary differences from the most junior up to associate levels were also not all that different. So why join the rat race of "publish or perish?"

And again, for those not familiar with the academic world, "publish or perish" is a popular phrase used to sum up academic culture, especially the American variety. Actually, that is not quite the right word, more like a kind of Hobbesian tribe, a "dog-eat-dog" mindset, though this is a bit insulting to dogs who generally are satisfied to play, and would only set to on each other if there were only one bone to eat. For humans, it is likely the opposite. The more they have the more they are likely to fight over a crust of bread. Perhaps I exaggerate, as is my self-confessed fault.

But in this instance I don't think so. This case concerns a seminar intended for "senior" graduate students—that is, we had finished all our coursework and other requirements and were now writing our dissertations. Our most conscientious and caring Dean arranged this seminar to be given by the most prominent sociologist (some would rate him as number one in the field) to advise us on what we should do once we are done with our dissertations and put ourselves on the job market. The dominance of commerce language is no mistake, but rather an essential part of the academic "culture." Tread carefully here. The language is seductive. It was used when masters put their slaves on the market in the town square as late as the 19th century in pretty much every known country of the world. In the twentieth century academic market setting, graduate students who slaved away either for very little money working for their professors who conducted their research using research grants that also paid a pittance, or paid their own way and as a result graduated with an enormous debt. To graduate, therefore, was to put oneself in a precarious position.

Go on then. You may think what you like. But yes, probably this has something to do with my never actually graduating. There's still time though. There was a *cause célèbre* when a university administrator discovered a criminal justice Ph.D. student who took 25 years to finish her dissertation, and that the School of Criminal Justice apparently approved the dissertation, giving it an exemplary pass with distinction— to the shock of the administrator, who later became the provost, that's right, Dr. Dolittle, most likely because of her exposé of the School's mismanagement of Ph.D. students.

***

The illustrious professor opened the seminar with this challenging statement:

"Good morning all. I am professor Godfrey Gardner and I am the most published sociologist in America, probably the world, though you should understand that publications anywhere outside of the USA don't count."

He leaned back in his chair and puffed at a cigar, that's right, a cigar, totally obnoxious, in those days allowed, actually had just been banned on campus, but this professor simply believed that his top rated status meant that the rules did not apply to him. One student, whether by protest or genuine medical reasons, got up, tried to wave the smoke from her face, and left.

Professor Gardner watched the student leave then continued.

"If you do not want to rise to the top, you may as well leave now. My talk is only for those who have the guts to go for it."

You are almost right if you think that I got up and walked out. I nearly did, but curiosity got the better of me. And there were no cats in the room.

He then opened a thick folder and began to read out a list of his most recent publications. And as he did so he held up the thick folder, shook it and said, "these are only for last year." He then passed out a few reprints of his articles. "Notice," he said, "that there are not a lot of different journals that I have published in. That is because I choose only to publish my papers in the top ten rated journals. The rest are a waste of time. In fact, most of my publications are in the top five and I average about four to five publications a year in that category. Any questions?"

There were seven of us; cowed, overwhelmed, scared out of our wits. One student got up the courage to ask, raising her hand just a little.

"Yes?" asked Professor Gardner, almost a yell it seemed to me. Talk about being full of himself!

"So how do you know what are the top rated journals?" she asked timidly.

"We do," answered the professor with a smugness that made me want to get up and slap him. And he continued. "All of us, your peers," and he grandly waved his arm around the table to illustrate his point.

But the timid student complained, "but you're way above me, how could you be my peer?"

"We are all in the same discipline. And those of us who are at the top of the discipline are surely those who know the difference between great journal articles and average journal articles. Otherwise we would not be at the top of our profession."

The timid student now looked even more perplexed. The great

professor seemed to be expounding a circular argument. But I could see that she dare not suggest such a thing. There was a good chance that one day he might be reviewing one of her papers for one of the top journals.

Another student sensibly tried to change the subject. His demeanor, was not unlike the professor's. Perhaps he was an ambitious student who was unconsciously aping the professor. "So what do you look for in a paper when you review it for publication?" he asked.

"Now that is an excellent question. As you all know, papers that are submitted to top journals are sent out by the editor for peer review. I receive many such requests every week. And once you enter the profession you will also. I have but one crucial rule in doing such review, which is..."

He waited for effect. Nobody dared fill in the blank.

"Always reject the paper. All submissions, in my view are competing with me. If that author gets published, it is one more publication that I must compete with. Additionally, I never say anything positive. Always, always provide extensive criticisms. To me, there is no such thing as a good paper....except mine, that is."

He finished off that remark with a very large, proud grin. And he cast his busy darting eyes around the class of students looking at each face in turn, except for me because I habitually look away and most often down, if I were in any way expecting to be called upon. We were petrified or maybe more accurately, mortified.

What my fellow students learned from this encounter with the grand wolf of scholarship, who knows. I have subjected you to this—as usual—excursion into the lower side of academic publishing because it forms the very spine of those two sacred goals sitting on the horizon, just beyond one's reach, tenure and promotion. Individuals undergoing applications for tenure and or promotion must subject themselves to peer review. Their colleagues (a vague and twisted term) must sit in judgment of you and decide as your "peers" (never mind that those without tenure are rarely allowed to vote on such actions) whether or not your academic record reaches the level of tenure, whether you are good enough to join the club.

And this brings me to the case that Colmes and I both relished and hated, because it revealed the impossible contradictions of the entire system of promotion and tenure, and worse, turned nice people into obnoxious people, friends into enemies.

***

But before we get to the case, there is one more issue that I should examine, well not really an issue, just a philosophical, or maybe political problem in the abstract sense, about who gets to be on top and who ends up on the bottom. I casually mentioned Hobbes earlier in this story. It was he, I suppose, who popularized the Western idea that no society could survive unless it was divided into the rulers and the ruled. This issue was, of course, obvious to our forebears of western thought, political and philosophical, though, the ancients (the Greeks and the Romans) probably did not draw a clear distinction between the two as we do today. Probably the modern term "ideology" achieves the same mixture.

In any event, the history of Western universities (and probably their ancient equivalents in Eastern and African civilizations) were founded on the rock of hierarchy. Their very definition requires it. They were and are institutions inhabited by those who at first sought after knowledge, and once gained, passed it on to their successors. And in universities, at least, the possessors of knowledge were inevitably those persons of authority, otherwise how else could one learn? Particularly as universities probably preceded books as we know them today. In the West, to make a very long story very short, universities had their early beginnings as repositories of knowledge in monasteries whose inhabitants studied the history of god in this world and transmitted various interpretations of it to the masses. Thus, was the hierarchy of the western world structured, probably of necessity, unless the modern repositories of knowledge (computers) overrun universities. But that is another story for another day.

I guess what I am saying is that I would not want you to come away from my story thinking that I am some kind of anarchist. Authority structures appear to be an inevitable necessity in universities and probably anywhere else where humans interact and exchange knowledge.

Now let's get on with the story. It is a story that is repeated many times over in most academic institutions that adhere strictly to the demands of tenure and promotion rituals.

***

One might think that, since the procedures and rules of promotion and tenure are well established, often in many university departments written down like laws, indeed some even "legislated" by faculty senates of various kinds, the process would more or less run itself, saving those who must make the decisions (thumbs up or down) from any personal responsibility for the final decision. And of course, the voting faculty who are on the relevant committee can vote anonymously (except in certain nasty circumstances) so as to avoid any personal responsibility for a thumbs down decision.

This case involved many highly motivated persons, colleagues of the assistant professor who was coming up for promotion and tenure. For those uninformed of these terms, "tenure" means that you get to remain in your "line" (position of employment in whatever university you are working) forever, that is, until retirement. This is the case in any university that has adopted the American system. The structure of this system has a long history, but let us just say, for the sake of brevity that its detailed history and benefits (especially to union members) are tied to union actions of the past. Most universities in the United States, especially public universities, adhere to this system. An increasing number of private universities do not. Generally speaking one comes up for tenure in the sixth year, and if denied, the candidate has one year to find a position elsewhere. Of course, if it gets out that one has been denied tenure, it is rather like having a felony on one's record. So finding another job at the same level is rather difficult.

But now to our case. It was one that Colmes relished because of its obvious complexities. The case had gone all the way up to the President, who had promptly sent it back again, directing that Colmes take it up. The various faculty committees that dealt with the case either had not read the rules of promotion and tenure procedures, or were motivated by personal animosities. Of course, the Provost was in an impossible position, also a situation in which Colmes could hardly hide his glee. She had tried to force the faculty committees to endorse the promotion and tenure, and they had refused, threatening that all hell would break loose if she approved it. Finally she had recommended to the President that the faculty opposition was so deep that he should deny the tenure but approve the promotion. Though "legal" this compromised solution revealed a distinct weakness of any administrator, in this case the Provost.

How could such a situation arise when all the rules and requirements were written down and stated very clearly? You either had the qualifications or you did not.

Colmes, of course, was most amused, and saw clearly the problem. The fact was that the candidate did not fit the unwritten requirement for promotion and tenure.

"What was that?" I naively asked my mentor.

***

This case concerned Derick Dempsey, no relation to the famous boxer, though his unremitting pugilistic demeanor would suggest so. And mindful of my earlier speech on ambition, it would be hard to say that his constant demand that he be tenured and promoted was the sole reason for his belligerence. Rather, his constant peppering of his colleagues, senior or junior to him, was in the form of pointing out their weaknesses, errors in judgement, their performance falling short of the level of scholarship that he considered was acceptable. That is, he considered himself to be the best example or an outstanding scholar in their field, that field being psychology. He constantly reminded his colleagues, usually by placing memos in their mail boxes, of his accomplishments, and these were without any doubt, impressive. It seemed that his papers were routinely accepted for publication in the top ten journals in the field of psychology, his specialty being counseling psychology.

As if that were not enough, he would post notices on the department noticeboard of the names of colleagues who had not published a paper in a leading journal in over a year. How he acquired such information was a matter of wonder, presumably he scrutinized the top ten journals looking for the names of his colleagues. It would be tempting to surmise that he was further acquainted with the journals because he was on the editorial review boards, except that he was not of sufficiently high rank to be invited into that elite group. That is, he was not yet tenured and certainly not a full professor.

A note on terminology is perhaps necessary here for those who are not familiar with the American university system. The word "professor" can mean anyone who is teaching in a university, but if used on its own to describe one's position in a university, together with the authorship of a journal article, it must not be applied to anyone who was not a "full professor" that signifies the highest rank, of course with tenure. This fact of terminology fed the severe disapproval by Dempsey's colleagues who were well aware that he routinely referred to himself as "professor" when his affiliation was required in describing his authorship in any journal article.

One morning, faculty came into their offices to find pinned on their office doors a memo from Dempsey. Again this itself indicates that Dempsey had no idea of what it was like to teach in a school or department, since many full professors or anyone with tenure routinely did not show up to their offices every morning. Many in fact posted a notice on their office doors indicating their office hours, some brazenly informing students that they were available only by appointment.

The memo read:

TO: All faculty
FROM: Professor Dereck Dempsey

SUBJECT: Lack of Courtesy

DATE: 4/12/2010

I have been informed that faculty do not appropriately acknowledge students when meeting them in the hallway or outside of classroom in public space. This conveys a lack of respect for our students who deserve better. At least I urge that all nod to convey recognition.

As you can imagine, routine faculty meetings were hardly routine. Dempsey almost always arrived late to the meeting, then delivered blistering speeches upbraiding his colleagues for their lack of punctuality, yet another indicator of their disrespect for others. The chair of the faculty was usually chosen by popular vote, show of hands or anonymous vote. However, things got so difficult that nobody wanted to be chair if they had to deal with the likes of Dempsey. This left Dempsey volunteering to chair the faculty, which generally had the result that faculty would not show up to the meetings, (an offense against the department by-laws) thus incurring yet another memo pinned to their doors.

***

There is much more I could report on Dempsey's character. But I think I have conveyed sufficient information to give you an idea of what was about to happen, and why Colmes was called in to avert the disaster that was destined to occur.

I sat on my wicker chair across from Colmes who looked up from his crossword.

"The trouble," said Colmes, "is that the by-laws governing the tenure and promotion procedures are silent in regards to character traits or physical appearance. Their omission, one assumes, is an indication that they are considered irrelevant. Is that not the case, Hobson?"

"Looks like it. And that's reasonable, isn't it?" I said, having once met Dempsey and immediately took a distinct disliking of him. He was truly obnoxious.

"Really, Hobson? Giving this obnoxious person tenure means that the rest of the faculty in the department will have to put up with him for the rest of their working lives. Many will choose to leave."

I responded with an unsympathetic remark. "Since most of them get a good salary and only show up to their offices when they feel like it, seems to me it's a small price to pay."

Colmes smiled and frowned. "Dear! Dear! Hobson. Such resentment is not becoming of you!" He looked at his watch and said, " we shall see. Dempsey is due here in ten minutes. What should I ask him, Hobson?"

"You're teasing me, Colmes. It's not becoming of you. I'm at the bottom of the ambition ladder, and I don't need to be reminded of it."

Colmes ignored me, as I deserved. "As you know Hobson, the holy trinity of promotion and tenure qualifications is Publications, Teaching and Service, in that order of importance. You know that, right?" His twitchy grin appeared.

"Right. And that seems reasonable, doesn't it? Though I think personally that teaching should always come first, given that I am a perpetual student who occasionally teaches when they are short of faculty."

"And service?" asked Colmes, frowning and leaning a little across his desk to me.

"I think that's bull shit," I said brazenly, even blushing a little that I used such language in front of a most proper Victorian gentleman.

"But you are right, Hobson. And that is where faculty who want to deny someone tenure usually focus their negative energies. If they don't like a candidate, they will look first at service, and if that fails, teaching, especially student ratings. The latter, by the way, are marvelously adaptable, especially if a professor teaches a very large class. If the teacher ratings allow open descriptive comments by students, instead of the more confining and protective (of the professor) numeric rating scale, one can always find some awful derogatory remarks. It only takes one or two students to do that, and there is fodder to use effectively against the candidate."

I remained silent in response to this cynical little speech. Everyone knew this, but one never heard it spoken out loud.

Colmes continued. "So we must create the opportunity for our candidate to contribute to his own demise, right Hobson?"

"I don't follow. From what I hear, he excels in all three categories. He gets great teacher ratings, funny, engaging, informative, listens to the students. What more could one ask for?"

"Indeed. Indeed, Hobson. And his service is exemplary. He serves on several University committees, Library, Outreach, Student welfare, and the local union, United University Professors, don't forget that, Hobson. Very important back-up in case he is denied tenure."

I shot back. "And he will be denied, right Colmes?"

"Indeed, you are right. That has already more or less happened. Remember there are several layers of approval needed. It starts at the department level, goes to the chair who writes a letter summarizing the faculty discussions and vote, then to the dean of the school, who also writes a letter and sends on the packet to the college level committee that sends on its recommendation to the provost, who refers it to the senate committee for tenure and promotion that deliberates and returns its final decision to the Provost, who then makes her recommendation to the President. In this case, President O'Brien has sent it to me via our friend Provost Dolittle. O'Brien, faint of heart as he has always been, does not want the responsibility of rejecting this guy because he knows it will lead to an awful mess, law suits and whatever else. Aren't you glad you're a nobody, Hobson?" ended Colmes unkindly.

I looked at my mentor and did what any sensible student would do. I bit my lip and shut up.

Colmes continued, and I was wishing he would shut up. "With this meeting we will find a solution, Hobson young man. You can depend on it."

I couldn't help thinking that Colmes was in a mild way a parallel version of Dempsey, in a kind of socially acceptable way.

There was a faint knock at the door. Colmes looked at me, amused.

"Enter!" he called and then muttered to me, "one would have expected a loud knock, don't you think?"

Dempsey, a person small in stature, with broad shoulders and upper body, most likely a result of gym workouts, tapering down to a narrow waist, to what I guessed to be skinny legs. He carried in his hands several psychology journals and carefully placed them on Colmes's neat desk. I quickly rose from my wicker chair and said, "I'm William Hobson, Colmes's assistant, please take a seat." I quickly retreated to the overstuffed chair in the corner.

"Thank you Sir," beamed Dempsey, as he took his place on my wicker chair. "These are my latest publications." He pointed to the reprints on Colmes's desk, and tossed me a couple of extras.

Colmes coughed a little, clearing his throat. "Your resume is most impressive. Your writing voluminous and all of incredibly high standard," observed Colmes, licking his lips as if to hold back the drool.

"Thank you Doctor Colmes. Doctor, is it? Or professor?" queried Dempsey an a kind of solicitous though aggressive tone.

"Colmes is fine," retorted Colmes. "Now Dr. Dempsey, let's get down to business. You know why you are here?"

"Well as a matter of fact I don't," said Dempsey with a frown, "it's most irregular." He leaned forward as if to underline his dissatisfaction.

The bright light of Colmes's desk lamp reflected off Dempsey's balding head that was shaved to a stubble, along with a blonde, carefully clipped beard that had a slight ginger tint.

"The issue is that every committee and letter from your promotion and tenure process has recommended that you be denied tenure and promotion. Though one has recommended that you receive promotion without tenure."

"And the reason?" demanded Dempsey, "when it is surely obvious that on the three criteria of publications, teaching and service I am outstanding on all counts."

"I couldn't agree more," responded Colmes, "which is why your case has been referred to me."

"And your standing in this process is...?" queried Dempsey with a heavy dose of sarcasm.

Colmes tried responding to this aggression by pulling rank. "I am the university's distinguished multi-disciplinary professor."

"With what is your role exactly in my case?" demanded Dempsey his voice rising a decibel or two.

"The President's, shall we say, Envoy," said Colmes with a wry smile.

"And what is that?" insisted Dempsey.

"I solve insoluble problems," replied Colmes not giving an inch.

"And I'm an insoluble problem?" asked Dempsey with an additional layer of sarcasm.

"Exactly!" conferred Colmes.

I have to say that I found all this very entertaining. It was like the Dempsey-Carpenter face-off. Would it end in a knock-out? I stared at Dempsey. He looked a little like a boxer, with his solid upper body. But he didn't have a boastful personality or presence. He was simply an aggressive type with no social skills, who knew no other way to behave. If you simply ignored his aggressive demeanor you were fine. And I would hasten to add that he was not in any way a bully as far as I could see. He didn't bully people interpersonally to get them to do his want. All his "bullying" was the result of how people interpreted his silly memos. They were not directed at any particular person, the usual way of the bully, but to everyone in general. It is not certain, even possible, for one low on the hierarchy, to bully those above him.

Anyway, if one must use the term bully, it is more like the saying "bull in a china shop." He has no idea of the effects that his mere presence in a room have upon other people. Maybe someone should tell him?

Of course, at Colmes's direction, I had already researched Dempsey's previous jobs. Colmes was amused and I amazed that Dempsey displayed the same behavior at his previous place of employment at the University of Chicago department of psychology, where they made it clear to him that there was no way he would get tenure and this was in his first year there. And even more surprising is that the Dean and faculty of our psychology department were also aware of it, in fact had been warned, but they were so enamored with Dempsey's incredible publishing record that they ignored it when they hired him.

Now, Colmes began to chip away at Dempsey's brittle persona. I was curious as to what was my mentor's goal? To find a justification to deny Dempsey's tenure, or else find a way for him to be granted it, in spite of the overwhelming opposition by the faculty?

"Dr. Dempsey," began Colmes, leaning well back in his chair, "you must surely be aware that you have a, shall we say, negative effect on your colleagues."

Dempsey quickly shot back. "And what does that have to do with my record of outstanding performance on all three tenure require-ments?"

"Everything, Dr. Dempsey, everything," replied Colmes in his best Victorian English accent.

"But there is nothing in the formal procedures requiring that the candidate be likable," insisted Dempsey.

"Indeed. You are correct," said Colmes, leaning further back in his chair, tapping the fingers of his open hands together.

"So why have they voted against my tenure?" asked Dempsey, clearly frustrated.

"Because they don't like you," repeated Colmes, with an amused grin.

"But they are not allowed to deny me for that reason. I'll sue them! That's what I'll do!"

"You could," answered Colmes, and you might even win, though it would cost you a lot of money."

Dempsey fell silent. He squinted a little, I think his eyes were watering up. It was enough for me to feel sorry for him.

Colmes allowed the silence to continue. He was a master at this kind of manipulation. He made a small cough to clear his throat, but other than that he sat still, and quiet. For my part, I was on the edge of my seat on the otherwise comfortable overstuffed chair. Dempsey withdrew a handkerchief from his pocket and wiped his eyes. Now Colmes was ready to ask his next question.

"Do you live alone, Dr. Dempsey or are their family for you to go home to?" asked Colmes gently.

"I am alone. My wife and two kids left me some time ago." He looked down, then up and at Colmes. "I guess they didn't like me either."

Now I really felt sorry for him. Colmes leaned back in his chair, me on the edge of mine, wondering what would come next.

Dempsey made as if to leave. "Don't go," said Colmes quickly, "we have only just begun, but I do see a solution in the offing."

Dempsey sat back on the wicker chair and sighed. "Dr. Colmes, I don't know how I can make people like me. It's not fair. I do my job that is the very best. And yet they still don't like me, not my colleagues, not my bosses."

"Well, let's not get ahead of ourselves. Your bosses, for example, such as the Dean or Provost, neither like for dislike you, though they both regard your excellent resume with considerable appreciation. But they do not have to live with your everyday abuses and criticisms. That is what your fellow faculty do not like."

"So what can I do then? I mean, I am who I am, aren't I? I can't just change myself overnight. Anyway I've tried. And I couldn't. When I see poor behavior I have to call it out. I don't see what's wrong with that…"

"Well, I can, and obviously your colleagues do too. But I think you are right, it is unreasonable and pointless to expect you to be someone else."

"Then what is the solution, Dr. Colmes? What can I do?"

Colmes sat forward. "Dr. Dempsey. You are not gay by any chance, are you?"

Dempsey, enraged, jumped up and my wicker chair went flying

backwards. "How dare you!" he screamed. "How dare you!"

"Then I am right?" asked Colmes quietly.

"I, I..."

"Never mind answering. Here is the solution. You need to give your colleagues a reason not to hate you. It may be a bit much to hope that you get them to like you, but getting them to tolerate you is certainly possible. All you need to do is give them a good reason to do so."

"But I..."

"After all, isn't it rather pathetic on their part to get so upset because you distribute silly memos berating them to do this or that? Why don't they toss them away, shrug, and say, silly Dempsey, there he goes again," added Colmes.

Dempsey sat back in my chair and took a deep breath. "I have HIV," he muttered, and I detected a very faint smile. Then he glanced quickly at me.

"Don't worry," said Colmes, "Hobson is my trusted assistant and will not breathe a word of any of this, unless, of course you want us to."

Then Colmes looked back at Dempsey and said in his most careful and formal Victorian manner: "It may not be possible to get your colleagues to like you, but it certainly is possible to give them a reason to discount your annoyances."

Some weeks went by. Dempsey sent out an occasional silly memo. His colleagues smiled and nodded hello when they met outside their offices. A couple even came to his office to tell him how much they liked this or that of one of his publications.

The chairs of the relevant committees and the Deans revised their letters to the provost and Dempsey received promotion to Associate Professor and tenure. After two years he received promotion to full professor. And two years after that he died of a brain tumor.

Case closed.

13. The Stolen Dissertation

I have long hesitated to describe this case because it hits rather too close to home for my liking. Writing an original and worthwhile dissertation has been the bane of my life for the more than sixteen years of my graduate student life. I did manage to finish the dissertation of my first Ph.D. in criminal justice, but that was I think, now in retrospect a little easier than the one I am trying to do now in philosophy, or "mindfulness" as some of the younger students call it.

My problem is one that all Ph.D. students face. To put it simply it is that what the faculty asks of its students is unrealistic and essentially an impossible task to demand that anyone undertake. It is expected that all dissertations make a contribution to knowledge, add new findings to the accumulation of knowledge in their chosen field. Just pause for a moment and think about this. First of all, how is one to comprehend or even grasp what has gone before? The answer to this, the professor will say, is that this is why all dissertations must include a section at the beginning of their dissertation, a "literature review" that recounts everything that has been published before on the particular topic one has chosen for one's dissertation. Perhaps you can now also see why I have had trouble writing my dissertations, especially my current one in which I have been unable to even write a one page outline of my topic. The reason being, of course, that I cannot find a topic that does not repeat what has gone before. How can I possibly grasp everything that has gone before on my topic if I cannot find a new topic in the voluminous literature in the field that is in itself an impossible task, to say the least. These days there is more than just a bible or two to read and digest. You see what I mean? How can I do a literature review on my topic if I do not know what I am looking for? Do you see the impossible whirlpool that paralyzes the mind of any serious student?

There is much more I could say about this because, as you can see, I have given much thought to this problem. However this case is not about me, but about the foibles and vicissitudes that arise from this universal problem of academic life. That is, the problem of knowledge. Or, to put it another way, the twisted relationship between the old and the new.

I have never fully revealed to Colmes my thoughts on this matter. He enjoys making fun of me as the "never ending" student, as he likes to call me. And to this day I do not know what Colmes's dissertation was about, what field he studied, or whether he ever wrote one (and, given his dyslexia, how could he?). His entire academic background is shrouded in mystery which, as I have already related, drives the VP for human resources crazy in her vain attempt to somehow defrock him.

So while I was as usual sitting at my desk staring at a blank piece of paper, trying to come up with a dissertation topic, write a one page outline of what it would be about, I welcomed the bang on the wall of my office signaling that my mentor needed my presence. I arrived to find a student, about my age (an older or mature student), bright red angry cheeks, screeching in a way that was not appropriate for her age. Colmes sat at his desk, placidly munching a toasted scone, licking his lips, then sipping his cup of tea.

"Come! Hobson! Do join us!" he said, amused, crumbs of the scone falling down his carefully buttoned shirt and tie.

"The asshole stole my dissertation!" she screamed.

"And which asshole would that be?" asked Colmes, mockingly.

Her name was Shirley Anderson, and she sported a huge mop of red hair, a face freckled not unlike Little Orphan Annie, her green eyes were those of a demon, her slightly overweight body bristling with rage, one hand on her hip, the other waving what I guessed was her dissertation proposal. I carefully made my way around her to the overstuffed chair. I was a little taken aback by Colmes's mockery. She was clearly in no state to suffer such unsympathetic Victorian masculinity. And in response she quite reasonably, I thought, tossed her dissertation proposal on to Colmes's desk and it broke apart, the pages spreading all over, some on to his lap.

"My dear young lady!" quipped Colmes, "my deepest apologies. But from what I understand of your case, your dissertation was not stolen."

"How would you know? Has the Dean already turned you against me? You men!" She now stood upright, head back, her chest and slightly protruding belly thrust forward, her entire body dressed in a tightly fitting black stretch top and tights running down her slender legs. She reminded me of a male ballet dancer. Except that she was certainly no male.

"Please take a seat," said Colmes quietly, pointing to my wicker chair, "I apologize, and meant no offense."

I was surprised that Colmes apologized. He rarely apologized for anything he said or did. The idea that he could be wrong rarely occurred to him. I stood up from my stuffed chair and extended my hand. I felt sorry for her. I completely understood what she was going through. "I'm William Hobson, Professor Colmes's assistant," I said calmly.

Colmes gave me a quick sideways look, a mixture of annoyance and approval. The student needed to be calmed down.

She turned her freckled face towards me and said with a delightful smile, "pleased to meet you, and I'm Shirley Anderson. And I'm not happy right now."

The room fell silent. Shirley looked back at Colmes who coughed a little to clear his throat.

"Miss Anderson," began Colmes.

"You can call me Shirley," she answered, "and I'm very upset as you might have noticed." She managed a faint smile, though I detected water in her eyes.

Colmes began to gather up the pages of her dissertation proposal. Shirley leaned across the desk to help. Their eyes met and I could have sworn there was a spark.

"What I was pointing out before, Shirley, was that technically speaking, I do not think that your dissertation was stolen, at least going by what the Dean told me."

She was about to interrupt, I could see, but then fell back in the chair and waited for Colmes to finish.

"Rather, it was your idea that was stolen. I know that sounds a bit pedantic, but that is surely what you meant as well, is that not so?"

Shirley wriggled a little on my most uncomfortable wicker chair. "I suppose that's right, she said. "But either way, it's not allowed, is it? I mean. The Dean or the chair of his dissertation committee should stop him, right? I mean, it's clear that he stole my idea, and you know it took me maybe a year to come up with it."

Boy oh boy! Did I feel for her! I certainly understood where she was coming from. And I was about to say so, when there was a knock at the door and in burst another student with whom I was somewhat acquainted, having served with him as student representative at the school of criminal justice faculty meetings. I rose, and expected that Shirley would also, given that it was very likely that Colmes had invited the evil doer to join us.

"I'm Sullivan. Tom Sullivan. And I didn't steal nothing," he blurted, standing in the doorway.

Shirley remained seated, fiddling with her dissertation proposal, putting the pages in order.

"Of course not," said Colmes slowly, looking him up and down. "Do come in and close the door."

I stood and offered him my seat in the corner on the overstuffed chair. Of course, he was not going to let himself be put down there.

"I'll stand if you don't mind," said Sullivan.

"Fuck you!" mumbled Shirley.

I was shocked, and Colmes showed no emotion at all. "I have looked most carefully at both proposals," he said, "and I have to say that they are remarkably similar."

It was then that things took a most interesting turn, and I was surprised that I had not seen it coming. Time was to be the best advocate.

"I had this idea a long time before she did," claimed Sullivan, "at least a year ago."

"And I had mine longer ago than that. I can prove it. We were in that seminar a couple of years ago. I spoke up about my idea, even did a short presentation on the topic. And you were there, I remember it well," countered Shirley.

I sat back in the overstuffed chair and sighed. I could not see how this could be resolved. How do you prove which idea came first? Worse, how can an idea be stolen? What exactly is an idea? Colmes looked at me with a knowing glance.

"What is the idea, exactly?" asked Colmes directing his question to both students.

Sullivan stepped forward. "My dissertation is titled 'The Fallacy of 500 Delinquents.' "

Shirley quickly stated, "mine is called '500 Delinquents revisited.' "

"The titles do seem similar," noted Colmes, clearly amused. And what will be the contents of these dissertations?"

Sullivan quickly answered, "I will reanalyze the Gluecks' data and show that their entire method of collection and analysis of the data was biased by certain preconceived, unstated assumptions about the causes of delinquency."

Colmes looked across to Shirley. "The same," she answered, then added, as if an afterthought, "but I will probably pay more attention to female delinquents."

I should inform my readers here of just who "the Gluecks" were. They were, I suppose you could say, the modern pioneers of juvenile delinquency research in the United States, if not the world. They left behind them an enormous database of information collected over a number of years between the 1940s through 1960s. A husband and wife team, they won awards and medals of honor all over academia (Harvard especially) for their research and writings. Taking them down convincingly would be a huge undertaking, guaranteeing whoever managed to do it, a prestigious career, one that would surpass the Gluecks. That a mere graduate student could do it was most unlikely. The ideas of these two students were just a little too grand, was my guess. But then, who am I to judge?

Yet this dissertation topic had a most attractive advantage: it avoided the costly and time consuming necessity of collecting the data. The Gluecks had already done it, and left it in pristine condition. Of course, it would have to be digitized. However, if I wanted to be a troublemaker, I could have argued that neither of these dissertation ideas was acceptable because of the very fact that the student was not challenged to construct their own measuring instruments, as they were taught in their statistics and methods classes. In a sense, one could even argue that, because they were not collecting their own data, that there would be nothing "original" in their dissertations, and therefore did not qualify as adding to the body of knowledge already established in this field. It was nothing new. The Gluecks had already done it.

"The chairs of your respective dissertation committees are different, I take it?" asked Colmes.

Shirley quickly responded, "I have mine, Professor Antwhistle, and she is very much in approval of my topic."

Sullivan jiggled nervously from one leg to the other as though he were about to turn and leave. "I haven't formed mine just yet," he said sheepishly.

"I will recommend," announced Colmes in his Victorian morality mode, "to the Dean that both topics are acceptable, that there is little chance that they will be duplicate dissertations."

Both students remained silent. Shirley looked down, not entirely happy with this decision. Colmes noticed, and then added, "though I do think that both of you may find it useful to work together to set up the Glueck database for analysis."

"But, professor," began Shirley.

And Sullivan could not hold back a grin. "Sounds fair to me," he said.

Colmes continued. "I assure you both, that by the time you have set up the database and put together your methods, literature review and hypotheses, they will be quite different in their outcomes. Don't you think Hobson?"

"Indeed I do," I nodded with feigned enthusiasm.

"Then I think we are finished here," said Colmes as he dismissed both students. "And Sullivan, see that you get your dissertation committee formed before I change my mind."

This might have been the end of it, except that an unusual event was soon to occur that would ruffle Colmes's satisfaction with having easily solved this small case. Frankly, I could not see why the Dean had referred the case to Colmes in the first place. Well, that's not entirely true. Colmes had over the years managed to convey to all at the university that his services were indispensable, so whenever any case arose that was even slightly disagreeable, administrators and some professors would refer the case to Colmes.

***

Believe it or not, I had managed to type out a few pages of what my dissertation would look like. Having done a Ph.D. in criminal justice, and completed my dissertation, I was naturally inclined towards something, shall we say, theoretical, in my second Ph.D. in philosophy. At that time in the world of social science a theoretical dissertation (that is, no data collection) was beyond comprehension. The founders of the field of criminal justice were preoccupied with establishing criminal justice as a "science" which to them meant that every dissertation had to be empirical, that is you decided on a problem, you did a literature review of the topic, identified the gaps in the literature, formulated a theory, derived hypotheses to be tested, identified what data one would need to collect in order to test the hypotheses, adopt a measurement technique (that is, how and what data were to be collected) and that was it. Facts were established, your theory supported or not. This was all well and good, except there was one pesky thing that hovered over every such dissertation, which was that there was supreme disappointment, indeed, the likelihood that a committee would fail a dissertation, if the research did not produce positive results. This is why the demand for statisticians, as exemplified in the case of *The Student Body,* (case 15) was enormous, and why the only obligatory courses in criminal justice, were statistics and methods. Getting a significance of .05 or less was the ultimate achievement.

Forgive me. I have rambled on again. But I needed to share my thoughts with you here because the event that would turn everything upside down, well I exaggerate a little, was in a way a product of what I have just described.

It concerned a now elderly student (Prudence Wright) who was in her late thirties when she enrolled in the criminal justice program, in 1965 about ten years before I enrolled in the same program. She zipped through all the course work and passed all the qualifying exams, and then formed a committee and wrote her dissertation. Except that she did not quite finish it, or at least as far as I know, she may have written it but did not submit it, though it remains unclear whether she defended it or not. Rather similar to what I did with my criminal justice dissertation. I wrote it, finished it, defended it, but did not get around to actually submitting it through the formal administrative channels, with the result that I had finished my Ph.D. but had not yet graduated. As you know, I did all this so that my official status was still a student, so my F Visa would remain valid in the US.

One might say that life intersected with Prudence, who had pursued a successful career becoming director of the New York State Criminal Justice Services, a most prestigious position, for which in those days, a Ph.D. was not required, in fact might have been looked on as a liability. Toeing the line for the bureaucratic and political needs of the Governor of New York and other politicians, was all that was needed, and this was usually in the form of statistical reports that supported politicians' versions of the truth. Prudence was on the verge of retirement and now was moved to complete her Ph.D. by defending her dissertation that was completed some thirty years ago.

The Student Performance committee first considered Prudence's request and took the easy way out. It would be surely ridiculous to accept a dissertation for defense that was written thirty years ago. If it were accepted it would be a patent admission that the field of criminal justice had made no progress in those thirty years! However, the rules required that the case be forwarded to the full faculty for its consideration. And it was there that the impossible situation arose to which Colmes would be called to resolve.

The chair of the student performance committee presented the case, which took only a few minutes. The chair of the faculty was about to put the case to a vote when Professor Theodore Garcia, (Ted the Red, you may remember him from a previous case or two), who had remained silent throughout the deliberations, in his deep gravelly voice, called for a point of order.

"Before we vote, should we not give the student an opportunity to make her case? I mean due process, after all," he said.

"She had her say when she met with the Dean and he rejected it and sent her case to us for confirm," replied the chair of the student perform-ance committee.

"What about due process?" asked Ted, a lawyer after all. "Has anybody read the dissertation? Does a copy of it exist? And if so who has it? And does the original dissertation committee exist? Should it not be, with regard to academic freedom, the dissertation committee that makes this decision? Is there any law or regulation that says she cannot defend a thirty year old dissertation?"

The chair of the faculty gave a resigned sigh. "According to the Dean's administrative assistant, there is no record of her dissertation committee, but there is a record that she passed all other requirements with distinction. I would have to go back and look in my own files to be sure, but I think I remember being on her committee. It was probably the first dissertation committee I served on."

"Then do we have a copy of the dissertation?" persisted Ted.

"I do," responded one of the graduate student representatives, a heavy-set, woman in her mid-thirties, an NYPD cop who had taken advantage of the program that took in a select number of NYPD cops to do their master's degree. A deal made between the Dean of some thirty years ago and someone in the then Governor's office.

The entire faculty looked at her in amazement. The chair looked at her grimly.

"You're sure of that? I mean, how would such an old dissertation draft, in fact come to think of it any dissertation be in the hands of students?"

The faculty stirred, the scraping of shoes on the wooden floor filled the small meeting room.

"By Prudence Wright, is that the one?" replied the student rep.

"Yes, you mean there are others?" asked the chair.

"Sure. Is there something wrong with that?" she retorted defensively, "I mean, I'm only a masters student, so I wouldn't know."

"Well, I guess not. So where can we get this dissertation?" asked the chair feeling a little foolish.

"You mean," put in Ted, "that you guys do not have a copy of the dissertation, and you made your decision based simply on the fact that it was written thirty years ago?" growled Ted the Red.

This was Ted's usual manner with his colleagues. Because none of them were lawyers, he considered himself to be surrounded by know-nothings, people who had no idea how the real world worked.

"I guess not, " answered the chair, slightly embarrassed.

"Well, we're not," asserted the chair of the student performance committee. "It was written thirty years ago, was not defended, so why do we need to look at it? The statute of limitations is eight years, if I am not correct. And that's a rule of the university, not confined to this school."

Silence again, then another scuffling of shoes on the floor.

"That may or may not be the case," answered Ted, sitting up straight his tall body rising above everyone else, even sitting at a conference table. "She has a right to be heard, to make her case."

"But she's no longer a student," argued one of the faculty.

"Actually, technically, she is," responded the chair. "It seems that the university has allowed her all these years to enroll as a dissertation student. She paid her fees every year, so therefore technically maintained student status."

"Then we owe it to her as a faculty to at least read the dissertation before making such an arbitrary decision. Statute of limitations be damned," pronounced Ted, now a lawyer speaking for the defense.

"But she doesn't have a dissertation committee," complained another faculty member.

"Isn't that our fault as a school for being negligent?" insisted Ted.

The chair sighed again. "Well, I suppose we should also recognize her service to the New York State Division of Criminal Justice Services, and recent years as its director. She makes us look pretty good," said the chair seriously, but then immediately regretted it.

Several faculty spoke out, each annoyed and resentful. Their complaint was of course, that what she did in her work as a bureaucrat had nothing to do with academic achievement. The school of Criminal Justice achieved its top ratings not by what its Ph.D. graduates did in the workplace, unless they were in academia of course, but by the number of publications its academic faculty produced every year. The school of Criminal Justice was an academic school, not a training school.

Ted spoke up. "I move that the student be invited to meet with faculty of her choice to form a new dissertation committee and, should the committee approve the dissertation, to arrange for its defense."

The student representative seconded the motion and it passed with no objections, and with one abstention. The one abstention was normal being that it was from the one faculty known as the "great abstainer" who always abstained and had never been known to vote for or against a motion.

The matter appeared to have been resolved and the chair moved to close the meeting. He called for a motion, and just as he was about to call for a vote to pronounce the meeting over, the Dean's assistant slipped in the door, whispered in his ear, and dropped a thin folder on the table. The Chair's cheeks went a little red. He opened the folder and stared at it.

"Well?" said Ted, rising as though the meeting had ended, "I have a class to teach."

The chair looked up and said, looking at Ted. "I think you better stay. It seems that Prudence defended her dissertation thirty years ago. She just did not get around to submitting the final forms to the administration, or submitting the required copy of the dissertation formatted according to the university's strict rules."

"Did she claim she had a Ph.D. When she applied for the prestigious position at the Division of Criminal Justice Services?" asked one of the new assistant professors, trying to make a contribution.

"I can answer that," said the NYPD student. "She definitely did not. The story among the students is that she would not have got the job if she had a Ph.D. Would have been overqualified."

This small bomb caused a rippled of talk and consternation among the faculty.

"Then it seems that this is simply a small formality, and we have wasted all this time over a simple rule violation?" asked the chair of the student performance committee.

"I do not see that this changes anything," said the chair of the faculty. "She can't be granted a Ph.D. based on a thirty year old dissertation, defended or not. The research will be thirty years out of date. Every dissertation must make a new contribution to the field. To accept this dissertation would be to admit that the field has made zero progress in thirty years."

"Might be close to the truth," muttered Ted, now the cynical lawyer.

"Do we know what the title of the dissertation was?" asked someone.

The chair looked in the folder that the Dean's assistant had left him. "A Re-analysis of the Gluecks' study of 500 Delinquents."

***

I was surprised when Colmes actually came to the door of my office and knocked lightly as he entered. Strange. Usually, I was beckoned by a shout of "Hobson!" or that knock on the wall that divided my office from his. This must be something special. And it was!

We have a case that hits close to home," said Colmes, "or at least close to your home."

I looked up from the second page of my dissertation draft. "Really? You mean about Australia?" I asked thinking he meant that kind of home.

"Of course not. Your dissertation. Come to my office and I will fill you in. An impossible situation, a most attractive and enjoyable case, indeed. Though I can see no solution at the moment. Indeed I cannot."

What I have described to you so far I have taken from my notes that I took when Colmes filled me in on the case. It was indeed a little too close to home. I had the sense to make sure that I had submitted my first dissertation on criminal justice before the eight year statute of limitations ran out, though I am not sure whether there was such a statute way back then.

"So what do you think, Hobson. Should they make her do her dissertation over again, same topic or new topic?" asked Colmes as he settled into his desk chair, I on my wicker chair.

"I don't think that is quite the issue, is it?" I said coyly.

"My goodness, Hobson, you are sharp this morning. What are you getting at?" Colmes asked, as if he hadn't a clue.

"It's the topic, right? I mean, this would be the third Gluecks dissertation. There's something fishy going on here."

"Indeed, Hobson. Indeed!"

It was mid-morning and I heard the welcome sounds of the clinking of cups and saucers, and sure enough Rose the younger appeared, her hair tied up in a bun, knitting needles stuck through it, eerily just like her mother. She placed the tray on the edge of Colmes's desk and we each took our cups and plates, each plate with a scone broken open nicely, little pots or jam and clotted cream. Colmes reached out and grasped Rose's hand as she was about to lift the teapot and pour the tea into our cups. "Rose, my dear, let me do it. You sit over there on the overstuffed chair."

Colmes smiled, but it was a sad smile, and then I realized that it must be the anniversary of Rose the elder's passing.

"Thank you Colmes," Rose answered and sat herself down in the old chair, now starting to show its age. "I know," she said, "it's two years to this day."

"Indeed," said Colmes, "indeed, she is missed so much. I have survived that terrible day only because of your continued presence, my dear." He poured the tea in our cups and got up from his chair, I hate to say it, but he was showing his age. It was obviously an effort. But he managed it, even though his hand shook quite a bit as he poured the tea, then carried the tray to Rose in the corner, and placed it on the small side table that had been added some years ago for a chess board.

"And what case is about to be solved today?" she asked brightly, putting down her tea cup and taking out her knitting.

"It's the case of a stolen dissertation, and it looks as though it may have been stolen at least twice," said Colmes. "But I will spare you the details because the case is really about the impossible deliberations of the various criminal justice faculty, indeed, the very foundations that justify the existence of a university."

Indeed, I was in full agreement. And I admit that at times I regretted that I had spent so much time dithering about in academia, on a kind of treadmill, gaining knowledge, imparting it to other students, but for what end? Worse, in my most cynical moments, were we students getting our moneys' worth?

Colmes put down his tea cup and looked at his watch. "They will be here any minute," he said, looking to each of us in turn.

Rose took the hint and quickly finished off her last mouthful of scone with jam and cream, gathered up our cups and returned them to the tray.

"Stay if you wish," said Colmes, looking at her, with a most wistful look, touching her arm lightly as she reached for the tray. Looking back on our many years together, I think that this was probably the most loving moment that Colmes had revealed. It made me sad, feeling that time had passed us by way too quickly. And maybe it was this feeling that caused me to write up all these cases. His wisdom and insightfulness will be there for posterity. Perhaps forgotten, but always there to be remembered, if you see what I mean.

At that moment, there was a slight scuffle at the door and a loud knock.

"Enter!" called Colmes, then quickly turned to me, "Hobson would you be so kind as to bring some chairs from the kitchen? We will need three more."

"Three? It's going to be kind of crowded," I complained.

"Yes, but I don't want them to feel too comfortable," answered Colmes as two angry students marched in, the Gluecks students as we had started to call them, Shirley Anderson and Tom Sullivan.

"I thought all this was over with," screeched the red headed Shirley. In another world I might have been attracted to her. But she was such a heavy looking woman, though not so big and not fat either. Her presence just made you feel like she was pushing you, weighing in on you. Maybe that's what it was. She worked out at the gym every day.

"Right!" complained Sullivan. "What's this all about?"

I returned with two chairs but they appeared not to notice. I placed one in front of each of them, then returned to the kitchen for another and placed it beside the overstuffed chair. I was a little puzzled but dared not raise it with Colmes. This seemed to be too many chairs. There were to be the three students, so who else?

A gentle knock came at the open door and in came the mature student, Prudence Wright, confident, quite tall and slender, could have been a basketball player when she was young. Confident, a heavily made up face, well powdered, and a faint odor of lavender. She squinted a little, enough to suggest that she was wearing either ill-fitting contact lenses, or that she had some kind of eye condition.

"Ah!" said Colmes, "Thank you for coming at such short notice. May I introduce you to Shirley Anderson and Tom Sullivan, I think it would be fair to say that they are admirers of your work."

Prudence nodded at the two students, then looked at me. "I don't know what this is all about," she complained. "I thought we were meeting about the university processing my application to be awarded my Ph. D. Based on my dissertation that was passed with distinction and defended successfully."

"That is partly correct," answered Colmes. "By the way, please meet William Hobson here, who is my assistant, and these two students are Shirley Anderson and Tom Sullivan who are in the midst of writing their dissertations which happen to be on the very same, or should I say similar topic as was yours."

"Really?" asked Prudence, surprised, "I didn't think anyone but me had any interest in the Gluecks, that they were, by academic standards, stale meat."

"Not at all," responded Colmes, "and by the way, have you brought a copy of your dissertation, as I requested?"

"I have. But I don't think it was necessary. Years and years ago I donated a copy of it to the school of criminal justice library. At the time no-one seemed the slightest bit interested," answered Prudence.

From an expensive looking polished leather satchel, Prudence retrieved a thick, bound book, "letter size" as they say in America, typed, double-spaced as required upon submission, along with many other strict formatting requirements, margin widths, page numbering, front matter and the rest. She offered it to Colmes, but before he could take it, Sullivan snatched it away and immediately leafed through it. He then passed it to Shirley who did the same.

"Looks the same as the one in the library," observed Shirley. I have a copy of it."

Likewise," said Sullivan.

"Then how do your dissertations differ from mine? And why are they letting you do this?" asked Prudence adopting her bureaucratic manner honed as a thirty year New York State bureaucrat..

"Why? What does it matter to you?" asked Sullivan, defensively.

"Because I had the devil of a time getting my dissertation approved way back then. The eggheads claimed that my dissertation was not adding anything new to the field because I was simply using already collected data, and it was the view then that for a piece of research to be new, one had to collect one's own data."

"And did you find out anything new?" asked Colmes.

"Not really. Basically corroborated what the Gluecks did. Corroboration is just as important in science, especially social science, as it is to discover something new. At least that was my argument to the dissertation committee thirty years ago and they, after a few days, approved it."

"Do you have proof of the approval?" persisted Colmes.

"Here is the memo from the Dean's secretary at that time."

Prudence handed a letter to Colmes who read it quickly and handed it back. "This is an important document. I suggest that you make a couple of copies of it and submit it to the Dean," advised Colmes.

"I already did that, when I made my initial request," answered Prudence patiently.

"So what's all this to do with us?" asked Sullivan with a touch of belligerence.

"Yes, why are we here?" added Shirley.

"Do you both have copies of Prudence's dissertation, or have you consulted a copy of it directly?" asked Colmes.

"I don't have a copy, but I've of course read it in the school library. How else could I do a dissertation on it if I hadn't read it?" replied Sullivan.

"I have my own copy," said Shirley, now growing impatient.

At that moment, there was a knock at the door and Colmes called, "enter," then rose from his chair to welcome Professor Maxwell

Dunstan the renowned campus statistician.

"Well now, Dunstan, it's so very good of you to come. May I introduce to you three devoted students, Shirley, Tom and Prudence."

The three students twisted around to see who it was. They all had heard of him, and Prudence thought that she had consulted him originally, but then it emerged that Dunstan was not at that time on the faculty.

Then Colmes did something that surprised me. He got up from his seat and insisted that Dunstan take his place, and walked around the desk to take up the spare seat.

Professor Dunstan sat back in Colmes's chair, delighted. "How can I be of help?" he asked.

"Now that you have read the Prudence Wright dissertation, please tell us your opinion," requested Colmes.

"Well, for something written thirty years ago it's very solid. However it used the early version of analysis of variance to analyze the data, and the procedures of probability statistics have progress somewhat since that date."

"So had you been on Prudence's dissertation committee you would have passed the dissertation?" asked Colmes as though he were cross examining a witness.

"Certainly," said Dunstan with an air of impenetrable confidence.

"And what about now?" continued Colmes.

"Well, that's a sticky question. But given all that's riding on it, I would accept the dissertation, maybe with the provision that the student defend it again in front of a new committee. But I could be talked out of that."

"So you're saying that it is of sufficient quality to receive a passing grade?" pressed Colmes.

"Yes. But here is also another important reason why it should be officially passed," said Dunstan.

"And what is that?" asked Colmes.

The three students sat mute, looking down, as though they were the objects of the discussion, which in fact they were.

"Given the two dissertations by Anderson and Sullivan respectively on the Gluecks that are now in process, it will be very important that they be able to show that their dissertations are clearly an improvement over a previously published, that is an approved dissertation, that of Prudence."

"I take it," said Colmes looking at Shirley and Sullivan, "that each of you is doing the usual literature review of any other studies that have been published on the Gluecks?"

Sullivan mumbled, "yes of course." And Shirley nodded assent, then added, "and besides Prudence's there are none others that have actually re-analyzed the Gluecks data."

"Now wait a minute," said Colmes. "Is it acceptable for dissertation students to actually replicate a previous study? This does not seem to add any new knowledge to the field."

Professor Dunstan smiled, almost laughed. "A good point, but we have come a long way since thirty years ago when Prudence here, I'm sure, had a hard battle to get her dissertation, basically a replication of the Gluecks study, accepted as adding to the knowledge base."

"You're darned right about that!" exclaimed Prudence.

"These days," added Dunstan, " we realize that replication of a study is just as important, maybe more important, than the original study. Because results are all the product of probability statistics, there is always the chance that the analysis was defective in some way or another."

"But," retorted Colmes, almost chuckling, "what of these two," he gesticulated to Shirley and Sullivan, "they can't be allowed to do the same thing, can they? I mean they may just as well co-author the one dissertation and count it as two!"

Shirley and Sullivan stirred uncomfortably. But they were immediately saved by Dunstan. "The solution to that small difficulty is for each of you to use a different type of probability statistic. Prudence here, used what we would call today a primitive version of the probability statistic of analysis of variance, but it was the only one available at the time. I would suggest that Shirley use multiple linear regression analysis, and that Tom use either multiple logistic regression or multivariate analysis of variance, a more sophisticated version of the original. It will be most interesting to see how their results will compare."

By this time I was nodding off in my corner on the overstuffed chair. It all seemed to me like a kind of fraud. I might be old fashioned, but I could not see any creativity in these dissertation proposals. They were basically copying someone else and each other. They each complained that their own dissertations or dissertation ideas if one could call them that, were stolen, but ironically, I think they were both stealing those of the Gluecks of the 1960s, as did Prudence in the 1980s.

I can see the scientific argument for the importance of replication. But that should be after one has done a dissertation that contains something new. Maybe I'm old fashioned. Maybe I'm asking too much. Maybe this is why I spend years trying to come up with a dissertation idea.

***

It is probably unnecessary to relate the final outcome of this unmemorable meeting of minds. Colmes of course had set all this up in advance. He had Dunstan in his pocket, so he simply went directly to the Dean of the School of Criminal Justice and explained that Professor Dunstan had agreed to chair both dissertations of Sullivan and Anderson respectively, that each would be contributing innovative and unique methods of reanalyzing the Gluecks' data. And that the mature dissertation of Prudence Wright was in fact defended originally and successfully, so all it required was for her to submit a properly formatted copy of the dissertation to the administration along with the official forms signed by the Dean. The case was never returned to the faculty and no one asked what became of Prudence and her dissertation.

I admit that I am a bit of a touchy person. Colmes has managed to knock a lot of that out of me, but I still on occasion tend to take offence if I think I have been slighted in some way. And yesterday, at that unmemorable meeting I did take just the slightest of offence, when Colmes introduced everyone to Dunstan, except me. I know that I had met him once or twice before, but given Colmes's commitment to Victorian manners, he should none the less have introduced me.

The fact is that I think Colmes is losing his edge just a little. I do not know what is wrong with him, but he has not been quite up to it in recent days. He was slow to get up from his desk chair yesterday, and seemed to be puffing and out of breath by the time he walked around to the other side of the desk and sat on the vacant chair.

I got up from the three page rough draft of my dissertation concept, and decided to have it out with him. No, I don't mean that, I mean ask him if he's okay. I knocked on our office wall and heard a muffled answer of "come Hobson." I entered and made directly for my wicker chair.

"So all ended up well after yesterday," Colmes said well satisfied, though lacking that usual excessive pride over his own achievement. "I spoke with the Dean and he was most pleased to have it all fixed, and the prospect of three more dissertations coming out of his top rated graduate program.

"He said it was *his* program? I asked with a little petulance.

"Now, now, Hobson. Don't be such a moralist," Colmes said with a frown.

"Purist, more like," I retorted. "There wasn't a trace of creativity or a chance of anything new in any of those dissertations finished or unfinished,"

"Really, Hobson. Have I not taught you anything?" said Colmes frowning again.

"You have taught me much, especially the demand to maintain the highest of standards," which you obviously have not applied to your other students.

"Are you accusing me of double standards?" ask Colmes, raising his graying eyebrows, a slight sparkle in his glance.

"I am!" I announced as though from a pulpit.

"Then I am most flattered, since that is the very basis on which the entire academic establishment rests," he said now eyeing me with a kind of superior amusement.

"Are you OK?" I asked, suddenly remembering why I came to see him.

"Indeed I am, Hobson. Are you?"

Colmes started to breathe quickly as though out of breath.

"I don't know," I answered. "I'm confused."

There, I had bared my throat and waited for the final blow.

Colmes appeared not to notice. "These three cases," he said, "simply reveal the double standards and, when applied in practice among weak humans, the unavoidable duplicity built into academic life…"

I blinked and for a moment thought I was going to break down into tears. And then he continued, a furrow in his brow.

"The fact is, Hobson, that in academia, there is a fine line between sharing and stealing. If you do not believe me, read the history of the discovery of the DNA double helix."

"So the dissertations. Nothing was stolen, everything was shared?"

"Exactly, and the magician disguised as a statistician waved his magic wand and presto! Each dissertation was different. Problem solved. The next day is a new day."

Colmes said this in his typical enthusiastic way. This was the old Colmes I knew. And suddenly I felt much better and got up to leave.

"I'm okay," I called with a smile.

"Me too, Hobson!"

And I went back to my dissertation draft.

14. Overruled

For those of you who have not experienced the delights, dalliances and unfortunate disappointments of university life, I apologize in advance. But before I relate this case, I must take the time to ensure that all my good readers—and I am flattered that you have chosen to read me—are well informed of the circumstances in which this particular case arose. And at the risk of repeating myself once again (now there's a silly double something or other) this case is not at all special, one that is repeated every day in every university, maybe even high schools.

The case itself concerns a student who appealed his grade (it was a 'he', as far as I know from Colmes, though he would not bother to specify because in Victorian manners everyone is a "he" until proven otherwise). This was an undergraduate student who had queried the correct answer to a particular multiple choice question. It had been automatically marked as wrong (sorry, incorrect, one must avoid the bullying connotation of the word 'wrong'). In these multiple choice tests (for those who took a test so long ago you may have forgotten or maybe never took a multiple choice test) one is provided with a question, then a range of usually three or four possible answers. One must choose the correct answer. There is only one designated answer that is correct. And it is the professor who has set the exam and who has decided what is the correct answer.

Now, as you may have experienced yourself, it is quite common for there to be some ambiguity as to which is the correct answer. In fact, a smart student may argue or think too much about the meaning of the question, and decide that it could be one or more of the possible choices. For the professor, making up these questions is a challenge because one does not want to provide incorrect choices that look obviously incorrect.

It makes the test too easy. The choices therefore have to be kind of similar. The trouble is that a smart student (well, not exactly smart, let's just say argumentative) can easily show that their answer was 'as correct' as the designated correct answer. This embarrassing situation is generally solved by pointing to the "fact" that the majority of students in the class chose the designated correct answer, therefore the student's incorrect answer is incorrect. This is a weak argument against the protesting student because, as we know, majorities are not always right.

The solution to this weakness of such multiple choice tests is to distance the creator of the exam as far away as possible from the examinee, so that the examinee has no one in particular to argue with. Thus, these types of exams have flourished since the growth of computers, and now with the facility to take them online. "One cannot argue with a computer." As an aside, if you have ever been a student in recent or past years, you would know of some people who say that they are good or otherwise at taking those kinds of tests. It is likely that there is a skill that one can learn in order to get high grades in such tests that may not have all that much to do with one's understanding or knowledge that the test claims to measure.

But enough. As you can see, I have taken up too much time with this topic that I obviously feel deeply about. This case is not about me, so I know I must get on with it.

***

Because there is much at stake when examinations are administered and graded, there are many rules in place that expect that some students will complain or appeal their grade. When I say 'rules,' they are expressed in practice as procedures, just as criminal law is administered according to criminal procedures. They are interdependent. The procedures to be taken when a grade is appealed may vary across disciplines and schools or departments. But the general procedures are as follows and in this order:

1. First appeal to the professor who set the exam.

2. If not resolved, appeal to the Chair of the Department, who may

take the case to the department or college faculty's "student performance committee" or something similar.

3. If not resolved appeal to the Dean of the school.

4. If not resolved appeal to the Faculty Senate, which usually has a subcommittee that deals with "student performance."

5. If not resolved, give up. Or in special circumstances…

6. Appeal to the President, bringing a lawyer along.

7. Give up.

These are the rules of procedure for appealing a grade. But they do not tell the whole story, or should I say that the story is buried within the procedures. The ambiguity, or mystery more like, lies with the meaning of the word "rules" which hopefully will become clearer as I recount the case.

***

Francis Shoham suffered from a high anxiety complex. The class was Philosophy 101, all about Plato and Aristotle and the various dialecticians. One might argue that, if ever there was a subject that would not lend itself to a multiple choice exam it would be philosophy where every idea and concept was subject to minute dissection and where words were open to many different interpretations and meanings. But one can understand a professor, in this case a junior teaching assistant called Simon Jefferson, would lose a great deal of time grading over a hundred essays on such topics as justice, shadows in a cave, and the like. Besides, the young professor had not himself made up the test. Rather it had been handed down to him from his supervisor, Distinguished Professor Alice Armstrong who had constructed it decades ago. So it was a well tried and used test that had survived the "test of time," as one might say. Over the years it had been queried, and in response the wording adjusted, sometimes to account for changing times, though of course, the subject matter has remained the same for a few thousand years. And over the last few decades as computers became more accessible and user friendly, and the software improved, Professor

Armstrong had adapted her test to the cyber world and had administered it online for some twenty years. Indeed, the university's computing center established an entire wing that dealt only with computer test analysis. It was a wonderful labor saving device, and what's more it put a lot of distance between the professor and the student. There was little argument over any of the questions, and Professor Armstrong was proud of the fact that over those decades no student who appealed their grade had taken it beyond her. She had been able to discuss the students' incorrect answer and convince them why it was not the correct choice. And especially over the past decade, she had been able to resolve queries and complaints completely online, without having to meet with the student at all.

But right from the start, the case of Francis Shoham did not fit that pattern. And although the online test did not offer a section for a student to add any explanation or query about any of the test questions, the teaching assistant's email address was easily found. Thus it was that the high anxiety of Francis took over almost as soon as he had answered fewer than a half dozen questions. One might think that a student would make a complaint after the test results were received, and if the grade were lower than expected, to then complain about the ambiguity or inconsistency of the questions. But Francis shot off an email right away, pointing out the ambiguity of various questions, not just one particular question, but several of them. He had made notes as he went through the test, listed them in an email then after he had finished the test, though one could hardly call it finished, rather that he was timed out, even though in principle the test was not timed and in fact students were also allowed to save their test and complete it at a later time. But not Francis. He was so energized and upset with the total and obvious unfairness of many of the test questions to which there were no clear answers or certainly no single answer it seemed to him, that he just could not sit long enough at the computer. He jumped up, stormed around his bedroom, even screamed at the computer, then sat down and shot off his email full of complaints, all very, very detailed.

Of course, the email went directly not to the Distinguished Professor, who was most likely away at her weekend house in the Berkshires, but to her teaching assistant who was the named teacher of that course, Simon Jefferson. Upon opening the email, Simon stared at the long, carefully organized list of queries to some sixteen questions, which was about half of the questions of the test. It seemed endless as he scrolled down to the end, where Francis had accused the teacher of incompetence, and demanded that he be allowed to meet with him and discuss why he had been unable to finish the test properly. It was the fault of the test, not him.

Simon stared at the email and decided to put it aside for a day or two, while he thought about what to do. However, next day he received another email from Francis asking why he had not responded to his email, pointing out that the lack of response had heightened his officially diagnosed high anxiety state, and that it was essential that he be allowed to speak with his teacher.

This caused Simon a little concern, so he decided to forward the emails from his student to his supervisor, Distinguished Professor Alice Armstrong asking for advice.

***

Professor Armstrong sighed when she opened the email from Simon. He had been an excellent teaching assistant and she could see no reason to question his actions to date. The student emails, however, were another matter. She of course dismissed all of the student's criticisms as those of a raving lunatic, and shot off an email to Francis advising him not to respond to the student, but simply allow the grade that the computer would give him, most likely an 'I' (for incomplete). Though, and she did not know this at the time, technically, Francis had completed the test, because in a fit of rage, he had answered all the remaining questions checking off answers randomly.

Thus, when Simon collected the graded tests from the computer test analysis department, he looked through the grades and saw that Francis had received not an 'I' but an 'E'. This meant that Francis had failed the test. The university's grading system did not have an 'F' in its system because, during the days of student protests in the 1970s, students had complained that an 'F' was hurtful and degrading to a student. So it was expunged from the registrar's list of grades, and replaced with an 'E'.

However, this grade would already have been automatically sent to Francis, who, when he received it would no doubt raise hell that his professor had not responded to his query about the test. Mindful that Teaching Assistants were fair game among students, Simon immediately shot off an email to Francis informing him that there had been a computer glitch and that he was welcome to take the test again, providing him with a password to log into the test and take it over. Simon was a little nervous that he had acted without first getting Dr. Armstrong's approval, but had worried that she would be annoyed at being disturbed at her beloved retreat in the Berkshires.

Surprisingly, Francis in fact did log into the test and took it over. This time, he went through the test and answered all questions by checking off the second choice in every question. He would demonstrate to his examiners that the test was nonsense. And to some extent he was right. The next day, the computer returned a grade of 'D' which, technically in the university's grading system was a passing grade, since 'E' was a failing grade.

Of course, Francis was not going to give up any time soon. He was, after all, officially and medically disabled by his high anxiety state. The professors could not brush him aside so easily.

***

Francis persisted. He lodged an appeal with the philosophy department's chair, who quickly referred it to the appropriate faculty committee on student performance. This committee only met once a month, so time passed, and Francis became more anxious. His appeal was, of course, rejected, and it was automatic that the Dean of the college of arts and sciences would also reject it. The thought that an administrator would overrule a decision made by faculty was indeed horrendous. The Dean did however, take the time to see the student, so Francis found himself in a very nervous and anxious state in the Dean's spacious office unable to stand still, jigging around as though he needed to go to the bathroom. He listened to the Dean's lecture on having to accept the faculty's decision as final, and the usual advice that he should study the course materials more diligently, and so on. And when the Dean finally stopped, Francis jigged over to the Dean's desk and said, taking from his pocket a crumpled piece of paper, "I have a medical disability. I can't do these multiple choice tests. They discriminate against high anxiety students," and threw the crumpled letter on to the Dean's desk.

For one brief moment, the Dean considered accepting the appeal and overturning the grade. The kid had a small point. No allowance had been made for his so-called disability. But in point of fact, the Dean did not want to be the one who overruled a grade given by a professor. And there, in a nutshell was the problem.

"If you wish, " replied the Dean, "I will send on your appeal to the senate committee on student performance. It is they who have the final say. But my advice to you is to accept the grade. It is a passing grade after all. And in my experience I have never known a faculty committee to overturn a professor's grade."

Francis jigged back and forth, picked up the crumpled letter from the Dean's desk, and, prancing like a nervous horse waiting to start a race, backed away from the desk and cried, "send the appeal. I may be disabled, but I will not give up!"

And he departed, slamming the door behind him.

The Dean immediately called in his secretary and dictated a memo, referring the appeal to the senate committee on student performance. He was so pleased that it would not be him who had to decide this case. Thank goodness for committees, he thought.

***

The senate committee on student performance was composed of four or five people, depending on whether all members showed up to the meeting. The chair of the committee was Assistant Professor Alex Turret, an eager young professor who was coming up for tenure so was doing everything to establish an outstanding record of service, and chairing a senate committee was an excellent way to demonstrate his devotion to the university. He was a bright young fellow from the mathematics department. The other members were from random departments, but of course, none from the philosophy department. Had there been one such member, they would have to recuse themselves from this case because it was from their own department. The committee must do everything to protect justice and impartiality.

But more importantly, the committee, composed entirely of faculty old and young, must above all things protect academic freedom, to which every professor had an inalienable right. This was (and is) an absolute. This right, automatically applied to every case and circumstance throughout the university and every other university in America for that matter, trumped every other claim to justice. So we can see that the committee, before it even meets, has its hands tied. It cannot overturn a grade applied by a professor, if that professor will not agree to it. It would be a grave infringement on academic freedom. Professor Armstrong was adamant when called at her Berkshires retreat, that she would not support any grade change request that came from any student, she didn't care what disability he claimed to have. She had academic freedom to preserve. And that was that.

Where this sacred principle came from is a mystery, given that universities in America and elsewhere in the Western world, have their ancient origins in the opposite absolute: that they must put forth the teaching of Christianity (and before that, the bible, and before that the Greek philosophers) which depicts an academic history without academic freedom at all, but rather a strict recipe of what can be taught and what cannot. Teachers throughout history have been castigated, burned at the stake and whatever else if they deviated from the set biblical premises of academic thought.

I could go on and on about the condition (disease) of academic freedom on today's campuses. But that is for another day. For now, we must understand that the cards were stacked very much against Francis. The chances of getting his grade overturned by the senate committee were nil to none. In fact, he had only one chance, and that was with my mentor, Thomas Colmes, who—though I would deny it I were asked— looked upon academic freedom as a joke, like worshipping a totem pole (excuse my cultural appropriation here, but it is the most accurate way to describe the shibboleth of academic freedom).

***

While Francis's highly anxious state in his confrontation with the Dean could have been interpreted as his not listening to the Dean's advice to give up on his case, in fact, Francis departed even more determined. He returned to his counselor and described to her the rigid and immovable positions that the various faculty and administrators had taken. Was there no other avenue?

"Well, Francis, you have got yourself into quite a mess," said his counsellor with a kind smile.

"Cecilia," pleaded Francis in a quiet voice, "is there nothing I can do?"

"As a matter of fact there is," replied the counsellor. "I know of a colleague, actually I consider him to be a very good friend not just of me but the university. He's a kind of ombudsman."

"Please, tell me where I can find him. Can I send him an email or something?" asked Francis.

"I think it is better that you just pop in and see him. His office is hidden away in the tunnels underneath the lecture centers. Do you know your way around the tunnels?"

"Tunnels? I didn't know there were any," answered Francis, a little doubtful. Surely such an important person should be in a big office above ground, he wondered.

Cecilia stood up from her desk and grabbed a light jacket. "Come on, I will take you to see him. He's a bit, shall we say, odd, no, intense is the better word. But don't be scared. If he's on your side, and I know he will be, you are sure to win out in the end. Come along now!"

Rather rattled, Francis hurried along like a little puppy trying to keep up.

***

Three loud bangs on my wall called me to Colmes's office, which I was pleased to do, having sat for some time staring at my one page outline for my dissertation. I entered and saw that my wicker chair was vacant, though moved a little to the side of Colmes's desk. Cecilia sat on the overstuffed chair in the corner, and a young man walked nervously to-and-fro in front of the desk.

"Hobson! Thank you for joining us. You know Cecilia, I believe," Colmes almost smiled as he looked across to her, "and this is Francis a student who is having trouble with the philosophy department, a department that you know quite well."

"Pleased to meet you all," I said as I took up my chair and added, "happy to help in any way I can."

"The problem it seems is a disagreement over a grade and a professor, a professor Armstrong, I believe?" Colmes hesitated and looked to Francis who was too busy jigging around to answer. But the question was directed to me.

"Oh yes, I remember her. Always out of town at her Berkshires retreat," I said with a slight disapproving smirk.

"Exactly!" cried Francis as he jigged about. "That's what I'm talking about. They won't listen to logic!"

Cecilia got up from her chair. "Looks like things are getting under way. I have another client to see. So I will leave you to it."

"Indeed, Cecilia. And my best wishes to Chioma."

"Of course," she said with a very big smile, and left.

Colmes turned to Francis. "Now young man, let us see if we can fix this mess. What would be your idea of a final solution?"

The choice of words was perhaps not quite appropriate. But Francis did not seem to mind.

"They should let me take the test over, but a proper test without multiple choice. Just short answers," said Francis as he pranced about the office.

"Well now. That may be the ideal solution, but it will not guarantee you a better grade, will it? Converting multiple choice questions into short answer questions would be time consuming. Professor Armstrong would resist, and her teaching assistant would not be happy with this extra work. More difficult, other students who did well on the test may complain that you are getting special treatment."

"But I *am* disabled. I should receive special treatment;" complained Francis.

"Indeed," answered Colmes, a small twitch at the corner of his mouth, "indeed you are."

It was not altogether clear to me what Colmes meant by that unnecessary comment. I took it as slightly sarcastic, though Francis did not seem to notice.

"However," Colmes continued, "your handicap is not specific to the particular type of test, it seems to me, but applies to all types of tests, multiple choice, true or false, short answer and so on. Do you not agree?"

Colmes sat back in his chair, his finger tips of each hand touching.

Francis stopped his jigging for a moment and faced the Colmes's desk. "Then what do you recommend?" he asked, evading Colmes's original question.

I could see that my mentor was enjoying this back and forth, leading Francis in a particular direction, though I could not for the life of me imagine where. I rose from my wicker chair and moved to the overstuffed one in the corner. It was my way of informing Colmes to leave me out of the conversation. I preferred, as always, to be the observer, or recorder, not a participant.

Colmes leaned forward. He had an answer, though I could not yet see that it would be a solution.

"The only solution I can see, and it may seem like an impossible solution, is for your grade to be changed. Taking any other test or taking it over will not solve the problem. You will still end up with a D, or worse," said Colmes with a serious frown.

"But Professor Colmes, I can't have the D on my record. What am I to do? Cecilia said you would find a solution."

"What grade would you ideally like to have?" asked Colmes, an amused look of anticipation on his long face.

Francis was taken aback. "But, but, I told you, I can't take that test over again. Besides they will not let me."

"Would you be happy with a B?" asked Colmes, ignoring the protestations of his client.

"Well, yes, of course. I would," replied Francis suddenly standing still. His anxiety had magically fallen from him, as though a big cloak had dropped to the floor.

And now came the most incredible and shocking solution. Colmes looked across to me, sitting comfortably in the chair.

"Do you think you could get a B on such a philosophy 101 test?" he asked me.

"Who? Me?" I asked with a stammer. "You mean I could take the test in his place?" My face went red and I was unable to say anything else, I was so flabbergasted.

Francis started prancing around again, almost dancing, first up to me, then up to Colmes, indeed, right up to his chair behind the desk. Colmes recoiled and pushed himself back out of the way.

"More or less," answered Colmes, turning to Francis. "Mr. Shoham," he said sternly, "sit down on that chair and listen carefully to me."

Francis automatically did as he was told, though his legs continued to jiggle while he sat.

"I am going to inform Cecilia that you have agreed to retake the test under my supervision. I will request that Professor Armstrong or her TA provide you with a new password so you can access the test online. When you receive that password you will come to my assistant Hobson's office and take the test under his supervision and of course with the appropriate assistance given your disability. Is the test timed or not?"

"It is not timed," answered Francis.

"Excellent!" said Colmes. "Then go next door with Hobson and give him your contact details. And Hobson, you had better bone up on philosophy 101. Knowing you, I am sure you still have your notes from, how many years ago? About eight?"

I did not answer. It was eight, maybe more. And yes, I still had my notes. It's possible that I had even taken that very same multiple choice test all those years ago.

***

I must say that I found Colmes's so-called solution most upsetting, and quite frankly immoral, unethical, and a scurrilous attack on the very foundation of academia. No, not an attack on academic freedom, but an attack on the backbone of any organization whose mission is to teach, impart knowledge, and most important maintain standards of excellence (I hate that word, but here I am forced to use it). If people may cheat their way through any organization, but especially a university, then what is it all for? Who can believe what the university says it does? Am I a better person for having graduated from the university, or a poorer person for not having done so?

Let's not go down that path. The cynics would say that universities are an unnecessary luxury of "advanced civilizations." Some would say that the entire system of universities is a con-game. Its inhabitants talk amongst themselves and what do they produce of value? Nothing except talk. And people learn to talk without going to university.

But enough of this bitterness. My mentor certainly challenged me this time. He appeared, and maybe it is in fact really him, not to care about the values of honesty and excellence in education. He was focused on a small slice of the present: solve this kid's problem without upsetting the slow grinding machinery of the university.

Was he asking me to actually take the test on the part of this unimpressive student? He did not come right out and say it, but how could I do otherwise if I am sitting with him going through each question, advising him on what the question was asking, and how could I do that without hinting or even telling him what the right choice was?

Why don't you ask Colmes, or even refuse, if you are so concerned? You may reasonably ask. To which I have no answer except that I have some kind of faith in the intellect or genius of my mentor that he would not do anything that would harm me. At least not intentionally. Though he certainly was capable, with his Victorian mentality, to make me do something "for my own good."

I keep describing Colmes as Victorian. But I suppose that is not accurate because, as we all know, the supposed stern morality of Victorians, especially the men, was all a smoke screen. They easily justified the indescribable horrors of war, colonialism, criminal (and I mean *criminal*) justice, not to mention slavery white and black, and the preposterous idea that it was they, the men of Victoria who abolished slavery. Their "morals" were indeed, very demanding, but most men were up to overcoming them. And here I preach, sitting in the same cesspool of Victorian morality. If only morals were black and white. On the surface they are. But prick them a little and they turn into many shades of gray, blue and whatever else.

I give up. I will just help save this one kid fix his grade. It's an act of kindness, is it not?

Besides, my mentor sees a bigger picture. I am helping maintain a great institution of learning, my university.

***

After a couple of days I received my beckoning knock on the wall and I quickly appeared in Colmes's office.

"This is the test password," he said handing me a small slip of paper, looking at me with some slight amusement. "You do not have to do this," he said slowly, "but I assure you that it is the most reasonable and least damaging of all solutions available."

"Basically, you are having me take the test for him," I answered, my voice clearly conveying my lack of enthusiasm.

"I do not think that is quite what it is, though there is the danger that Francis will lean on you too much. That will depend on his state of mind and attitude. But you can surely, with your obvious social skills, groom him for the test, encourage him to make his own choices. If you can do that, then I do not see that any harm has been done."

"But what of the TA and professor Armstrong? How did you get them to agree to this?" I asked with a frown.

"I first spoke with Simon the TA, and he was more than agreeable. In fact a little too eager. He just wanted the case over and behind him. And he did admit that there were probably some questions in the test that had ambiguous answers. Though he pointed out again, that of the whole class Francis was the only student to complain, at least this semester. There had been only an occasional complaint in recent years."

"And professor Armstrong?" I persisted.

"Well, that was a slightly different matter. I suggested to Simon that maybe we did not need to raise the issue with her. After all, Simon had her complete confidence, and she enjoyed her Berkshires retreat largely because Simon took care of all the teaching demands."

I sat down on my wicker chair. "You're kidding! You did that to the poor guy?" I asked showing my concern.

"You know the old saying. What you don't know can't hurt you," quipped Colmes dragging out one of his Victorian pieces of wisdom.

I sat quietly and looked down. Perhaps he was right. Certainly, my impression of Dr. Armstrong was that she couldn't care less about the day to day workings of the university. She just wanted to spend her time at her Berkshires retreat, writing her books, a well-known expert on Aristotle. I took a deep breath and stood up before Colmes.

"I see you haven't started your crossword this morning," I said.

And then I turned and went straight to my office, where I found Francis in his usual high anxiety state, standing at my door.

"Come right in," I said with a bright smile. "Here is the password for the test. Let's hope this time it will seem a little easier."

"I hope so," Francis mumbled, trying not to smile.

"Now if you just sit here," I had to clear some books off the spare chair, "in front of the computer and log into the test we will get started."

"Okay. But I'm not sure I can go through with this…" mumbled Francis, "it's my fourth attempt."

"Not really," I said cheerfully, "only your first attempt was serious. The others were acts of protest."

Francis appreciated that remark and I think he took it as a kind of compliment. In any case, it had the effect of calming him down somewhat, and he was able to log into the test. The first question popped up, and he sat there staring at it. The instructions at the beginning however, were still visible. I read them through quickly. It said that returning to earlier questions was allowed. That was important.

"Okay, now Francis. Here's a trick I learned a long time ago with these tests. It looks like it will let you return to an earlier question should you want to. So what you should do is to quickly go through and answer whatever questions you think you can answer and skip those you need to think about. That way you at least can be sure that you have answered all those you know you are right on."

"Oh. I didn't know that. I can do that. Thanks. Makes it a lot easier."

I sat with him and when he paused too long at a question, I urged him to leave it and go to the next. So far he did not waste time asking me what this or that question meant. So far, so good.

It was not long until he had answered most of the questions. Now it was time to return to the difficult ones of which there were only five left out of what I roughly estimated to be about forty questions.

"I don't think I can do the ones I have skipped." he said, standing and fidgeting, wringing his hands.

"Come, sit," I urged, still smiling more generously than I ever do. "I'd guess that you have already easily passed the test. But just to make sure, why not give the remaining five questions a go?"

I quickly looked back at the test instructions. Some tests subtracted a point or more for wrong answers, a technique used to stop students from guessing. This test did not do that, so he was free to guess wherever he wanted.

"This question about Plato," said Francis as he sat down in front of the computer again. "I don't understand it. I mean forms could be correct and so could shadows, don't you think? I mean, the question is ambiguous."

"It certainly is," I agreed. "They need to update the test and fix these matters. But for now, let's just get it done. Choose one and move on to the next question you skipped. That's what everyone else most likely did."

"Really, they should be ashamed of themselves," mumbled Francis, as he checked off 'forms' and moved on.

And so, the test got done.

***

We heard nothing more from either Francis or Simon. And certainly nothing from Professor Armstrong.

15. The Student Body

The body. What an evocative word. I was sitting back on the overstuffed chair, sipping a cup of tea, while Colmes sipped his, pretending to finish off his daily crossword. "The student body, Hobson. That's what is up for grabs," he said. "Do you not agree, Rose?"

Rose the younger sat in my wicker chair, leaning forward elbows on Colmes's desk, her chin resting on her clasped hands.

"Just whose body are you talking about, Colmes?" quipped Rose, always ready for a little spar with the master.

"Well certainly not mine," grinned Colmes (he grinned only in response to two people I have known, Rose and Rose's mom Rose the elder who had by now passed away).

"Mine is up for grabs, to the right person," I joked.

Colmes looked across to Rose, and she to me.

"You two are a couple, then?" Rose said mischievously."

"Indeed we are, but not of the body," said Colmes. "We have the perfect relationship which is that we are joined at the mind, not the body."

I must say, his good humor of the morning shined through; a most unusual event.

"Great and greater minds think alike," I added, trying to go one better.

"Well, now," said Rose the budding philosopher, "is it not a fallacy to think of the mind and body as separate entities?"

I put down my cup of tea on its saucer and leaned across to place it on Colmes's desk. I was about to announce that it was far too early in the morning to be philosophizing about imponderables such as the mind-body problem, when Colmes put aside his crossword with a flourish and announced, "we are about to face that very problem not as philosophers but as problem solvers. We will not need a philosopher to solve it. We will need clear thinking and, of course, a certain amount of manipulation, mental and otherwise."

I looked at Rose hoping she would be as puzzled as was I. And fortunately she was, though she had a big smile on her pale Russian face, accentuated by her brightly painted red lips.

"What?" she asked.

"You may well ask, Rose," answered Colmes. "We are about to face a mind-body problem. I am expecting my client who is vexed by this problem but does not quite know it, to arrive any minute."

"And he is concerned about the student body? I assume you mean the body as in body corporate or something like that?" I asked showing off a little in front of Rose.

"Not quite, but you are close," muttered Colmes.

Annoyed by Colmes's who's-who game, I asked, "so who is it coming? Do I know him?"

"Indeed, you do. It is Professor Maxwell Dunstan from the mathematics department."

Rose got up from my wicker chair. "I don't think I need stay for this." She gathered up the cups and saucers and made her way out to the kitchen. "There's a bit of cleaning up to do."

"Yes, well," smiled Colmes, "I have a little cleaning up to do with Professor Dunstan.

"He has a mind-body problem?" I asked with a silly grin.

"One might call it that," answered Colmes.

As it was, I, like many on campus knew of professor Dunstan, though I had never needed his services.

***

Maxwell Dunstan was the only statistician in the mathematics department in the college of arts and sciences. He suffered from an inferiority complex, so my fellow students told me, all of whom had consulted him at one time or another. His services were in great demand as an adviser for many dissertations in the social sciences. Although there were quite a few statisticians in the social sciences, the unrealistic demand that every dissertation must have findings that produced statistically significant results was considerable. So it often fell to professor Dunstan to come up with a procedure that produced a probability of .05 or better. As one could imagine, this took some ingenuity on his part. Thus he was well known around the university as a kind of savior. Students went to him when all else failed, and faculty on the students' dissertation committees were routinely very much relieved and accepted his advice and procedures without question. Unfortunately it was this simple fact that caused him to suffer his feeling of inferiority, because his colleagues in the mathematics department made fun of him. They claimed that statistics wasn't real mathematics and had opposed his tenure, but the Provost overruled them. Which of course worsened his rejection by his colleagues.

Professor Maxwell was, however, a dedicated scholar and academic. He loved the university so much it made his rejection by his colleagues a minor matter. He was proud of the great service he provided to many faculty and students alike. He took collegiality seriously. Indeed, he believed in the university with all his heart and soul.

There was a faint knock at the door and I stood up from my place on the overstuffed chair.

"Enter!" called Colmes.

Professor Dunstan entered, a thin young man probably late thirties, of medium height, black hair, straight and parted to the side in early twentieth century style, dark brown eyes behind thin rimless glasses. He walked up to Colmes's desk and extended his hand. Colmes took it warmly, well, for him that is.

"Welcome Professor Dunstan. Thank you for coming. I heard your, shall we say, impassioned speech at the senate meeting yesterday."

"Please, call me Max," he replied with a thin smile. "I got a bit carried away," he answered apologetically.

"No need to apologize," said Colmes, "please take a seat. "And this is my esteemed assistant, Hobson," Colmes said, nodding in my direction.

"Yes, I think we have met at various times in the past," I said with a smile.

"Ah yes," said Dunstan, "a criminal justice dissertation, wasn't it?"

I blushed with embarrassment and nodded back, wondering what this mind-body problem would turn out to be. And since he showed up at Colmes's request he probably did not know that he had any kind of mind-body problem. In any case, since I have the advantage of hindsight, this is a good place to tell you of the impassioned speech to which Colmes referred. Embedded in that speech was the mind-body problem as Colmes had insisted on calling it.

***

The leading issue on the Senate's agenda was one put forward by the Vice President for University Development, the money raising arm of the university administration. An esteemed alum, whose name remains a secret, had bequeathed forty million dollars to build a new football stadium for the University's football team on the condition that it would maintain Division 1 status.

When Professor Dunstan heard of this, he was incensed and sent a memo to the Chair of the Senate that he was strongly opposed to the university "going commercial" as he said, sacrificing its mission as a university to develop academic curricula, providing a place where minds could meet and the minds of students be developed and challenged. He was invited to address the senate to make his case. The senate was always open to new ideas, wrote the chair of the senate.

The Senate meeting opened, the VP for development made his case for the new stadium, pointing out that although its building would cost much money, it would more than pay for itself with ticket sales. In fact, he claimed, it was the physical education side of the university, the team games, that brought in twice as much money than the rest of the university with its research grants.

Professor Dunstan was prepared for just this argument. Here is a rough outline of his speech, as described to me by various students and faculty who attended. Apparently, Professor Dunstan had stayed at the back of the room, as though he did not belong at the meeting, and as he spoke, began slowly to edge further and further up the aisle between the rows of chairs. Most did not bother to turn around to see who it was making this impassioned speech, until his voice screeched and all wanted him to sit down and shut up.

Here is the gist of his speech:

"This is a public university. We do not need massive donations. We do not want to be driven by enormous amounts of money as are the very sick preoccupations of the Ivy Leagues with their bloated endowments that they rarely spend on their students...

"It is true that the Victorian saying, in *corpore sano— healthy body healthy mind*—is worth acknowledging in universities and all educational institutions. But the pushing of bodies beyond endurance as in football, a violent sport, is not healthy, and emphasizes extreme competition...

"The original universities, beginning in the early 11th century, were monasteries. The monks looked on their bodies as sacred, so much so that they had to be hidden away, cloistered and isolated to avoid distraction or infection. The mind fed the body, not the other way around.

"Students are at universities for only a brief period of their lives. Academia is a place for thinking. Not doing. There is a lifetime to do that."

And so it went. In response the VP for development and various other administrators repeated that the physical education side of the university more than paid for itself, and indeed, since the state government had cut its financial support of the university every year, the university had to find money from other sources if it were to field classes of small size, maintain a good standard of teaching, maintain the excellence it boasted daily. Some departments could not pay for themselves with outside research funds, a good example being the department of classics. Without outside money such programs would have to be closed, especially as there were very few students interested in the classics. And what would be a university that did not have a department of classics?

It was unfortunate that Professor Dunstan got very worked up with his speech. It seems, so my informers told me, that he lost it towards the end, started yelling and accusing the university administration of being only concerned with money, that they didn't give a damn about students, not to mention faculty. In the end, so I am told, Colmes, who had been sitting quietly in the row behind him, gently guided Dunstan out of the room as he ranted and raved at all the faces gawking at him. And apparently none had spoken in favor of his position. Most had remained silent, simply waiting for the vote.

By the way. Colmes had never mentioned, not even when Dunstan came to his office, that he was there at the meeting. I discovered all of this much later.

***

Colmes began by inviting Professor Dunstan to join us for a cup of tea, to which surprisingly he happily assented. This annoyed me because we had only just had our morning tea. Colmes gave me a quick look, and I scurried off to the kitchen behind door two, and passed on the request to Rose the younger who was pottering around the kitchen, practicing her knitting, trying to reach the level of expertise of her dear old mother.

"Our mind-body problem has arrived," I said to Rose jokingly. "Colmes wants cups of tea all round."

"Nothing like a good cuppa to get the old body working," said Rose, copying the Russian accent of her mom. She put the kettle on and I turned to join the party in Colmes's office. Then his voice came loudly down the passage asking for an additional cup of tea for the Provost, and a kitchen chair for her to sit on.

I returned with the chair and plonked it down in front of Colmes's desk, and nodded with a smile to Dr. Dolittle, muttering "very good to see you again," and dropped down on the overstuffed chair in the corner. Professor Dunstan watched me with some amusement, then turned to the Provost, expectantly, but she simply addressed Colmes.

"So where are we now with this somewhat regrettable situation?" she asked.

In the presence of the Provost, Professor Dunstan seemed to shrink in size, withdrawing his thin body as much as he could into my wicker chair, his arms crossed hugging himself as though he were in a cooler. Her officious tone that she always used when addressing Colmes did not help things either. In fact, I wondered why Colmes had invited her, but no doubt he had a well thought out reason. Colmes leaned back in his chair.

"As you may well know," said Colmes with a strong, solid Victorian accent, delivered with a frown at the Provost, "my sentiments are very much on Dr. Dunstan's side."

"No doubt," said Dolittle, laced with sarcasm.

"But I do understand," Colmes added, "that the university, the body corporate one might say, has a money problem, always has and always will have," and it is the often unpleasant role of the upper tier of administration to make hard choices in order to keep the university alive and well."

I leaned back in my overstuffed chair and waited for Dunstan to respond. But he did not. He just sat there, hunched up, looking at the floor.

"So it's not so much a mind-body problem as it is a money-body problem," I thought of saying but did not.

"I do value the one and only thing we appear to have in common," said Dolittle, looking at Colmes and I must say in a surprisingly friendly way, "and that is the football games, sitting among the students and many parents, cheering on our team. Our purple and yellow colors fluttering in the wind, our school anthem played by the college band..."

It was as though Professor Dunstan were not even sitting there, right between them. And from my perspective I could think of nothing worse than having to sit among a mob of half crazed cheer leaders and barrackers. Whenever I see such crowds at big sports events, I think of the news reels of Hitler's speeches in the Sportplast of Berlin. But I could see their point. It gave the students a sense of belonging. It was certainly a student body. Very much alive, very much ready to act. It was little wonder that the protests against the Vietnam war came initially from students at universities everywhere. But the underside was—and I hate to say this because it makes me seem old—that for students, action comes first, followed only later by words. Yet paradoxically, the words of ideologues such as Marx and others, worked like kindling in the minds of the young. A healthy body indeed. The body came first, the mind second.

But now, you see, I have wandered off the path. Here, sitting at Colmes's desk, was a young professor at the height of his powers, an excellent model for his students, a tremendous source for so many frustrated and intellectually timid dissertation students, with nothing to say, having said it all the day before in anger at the Senate meeting. How could my mentor callously allow this situation to arise? Or worse, had he intentionally engineered such an outcome?

Colmes cleared his throat with a small cough. "Doctor Dolittle, perhaps you could explain further to Professor Dunstan how the funds will be used and perhaps how he might also benefit?"

"Yes, of course," answered the Provost. "I have just come from a meeting with the Dean of Libraries and the VP for development, and am pleased to report that we have arranged to use some of the funds to renovate part of the ground floor library, near the reference section and to construct a special glass enclosed office and study where students can sit with their professor and receive one-on-one instruction and advice."

Professor Dunstan remained hunched, though there was a slight flicker of apprehension in his eyes. Colmes eyed him carefully and added, "of course, I am sure you have already surmised that the stadium will be built. There is nothing to stop it, and probably it is all for the best anyway, given the way universities are competing with each other these days. We admire—and I know I also speak for the Provost here—your dedication and concern for the future of our university's pursuit of excellence. But that pursuit requires money, and the stadium is guaranteed to help with that problem."

Seeing that his remarks only got the faintest response, Colmes added, "believe me, as I demonstrated by my presence at the Senate meeting yesterday, and continue to assure you today, I completely agree with you. In fact I would go much further than you. A university can foster a healthy body through its gymnasium facilities without forcing aggressive competition on the field, which, I have no hesitation in saying, promotes nothing less than legalized violence. And worse, promotes rigid stereotypical us-against-them psychology that justifies violence of one against another. The rules of whatever game are there to whitewash the violence."

The room fell silent. Professor Dunstan uncurled himself from the wicker chair and sat up more or less straight. And now I was moved to have my say, stimulated as I was by my mentor's speech.

"Don't doubt his support," I said with a serious smile, "Colmes hates going to senate meetings, and only does it when the situation is serious enough to require his presence. Supporting you was one of those situations." I could have added, as I think I have mentioned in other cases, that Colmes frequented the gym daily and worked out on several of the machines. Though I must say that of late, I have noticed that his visits there have not been as frequent.

Professor Dunstan was at last stirred to speak. "Thanks for your support. I feel better already. I made a fool of myself yesterday. No one spoke up for me," he said forlornly.

Now it was the Provost's turn again. "I can say that I speak for the entre university that we value your dedication to your work, especially the additional work you do in assisting dissertation students from every corner of the campus, for it seems almost every discipline needs someone like you. The special office we have in mind will be for your exclusive use, as often and for as long as you wish it. It is the least that we can do, and..."

Professor Dunstan sat up and at last became somewhat animated. He had come out of his slump. It is important to understand that this offer was one of amazing, shall we say, generosity. To have one's own office inside the university library that was already suffering from lack of space, was no small thing. It would be the envy of the rest of the faculty. Many faculty had asked for such an office. The best they ever got was a desk-shaped cubicle with their name on it.

The professor was overwhelmed. He had his say yesterday. Many—who knows how many—were in secret agreement with him. But the very failure of so many to speak up simply demonstrated to him, as he was now coming to see, that the problem of money and the university was a problem that persisted for generations, and that one small voice such as his could make little difference. What was the word that the sociologists used? Structural, like structural racism. Without money, the university would collapse in upon itself. And if it did, who is to say that what may replace it would be better? Or would we be better off without universities? In the meantime, he was and would be very happy doing what he was doing. Meeting with students, helping them solve their research problems. Teaching them how to make of science facts that one could feel comfortable in following. He was about to say thank you and this was all wonderful, when the Provost coughed a little and continued where she had left off.

"And I have already put your name forward to the Senate Committee on Promotions and Tenure, for promotion to Full Professor," she announced as she stood up from her kitchen chair and put out her hand. "Congratulations, and keep up the good work!" She reached out and before he knew it, Professor Dunstan jumped up, grabbed her hand in his and squeezed it with much affection and gratitude. He could hardly wait to get home and tell his wife, who was, as a matter of fact, a graduate student in the department of sociology just finishing off her

Ph.D.

And with that, the Provost stood and put out her hand to Colmes who almost smiled as he took it and touched it ever so lightly to his lips—a true Victorian. Dolittle quickly withdrew and left without further word, followed by Dunstan, running after her as would a well-trained dog.

***

"Mind over matter," don't you think?" quipped Colmes.

"Surely the reverse," stated Rose the younger with the same forcefulness of her mom.

I sat in my corner on the overstuffed chair and decided to keep out of it. For one thing, I was not sure what, if any, Colmes had contributed to the solution of this problem. It was more like a case of a problem solving itself. All it needed was time.

"So how did you get the Provost to fork over those goodies for Dunstan, and how did you know he would go for them?" persisted Rose.

Colmes sat back in his chair. "A simple matter of human weakness," said Colmes. "To start with, I knew, well everybody knows, that the Dean of Libraries is a whining, complaining individual who has managed to garner the dislike of many in the administration. So it was a simple matter to suggest something to Dolittle that she would enjoy imposing on her nuisance of a Dean of Libraries. Dolittle is a spiteful bitch as Hobson and I know, don't we Hobson?"

I nodded in assent. I did not say anything because quite frankly I was uncomfortable when Colmes spoke like this. It was a smugness that every now and then emerged, and unbecoming of a great man, which he almost was.

"And Dunstan, poor little man?" pressed Rose.

"Yes, a bit of a wimp who had his ten minutes of glory in the senate meeting. It was an obvious deduction that he would go for such an attracttive offer, especially sitting opposite Dolittle, the Academic Provost, who is held in awe by all faculty, no matter what their status. An academic provost, no matter who it is, has an immense amount of power. She can make or break whole departments and even colleges or schools, let alone individual faculty. Is that not right Hobson, my boy?"

I nodded again in assent. Rose looked at me, amused. I stood and said, "Well I must be off. I have a dissertation to write," and departed.

16. Celebrity Cook

It may come as a surprise to you that Colmes always wore a double breasted suit, mostly dark navy, lightly striped, a white handkerchief in his top left pocket, though no suspenders underneath, at least I don't think so, as it was rare that he allowed the jacket to be unbuttoned. I have been describing him as Victorian in his ways, but I suppose his dress is more early 20th century. Yet lately he rarely wore a tie, the top button of his pale blue long sleeved shirt undone revealing the thick hair of his chest. It goes without saying that there was no computer on his desk, indeed, only an old fashioned blotter on which he wrote the occasional note with his old fountain pen. Apart from a telephone that he grudgingly used, there was only one other object on his desk, which was an ashtray. When I look back on my cases that I have described so far, I am amazed that I omitted this small but significant fact. He was a chain-smoker, Phillip Morris cigarettes and the occasional cigar in our early days, until the campaign to extinguish smoking finally made it illegal on campus. Fortunately, I was never a smoker. I found it disgusting and almost declined Colmes's offer to me of an assistantship because of it. In fact, I made it a condition when he hired me, that he give up smoking. He hung on though, until the campus finally issued a directive that there be no smoking on campus. It has been some years now that he quit, but he still keeps the ornate ashtray on his desk as a reminder of the good old days. And the smell of tobacco still remains embedded in the furniture and walls of his office.

I recount all of this now because the case I am about to describe demanded the skills and know-how of someone from the 21st century, not the late 19th century that Colmes emulated. So one would think that this case was beyond his skill set. Even so, my faith in Colmes was such that it was I who brought this particular case to him. I did it after much hesitation, not so much because of his technology phobia, but because I thought that his personal health was deteriorating. There were just a few small signs, one that he was going to the gym less often, the other that he seemed a little out of breath when he got up from his desk. I wanted to ask him if he had been to a doctor, but dared not, for fear he would take it as an insult. He was a Victorian, proud of his physical fitness and his tall straight body of an aging man.

***

You may remember case 12, *Circle of Truth,* in which I described the seminar that I attended of the world's top sociologist, Godfrey Gardner. And at the beginning of the seminar, I mentioned that one of the students abruptly got up and left the seminar because of Gardner's first outrageous comment. That student a year or so later appeared at my door. This was most unusual because hardly ever did anyone take the time to come to my office. No one knew where my office was for one thing, and to find it was another, given that it was tucked away next to Colmes's, deep in the tunnels beneath the university. My door was always open, indicating I suppose that I was hoping someone would come in and save me from having to stare at the current draft of my dissertation proposal.

"Do come in," I called. "Richard, isn't it?"

"Right. Just call me Dick. Dick Smith," he answered.

I was a little embarrassed because I never had a visitor to my office before, so I did not have a second chair to offer him. All I had was a small stool that I sometimes used to stand on to reach up to a high shelf of my bookcase. "Hope you don't mind," I said, "but please take a seat." I indicated the stool. He smiled a little, though it did not hide his serious wrinkled face, rough brown beard unevenly clipped, a rich crop of wavy hair, a young man who looked quite old for his age. He was dressed in ill-fitting clothes, most likely bought at the Salvation Army store, gray pants, dark woolen sweater knitted in a rough style that reminded me of Rose the elder.

"I need to talk with Professor Colmes. I understand that you're his research assistant?" he asked.

A short fellow, but clearly stocky, he gave the impression that he was always ready for a fight.

"I am. And what is the problem you wish to discuss?" I asked in an unwarranted almost unfriendly way. For whatever reason I felt uncomfortable with his presence and he sensed it.

"Don't worry," he said, smiling, "I won't hurt you. Just because I did time, doesn't mean that I'm some kind of creature that walked out of a horror movie."

It was then that I realized who he was. The School of Criminal Justice had a program in which it admitted a small number of ex-cons, usually one a year, into its program *gratis*.

"Of course not," I mumbled most embarrassed. "So what's the problem? Oh, and now I remember. You walked out of that dreadful seminar with Gardner."

"Right, and that's what I want to talk about," said Smith.

"That was a year ago. I don't see what you're getting at," I replied .

"I think Gardner is a fraud, but I can't prove it," said Smith with a deep frown, "and I hear that this is what Colmes is good at."

"I don't know who you have been talking to, but yes, you are right. It does sound like something he might be interested in, and absolutely yes, it would be great to see that asshole get his comeuppance."

I knocked on my wall to see if Colmes was available, and immediately received the response "Hobson!"

"Looks like he's in. Let's go see him," I grinned.

To my surprise, Colmes got up from his chair and met us as we came in, putting out his hand to Smith. "Dick Smith, I presume," smiled Colmes with a devilish grin meant for me.

"Professor Colmes, at last I have met you. I have heard a lot…" said Smith as I broke in. I was beginning to feel left out. It was as if they already knew each other.

"Colmes, this is Dick Smith, he's in the Criminal Justice School's ex-con program," I announced feeling as though I had been upstaged.

"Yes indeed," answered Colmes as he returned to his chair and I showed Smith to my wicker chair. "I have been expecting you."

I sat on the overstuffed chair in the corner, as usual, and as I did so, I called out, "how could you know that? He only just now came to me in my office." Smith was also surprised, but I could see he was trying to hide it.

"My contacts inside," said Colmes with a hint of mystery, "no doubt they sent you to me?" asked Colmes.

"Well, yes, though Professor Colmes, I like to keep it quiet that I still communicate with insiders. You know. Once a con always a con. It's hard to get over the prejudice," answered Smith.

"Indeed, indeed," said Colmes.

"And it's about the prejudice against ex-cons that this is about, kind of," said Smith.

"Do tell," said Colmes.

"He wants to take down Gardner!" I burst out.

"Now, now, Hobson, let's not get ahead of ourselves. Smith, tell us the whole story and why you need our help." Colmes was so thoughtful to include me as part of the help. I felt foolish for having jumped in as I did.

"This guy Gardner, I think he is a fraud, but I can't prove it," said Smith.

"Pardon," said Colmes with a small cough clearing his throat, "but that does not sound very scientific. One should not begin with a conclusion, you know."

"OK. Then let's call it an hypothesis," grinned Smith.

"Indeed! Indeed!" affirmed Colmes with, for him, a big grin.

Smith continued. "Gardner published a paper in the American Journal of Sociology…"

"One of the top ten," I put in.

"…claiming that a sample of youths of university student age, 18-24, convicted of a crime and sent to prison had an average IQ of 85 compared to a similar sample of university students whose average IQ was 105. The findings, he claimed were well beyond the point .05 percent level of probability. In other words that cons, like myself, are dumb shits."

Colmes remained expressionless. "And how do you intend to prove otherwise?"

"Well, I contacted Gardner and asked for his data set so I could replicate his study."

"What do you mean by replicate? If you use his same sample, how can you expect to find different results? The errors, or error, may simply be one of sampling," pressed Colmes.

"Right. But any statistician worth his salt, can reanalyze data and come up with different results," countered Smith.

"That is a cynical view, if I may say so," observed Colmes.

"Fair enough," said Smith. "In any case, he refused to release his data. Claimed some kind of privacy rights of the subjects of the study."

"And how do you plan to get around that?" asked Colmes.

Smith appeared to ignore the question. "Anyway, I decided to get my own matched samples and replicate his study, which made my dissertation."

"And?" queried Colmes.

"I found no significant difference in IQ between the two matched groups," answered Smith with much satisfaction.

"Then you have solved the problem, have you not? Simply publish your findings and this will be sufficient to counter Gardner's cooked-up study," said Colmes with a challenging smile.

"Easier said than done. I submitted the paper to several of the top journals and it was roundly rejected by all. Some of the nastiest critiques came from Gardner, even though all the top journals are supposed to be blind peer reviews. You can always pick who wrote them, especially Gardner."

"Are you sure it was Gardner?" asked Colmes.

"Sure sounds like him," I interjected.

"Then, maybe your study is flawed," said Colmes staring hard at Smith.

"Maybe. But if it is, so is Gardner's," said Smith with a deep sigh. "I mean, I applied his own methodology exactly, and wrote up the paper for each journal, just like his. And of course I cited him profusely."

"Hmm," opined Colmes, "this is indeed an interesting problem. Let us meet this time again tomorrow while I think about it. "

Smith appeared disappointed. He sat as though he did not want to leave.

"Come," I said, "we can talk more in my office. I assure you that Colmes will think about it and will as usual come up with a solution. You can bet on it."

I stood by Smith as he reluctantly rose, thanked Colmes, and we turned to leave. And just as we reached the exit, Colmes called out, "what is Gardner's university?"

"Chicago, of course," called Smith, dejected and angry.

"Oh, and would you be so good as to leave a copy of your rejected papers with my excellent research assistant Hobson, before you depart?"

***

Now, while it is probably unnecessary for me to recount this gossip, and I warn you that is all it is, but the student rumor— and come to think of it not just confined to students—has it that Gardner in his youth, before he entered university set fire to a house in the Chicago's West side, West Garfield Park. It occurred during the 1980s when school desegregation was at its height and school bussing was introduced causing considerable racial conflict. Two persons, so it was claimed, though the bodies were never found, were killed in the house fire. Gardner, however, always denied this accusation, though he admits that he was in the area when it happened. That was a reasonable explanation because in fact he grew up in that area and was one of the minority of white students who attended the local high school. And in his defense, there was a report deep in the pages of the *Chicago Times*, of his arrest, his brief interrogation at the police precinct, then release. The

article in the *Chicago Times* did not shrink from pointing out that, had
Gardner been black, he would have been locked up, charged with the
crime, then interrogated until he confessed. Not to mention that house
fires in that area then, as of now, were common, not surprising given
their poor condition, in fact every tenement was a fire risk.

I tell you this as a kind of anticipatory defense of Gardner. Maybe
his early impoverished background had something to do with his obsession with clawing his way to the top. Of course, Smith also knew this,
and he joyfully recounted the rumor to as many others as would listen.
He even embellished it when passing on the rumor to me, claiming that
Gardner was also involved in the killing of great basketball star Ben
Wilson.

I find it amazing that the mixing of fact with fiction enjoys a rich
life among people who would otherwise describe themselves as "social
scientists" as would all those who inhabit this university (except the
philosophers and creatures of the English department). Yet it is in
universities that movements and protests so often occur when facts do
not quite match the fictions that live in the heads of young (and even
older) students. Protests and demonstrations, especially those that are
violent, serve to embellish the factual claims of the protesters. But here,
I begin to sermonize. After all, I'm doing a philosophy Ph.D., so I
suppose that puts me in the faith or faithless (no difference there)
categories.

What does this diversion have to do with the case? A great deal. It
offers an explanation both for the extreme antics of Gardner who indeed
has clearly demonstrated in his seminars that he will do anything to claw
his way to the top and stay there, but even more extreme, once on top to
keep all others down. If you have the power, use it. A bit like Caligula,
though he used it for fun, not domination, which produced far more
dreadful results. Although, I must admit that in Gardner's seminar, I felt
as though we were being played with. Could Gardner be deposed as was
Caligula?

I knew that Colmes was up to something when he casually dismissed Smith and me, promising to "think about it." Of course, he had already thought about it and was up to something for sure. After Smith departed my office I picked up Smith's paper and read it through quickly. It looked perfectly reasonable to me, as far as these boring empirical studies went. Then came the familiar knock on my wall beckoning me to Colmes.

"Now, Hobson, I have an important errand for you," he said with a mild smile, well not a real smile, just a flicker of the corner of his mouth.

"So I am your errand boy," I quipped, feeling a little belligerent after the Smith interview.

Colmes ignored my most unnecessary remark. "I need you to visit Coxsackie prison."

He paused awaiting my response.

"And?" I asked.

"Meet with an inmate by the name of Tiro Sellin. He will have something for you, or should I say, you will need to write down what he tells you. We can't risk passing something from inmate to visitor. They might get suspicious."

"And what will it be, then? I mean, why can't he phone you? Inmates get phone privileges these days, don't they?"

"Indeed, but too risky. He will give you a password. How he will do that I am not sure. It will be a coded message of some kind."

"And the password is for?" I asked.

Colmes ignored the question. Instead he said with a wry smirk, "and by the way he is blind."

I looked at him in disbelief. "How? I mean why?" I stammered.

Colmes grinned. He truly loved doing this to me. "I thought you would never ask," he said. "Tiro is an old friend of mine from Philadelphia where I played cricket for a few years while I was a student or not really a student, trying to decide what to do with my life."

I sat on my wicker chair and leaned forward elbows on his desk, completely overcome. This was Colmes, the person known rarely to talk about himself, about whom practically nothing was known about his past. I was quite taken aback. Though now in retrospect I think that it was at a stage when his health was deteriorating for reasons then not known to me. Colmes continued.

"He was always a bit on the shady side, and I found that, well, fascinating, exciting maybe. He would frequently show up to our meetings at the local cricket club, had lots of money, pay for our drinks, even meals and think nothing of it. Then he would disappear for a few weeks and show up again and splurge his money on good food for all of us."

"And all this when he was blind?"

"Indeed," said Colmes.

"Tell me more, I urged. Where did he get his money?"

"That I do not know. But I do know *how* he got his money" answered Colmes.

"There's a difference?" I asked, perplexed.

"Indeed. You see he was, and still is, a cyber sleuth of the first order." Colmes looked at me amused.

"You mean a computer genius?" I asked getting tired of my own questions.

"Of the first order. He can track down anything on the internet or even on the inside of a desktop computer," said Colmes pleased with his own apparent acquaintance with this rapidly growing field of information technology.

Yes. I know. Colmes, who had to be cajoled and nagged to install a telephone on his desk. Let alone a computer. I was amazed. And still am. "Don't tell me," I said almost breathless, "he has hacked into Gardner's computer account at University of Chicago and…"

Colmes cut me off and finished my sentence "…did not download the database in question because he did not know what one. There were several files, some quite large and it would have taken too long to download them."

"Then poor Smithy," I said with warranted familiarity, "will have to commit a crime by hacking into Gardner's account and downloading the file in question."

"Indeed, Hobson. Indeed."

"And Tiro did all this while inside the prison?" I asked with admiration.

"Indeed again. You know they have an excellent rehabilitation program in prison and one part of that is teaching them about computers. Funded by IBM as an outreach program. Quite an irony, don't you think Hobson?"

"Indeed, I do," I replied, dumbfounded.

"Then off you go, Hobson and do your part. Get the password, and the username, the latter is already available in Gardner's email address."

"You know about email?" I asked mockingly.

"I know far more than that," he answered staring at me in a way that hinted lightly of a threat. "Now, off you go. And be careful of your terminology when you speak to Tiro and later to Smith. And especially with Smith, do not use any word that hints of breaking in, or of a crime, or whatever. Understand?"

I nodded assent and stood up to leave.

Colmes continued. "And when you have the information needed, contact Smith and bring him here to work out the next steps. This will need to be done very carefully."

I nodded assent again. And I was on my way to Coxsackie.

***

About thirty miles south of the university, the freeway gradually rises, cut into the side of a slope that marks the beginning of the Catskills, a low mountain range, most of which, on the eastern side, has been cleared of forest. Coxsackie prison lies at a distance and its view from the freeway is as though on an architect's map, square squat buildings, roadways and fences connecting them and protecting them from visitors and inmates alike. Every time I visit I shudder at the sense of isolation, as I drive off the freeway, the prison sitting alone, surrounded by rich green meadows in spring and summer, or desolate stretches of the dark frozen fields of winter. I know this place and hate coming here. On and off over the past dozen years or so, I have ventured in to do my charitable part to teach an occasional class to those inmates who were studying for a B.A. degree or something like it. It took a long time until I could feel comfortable standing before a small class of inmates, some of whom may have committed atrocious crimes. The crimes they may have committed of course, were in my imagination. And some of them knew it, approaching me with a quiet glee when they sensed my fear.

On this day, however, my mission was quite different. I did not find the security procedures demeaning, or threatening, even though the rough hands of the guards sometimes hurt when they checked my pockets. I was ushered into the visiting room and took up my seat at the long counter where I awaited the arrival of the mysterious Tiro Sellin. I looked around and saw several others either waiting or talking with inmates across the counter. The noise of chatter echoed in the sparsely furnished room, everything shiny and excessively polished, the din of metal chairs banging and sliding on the bare wooden floor also highly polished.

I heard the clanking of security doors opening and closing, and soon enough, my client, or whatever he was, appeared at the door and waddled towards me, reminding me of a penguin. He knew who I was, I do not know how, and I don't know why he looked around the room because he was supposed to be blind. However he did feel around a little for the chair that was opposite me and sat down, making himself comfortable.

"You're Tiro Sellin?" I asked, rising to shake hands.

"So how's my old mate Colmes?" he asked as he stretched out his hand and we shook. He held on to my hand tightly, turned his head in the direction he thought was my face and I felt a small slip of paper rub against the palm of my hand.

"He's fine, Mister Sellin" I said. This was a small fib, because in my personal opinion Colmes was not in that good of health at all.

"Please, call me Tiro. We had some great adventures together," he said with a gleeful laugh. "You wouldn't believe. I remember the time we went to the Casino, that was…"

As much as I would have liked to hear those stories, and perhaps one day I would return to hear them, I was here on business and wanted to get it done as quickly as possible. I had a dissertation to write, after all. Besides I hated being locked up in a prison. A contradiction, I know. After all my office was not all that different from living in a prison, the President of the University Finneas O'brien had even famously said so (I know, I've told you this before, which shows how strongy I believe it to be true). But I was there of my own accord—a huge difference.

"So our business has concluded?" I broke in.

"Don't you want to know how I came to be blind?" he asked.

"Not really," I bristled.

"I see, *sagor nahor,*" he said, "that Colmes's Victorian manners have not rubbed off on you."

I sat back and took stock of myself. I was being a bastard. Why not be friendly? Never know, his services may be wanted again. "I'm sorry," I murmured, looking around as if all were listening. "It's this place. You know, I mean, of course you know."

"We were breaking into a safe, " whispered Tiro with a grin as though he were taking me into his confidence. I remained silent but leaned over as if I were expecting him to whisper in my ear. "Colmes had an oxy torch cutting a hole in the safe door. Don't know if you've seen this, but the cutting throws off huge sparks. Colmes, of course, was wearing dark protective glasses. I was kneeling right next to him and just as the big hole was done, the torch gave off a huge spark and it hit me in the eyes."

Tiro stopped, expecting my response.

Naturally, I was speechless. "You, you mean you and Colmes, you were, he was, I mean…" I stuttered.

"And that's what blinded me," continued Tiro, acting as though he had merely told me the weather forecast.

I leaned heavily back in my chair. The legs squeaked on the

polished floor. Tiro grinned. I took a deep breath, and looked at him now, more closely. I realized then that there is so much that is lost about a person when they are dressed in bland prison garb like all other inmates. Still, I could imagine him all dressed in civvies. It would not be unlike Colmes—sorry for the double negative—a kind of dapper Victorian outfit, nicely ironed gray lightly striped pants, tweed jacket perhaps, cream shirt with broad tie knotted loosely. A monocle perhaps. I smiled inwardly at this fit of silliness. Being in a prison did things to me. But the face would be the same. A tiny face and head, grizzled features behind a gray beard, trimmed to a medium length. And, though he was sitting, I had noticed as he walked in that he was very short, and bandy. So short that my mind, now almost out of control, shot a vision into my eyes of Colmes and Tiro as a Laurel and Hardy couple. Then it occurred to me that Tiro's build was rather like my own. Short, wiry and nimble. I was unable to hold back a grin.

"You think that's funny?" asked Tiro.

And now I had to wonder, how did he know that I grinned? He's blind, isn't he? Or maybe not? Though I have heard that blind people develop a sixth sense or whatever. Probably a popular lie. I nervously found myself rubbing the palms of my hands with my fingers and then remembered the piece of paper that Tiro had passed to me.

"Flower," said Tiro in a loud voice. I looked at him with consternation. "It is the key to any gardener, is that not right?" he added.

I looked at the piece of paper on which was written SAGINAHOR, letters scrawled roughly as though written with one's eyes closed.

"That's what you said before," I muttered.

"Said what?" Tiro asked.

"Sagi Nahor!" I said loudly, and everyone looked around.

"Shhhh!" whispered Tiro. "It means 'perfect light' and other things as well."

"So?" I asked getting back to my impatient self.

"Colmes says he has a friend in your university computing center," whispered Tiro. "If FLOWER doesn't work, and there's a good chance it won't, tell him to use SAGINAHOR."

"All right," I mumbled. I didn't really get it.

"You will need FLOWER to enter. You can get his username from the University of Chicago's web site, believe it or not. That professor, he is a wolf of a man, that is for sure," said Tiro with his big bearded grin.

I repeated everything over and over. I had no writing implements or paper upon which to write because they took everything at security. And there was a good chance they would search me on my way out.

"Got it?" asked Tiro showing some concern.

"FLOWER? It's kind of obvious, isn't it? You sure it will work?" I asked.

"No I'm not. Since I entered his account, it's slightly possible that the university's security system, which is basically non-existent, picked it up and he may have changed his password."

"And that's it, then?" I said in consternation. I was about to get up and leave, sure that this guy was slightly mad and useless to us.

"No. It's not. As Colmes will tell you, you always need a backup plan. Right?" said Tiro, seeming to lean over my shoulder.

"And that is?" I asked impatiently.

"Sagi Nahor," grinned Tiro.

"I don't see it," I squinted to press home my frustration with this silly man.

"That's the password to professor Alfred Smith, a professor in the University of Chicago's department of philosophy. I looked up the listing of faculty that is also on line, and gave him a computer account. Then I copied Flower's databases into that account. There are quite a lot of them."

You can imagine. I was dumbfounded. I gulped more than once in amazement as I tried to find the words to respond. "Tiro, I don't know what to say! I'm speechless."

"Think nothing of it," he said. "Colmes and me, we go way back."

"Thank you, Tiro. Got to run!" I cried, eager to get out and write everything down so I wouldn't forget. "Thank you for your immense help, and the very best from Colmes."

I quickly departed without another word, leaving Tiro staring blankly, a grin so large one could see it through his beard.

***

Upon my return to Albany I dropped off the rental car and went straight to Colmes's office. I avoided contacting Smithy because I was not sure which way Colmes would go. Maneuver Smithy into illegally penetrating the University of Chicago computer system and thence hacking into Gardner's files, or find someone here who might take that risk? Certainly, if Smithy was caught, being an ex-con it would be good-bye for several years, especially as the woke generation that was rapidly overtaking universities were now classifying computer hacking as an act of violence and arguing that it should be punished as severely as physical violence.

I was surprised to find Colmes lying flat on the floor of his office, right where my wicker chair usually stood.

"Come, Hobson, take my chair at the desk. I will not be a moment. He was raising one leg, kept straight, a few inches or so, dropping it slowly, then the other. There he was, his late Victorian double breasted jacket still buttoned up, his suit pants folded in at the ankles with bicycle clips.

"What's going on?" I asked.

"Getting a bit weak at the knees, Hobson. A sign of aging, is it not?"

"But you used to go to the gym every day. Have you quit that too?" I asked as though I were his health advisor.

"I only go to the gym to maintain my contacts with important people, that is people who I consider important to my work. I don't exercise seriously there. Just casual" he answered, a little out of breath, his usually pale gray face now flushed at the cheeks.

"Have you been to a medical doctor?" I asked, choosing my words carefully. "I mean, are you Okay?"

"Medical Doctor? You mean Quack?" he answered looking to be challenged. "I already know what they will say. 'Reduce alcohol, reduce sugar, reduce salt, no saturated fat, eat tasteless vegetables, eat a balanced diet, drink tasteless water until it comes out of every orifice.' What kind of a life is that?"

By the time Colmes had finished that long sentence he was almost out of breath and he let his leg drop with a small bang. "Satisfied?" he snapped. "Where is Smith by the way? I asked you to bring him with you."

I stood looking down at this amusing piece of Victoriana having, for him, a temper tantrum.

"Colmes," I ordered sternly, "that's enough! Stop that silliness and get back to your desk! You look ridiculous down there." I wanted to put my hand over my mouth indicating that I was sorry I said what I said and in the manner I said it. I was standing above his head as he looked up, his eyes strained to look back over his skull.

Then to my surprise, he raised his hand and said, "help me up, Hobson." I took this to mean that he had forgiven me my insolence. Though I hoped also that he would take my advice and get himself checked out properly. I grabbed his hand and pulled him up.

"So Tiro came through?" asked Colmes as he unruffled his suit, removed the bicycle clips from his pants and sat down at his desk.

"Well, that and more. He gave me two passwords, I think."

"What does that mean, Hobson? Either he gave you passwords or he didn't"

"One is for Gardner's account. The other is for a professor Alfred Smith some random professor at University of Chicago. Tiro opened an account in his name."

"And why did he do that?" asked Colmes as he opened to his *Times* crossword.

"Just in case the Chicago University security system noticed his use of Gardner's account and changed the password."

I found myself getting annoyed again. Colmes asking all these questions as though he didn't trust me to have thoroughly carried out his instructions.

"Tiro also advised getting a computer whiz to do the job. He said that you would no doubt know someone."

"Indeed, I do," said Colmes with that satisfied tiny smirk.

"Let me guess. Cecilia," I said, with a touch of micro aggression.

"Excellent Hobs! Excellent! In a way," he said pensively, "she does what I do. She solves psychological problems of her student clients, and to do that she needs access to all kinds of information, some of it often shielded by obtrusive and excessive privacy laws. It was I who urged her, against her counselor's advice, to do a combined major in computer science and counseling."

"You would put her at harm's way? I mean, it's Dick Smith's beef. Let him take the risk."

Colmes frowned, but I could see that he too was a little worried. I continued to press the point. "After all, what do we care if Gardner is an asshole? There are hundreds or even thousands like him all over academia. Why should we stick our necks out for a chagrined graduate student like Smith, who had his paper rejected by a top journal?"

"I see your point," agreed Colmes. "Too bad we do not know whether Smith's accusations will be corroborated."

"And now we have come full circle," I sighed.

"Once again, Hobson, you are perfectly on point," praised Colmes, indeed most unusual.

We both fell silent.

Then it came to me. It was in fact so obvious I could have kicked myself for having been so preoccupied with being annoyed at Colmes for treating me like some fresh undergraduate, made worse by my impatience with Tiro.

"Tiro has done it for us," I said self-consciously.

"How? Why would he do that?" asked Colmes whom I was sure already knew the answer.

That second password, sagi nahor…"

Colmes interrupted. "Yes, perfect light, but a common saying referring to the blind, an opposite of sorts. What about it?"

"That was his password hint for the second account he opened in professor Smith's name," I continued.

"You already told me that," said Colmes looking amused.

"Well, he said that he had copied all Gardner's databases into that account, that is actually Tiro's account. So all Cecilia has to do is download the data from that account and not bother trying to enter Gardner's account at all. So there's very little risk until they discover Tiro's fake account. Which, according to Tiro is very unlikely."

"In that case, Hobson, I think we can leave Cecilia out of it, and go straight to Smith. Let him carry the burden of his resentment and urge for retribution," mused Colmes.

Why not share the risk?," I mused aloud. "Perhaps Cecilia could be on reserve in case—I am choosing my words carefully here—Smith is unable to log into Gardner's account and download his databases."

Colmes sat back in his chair his hands wide open, fingers spread apart as usual, tapping them together. Then he leaned forward and said with a determined satisfaction, "let's do it, Hobson. Arrange for Cecilia and Smith to meet us here tomorrow morning, or any time that suits them."

Had he forgotten my other point? Why pick on Gardner? Even if he is shown to have cooked the books of his database, why pick him out of thousands? Is it just his bad luck that we got him? The same as getting caught speeding? I felt a bit like the cop who hides in a laneway with a speed camera, then zips out to catch a speeder, one of many. There was no way to ignore the fact that we were, in fact, enabling Smith who was motivated, if not by revenge, by the same motivation as Gardner: It was one fewer with whom Smith must compete. I must say, there is a nice symmetry to that.

***

You can imagine how pleased I was. I had won a kind of battle, not really a battle, let's say a challenge of my Mentor, and he not only had recognized it, but was in very pleased with my performance. Of course, my successes were also his, whereas his successes were not mine, if you see what I mean. It's a matter of hierarchy as I have repeated so often throughout my cases.

I arranged for the meeting and purposely made it so that they did not meet with me prior to entering Colmes's office. We would all show up there at the appointed time, which happened to be the afternoon at 4.00 pm., about the time for afternoon tea.

So pleased was I with Colmes's recognition of my talents, I showed up in his office a little early. He did not even look up from his *Times* crossword puzzle, though I think I heard him mumble "afternoon Hobson." I walked past him through door number two to the kitchen and retrieved a chair, noisily placing it beside my wicker one. I decamped to my usual place when there were guests, in the corner on the overstuffed chair.

Then Colmes mumbled. "We'll need another chair. I asked Dunstan to join us. Just in case Smith doesn't know what to look for."

We were back to the usual. It annoyed me. Why couldn't he treat me more like an equal, I mean respect me as a colleague? Even a friend? And surely we were friends? I noisily trotted down to the kitchen and retrieved a chair, making sure to bang the legs against the wall and doorway. Colmes ignored me. I might have said something that I would later regret, when I heard the clinking of cups and saucers in the kitchen, the sure sign that Rose was preparing afternoon tea, scones with jam and cream of course.

Colmes looked up. "You better tell Rose that there will be three guests this afternoon," then went back to his crossword puzzle.

I did what I was told, then briefly slipped back to my office to retrieve my little stepping stool to use as a coffee table beside the overstuffed chair. All three guests arrived just as I was at Colmes's door. "Welcome all," I said with a forced smile, "go right in and take your places at Professor Colmes's desk." They did as requested and I sat quietly in the overstuffed chair, waiting expectantly for Colmes to acknowledge their presence, and more importantly for Rose to appear with the afternoon tea. At last, Colmes looked up from his crossword, folded the paper, and placed it carefully in his desk drawer.

"Well, now," he said, "Hobson and I have thought carefully about this venture, indeed a risky one and concluded that the safest way to move forward is for Mr. Smith here to take the first step which is to open Gardner's account using the password that we have obtained, and his username which I understand is publicly available."

Smithy interrupted. "That's no problem if you have the password. I've emailed him many times, as you might guess. He has at least two different emails, so I will try each one and hope it works. So what's the password?"

Smithy was clearly excited and champing at the bit.

To my surprise Colmes produced a small blackboard from the drawer of his desk and a piece of chalk, beckoning to me to take them.

"…write the first one down, Hobson."

I wrote in big letters FLOWER turned the blackboard around and showed it to our guests.

Cecilia raised a finger and said, "excuse me, but really, FLOWER as a password? Gardner must be pretty dumb to use a common word like that, especially with a name like Gardner."

Smith stirred in my wicker chair, and Dunstan looked on amused.

"Well, the password isn't exactly FLOWER," I called from my corner. You have to play with the letters.

Then Cecilia's cheery face lit up. "Oh, I see, this Gardner, he's a big shot, tramples on all who get in his way, right? A wolf and proud of it!"

"Exactly!" Chimed Smithy. And Dunstan even stirred a little indicating his agreement. No doubt he'd had dealings with Gardner, given his notoriety, and being an expert statistician and all. In fact, he was naturally suspicious of many at the top who were just a little too successful with their publications. Many of their papers were very ordinary, wreaking of data manipulation.

"What are you getting at, Cecilia?" asked Colmes who I am sure had already guessed what it was.

Cecilia responded quickly. "I'm thinking that he has made up his password with a word associated with his name, a gardener, what does he do? He grows flowers. Then he does what lots of people do when they are sick of using passwords they cannot remember, they simply write the favorite word backwards. And in this case FLOWER becomes REWOLF. Get it?"

"It's exactly the sort of game my inside source of these passwords would play," said Colmes, "I think you are probably right. And given my informant's own circumstances he would certainly not want to pass the actual password to Hobson here who met with him. But he also gave us a second password plus username, in case the first one failed. It is SAGINAHOR."

"Oh," chirped the now excited Smithy, "your informant is blind?"

"Well, in a way yes, he is," answered Colmes evasively, "why do you ask?

"Because it's a popular Hebrew expression that literally means perfect light, but refers to its opposite, that is blindness where there is no light," answered Smithy, glowing with pride.

Colmes nodded to me, a signal to write SAGINAHOR down beneath FLOWER on the blackboard.

"And the username?" asked Smithy.

I decided that it was time that I had my say. "You're not going to believe this, but it is the real name of a Chicago Professor of Philosophy. He apparently does not know he has a computer account. Our blind informant has now given him one," I replied with an equal amount of pride..

"So what's that for, then?" asked Smithy.

"In case you fail with the Gardner account," I quickly replied. "Besides…"

I was about to spill the beans that our blind informant had already copied all Gardner's databases into his own account, when Dunstan, who had sat quietly amused all this time, intervened.

"Let's be careful what we are talking about here. Exactly what is it that you want to download and why?" he asked.

"Gardner's been cooking the books," announced Smithy with an air of moral rectitude, "and it's time he was held to account.'"

"What, exactly does that mean?" asked Dunstan as though he were quizzing a student in a dissertation defense.

"I don't quite know yet, but I will once we have the evidence," said Smithy defensively.

I was beginning to see why Colmes invited Dunstan to attend.

"And what would you consider evidence, in fact, what will having Gardner's databases tell you?"

"Well, I will use the same statistical analysis he used to test his hypotheses and see if they come out the same."

Dunstan gave Colmes a worried look, then returned to his cross examination of Smithy.

"I seriously doubt that you will be able to find out whether he has been cooking the books, as you call it. There is already a version of Gardner's database floating around, isn't there?"

"That is correct," I said. We had a small problem relating to that database in a previous case. I glanced quickly over to Colmes, but he remained passive.

"Then maybe you should start with that?" asked Dunstan addressing Smithy, who looked a little crestfallen.

"However," I added, "our inside source says that there were several databases in Gardner's file. "Perhaps comparing the databases might reveal something?"

"It's probably worth a try," said Dunstan in a more positive light. "What you need to look for are manipulations of the sampling. And you will get that by looking at the number and pattern of missing values in each database. Obviously if you have matched samples, the way to reach a level of significance that you want, is simply to drop certain cases from your sample until your analysis produces significant results."

OK," responded Smithy. "I'll have a look at the two databases that are floating around among the students."

"Don't bother," said Dunstan, "I have consulted for both those dissertations and can tell you that they are identical. You will need more than two. Of course, if he is smart, and we all know he is, I'd be very surprised if he retained all the databases that he tried with his manipulation. Assuming, of course, that he's been cooking the books as you call it."

"I have another appointment," said Cecilia. "I don't think I am needed here anymore. Good luck and be careful!" she said cheerfully, turning to Smithy. "I don't want you coming into me all depressed."

Colmes stood, struggling a little to rise up to his full straight height. "Thank you for coming my dear. And my regards to your mom."

This left an empty chair between Smithy and Dunstan. Silence reigned as we all, I suppose, were thinking how hard it will be to get the son-of-a-bitch. Then the silence was broken by the clinking of cups and saucers and Rose the younger appeared through doorway number two, with a large tray of the essential scones with jam and cream, pot of tea. And matching cups. She placed the tray on Colmes's desk. "Help yourselves," she said with a faint smile, and quickly returned to the kitchen.

Dunstan, who had become a frequent visitor to the office, lunged forward and helped himself. Smithy sat back a little embarrassed. I could see that his eyes were almost popping out at the sight of the jam and cream.

***

I felt a little sorry for Smithy who left our meeting a little crestfallen, though the scones had cheered him up a little. Being an ex-con, he knew that he had to look after himself, and decided to wait a little until making the attempt to acquire Gardner's files. In other words, his vengefulness against Gardner had been softened by Dunstan's words of caution. Instead of rushing in and claiming to all that Gardner was cooking his data, he would wait a while then quietly access the databases, download them and examine them according to Dunstan's advice.

Unfortunately, in the time that lapsed most likely Gardner had been informed that his computer account had been hacked, since the REWOLF password did not work. Smithy quickly switched to the SAGINAHOR password of the unknowing Alfred Smith, which worked. He was suddenly confronted with a screenful of files which he proceeded to download. They were all EXCEL files, which for those unacquainted with the arcane language of Microsoft, were database files that could be opened using Microsoft's software of that name.

We need not go into the details of Smithy's search. It is enough to say that there were some thirty files, all of them a different version of the original. Fortunately, each file was dated so Smithy could roughly link particular files to particular publications of Gardner in the order as they appeared in his favorite top journals. True to Dunstan's advice, the number and location of missing values appeared in different amounts and places according to the different publications that Gardner had developed. He went back to Dunstan who helped him formulate a letter to the editors of all the ten journals in which Gardner had published, recounting the missing values patterns and questioning the veracity of Gardner's entire work. Dunstan insisted that Smithy return to Colmes and me to further discuss to whom the letter should be sent. And so we met, this time me on my wicker chair, Smithy on a kitchen chair just beside mine. This time, there would be no tea with scones. This was serious business.

Colmes looked over the draft and passed it to me. It looked awfully like a time bomb.

"Are you sure you want to go ahead with this?" asked Colmes talking almost like a father would speak to his son who was about to go to war.

Smithy sat silently, looking straight at Colmes. "I've been through a lot. You know that. Your mate in prison. I know all about him," he said in a quiet and calm voice.

This really took me by surprise. It should not have. Colmes had often said to me that there was an extensive subterranean communication system among cons and ex-cons. Nothing organized. Simply a system that emerged on its own, so to speak, kind of like when you look at droplets on top of a basin of water that seem to float aimlessly around and eventually joining up to make one large bubble then in a flash disappear into the body of water.

"Let's look at this situation carefully," said Colmes in a controlled monotone. "If you send this bombshell to the editors of the various journals, the first thing they will think about is how it will affect them. And of course, they are the final gatekeepers, so the buck, as we say, is on them. My guess is, and I admit it is a cynical one and perhaps reflects my lack of experience in this kind of humiliating exercise of submitting one's thoughts to a panel of so-called peers who mistakenly, or perhaps purposefully believe that only justice can be done when a group of superior peers passes judgment upon the work of one who is not in their club."

Good grief! I thought to myself. Is this the detached, scientific and rational mind of Colmes? His assessment seemed to be not so much cynical, as he admitted, but bore a distinct element of resentment. A chip on his shoulder, some might even say. Never, never would I have thought that of the supremely confident Colmes. Surely it was not that which drove him. I now began to worry that perhaps something was wrong with him. In fact, I had noticed his physical health appeared to be deteriorating. His trouble standing up from his swivel chair. A shortness of breath at times. And he coughed perhaps more than usual to clear his throat.

Smithy's jaw dropped as he looked back at Colmes. I saw a twinkle in his eye and could see that this small speech of Colmes had buoyed him considerably. "So you think I should do it?" he asked with an expectant grin.

"No, I do not," answered Colmes with what for him was quite an amused smile. "Rather, I think you should attack him on a playing field where the odds are a little more evenly distributed."

Smithy was puzzled, as was I. Then Colmes continued.

"You should address a brief letter to the Editor of the Chronicle of Higher Education, attaching the notes in your draft letter to the editors of the relevant journals. There, your chances are much better that you will be listened to, if not for the actual content of your case, but for the very big scandal that it will create in all of academia. There are many, many researchers in academia and elsewhere who have much to hide, isn't that so Hobson?"

This request for agreement took me by surprised. I mumbled back, "I should say so," and looked expectantly at Smithy, who sat there absolutely glowing. I could see his mind churning away.

Then Colmes leaned forward and said, "and by the way, you should sign the letter in your own name of course, but request that your name not be published with the letter, for fear of reprisals. That will create a nice atmosphere of mystery and evil."

The great satisfaction that Colmes displayed in saying this was astounding. And Smithy lapped it up. Though surely he understood that he himself was in much danger. An ex-con, accusing a superstar was unlikely to be believed.

***

Godfrey Gardner was mildly upset when he learned that his university computer account had been hacked. University computer systems are popular targets of hackers, often times by young smart-ass students doing it for the fun of it. In a way he admired them for having the guts to go for it, and looked upon the incident as a small price to pay for the immense convenience that computing systems provided, making his life much easier to collect data, analyze it in a matter of minutes instead of hours. After all, it simply required that he change his password, and the university computer authorities were always nagging their users to use passwords that had a high level of security.

On this morning, however, when he came into his office, someone had left a copy of the *Chronicle of Higher Education* on his desk. On the bottom right of the front page he saw a headline that read, "STAR PROFESSOR COOKED BOOKS, says student." Gardner picked it up carefully read the short but inflammatory article:

Albany, Monday 10, 2010. Schumaker graduate student, name withheld at his request for fear of recriminations, has accused disting-uished professor, Godfrey Gardner, University of Chicago top rated school of sociology, of having altered his databases, in particular intro-ducing missing values into certain versions of the databases according to the hypotheses he claimed to be testing. Gardner is renowned for his research on the intelligence of prison inmates, purporting to show that the I.Q. of prisoners, regardless of length of time in prison, was ten points or more lower than those of a matched sample of individuals who have never been convicted of a crime or incarcerated. Attempts to contact the professor by the *Chronicle* have so far not managed to find him in his office. We recognize that these are serious accusations and the *Chronicle* is committed to investigating this accusation to the fullest extent. To this end we have engaged the services of a nationally known statistician to look into these databases that are currently in the possession of this student who has refused to reveal how he came into possession of Gardner's databases.

Stunned, Gardner dropped the paper on his desk, and instantly his phone rang, as it would the rest of the day. But he automatically picked up the phone.

"Godfrey?" asked the voice, familiar but Gardner was not sure who it was.

"Yes, who is this?"

"Max Dunstan, Godfrey. I'm told you are in a spot of bother."

There was no love lost between these two men. Because, of course, they were in competition, even though technically speaking Dunstan was in a different field, of mathematics, though he did most of his scholarly work in the field of sociology, Gardner's sacred domain.

"No bother. I have nothing to defend. I don't know who this asshole might be, but he's going to pay for it, I'll see to that," answered Gardner. "Anyway, what business is it of yours?"

"Well, the *Chronicle of Higher Education* has hired me to invest-igate whether there is any substance to these accusations. So I thought I'd better start with you."

"Forget it, Dunstan. It's all bullshit. Why would I want to fudge my data? I'm at the top of my field. All done by publishing my work in the very best journals. If you say my work is crap, then you are saying the work of my peers who have judged my work, is also crap."

"Look Godfrey, I don't want to get into argument with you. All I need to do is to have a look at your databases and if there is nothing wrong as I'm sure will be the case, then all's good and you have nothing to worry about," assured Dunstan.

"I'm not worried about anything," answered Gardner. "My peers have judged my work A1. And that's that. As for the accusations and the rest. Bring them on. All publicity is good publicity, negative or positive, as I've said many times."

"But Godfrey, I can tell you that your accuser, and there are others, is out for your blood," warned Dunstan.

"Bring it on. It will make me even more famous, if that is poss-ible," bragged Gardner.

"Okay, if you say so," replied Dunstan. "Then would you mind sending me copies of all your databases, that is, those related to the comparison of intelligence between prisoners and non-prisoners?"

"They are not available to the public. In fact they are the property of the University of Chicago, so you will have to get permission from them. Besides, I have not written anything on that topic for some years now so have not looked at the databases. It's entirely possible that they have been routinely erased from the University's computer system."

Gardner hung up the phone, a self-satisfied smirk on his unplea-sant, closely shaven face that looked like the stamped image of a coin attached to a pink bald head.

Unbeknownst to Gardner, Dunstan, anticipating this problem, had already contacted the University of Chicago Computing system chief and established that the databases were in fact still in Gardner's account, and received the assurance that they would not be deleted unless requested by Gardner. They did, of course, refuse Dunstan's request for a copy of Gardner's databases.

In any case, the *Chronicle* followed up with a more detailed account of how the databases were manipulated by Gardner, so it seemed as though Gardner's goose was cooked, as they say. And there was worse to come.

***

It took several weeks for the editorial boards of the top ten sociology journals in America to meet and discuss the Gardner case. This was not because of the organizational challenge since boards of the journals were mostly made up of the same top ten people. And of course Gardner was one of the board of every top ten journal, and president of half of them. The delay in getting all together was caused by the reticence of several members who were busy making sure that their own databases were safely tucked away, out of sight, and certainly beyond the tentacles of any computer system.

Gardner vociferously attacked the *Chronicle* accusing them of doing the same as the burning of books in the middle ages. This had nothing to do with the issue at all, but of course that was of no concern. And the *Chronicle* immediately understood what was at stake and came very close to recanting the story.

Then came the predictable demand, that the accuser step forward and it was this demand that, incredibly, finally led to Gardner's downfall.

Naturally, Smithy had been waiting nervously on the sidelines. There was much that the media would love if they got their hands on it. Dunstan, complicit in the release of the accusation, appointed to evaluate the accusation. An ex-con who was the accuser. A shadowy figure (Colmes) who orchestrated the entire plot, and the illegal hacking of the

University of Chicago's computing system by the accuser's confederate a current inmate in the local prison.

The climax came when, in an attempt to sway public opinion, Gardner agreed to a TV interview for the *Chicago Evening News,* which had, as had other news media, picked up from the *Chronicle* article. Throughout the interview, Gardner repeated many times how many publications he had, and how he was at the top of his profession, and how, if the media listened to the secret accuser, who obviously carried a grudge of some kind, the entire system of peer review would collapse and we would then never again be able to believe the research published in scientific journals. The entire edifice of knowledge and science was under attack!

At this climactic point of the interview, Gardner turned to face the red light of the camera and said with a deep voice and a haughty very serious face:

"I demand that this scurrilous accuser step forward and act like a man, not like a pathetic frightened little girl! Stand behind his accusations and take what is coming to him!"

The camera instantly switched back to the interviewer, a seasoned reporter of many years' experience.

"And there you have it," she said looking into the camera. "You decide!"

Fade and Out, as they say.

The next day Gardner was invited to meet with the University of Chicago's President where he was fired for his inappropriate sexist comment on prime time television, an offence that required the swift and severe punishment that matched it.

Dessert had been served.

17. The Slap

Physical objects, family heirlooms, for example, come with memories and sometimes stories attached. As they are passed from one generation to the other, their handlers can effortlessly add their embellishments, shaping the past into an understandable journey into a present that logically, it seems, leads to a future. Family photographs and portraits offer the same promise, and when connected to ancestry charts, provide some comfort for those who are convinced that, because there is a structured past, it must lead to a structured future. That future, however, cannot be known until it has passed.

I begin this case in this silly philosophical manner—I am after all a student of philosophy—because I have had to rely on the recollections of Colmes concerning this entire case for it occurred well before I joined him as his research assistant. A number of the other cases I have described relied somewhat on Colmes's recollections, although they were, mostly, cases in which I may have been tangentially involved. Furthermore, this case is of considerable interest because it was probably the first case that Colmes "solved" (a bit of an exaggeration), but certainly one that led him into the permanent role of problem solver for the university.

The case occurred in the 1970s in a class that Finneas O'Brien was teaching. He was then a professor who had been acting Dean of the School of Criminal Justice, and was about to be made permanent. A decade after that, he would become the President of Schumaker university. This was also in the era when the Schumaker School of Criminal Justice was establishing itself as the top criminal justice program in America (there were only two or three others to compete with), and prided itself as the pioneer that actually invented the entire academic discipline of criminal justice. It was not a leader in its field. It *was* the field. At least that is how Finneas O'Brien portrayed it, and there was little or no opposition to this brazen self-promotion both of the School, and himself, being especially new to academia, who had never written a dissertation. (Okay, no snide remarks, that maybe there's hope for me yet).

One of the interesting outcomes of this self-portrayal of the School was that it excitedly embraced all things new, not so much in criminal justice since the school itself was the icon of new-ness. Rather, it looked farther afield for ideas and research that could be imported into this new field, and those ideas naturally came from its academic siblings, the social sciences (including law, though Ted the Red would not agree, certain that Law was a cut above and certainly wiser and more logical compared with the social sciences). One of those ideas, or rather fads we might call them now, was a new way of teaching, probably based on the popularity of Rogerian therapy whose single principle of therapeutic technique was to repeat as a kind of question exactly what the patient said. So if a patient said, "I have a terrible headache," the therapist would respond, "terrible headache?" and so on.

The new way of classroom teaching was called a T-Group. It went one step further than Rogerian therapy. The whole idea was to empower students to talk. The teacher was simply, one might say, a "sounding board."

Now those of you who are or have been teachers or have worked with or within groups in various capacities will find this quite surprising. Imagine going into a class—a graduate class of bright students, the professor famous in his own right, in which the professor sits down with the group of around a dozen—and starts the class without saying anything. Not even telling them "this is a T-group Class" or "This is a T-group class, and it's up to you to speak, not the professor."

Those of you who have ever taught a class no matter at what level, would know that one must prepare for a class. Many teachers are very conscientious and have reams of notes and class lessons planned. Others wing it a little, but there is always some kind of syllabus or description of what topics the class will cover. Such preparations were dismissed by the proponents of T-groups on the grounds that they unnecessarily interfered with the initiative of the students. They argued that the whole goal of teaching was to get students to think for themselves, regardless of what the subject matter was.

I should also add that, to the extent Colmes described it, there was quite a lot of sniggering and criticism of O'Brien for teaching this class. This was because his fellow faculty came, with the occasional exception, from the criminal justice world, and therefore held a low opinion of anything that sniffed like hand-holding. According to Colmes, the rest of the faculty thought that the new teaching method came from O'Brien's academic background which was a masters degree in social work. Forget about the fact that he had run Sing-Sing prison for a decade! Social workers were hand-holders and hand-wringers. And that was what T-Groups were all about.

Events would show that it was not quite like that.

***

Teachers also know that you can walk into a classroom and within a few minutes or less, get a feeling for the atmosphere of a class. The atmosphere is essentially set by the teacher who is the acknowledged expert. That is, in academia especially, it is the professor who is assumed to contain the reservoir of knowledge, the students the sponges that are supposed to absorb it. There are certain signs and signals that one can depend upon; in fact, often these signs impart the atmosphere of the entire university.

The classic sign is the presence of a mini rostrum, an immovable lectern upon which the professors place their lecture notes, room behind it so that the professor may walk back and forth and around the rostrum, keeping a safe distance from the audience that, in its most developed form, appears as a theater. Indeed, many universities call them theaters. Which they are, of course, inviting the lecturer to play the part of expert, entertainer (to hold the students' attention) and messenger of the truth. If this sounds a little like going to church, this is no accident. The majority of modern universities have their roots in ancient religious orders, monks of a variety of religions, cloistered away, nestling with the knowledge that they believe to be the truth. Protecting it from the masses, imparting it only to the chosen.

In a complex way, the same system dominates universities. Certain examinations and accomplishments are required by all universities for entry (unless they are completely open, a system experimented with on occasion but usually abandoned as unrealistic). In the 1970s it was totally and completely impossible to accept the assertion by the generation of students of the Vietnam War era that chimed "never trust anyone over thirty." There were very few professors in the 1970s, at least full professors, who were under 30.

But unlike the direct attacks on authority of the Vietnam War protests, the more insidious attack came in the form of a viral infection that quietly entered universities under a number of guises. The T-group was one such virus, spreading the doubtful ideas of the progressive psychiatrists of the time, translated into the classroom by teachers who perhaps had become disillusioned by the unrealistic expectations of their students. After all, professors were expected not only to produce new knowledge, but to impart old knowledge to an audience whose motto was "out with the old."

I relate all of this just as Colmes told it to me. Today I have the advantage of hindsight and can write up the case dispassionately, at least I hope so. You may be surprised that, when Colmes was telling me all this he was quite excited—for him that is. I wanted to ask him whether he was involved in the Vietnam War, but I could never get up the courage to ask. I hoped that one day he would open up to me. In fact, much of his past is just as much a mystery to me, as it is to his opponents in the university of whom there are many, as I have at various times noted in other cases.

So now, imagine yourself in a classroom that is small with about thirty chairs set up in rows, arranged with the expectation that the professor will stand at the lectern out front, backed by a blackboard that runs the full length of the classroom. It is there that the professors will write the most important points they make as they lecture. If the professor is a stickler for time and the quantification of knowledge, they will disallow any questions during the lecture and only, if pressed, allow questions at the small amount of time saved at the end of the lecture.

On this day, the third meeting of the class, the students trickled in. The last two meetings were disbanded after fifteen to twenty minutes of silence in which no student spoke. The students entered the classroom sauntering to-and-fro choosing a chair and then trying to set it up where a circle of chairs will be arranged. At last a more assertive student enters and takes charge of setting up twelve chairs in a circle. O'Brien always comes at least five minutes late, thus forcing the students to arrange themselves without his having to assert his authority. He enters the classroom and finds that the students have seated themselves leaving one chair empty, obviously for him, thus acknowledging his place of authority at the "head" of the designated circle.

O'Brien limps in, leaning heavily on his walking stick, walks into the center of the circle—a mistake, or seeming so because it made him the sole focus of attention. Authority was very hard to get rid of! He glances around the circle of students, goes to the empty chair and with some difficulty lifts it up and takes it across to the other side of the circle and tries to push it in. The students of course, make room and there is a loud clatter and echoing dings as the metal legs of the chairs scrape on each other and on the linoleum covered floor. He hangs his walking stick over the back of his chair and there he sits, expressionless, though his intense gray eyes scan the circle of students.

Silence.

Not even a giggle as there were in the last two sessions.

***

All of the above is how Colmes described it to me. Then, as if to emphasize the event, Colmes actually jumped up out of his chair and started walking back and forth telling me what happened next, throwing his long arms around as if he were announcing the winner of a wrestling match. I was on the edge of my wicker chair, just as excited as was he. But then he stopped, with a mischievous gleam in his eyes, and stood in front of me, his hands on his hips looking down.

"Now those twelve students," he said, "they were a moribund lot. Pathetic! That's how Finneas described them."

"Before or after this supposedly memorable event?" I asked having trouble to hide my sarcasm.

"Before, Hobson, of course before!" said Colmes loudly. "And he told me there was only one that looked like she had any go in her, but even she never said anything."

I was about to ask him who that might be, but he suddenly began walking to-and-fro again.

"You know, Hobson, everyone said he brought it on himself," Colmes cried with a frown. "It was nothing of the sort. Nothing of the sort!" Colmes gesticulated. I thought I even detected a little sweat on his forehead.

"Colmes! Calm down. What's got into you?" I said in my most brotherly voice.

"So they called me in," said Colmes, still walking back and forth.

"What for, Colmes? You still haven't told me what happened. The event, Colmes. The event!" Now I was getting worked up.

Colmes stopped right in front of my wicker chair, leaned down and said right in my face, "she slapped him!" He raised his right hand and swung at to my face, stopping so that I received just a little tap.

I recoiled in horror. For a moment I thought—how could I have thought?— that he had slapped me over the face.

"Yes, Hobson, you have experienced the terrible event. After some twenty minutes of silence, and by the way Finneas had told me that this time he had resolved to sit there the whole three hours if he had to until a student talked."

Then a young woman somewhat older than the other students stood up noisily from her chair walked purposefully across to him from the opposite side of the circle of students, raised her hand and gave him a hard, sharp slap over the face, so hard it knocked off his glasses, he almost fell off the chair, and his walking stick flew off the back of the chair and fell to the floor with a clatter."

"Good god!," I exclaimed.

"And that's not all," continued Colmes more quietly and measured.

"She dropped her knitting when she hit him."

"Oh no!" I gasped. "Rose! It was Rose the elder!"

"Indeed, indeed," nodded Colmes as he went back to sit at his desk. "But that's not the end of it," continued Colmes, "it's more like the beginning of it." Colmes stopped, waiting for my predictable question.

"Really? Then what happened next? Certainly so far I am puzzled how you came to be involved," I politely asked.

"Mind you," warned Colmes, "I surely don't have to remind you that I have put together this description of the event from talking to the students who were in the classroom when it all went down."

"Go on, Colmes! Damn you!" I nagged. "Next! What happened next?"

"There is some disagreement about what happened next, both from the rest of the students who were there, and from Rose and O'Brien. Anyway, the outcome was that Rose's face collided with O'Brien's walking stick as it flew off the back of the chair and broke her nose. The campus ambulance was called, and well, you have seen the rest. She ended up with a bit of a beak nose. The bone was smashed in several places. She had some sort of calcium deficiency that weakened the bones in her face, especially her nose."

"And she sued?" I guessed.

"Not quite!" answered Colmes teasing me no doubt.

"Colmes come on! Tell me the whole damn story," I pleaded.

"Finneas claims that he grabbed at the walking stick to steady himself and save him falling off the chair and on to the floor," said Colmes sitting back in his chair. "And Rose claimed that he wasn't trying to steady himself, that he clearly grabbed the walking stick and swung it directly at her face. It was certainly a terrible blow, according to Rose and some of the other students."

"So I can understand Rose thinking that O'Brien did it on purpose. What about the students?" I asked.

"As one would expect," answered Colmes. "Those dressed as males believed O'Brien's version. Those dressed as females agreed with Rose."

"If they thought he did it on purpose, did they call the cops?" I persisted.

"One of them called the campus police, who then called the campus ambulance. The medics came instantly, loaded Rose into the ambulance and took her off to the hospital, which is where I first met her," answered Colmes, a slight wistfulness in his voice.

I regretted pressing him so hard. I had not fully appreciated how much Rose meant to him, and she had passed away quietly a couple of years before Colmes told me of this case.

"Rose called you, to get advice on seeing O'Brien?" I persisted.

"Not at all. It was my old friend Finneas who called me in to manage the case and save all from embarrassment."

"You mean, just out of the blue? You were then one of the regular teaching faculty?" I asked a little astonished.

"Good god no!" exclaimed Colmes. "I thought you knew that we became friends when he was warden of Sing-Sing. I helped him deal with a lot of very nasty cases of crime and violence in and out of the prison.

"So, because it looked like a case of violence, the first person he thought of was you?" I asked with an approving voice.

"Probably," mused Colmes, "probably."

Colmes stood up from his desk and started to walked around the room again. I could tell that he was irritated, that maybe he regretted describing this case to me.

"We can stop there if you want," I said to Colmes, putting aside my laptop. He ran his hand through his thinning hair, and was about to continue, I think, when Rose the younger appeared at doorway two with afternoon tea.

"It sounded like you needed this," she said with a most endearing smile.

"My dearest Rose," said Colmes as a father would to a daughter, "indeed we do." His Irish eyes twinkled a little, though his entire demeanor was quite subdued, even sad, I thought.

"Would you mind if I joined you?" asked Rose, putting down the tray in front of Colmes, and producing her knitting from her hair bundled on top of her head. "I have heard most of what you have been telling Hobson. Perhaps it has something to do with why I am here?" she asked mischievously.

"Here, take my wicker chair, and I will sit in the corner where I belong," I said half-jokingly.

"Now, now Hobson. No whining…" scolded Colmes.

I was about to answer, "I'm not whining," and fall into the trap of behaving like a pouting child, but stopped myself just in time.

Rose took her seat on my wicker chair, we all poured our tea from the floral teapot and our cups clinked on their saucers.

Colmes folded his arms, a sign some say, of defensiveness.

"Come on Colmes," I said showing off to Rose, "out with it. How were you involved, how did it become one of your favorite cases?"

Colmes looked across to Rose, I have to say, a kind of prideful glow in those Irish eyes. I looked at Rose and decided that she also had those gray Irish eyes, did she not? Why was it that I was only now noticing this obvious detail after having talked and worked with Rose the younger for quite some time. I tried to remember the color of Rose the elder's eyes, but admittedly I could not. Then I realized that it was difficult to make out the color of Rose the elder's eyes because she applied considerable powder and makeup to cover over her wrinkled face, and her cheeks were permanently swollen as though she had been hit hard in the nose and face by a football. I wondered whether this may have anything to do with O'Brien's walking stick.

Colmes leaned forward and continued his story. "According to

Finneas and some other students who were willing to speak to me in private, Rose, after slapping Finneas hard over the face, was still inexplicably angry, and lunged at the walking stick. Finneas made a grab for it, but he was hampered without his glasses. His open hand grabbed instead a handful of Rose's breast, she screamed and pushed it away, and Finneas lost his balance, gripped her woolen skirt or dress or whatever it was, and pulled her down with him, she hitting her nose on the metal chair leg, the two of them ending up on the floor, Finneas half on top of her, his left hand still gripping her breast, his knee bent up in between her legs."

Now I could see where this was leading. Colmes coughed a little to clear his throat, and took a sip of his cup of tea.

"My poor old mom," cried Rose.

"She wasn't so old then," smiled Colmes and continued his story. "As it happened, I was a volunteer medic for the campus health service and I heard the call come in, but it was not my turn on ambulance duty, so I didn't think much of it. Soon after that, I received a call from Finneas asking me if I had heard anything. I asked, 'like what?' and he told me of the accident...."

Colmes stopped again, and took another sip of his tea. And then continued. "Finneas asked me to go to the hospital and make sure Rose was okay. She was a recent immigrant from Russia and probably had no one to look out for her. She was a bit older than the rest of the students so probably had no close friends."

"That was nice of him," said Rose with a sweet smile, as Colmes continued.

"I did as he requested and found Rose stuck in a cubicle in the emergency department of the hospital. She was in a kind of delirium, maybe caused by the drugs the medics gave her in the ambulance. Unfortunately, she was calling out in her loud Russian accented voice that she had been raped. She tried to get up from the bed but fell back. Her face was barely visible under the bandages, now stained with blood, wound around her head to cover her nose, which, as it turned out was broken into many pieces. Naturally, when the medics heard the cry of rape, they rushed into the cubicle, pulling back the curtain that separated it from the rest of the emergency department. 'O'Brien! That piece of shit! He tried to rape me!' she cried."

"Oh my God!" cried Rose the younger.

"The medic who entered was soon joined by the campus cop, Larry Cordner. You know him, of course, Hobson," said Colmes.

"Indeed I do," I replied.

"Fortunately," continued Colmes carefully, "well, for this particular case I mean. In those days there was no such thing as a 'rape kit' or any set procedure for recording the complaints or accusations of rape by alleged victims. And Rose was holding her crotch and calling out Rape! Rape! I looked at Cordner and told him that as far as I knew, there had been an accident in her class, that she had in fact attacked the professor completely out of the blue, they had both fallen down on to the floor and she banged her nose on the metal leg of the chair. There were twelve students in the class at the time, two of whom had informed me of the accident. "

This last part, of course was a lie, but I trusted Finneas's account that it would be accurate."

"And my mom? What did she do next? Or more accurately, what did you bastards do to her next?" asked Rose, knitting furiously.

"The medic gave her an injection that calmed her down, and as she dozed off she asked for her knitting. And it was at that point that I knew she was going to be okay," answered Colmes.

"And that's it?" I asked.

"Pretty much. After she dropped out of consciousness, the medic gave her a quick examination—Cordner and I turned our backs of course—and concluded that there was no evidence of rape. However, the accusation of rape was almost as bad as the real thing, against a person like Finneas, upwardly mobile as he was. So I stayed by Rose, and eventually convinced her that no good would become of publicizing this accusation, that it was made during a period of delirium. Cordner informed the medic that he would take all necessary steps to investigate the rape charge, thus relieving the medic of any responsibility for the accusation. After all, Cordner was the police. And that was it."

"You mean the medic examined her while she was out to it? Without her permission?" asked Rose the younger with a gasp of disbelief.

"Things have changed," muttered Colmes.

Rose and I looked expectantly at Colmes. "Perhaps there is a little more you could tell us, Colmes? Especially for Rose here. It was her mum after all…" I immediately regretted my condescending manner.

"My word, Hobson, you are becoming quite offensive. I hope this is not an indication of what you will be like after I'm gone," said Colmes, with the tiny hint of a smile.

"What? You're not…." I stuttered.

"Of course not. My dear Hobson, you do take things much too seriously," said Colmes as he smiled a bigger smile and looked directly at Rose, who looked up from her knitting and returned her much sweeter smile.

Colmes continued. "As I know you both must have observed, I was much attracted to Rose. She was admitted into the hospital and they did extensive surgery to repair her nose that was broken in many places. I stayed with her night and day, read Tolstoy to her—his *Confessions* she liked very much, though I don't much care for them myself—then took her home here, in my office-come-home, which was built out of the generosity of my dear friend Finneas in appreciation of my having saved him from the dishonor that probably would have destroyed his chances of becoming president."

"So you really are my Dad," muttered Rose as she put down her knitting, the needles in her hair, and began gathering up the cups and saucers. And as she leaned over to take Colmes's cup, he gently took her hand and pulled her to him, then kissed her lightly and gently on her cheek.

"Indeed, indeed," he said.

18. A Rape Advantage

Obviously, the heart of any university is its faculty. That is, the professors, and of course their underlings, the teaching assistants without whom all universities would collapse. The T.A's who are paid well below any estimate of a minimum wage, do most of the grudge work of teaching. That is, assisting in lectures to the undergraduates, often in classes of a couple of hundred, dealing with the complaints and nuisance questions, and acting as the professors' secretary and gatekeeper, protecting them from the hordes of student that they so much deplore, yet cannot survive without them. This unfortunate circumstance is especially the case in what are classified as "research universities" where the supposed overriding mission of the university is to publish research, become the recognized authority on particular subjects. Translated into common language that everyone can understand, what this comes down to is money.

The most successful professors write research proposals and submit them to the many grant giving organizations, whether it be private (e.g. the Ford Foundation, Rockefeller Foundation etc. etc.) or the most likely source, the Federal and state governments. Massive amounts of money are funneled into universities, much of it to research assistants (who may also teach because they must have some teaching experience in their resume if they want to go on to a successful career in academia).

Finally, there is also a very well established practice in Research Universities, for professors who get large research grants, to "buy out" their teaching time. The rules about how many courses one may buy out vary according to universities and even departments. So you can see the very strange situations into which students innocently step, especially ambitious graduate students. The university is there to educate students, without whom there would be no point in having a university. Yet, its faculty in general (there are many exceptions, and there are private "teaching colleges" that do not do research and are proud of their teaching) are mostly annoyed by the presence of students, especially undergraduates whom they consider it beneath them to teach. Again, this is why graduate students "Teaching Assistants" bear much of the teaching load of a university.

I began this case with this very short outline of who "the faculty" are, because one can see that the entire setting is a very competitive environment in which professors compete for (a) money and (b) recognition. It is no wonder that, during the student protests in the late 1960s and early 1970s, students demanded a voice on faculty meetings and committees. Little did they know what they were asking for.

This is also another case for which I do not have first-hand information. It occurred at a time before I came under Colmes's tutelage, so I have had to rely on his recollections. It occurred when Finneas O'Brien was not yet President, but was the Dean of the School of Criminal Justice. It is also one of the strangest cases because it revolved around a most unusual issue concerning the Dean's appointment.

At the end of the school year, it was the custom for the faculty of the school to meet and discuss the Dean's performance and decide whether or not they should be allowed to continue on in their position for the following year. When I have mentioned this to others in academia they have responded in disbelief. Yet all the senior faculty (of course they were the only ones whose votes really counted, though this case suggests otherwise) were adamant that this annual assessment of the Dean's performance was clearly stated in the school's bylaws. Though, as Colmes informed me, he was never able to locate a copy of the school's bylaws and came to the conclusion that there were none, at least none written down.

In fact, this was a strange faculty. Colmes told me that the senior faculty also asserted quite some weight and that they had every year refused to allow the Dean to teach, on the grounds that he was not up to standard either in terms of teaching or in his academic prowess (no publications in top journals). Even Colmes expressed his astonishment at this apparently routine practice of the senior faculty who every year in the annual assessment of the Dean issued this mandate.

And now, to our case.

It occurred in the first year of Finneas O'Brien's Deanship having moved into the position after serving on the teaching faculty. It also came in the year after that difficult case of *The Slap* that I described previously. And so in the final faculty meeting of the year, after having dealt with the various topics and issues concerning students, and reports from the several committees—the student performance committee, the undergraduate curriculum committee, the graduate curriculum committee, the promotion and tenure committee, the library committee, the planning committee, the computing center committee—the question of the Dean's performance was placed on the table by the chair of the faculty, Morris Fartsworth, a rotund, jolly fellow, according to Colmes, who had trouble taking anything seriously. And perhaps he was just the right person to chair a faculty that was about to make an assessment of the Dean's performance, on the basis it seems, totally unrealistic and surely against all administrative rules and regulations, that they, the faculty, had the power to dismiss the Dean should they decide that his performance was not up to scratch. It seemed, according to Colmes, that the faculty was on the verge of sacking Finneas, for vague reasons, supposedly about his former teaching (remember the case of *The Slap*) but truly was more about the refusal of the Dean to submit to the Provost their relentless requests for increases in their already bloated salaries.

Of course, this Dean assessment was totally irregular and ran against the entire establishment of the university system. The only person who had the power to sack, or for that matter to hire, a Dean was the President of the university. But, reported Colmes, these faculty were very proud of the fact that they carried out this annual assessment of the Dean's performance for it demonstrated their complete devotion to democratic ideals, that it was the faculty who must take charge of the education of their students, not a single authority, a dictator if you like, such as a Dean who was routinely appointed by the administration. It was the faculty's right, they asserted, because they understood much better the needs of the students, and they conducted the research that provided the financial needs of the university. Of course, the hypocrisy of this most moral assertion was that the majority of these professors brought in as much research money as they could to buy out their courses and thus avoid teaching the students that they morally claimed was their first priority.

So said Colmes, with that superior smirk of his own. And as a long time student, I have to agree with him, though I can also see the other side of it, that universities would collapse if it were not for the use of slave-like graduate students to teach a good portion of the classes. But that is another issue for another day.

"We now move on to our final topic, the annual Dean's assessment," announced Fartsworth with vigor and a big smile.

"Point of order," requested a junior professor who sat away from the big table and in a corner of the room. She knew her place.

Fartsworth leaned to the side so that he could see who it was. "Yes, and what point is that?" he asked again with a grin.

"My point is that this Dean is a known rapist and should be drummed out of the university immediately," she answered.

There was much scraping of shoes on the wooden floor, as all those sitting around the large conference table squirmed and tried to think of reasons why they were not asking to be heard. In fact, no one responded to the young professor's demand.

The chair responded, as was his duty. "I do not believe that you have actually raised a point of order, because we have not begun discussion so that there is no point to request an order for," garbled Fartsworth. This answer generally received a positive response in the form of mumbles of 'here, here' and so on.

"I second that motion," called out a student representative.

"There is no motion for you to second," retorted Fartsworth, his big brown eyes and jolly round face enjoying this silliness.

"OK," said the assistant professor from her seat in the corner. "I move that the Dean be sacked immediately, because he is a rapist."

"I second the motion," called the student.

"Discussion?" asked Fartsworth, still jolly, regardless of the shocking circumstances.

Ted the Red a very full professor (you remember him, a mate of Finneas) stirred his long lanky body and in his deep gravelly voice said, "I move that the two student representatives at this meeting be requested to leave as the bylaws to not allow students to vote on the hiring or firing of professors. They are not qualified to make such a judgment upon our professorial peers."

"Is there a second to that motion?" asked Fartsworth.

"Point of order," called the young professor in the corner, "we have not finished out discussion of the previous motion."

The jolly chairman now became a little less jolly. In fact, according to Colmes (by the way, how did he know about this since he was not in that faculty meeting at the time?), his face went red, not from jolliness, but from frustration. "I ask again," he said, ignoring the young professor, "is there a second to that motion to remove the students from this meeting?"

"Second," called another young professor who sat at the table right next to Ted the Red. It was clear that he had decided to hitch his sails to that renowned professor.

"All those in favor?" called the chair, with quite some relish. The students stayed in their places at the table, showing no signs of leaving.

All faculty except the young professor in the corner called "aye"

"Wait a minute!" she called loudly. You can't do that! What about discussion?"

"Not needed," answered Fartsworth with a very big grin. "As chair, I respectfully request the students to leave this meeting."

All eyes were on the students. They did not budge.

"This is disgusting!" cried the young professor in the corner. "You'll never hear the end of this!" she yelled and got up to leave.

The meeting was suddenly at the point of pandemonium . "You better leave or I'll throw you out," threatened professor Garcia (you remember, Ted the Red) moving out of his chair and leaning towards the students. The chairman Fartsworth leaned over and grabbed his arm. "That would not be wise," he said, but still quite jolly. "I order this meeting to come to order!" he cried, now grinning at himself really, when he looked around the room and saw that no one was listening to anyone, and everyone was calling out and some even swearing. Some jumped up to leave and their chairs noisily flew backwards. Now there was pandemonium.

The young professor hesitated at the door, in a way rather pleased that she had caused this, then opened the door to leave, whereupon she almost ran into Colmes who stood at the doorway and, so he says, immediately everything stopped and all stood or sat where they were, gaping at him as he eased his way past the young professor. According to Colmes (doubtful) some of the meeting participants seemed a little embarrassed for allowing the pandemonium to develop, but others took his presence as an intrusion, though how Colmes divined that, I do not know.

In any case, Colmes muttered with that slight condescending smile of his, "I hope I am not interrupting something?"

"I jolly well hope so!" exclaimed the relieved and jolly again chair, "do come and join us, and let us all be seated."

The meeting participants were so flustered by these events, the presence of Colmes, his tall Victorian demeanor in his tightly buttoned double breasted suit, overwhelming all with a sense of decorum, that they obediently and quietly took their seats again. Colmes chose to sit with the young professor in her corner away from the table. He raised a finger to get the Chair's attention and politely said, in his fake English accent, "May I address the meeting briefly? I know that my presence here is a surprise to you all as you were not forewarned..."

"It is a little unusual. But I do not think there is anything in the bylaws that forbids our listening to a visitor if the issue is of some importance and relevance to our deliberations," answered Fartsworth in his best chairmanship manner. Of course, Colmes would say that no doubt Fartsworth was inspired by his Victorian presence (as I would characterize it).

***

Now what Colmes said next, I insist is exactly what he told me. This I was careful to write down verbatim as he talked, puffing one of his favorite cigarillos and sipping an Old English Sherry.

"I was seduced by the charge of rape," announced Colmes.

The room fell silent. The young professor shifted away from him as though this information had made him unclean. All sat still, seemingly mesmerized by this outrageous announcement. He waited for what seemed like many minutes, but was really only a few seconds. Though it was enough to have all in the room sitting on the edge of their seats, hoping for him to say something even more terrible.

"The young professor here," said Colmes turning to her, who now sat leaning away from him her arms folded tightly across her chest, "what is your name my dear?"

"Gloria Watkins," she answered compliantly, but with a look of terror in her blue eyes, her pale blond face reddened from a mixture of embarrassment and anger.

"Yes. How nice. Well now professor Watkins, let me assure you that no rape was ever committed or contemplated by your Dean Finneas O'Brien."

"Goodness me!" I said to Colmes, as I wrote furiously to record everything accurately, "surely she got up and slapped you or something." But Colmes did not even bother to answer me because he knew that I knew that she was cowed sitting right next to the proud, self-assured and condescending Colmes.

"The victim, that is how you think of her I am sure, was never raped by Finneas O'Brien although they were indeed in close contact when, and I emphasize this, that she, Rose Kolzakova, slapped him hard across the face knocking off his glasses and causing him to fall from the chair as he grabbed for his walking stick to save himself...."

"Yes, Yes, we've heard all about that," interrupted one of the student representatives. "She said she was raped and that's that. We don't need any more proof."

This blatant assertion that ignored the rule of law stirred Ted the Red into action. "Need I repeat, presumption of innocence, reasonable doubt..."

"Blah, blah, blah..." broke in Professor Watkins, "you men, you use the law to hide your disgusting deeds."

"Order, order! "called chairman Fartsworth. "This is not a trial, it is a discussion. Please show our guest some respect. Continue Professor Colmes."

"Bull shit!" yelled professor Watkins, "there were twelve students in the room and eight of them said O'Brien raped her. That's all the evidence we need to tell our upright Dean that we no longer require his services."

"If I may continue?" asked Colmes, now standing and, as I can imagine, he began to walk around the meeting room. "I would like to get back to my opening remark. Seduction. It is the key to this entire series of events. Perhaps none of you know that it was I who was called in to the unfortunate event, and it was I who accompanied Rose Kolzakova in the ambulance to the hospital, and it was I who stayed with her during her entire time in hospital, which was several days and nights while she had surgery to mend her very broken nose. And let me quickly add that Professor O'Brien did not break her nose, but that she hit it on the metal chair leg as she fell down..."

"She was raped," insisted the angry Professor Watkins, "otherwise why would she suddenly get up in front of the entire class and attack him? She must have had a reason, and what other reason can one think of than having been raped by a well-known predator."

"But she was not raped in the class," insisted Colmes who indicated to me that he regretted his mistake of entering into her line of argument, when it was so obviously false.

Inevitably, Watkins retorted, "so you don't deny it? She was raped and so took it out on O'Brien in class. It was supposed to be a therapy group after all, and that was her therapy." Professor Watkins was sounding more and more confident.

Then Fartsworth thought it was time he said something. "We are not really getting anywhere. What is it that you had to say? Why did O'Brien ask you to address us?"

Colmes walked to what was somewhere at the head of the table and stood beside Fartsworth. "The fact is that I fell in love with Rose the minute I sat beside her in the ambulance on its way to hospital. She kept crying rape! rape! And I kept comforting her. It was the way she said it, and the way she talked when she woke from a deep sleep after her first surgery. Her rough deep voice, her marvelous Russian accent, her no-nonsense approach to life, her obvious toughness having survived impossible living conditions in St. Petersberg her original home, and above all, her knitting. Rape! Rape! What else can one ask of a woman?"

"You said that?" I asked Colmes in disbelief. "You actually said that?"

"Hobson, Indeed. Indeed I did, or close to it. Doesn't it make you proud to be my apprentice?"

Quite frankly, I still do not believe it. But anyway, it must have worked, because no one apparently stirred, they were spellbound by his small if slightly offbeat love story. Even Professor Watkins appeared to be moved.

Colmes continued. And here was the bombshell.

"When Rose was well enough to leave the hospital, I called for a cab and we drove to a small Russian orthodox church where I had arranged for the local Ukrainian priest to marry us. And we have lived happily together since in my apartment that happens to be on campus."

I was stunned. But I should not have been. I had of course assumed that they were a couple for as long as I could remember. I just never knew that they were married, and a religious ceremony to boot!

The faculty apparently were even more stunned. Technically, of course, it was a no-no for a professor to have sex with a student. But getting married seemed to be a widely accepted solution to that no-no.

"And O'Brien?" I asked. "Did they sack him as Dean?"

"Well, that's the amusing part of the story, Hobson. O'Brien had given me the task and the letters to go with it, to inform the faculty at the meeting that he had negotiated with the Provost an ironclad commitment for the school to be allocated two new faculty lines to increase their faculty size. Admittedly I probably should have announced that at the beginning and I would have been in and out of there in a minute, but then O'Brien's charge of rape would have been left uncleaned, if you get my point."

Colmes left the faculty meeting immediately after he announced the new faculty lines. On his way out the door he heard Professor Watkins say, "I move the meeting be adjourned."

And chairman Fartsworth announced, "So noted. And is there a seconder for the motion?"

"Second," said one of the students.

Fartsworth had hardly managed to announce the meeting officially closed, when all the attendants, like horses let out of the start gate, hurried out, the professors without another word to anyone, off to hide in their offices, the two students to the cafeteria, talking excitedly as they went.

19. Hostage Crisis

Words matter. The pen is mightier than the sword. Words, words, words. Even in sport, many argue that the final arbiter is the psychological state of the those engaged in it, especially team sports, and it is words that determine that psychological state. That words are valued so highly is abundantly clear by the outlawing of drugs that alter the mind and body, thus undermining the power of words that matter. And, with the very large exception of the media, it is in a university where words are the most visible means of exchange, where their true power emerges from the depths of psychology to demand a sacrifice of one or many.

I know what you are thinking. There he goes again. Waxing and waning over academia. He must deride it so much! Even despise it! But in response I say that if those accusations were accurate, why would I stay in my position, a lowly one at that, for so many years, about forty if I am not mistaken? Let me give an honest answer. It is all because of my friend and mentor Thomas Colmes. Think what you like. Call me what you like. But I am proud of it. The two of us have affected the lives of many, all for the good, or mostly as good as it possibly could have been.

Defensive? Indeed, I am. For our consciences are not of course, like anyone else, entirely clean. Though my defensiveness that you no doubt have detected, is rather more confined to just this one case. It is a case to which I have alluded at various times throughout my description of Colmes's cases. This case was, like many others, buried in the banter of both Toekiarty and Bates when they came to Colmes's office. Yet they often mentioned nothing of anything that might even sound like a possible case as far as I could make out.

***

No sooner had Rose brought the afternoon tea, the phone rang.

Colmes was having a small coughing fit so I took the call.

"Professor Colmes office," I said.

"This is the president's office, is Dr. Colmes available please? The president would like to speak with him," came the trembling voice of his secretary.

"Just one moment, this is Hobson." I held the phone at arm's length and mouthed "Finneas" hoping Colmes would understand.

His coughing stopped, and he took the hand-piece. "Colmes," he said.

"O'Brien," came the familiar voice of his longtime friend.

"Finneas, jolly old son," said Colmes, "what can I do for you?"

Colmes sat back in his chair, took a sip of his tea and listened. Both Rose and I sat staring at him and then at each other. We had become very good friends. We were both a little worried about Colmes. But this chat with the President clearly gave him a boost and he began to move more quickly and purposefully. Back to his old self. After some ten minutes, that seemed like an hour to Rose and me, Colmes hung up the phone and turned to us with a very big smile on his face, yet accompanied by a very serious frown. "We have the case of all cases," he announced in a low voice.

Colmes said this of almost all our new cases, so I did not take his remark too seriously. "Oh? Really?" I asked almost with a yawn.

"You remember the young assistant professor Gloria Watkins who gave me a hard time over O'Brien's rape charge?"

"Indeed I do," I answered.

"That's how you and my mom came together, isn't that rightl?" added Rose.

Colmes looked down, a deeply furrowed brow. "Watkins and an ex-con student by the name of Felix Grouse have O'Brien and his secretary holed up in his office. They have barricaded the door and are demanding that the police come and arrest O'Brien for rape, and me as an accessory."

"Are they armed?" I asked feeling a little foolish that I had to ask that question. "I mean, what happens if their demands are not met?"

"This is the crazy part. They have issued a deadline of one hour from now, or else they will rape O'Brien to teach him what it's like," said Colmes.

Rose and I both turned a bright shade of red. "Good god!" I cried.

"Not God Not good!" cried Rose, holding back a smile.

"Has anyone called the police?" I asked.

"Not so far as I know," answered Colmes. "It's up to us to mitigate this crisis. And calling the cops, of course, is our last option."

"Indeed!' I said with enthusiasm

"The first thing we must do is contact O'Brien's wife, Chi-Ling. Rose do you think you could do that?" asked Colmes.

"Sure" replied Rose "should I bring her here?"

"Yes. And of course she must tell no one."

"Right you are," said Rose, and just as she was leaving Toekiarty appeared at the door.

Toekiarty immediately rushed in yelling at Colmes, "you've done it this time Colmes. You're not going to get away with this!"

"Do take a seat, Toekiarty," said Colmes quietly, "and how may I be of assistance?"

"I knew this would happen," she growled. "Your ex-con program was destined to cause violence and grief to my faculty. And now one of our lovely young assistant professors is in fear of her life."

Colmes calmly picked up his pencil as though he were to fill in his crossword puzzle. "Of course, you know that it is not my program but that of the Provost. And who is this unfortunate young professor?"

"Gloria Watkins. She's right now held hostage in the president's office by that disgusting ex-con Felix Grouse!"

Her voice was again so loud, I was sure that I could have heard every word in my office and maybe the one further down.

"And what is your source of information?" asked Colmes.

"Grouse, that's who! He phoned me in my office. It's an outrage! A dreadful outrage! What are you going to do about it?"

"My dear Toekiarty," sighed Colmes, "You have been misled."

And at that moment, Toekiarty's Washington Bates, her expert on critical race theory, who was never far behind her, came into the office. Colmes nodded at him and gestured to my chair which I quickly vacated and moved to my proper place in the corner on the overstuffed chair.

Colmes continued. "Grouse is a black criminal ex-con who has done time for rape and various violent acts. You cannot believe anything he tells you...."

"Wait a minute!" yelled Bates, clearly rising to the level of anger displayed by his boss Toekiarty. "Let me be sure of what I just heard. In fact I must write this down. You said, 'Grouse is a black criminal ex-con so you can't believe anything he says'. That right?"

"Close enough," said Colmes. "However you should know that the President called me and told me a completely different story. He said that Grouse and Watkins were in cahoots, and if anything, it was Watkins who was running the show. And their demands were certainly different from what your boss here is saying."

"And what's that?" asked Bates quickly glancing sideways to his boss, who pretended not to hear.

"Never mind. Let's hear what O'Brien had to say," answered Toekiarty more or less brushing Bates aside.

Colmes informed them of the demand and looked at his watch. Bates was outraged that Colmes would believe such a far-fetched story. He was sure that Watkins was behind it all though. He knew Grouse well and insisted that he was a kind and gentle person who would not hurt a fly.

Toekiarty, however, responded to Colmes immediately with the obvious, to her that is: "Then get your ass over to the cops and tell them to arrest O'Brien. You're shielding him because he is your buddy. Don't think I don't know. And it's very clear that you're an accessory. Consecrating O'Brien's marriage of his victim Chi Ling to make it look like nothing happened. Enough!"

I was most pleased to be sitting in my corner left out of this awful mess, the viciousness whizzing past me like a cloud of darts. Now all that would be needed to complete this imminent destruction of Colmes was for Provost Dolittle to show up, and all Colmes's enemies would be lined up against him.

Colmes replied calmly, "for the moment we do not want the police involved, unless you of course wish to speak with them?"

Toekiarty's face was almost bursting with anger. But she fought valiantly to keep her thoughts locked inside that bulging body of hers. Bates took it upon himself to speak on her behalf. "Quite frankly," he said, "the President deserves everything they have threatened him with. It will serve him right!"

Colmes looked at them both with detached amusement. "Perhaps you would like to switch places with Grouse?" teased Colmes.

I shrank back into my overstuffed chair when I heard this. It was reckless and surely provocative. And I ask you, could those two Toekiarty and Bates be any more provoked than they were already?

"The trouble with you people," added Colmes, "is that you see everything in black and white."

Now there was the final straw, surely. Bates took a deep breath and drew himself up in an effort to make himself bigger or taller or something. And Toekiarty instead seemed to draw her rounded head back into her fat neck a bit like a tortoise pulling its head into its shell.

I looked at my watch and gave a little cough. "It's almost time," and left it at that.

"Could you repeat that racist remark?" asked Bates, as though he were a translator of a foreign language.

Colmes picked up the phone and dialed the direct line to the President. Then he grimaced and held the phone out to me to hear. It was O'Brien's secretary. She was, apparently, hysterical.

"They, they've pulled down his pants!" she cried.

Colmes turned to his unpleasant guests. "You hear that? Is that what you want?"

"Call the fucking police!" yelled Toekiarty.

"Here's the phone, you do it," snarled Colmes, as he held out the phone.

Toekiarty shrank away and edged closer to the door. Which was a mistake, for at that moment Rose returned with Chi-Ling in tow.

"Chi-Ling" called Colmes, rising unsteadily from his chair. "I hope Rose has filled you in. I am on the phone with Finneas's secretary. It's not clear what is going on. "

"Let me speak to them," said Chi-Ling in a most authoritative and decisive tone.

Colmes handed her the phone and she almost took it with a snatch. "Hello? Let my husband alone, do you hear me? I want to speak with him immediately!"

I could just hear a male voice come on the phone. At first I thought it was O'Brien, but then realized that it was Grouse, who I think said, "he can't come to the phone right now he's busy."

Then Chi-Ling cried out, "doesn't anyone care about my husband?"

"Chi-Ling," said Colmes, looking her straight in the eye, you know we cannot call the police. It would have far worse repercussions."

"Worse than his being, ...being....gang raped?"

"Believe me," answered Colmes, I have known your husband for much longer than you have. Calling the cops would be far worse."

"Then what about the campus police?" asked Chi-Ling.

"They will just call the city cops. No, the best thing we can do is to wait," said Colmes calm and in control. "Let them work it out. Let the problem resolve itself."

"You mean, let the President get raped?" asked Bates in disbelief.

"That may happen, but then again, they are all intelligent human beings equally divided by gender. Who knows. Maybe they will resolve it differently," said Colmes unperturbed.

"The secretary," Bates asked quietly almost as though he didn't really want anyone to hear his question, "is she married, or... I mean... er... is there a partner?"

"If I know secretaries..." began Colmes, aware that he was in dangerous territory.

"And I know filthy men," broke in Toekiarty.

"Then I think we are on the same wave length, are we not?" continued Colmes, to the consternation of Bates, who I could see was rolling his tongue inside a most likely very dry mouth. And I admit that Colmes had me biting my tongue for fear that he himself was going to step in it.

Rose gently edged her way to door two. "I think I'll go put on the kettle and make a cup of tea. How many for tea?" She asked looking around the room.

Of course I raised my hand, and said "scones too," with a grin.

"Then you had better come and help," she quipped back.

Colmes did not answer but it was taken for granted that he would take tea. It was about time for afternoon tea anyway. Bates was too frightened to say anything more so he just raised his hand copying me. Toekiarty of course, could hardly wait for tea and scones, but would never admit it. "Just a little something," she said, "it doesn't seem right for us to enjoy tea and scones when those poor things are being held hostage."

"Hostage?" asked Colmes, "have you ever heard of the Stockholm syndrome?"

Bates shifted uneasily on his feet.

Colmes continued. "It was when a hostage, she happened to be a woman, wouldn't you know it, who was taken hostage in a bank robbery I think it was, and she fell in love the with violent leader of the gang that had taken her hostage. She even joined them."

Colmes had addressed this little explication at Bates and gave the distinct impression that he was telling Bates that he was ignorant. One could see the dreadful hate in Bates's eyes as he comprehended this cold and heartless piece of Victoriana.

As I have mentioned in many places I have spent much time trying to teach Colmes to be careful what he says in this day and age. Maybe a few decades ago ordinary people might have remembered or seen in old movies, the strict, almost stoic, practice of Victorian public morality. Colmes mimicked it, his entire social life was a caricature of it. In any case, it was clear to me that in the last ten minutes he had impugned the dignity of Bates, and insulted Toekiarty. Of this he was totally unaware —at least I think so. He is also capable of doing this on purpose just to get them angry and thus prone to error.

Now I know what you're thinking. Why don't the fools call the police and be done with it?

***

Gloria Watkins had already made a name for herself in the criminal justice world by publishing five papers in top journals every year for her first five years at the school, and was about to be considered for promotion and tenure. She even published a book and it was this book that made her a household name (well, a university-hold name) through-out the social sciences and criminal justice programs all over the United States, and even in Europe and the United Kingdom. In fact she had even received an invitation to speak at the famous Cambridge University School of Criminology, Cambridge England. Of course, such an invitation also carried with it an unstated offer of a position in the school. One could not obtain any more prestigious position in the world of criminology!

So one might ask, what is she doing threatening the President of a university, and worse, doing it with an ex-con collaborator. The answer is that it was her widely publicized book, Watkins appearing on every big talk show in America and even the U.K. The book recounted her no-holds-barred love affair with Felix Grouse while he was in prison doing time for a small number of robberies usually liquor stores or convenience stores. I say a small number, for the particular robberies for which he was tried and convicted were a tiny portion of the many series of robberies he had pulled off over a period of several months. He was sentenced to seven years prison, in the words of Judge Earnest Frost: "You are a blight on the good people in our neighborhoods. I would sentence you to many more years if only the law would allow it."

Grouse ended up in Coxsackie prison that was just forty minutes or so down the New York State thruway from Schumaker University.

Professor Watkins had been present when Grouse was sentenced. She was there with a group of her students on an excursion of various parts of the criminal justice system. In class later, she lectured her students as to the severity of the sentence, given that, the total amount that Grouse took in his robberies came to less than a few hundred dollars. Seven years for that? It was an excessive punishment, was it not? And to make it worse, lectured Watkins in a strong voice of authority, walking up and down the aisle of her students sitting in their desk-chairs, most with their heads down, weighed down by the guilt put upon them by their top ranked professor. Watkins was, of course, over-simplifying the entire case, and certainly, there were many retorts that might be made, that merely taking into account the monetary damage done, putting aside the injury and fright caused the victims of the robberies, especially as Grouse routinely used a gun, though never fired it. In any case, even if the gun were a toy gun, the fear inflicted upon the victims certainly should be taken into account. I could go on there, and should admit that this is me talking, not Colmes.

When Watkins heard that Grouse was placed in Coxsackie prison, she decided to write him a letter commiserating with him for the excessive punishment he had received, pointing out to him that she was sure that the real reason the judge was so harsh was that he, Grouse, was black.

Grouse replied with a long letter telling her of his sorrow, especially for his wife and five children, and saying in his own defense that he could not get a job and had to find a way of feeding them. And he didn't want to hurt anybody, and that was why his gun was never ever loaded. And thank goodness, he said, that the judge did not demand that he pay back the amounts he robbed. That would have taken food out of his children's mouths.

That letter, and many others followed, in response to Gloria's sorrow for his plight, though surprisingly and maybe heroically, he insisted that he was not punished so harshly because he was black. Such a position really annoyed Watkins and over the next several months, almost a year, she managed at last to get him to acknowledge that he had been the victim of racial prejudice of the worst kind, both inside and outside of the criminal justice system. But her most important accomplishment was to get him into the high school diploma program at the prison so that he could graduate high school and then would be eligible to join the Schumaker University program for ex-cons. To achieve this she had, in addition to writing him letters every week and receive his in reply, visited the prison frequently, even offering to teach occasional courses inside the prison, for free.

The book she published recounting her personal journey into prison and out, was a sensation, especially the memorable last sentence of the book which said: "I challenge judge Frost to visit Coxsackie prison, or any prison for that matter, to see the results of his mean sentences, the moral authority of which hides the human damage, anguish and suffering not only of the criminal sentenced, but especially of his family." I need not go into any more details of the book, especially the parts where she imagined she was his partner and described such scenes in unheavenly detail. It was as though they had really met and done it all together. All of this as she met and became good friends (according to her book) with Grouse's wife and gave her money to keep her family afloat until the happy day came when Grouse would be released.

Things did not quite work out that way, or at least they did, but at a cruel price. Grouse, who had become a perfect inmate, studied hard and got his high school certificate. He then took a number of criminal justice courses in the Schumaker University ex-con program, and was released after his second year of imprisonment. He did not go back to his family, but moved in with Professor Watkins who had been her guarantor into whose care he was released, the argument being that he had to be prepared for re-entry into the community, and that the first step was for him to stay away from his original neighborhood the culture of which the experts (that is Professor Watkins) claimed contributed to his being targeted as a criminal.

Watkins had heard much of Colmes, but steered clear of him as much as she could, given his reputation as an old fashioned individual who thought he was in the Victorian age. This she had not reconciled with the knowledge that he had also founded the ex-con Schumaker University program that provided a select few ex-con students with free tuition and a small stipend to get them by. It was this unresolved contradiction that surely resided beneath her outburst in the faculty meeting that I described in the case *Rape Advantage* in which she abused Colmes and called him a rapist.

I could say more about Felix Grouse, but I am most hesitant to do so. Recent criticism of the Watkins book has claimed that it is racist because it portrays Grouse as the placid, mild, and pathetically obedient personality which is, so they argue, the classic personality of the African slave—itself a stereotype. And there, you can see where, if I continued along this exposition, it would lead to that familiar circularity from which the philosopher in me has great difficulty breaking free. I think it best to leave off at this point and return to the heart of the case.

***

Provost Dolittle knocked lightly at the office of the Dean, newly appointed, the door always left ajar, signaling that all who approached were welcome to enter. This would last for a few months and then the Dean, no longer new, would keep his door closed, and there would be an aggressive secretary posted at her desk as close to the Dean's door as possible. Of course, when the Provost came by, all the minor personnel, that is, those not holding an academic appointment, felt an urgent need to rise and snap to attention, but that would reveal an awful soldier-like mentality, so they instead rustled papers, banged at their typewriters and computers, or answered fake telephone calls.

As soon as she entered newly appointed Dean Fartsworth rose from his large leather padded swirling desk chair to greet her.

"Welcome to my humble office," he said with one of his very big grins and as he did so his tongue darted in and out like that of a snake.

This was most appropriate for Fartsworth who was known among his fellow faculty as a liar and dissembler. How else could one rise so quickly from the level of an associate professor to that of Dean? Dolittle had offered him instant promotion to full professor (technically illegal) and a miserly extra $5,000 one time increase in his annual salary, which he jumped at, thinking that it had to be an easy job replacing the former Dean O'Brien who was now Schumaker University's first president with an Irish name.

"I have laid the groundwork for you. It is now up to you to carry it forward," said Dolittle.

"But I will have to get the faculty's approval, won't I?" answered Fartsworth, his tongue very active and leaving spittle all around his mouth and as far as his cheeks.

Dolittle stepped back a little to avoid any possible spray. "It is your prerogative as Dean to make administrative decisions. You have the power invested in you by me, your Provost, to change the name of the school to conform with the university's diversity and inclusive principles. The president has stated that the word "criminal" is a derogative term that stigmatizes those who have been unfortunate enough to be labelled as such. The university does not wish to appear that it favors such insensitive discriminatory language, which carries with it much damage to the lives of those who have been labelled as such."

Fartsworth splattered, "Provost, do have a seat," indicating the large metal chair in front of his desk, no doubt a product of prison labor.

"Thank you, but I must off to another meeting. And do understand that you have my full support and that of the Head of Human Resources and of course the President. "

"But Provost Dolittle. What do we call them, then if not , er, you know...?" asked Fartsworth with a sloppy drool, his tongue getting caught briefly on one of his protruding incisors.

"Nothing. Leave that to the professors to discuss in class. We will simply replace the word criminal in the name of the school with nothing," said the Provost, a very straight business-like face, and staring right into Fartsworth's pale almost dead eyes.

"So it's just 'The School of Justice' then?"

"Correct. Now I must be off. I have a very important meeting with the President coming up. He will be very pleased to hear the news that you are changing the school's name."

"But what about Colmes? I thought he was the reason the change was not made long ago?"

"That is correct," said the Provost with an most satisfied smile. "I am sure he will not be opposing it this time."

"Are you sure about that? He has a lot of sway with our faculty, you know," whined Fartsworth.

"I assure you he is not going to be a problem this time," smiled Dolittle. "Just get this done by the end of the week. All right?"

And she left, Fartsworth's tongue lashing and licking his lips, but saying nothing.

***

"Well now," said O'Brien with no less than a teasing smirk on his face, "who will be first or is it going to be a foursome?"

Watkins shrank back. Grouse, not a large person, stood in front of her as though to protect her. The secretary sat curled up in a corner of the office, whimpering.

"Well? What will it be?" persisted O'Brien.

"It's just you, the rapist, that we want. And your co-star Colmes," muttered Grouse.

O'Brien looked about the room. "Unfortunately, Colmes does not seem to be here. And my secretary would be a poor substitute, don't you think?"

"Asshole!" cried Watkins. "Go on! You can go!" she ran over to the whimpering secretary, grabbed her roughly by the arm and dragged her to the door.

Grouse quickly ran to the barricaded door and began to pull the chairs and table away. But the secretary screamed and wrenched herself out of Watkins, grip and ran back to her corner.

"If you stay, you'll be raped," warned Grouse.

"No she won't" cried Watkins. We're not rapists. We just want O'Brien to experience what he did to his innocent victims."

"But we've warned that we'll rape him if he does not accede to our demands," muttered Grouse in some consternation.

"Raping a rapist isn't rape!" announced Watkins with the authority of a preacher.

"What is it then?" asked Grouse, frowning and losing patience.

"It's punishment, pure and simple. It's getting what he asked for when he committed his horrendous crime. After all, you don't call the death penalty murder, do you?" Now Watkins, finding her stride, marched over to O'Brien and pushed her face right up to his. "Get it? It's retribution, evening the score, just deserts, name it what you like. An eye for an eye, a rape for a rape!"

"You are a criminal justice student?" asked O'Brien as he calmly placed his hand on Watkins' shoulder and pushed her gently away. "Who teaches you this nonsense?"

Watkins's face flushed and she pursed her lips. This was the ultimate insult. Here she was probably the most famous professor in the school of criminal justice, about to become tenured and full professor in less than six years, and this excuse for a president is calling her a student!

"How dare you!" she screamed, "how dare you?"

O'Brien looked at her blankly. He had no idea what he had said or done.

Now Grouse came up behind Watkins. "Come on, let's do him over and get it done with. He deserves it more than ever now"

"Tut! Tut!" cried O'Brien. "You already made me take off my pants and we have not heard back yet from Colmes. Perhaps the police are on their way this very minute?"

Grouse held back, gently tugging at Gloria's sweater. "Colmes was supposed to call us, and he hasn't," she snarled. "Our demands have not been met, so now we rape you. And by the way, I'm the top rated professor in the school of criminal justice, that shows how out of touch you are!"

O'Brien tried to step back. Grouse grabbed a chair and pushed it into him.

Watkins reached down to where she thought might be O'Brien's underpants.

At that moment the phone rang, and with some difficulty, O'Brien pulled away from Watkins, kicked the chair away and answered it. "O'Brien," he said.

The sound of a male voice with a slight Victorian accent could be heard. "It's Colmes!" cried Watkins. She snatched the phone away from the president. "Colmes, the rapist! I hope you are calling from jail?"

But all she got in reply was dial tone. "The filthy creep! He hung up!" She turned to O'Brien and once again put her face up to his. "Come on! what did he say?" she ordered, "or else!"

"Or else what?" teased O'Brien.

"What did he say?" insisted Watkins as her hands moved once again in the direction of his underpants.

"He said that the Provost was on her way to see him about an important matter. Something about a criminal... or criminal justice... or something else."

"Criminal?" queried Grouse, always piqued when he heard that word.

"That's what he said," answered O'Brien with a shrug.

Gloria pulled back and put her arm around Grouse. "Don't worry I'm sure it's nothing," she said softly.

"Then he hasn't gone to the cops?" asked Grouse.

"He did not say. But it was my impression that he was waiting for the Provost to arrive in his office."

Watkins banged her fist on the President's desk. "Our demands have not been met so let's get on with it. Once again she closed in on O'Brien and felt for his underpants.

"Maybe we should hold off until we hear what the Provost had to say with Colmes," mumbled Grouse.

"If you like," said O'Brien nervously, "I could call Colmes again and get more detail." He reached for the phone.

"Yeh. Let's wait," mumbled Grouse. "You never know."

"You're such a pussy," complained Watkins with a sweet smile. She turned to Grouse and gave him a hug. "Let's get away from this filthy monster and wait a while." Gloria took him by the arm and they sat on the floor next to the whimpering secretary, who instantly recoiled, hugging her knees into an even tighter ball.

Grouse took pity on her. "You don't have to worry, we're not here for you. It's not your fault you have an asshole for a boss," he said, trying to console her, but just making things worse.

"Felix, leave her alone," growled Watkins, "didn't you learn anything in prison? Don't trust anyone, even pathetic little shits like her." She looked at the secretary derisively. "I bet you let him screw you too."

"I'm married with two little kids," whimpered the quivering little girl.

"Yeh, well, you know with shits like him, that means nothing," snarled Watkins.

Then the secretary uncoiled herself and said in as strong a voice as she could, "anyway he hardly knows I exist."

"Well, that's what Gloria means, don't you sweetheart?" said Grouse.

Gloria looked at him with amusement. "This little man," she thought, "he's a little girl at heart."

***

Perhaps now I should say a little more about Felix Grouse, since his performance as a hostage taker was not quite up to scratch. After all, they had no weapons. He had complained to Gloria that they should at least have something to threaten O'Brien with, but she would have none of it. Not even a box cutter. She was against weapons of any kind. If their personal toughness and resolve could not intimidate him, two against one, a pathetic old man who hid behind his secretary, he with a gammy leg as well, they should not be in the hostage taking business.

In fact, Grouse had resisted Gloria's relentless cajoling that they give O'Brien a taste of his own medicine. And she had insisted that they had secret support from higher up, but she refused to explain exactly what that meant. And after all, Watkins was his professor. She had a lot of power over him, could see to it that he never graduated, since she was chair of his dissertation committee. Not to mention that she was a very aggressive person, in fact intimidated him. And he was well used to that, probably why he fell for her. He had been intimidated all his life, he swears he could remember his mother laying into him with a leather shoe before he was old enough to walk. Who knew what would have happened if he had a father. But he had no memory of him. So Felix was well used to being ordered around by women. One can imagine how he got on in prison. Raped every day pretty much, although he was gradually passed over because his assailants found him too compliant and passive. There was no fight in him. And it was this that Gloria had cottoned on to. They were a perfect match, one might say. At least that was so from Gloria's view of things.

The secretary managed to stop whimpering and Gloria put her arm around Grouse, offering him reassurance to the extent that she was capable of doing so.

Something of a stalemate had arisen. O'Brien managed to pull his pants up from his ankles. He stared at the phone trying to decide whether to call Colmes. From what he had read and seen about hostage takers, this pair in front of him did not seem to be the real thing. Not violent nor threatening enough. They looked like easy meat. He was half inclined simply to get up out of his chair and go to the door, pull away the furniture and escape. But why bother? They had no weapons, they did not have the courage to carry out their threat to rape him. What on earth did they think they were doing?

**

Rose brought us another cup of tea. I looked at Colmes waiting for some kind of sign, a twitch at the corner of his mouth, a quick blink of his lively eyes. But he gave no hint of any secret plan.

Toekiarty was now walking back and forth across Colmes's office, not realizing that she was following in his very footsteps, literally. Bates sat scribbling in a notebook. Rose and I sat in our corner, sipping our cups of tea. Colmes returned to his crossword. Finally Toekiarty spoke.

"Enough! I will not stand by and let one of my outstanding young professors be raped either by Grouse or your buddy, the rapist President," announced Toekiarty.

Colmes ignored her.

But Chi-Ling, ever the aggressive small person, proud of her academic accomplishments—meaning of course all of her academic accomplishments which included her marriage to the President of Schumaker University, stamped her foot as she rose quickly from her chair and turned to Toekiarty. I truly thought she was going to hit her or do something violent, by the look on her face.

"Would you please shut up!" she yelled. "It is my husband who is under attack, not your favorite faculty. It is your people who have threatened to rape my husband. He is the victim, not they. They are the hostage takers, kidnappers. What is the matter with you? You are so deranged!"

Colmes looked a little amused. The more conflict that occurred in front of him the more he enjoyed it. To him it was like watching a gripping movie. Rose and I looked at each other, and in an instant we connected, strangely I suppose, because it was via Colmes. And though I admit that I had admired Rose from a kind of psychological distance, I had never actually considered our closeness to be anything more than a psychological one. A friendship I suppose people call such a relationship. But our connection of looks was not psychological. It was, well, I have to admit it, kind of physical. We both sipped our cups of tea and sat back a little awaiting the drama to take its course. We saw Bates stop his note-taking and look up as though he wanted to enter the fray.

But then, there came a quiet knock on Colmes's door.

"Enter!" called Colmes.

A young girl, perhaps slightly overweight, a head of thick black hair, and swarthy face looking as though it had been under the sun for way too long, appeared in the doorway, a notebook in hand and a boxy looking tape recorder.

"Multi-disciplinary Professor Colmes?" she asked.

Colmes looked her up and down. She wore old gray baggy pants, a black tee-shirt covering a large bosom, at least large for a girl who was probably a college junior, and around her neck a voluminous necklace on which was threaded all manner of things, polished ivory-looking teeth, pecan shells, or maybe they were whole pecans, colored feathers woven into small discs and rings, and thin red and white markings painted on her arms and cheeks, though so faint they were hardly visible.

"Who are you?" asked Colmes in his usual threatening manner, then continued with a grin, "a Red Indian or something?"

Bates almost dropped his notebook. "Professor Colmes!" he cried loudly. "That is the last straw!"

"I am Kanontienentha, but everyone calls me Kana. Provost Dolittle sent me. I am the diversity editor for the university newspaper *Flotsam*," she said hurriedly, the words running together so very fast.

"And for what purpose?" asked Colmes. "As you can see I am very busy right now." He waved his arm around as one would on stage

"He's lying," interrupted Bates, "and you've definitely come to the right place. "I have recorded five glaring instances of hate speech."

Colmes looked with amusement first at Bates, then at Kana, then announced, "my goodness me! I must be losing it. I would have thought there were many more!"

Kana stepped forward and placed her tape recorder on Colmes's desk. "Do you mind?" she asked meekly.

"I do mind. The spoken word is sacred, to be enjoyed when delivered, unsullied by the distortions of writing or recording. Speech was not meant to be preserved as in a jar of formalin, and when revived its true taste is lost. Speech remembered is speech forgotten, its true meaning lost forever. Do I make myself clear?"

"All I did was ask," replied Kana with a blank face, "I didn't ask for a lecture."

Kanontienentha's refusal to be cowed by Colmes greatly cheered Toekiarty and her apprentice Bates. In fact, they clapped their hands lightly, Bates looking to Colmes hoping for another of Colmes's hate speech outbursts. But there was no time for it because as Colmes was about to take the bait, as they call it, Provost Dolittle appeared in the doorway. This gave Colmes the chance to look beyond Kana and ignore her in favor of the Provost.

"Ah. So I see that the two of you have met. Is the professor being cooperative?" Dolittle asked Kana.

"Not really. But it does not surprise me, from what I have heard," she replied. "He won't let me record anything. Even so, he has already insulted me and my race."

"I was just joking my dear," said Colmes with awful condescension.

"That makes it many times worse," said Kana with some satisfaction.

Colmes looked at her blankly. I hate to say this, but I am sure that he had no idea what he was saying or doing. He had walked into a minefield, and I could see that it had been set up especially for him. I tried to warn him by wriggling a bit to get his eye. Rose understood and stood to take his cup and saucer and mine to the kitchen, giving him a big nudge as she passed by him. But he seemed not to notice.

"I bring you news, which I suspect you will not like," said the Provost looking intently at Colmes.

Colmes pretended to work on his crossword puzzle.

"Pray, do tell," answered Colmes raising his head.

"I have just come from a most productive meeting with the new Dean of Criminal Justice, Morris Fartsworth."

"And?" Colmes muttered.

"He has agreed to remove the word Criminal from the name of the school. So this change will be made by the end of this week. He is meeting with his faculty as we speak."

"But you know that I objected to that some years ago when we dealt with that matter of the school's identity and its organizational location."

"In any case," said the Provost sternly, "I have spoken with President O'Brien. He says he has reached some kind of compromise or agreement with his captors. But they will not release him or his secretary until they hear directly from you, Colmes, in person."

"And what was the agreement?" asked Colmes. "After all, I have no wish to be arrested by the town police, of even the campus police, for facilitating a rape or whatever."

"The captors insisted that the agreement not be communicated over the phone. They wanted to make sure that all those involved be present to hear it directly, so there would be no rumors or distortions of the facts once revealed," answered Provost Dolittle.

"Then what are we waiting for?" asked Chi-Ling. "Let's get over there and set my husband free!"

Bates and Kana stared at her. It sounded to them like a kind of disrespectful theft of words from a well-known anti-slavery song. Nevertheless Toekiarty, Bates, Kana and Dolittle rushed out the door.

To my surprise, Colmes did not budge.

"Colmes," I said, "aren't we going there to free your old mate? "

"Yes," complained Chi-Ling, "we have to save Finneas !"

"Chi-Ling you go ahead. I am sure Finneas will be pleased to see you. And I assure you, he will be released whether I am there or not. And he will not be raped. I am very sure of that."

"I, I," stuttered Chi-Ling. She was about to plead again that he go when Kana stopped at Colmes's doorway.

"The Provost has told me that I must stay with you no matter where you go, until I have enough material to do an article on you," she said with a forced smile.

Colmes looked at me and to Rose as she returned from the kitchen. He sighed deeply and said, "all right. If it will make you feel better, I will come. But I can tell you now. I have figured all this out. I know exactly how this silly crisis came about. There never was a crisis. I can tell you that."

***

Chi-Ling was the first to reach the outer room of the President's office. She went straight up to the office door and banged it loudly.

"Finneas! Finneas! Are you OK?" she cried.

"Chi-Ling, my love! Do not worry I am fine. I have not been raped," he yelled.

"Then who is that crying?" cried Chi-ling.

"Oh, that's just my secretary. She'll be fine. They left her alone."

"Colmes! Where is Colmes! We want Colmes!" came the loud rasping voice of Gloria Watkins.

"He's on his way," called Toekiarty who had arrived breathless.

There was now a full contingent of persons, each of whom, with the exception of myself, had a bone to pick with Colmes. Actually, that's not quite correct, as I have had plenty of bones to pick with Colmes. It was not as if we were totally in agreement about everything. I often took the opportunity to correct him when I thought it necessary.

"This is Colmes!" yelled Colmes with all his Victorian might. "I demand that the despicable criminal Grouse and his prostituted female collaborator come out now. The game is up! I will never call the police as you fools demanded."

There was a long silence broken only by the scraping of Bates's pencil as he scribbled in his notebook.

Colmes turned to Provost Dolittle and muttered, "what a pathetic criminal Grouse is, thinking he can use the typical weakness of the female character to his advantage."

Kana fiddled with her tape recorder. Bates scribbled more in his notebook.

"Did you get all that?" asked the Provost.

"We did," both Kana and Bates answered in unison.

"Then that's it then. I think we have enough," she said.

"I will remember this day the rest of my life," chuckled Toekiarty gleefully.

The muffled noise of furniture being dragged away from the door now signaled that the hostage taking was at an end. The door opened, and there stood Grouse and Watkins, a little red in the face from moving the furniture, but arm in arm as though they were lovers, which they probably were.

Chi-Ling pushed past them and ran to Finneas who stood a little unsteadily behind his desk. The secretary remained curled up in a ball in the corner, still whimpering and sobbing.

Provost Dolittle went straight to Watkins and Grouse and gave each a little hug. "You have done well, I am so proud of you," she said.

Colmes stood back, his hands clasped together, his double breasted suit pulled tight at the shoulders. "All right, Dolittle, what kind of trick are you pulling? Congratulating a pair of kidnappers and extortioners? All your doing no doubt!"

"Indeed it is!" mocked Dolittle. "A little of your own medicine!"

I was truly startled. Never had I heard or seen anyone make such fun of Colmes. He stood rooted to the spot, his pale eyes almost closed by a heavy frown, his lips turned down in consternation.

Dolittle continued. "Bates, read out what you have, and Kana. Be sure that you have it all on tape.

"Actually, I have a lot on tape, the recorder has been running most of the time since I entered Professor Colmes's office," she said slyly.

And so, while my mentor had figured out early on that Dolittle had engineered the hostage taking and that the threat to rape O'Brien was a sham, he had not realized that the entire enterprise had been thought up by the Provost with only one goal, which was to corner Colmes and force him into complying with whatever she was about to lay on him.

***

Oh! How much I missed Colmes's office right now so I could

retreat to the overstuffed chair in the corner. But here, in the President's outer office, surrounded by the smug Provost, the ugliness of Toekiarty prancing around as though her team had won a great victory, O'Brien and his love Chi-Ling retreating to his office to lick their wounds, seemingly oblivious to the unfolding defeat of Colmes, the supposed loving couple Grouse and Watkins embracing each other, giggling with joy, and now Bates and Kana whatever her name was, standing tall (though as I have said she was very short), ready to reveal to all the horrors of Colmes's words of hate.

Bates, after a small cough read aloud:

"Grouse is a black criminal ex-con so you can't believe anything he says."

"The trouble with you people is that you see everything in black and white.

"Called Kana 'a Red Indian' or something"

"a pathetic criminal Grouse is,"

"the typical weakness of the female character…"

"That will do for now," interrupted Provost Dolittle. "I think, Professor Colmes, this should be enough to convince you that if we made these remarks public, as Kana here will do when she writes her article for *Flotsam*, your old time buddy O'Brien will have no other choice but to request your resignation. Your hate speech is far more extreme compared even to Nobel Laureate Sir Tim Hunt who was forced to resign for his prejudiced public statements about women not being compatible with science."

Colmes turned to look at each of those present directly one to the other, and then rested his stare at Toekiarty. He then unclasped his hands and put them in his pockets. "Do as you wish," and proceeded to leave.

Fortunately, or at least as far as I was concerned it was fortunate, President O'Brien saw Colmes departing and called out.

"Wait, Colmes! Wait a minute!"

Colmes turned. "I hope you were not part of the charade," he said in an accusatory tone.

"What was that?" asked O'Brien, pretending not to hear.

"He was not informed," said the Provost quickly, "for fear that the operation would be compromised."

Thus, the ruse was revealed to all present, much to the pleasure of Colmes's enemies, and much to the disgust to his supporters. O'Brien in his Churchillian stance, leaning forward on his walking stick coughed and seemed to growl at the same time.

The Provost quickly responded to the growl. "His hate speech, President O'Brien, it must stop. If the word gets out, the university will be irreparably tarnished."

Toekiarty would not be left out. "In the name of justice, equality and inclusion…"

"Names," interjected Colmes sarcastically, "it's plural…"

"Whatever," snarled Toekiarty. "This is the 21st century not the 19th century. We cannot allow hate speech of any kind to be used in this university. It is shocking in this day and age."

"We are of course all concerned about the name and reputation of Schumaker University," added O'Brien, "which has a reputation of excellence for its diversity and inclusiveness and especially the empathy it shows for those who are hurt by such speech…"

I could see that O'Brien was winding up to go on and give a lengthy and boring speech about excellence and empathy, but fortunately the Provost, bless her soul, saw things heading in that direction as she prattled, "I agree completely with our president, of course. And I would suggest that in the short term we request that Professor Colmes cease and desist from his hate speech, and that as a sign of good faith he agree immediately to the change of name of the school of criminal justice to simply School of Justice, a change that he has resisted for some years, and one that must be made if we are to keep up with the times. Surely he can see that using a stigmatizing and negative word 'criminal' is a form of hate speech that should not have any place in a modern and progressive university of excellence as is Schumaker University."

"What does it matter?" asked O'Brien. "Why was not the change made regardless of Colmes's opposition?"

"Because he had convinced all the faculty of that school that it would do them damage," added Toekiarty, eager to be part of this momentous occasion.

"I agree to the change," muttered Colmes. "I have never been against it."

And with that he departed, and uncharacteristically I chose to linger a while longer before following him.

Was this the end of Colmes?

20. The End of Colmes

I watched Colmes walk steadily away, his Victorian double breasted suit jacket buttoned tightly around him, his walking stick tapping on the floor, his head held high. I could not get a full view of his face because he had turned away so quickly in the middle of the ruckus that swept through the President's outer office as Toekiarty, Bates, Kana and Dolittle laughed and yelled as Bates repeated Colmes' hate speech, and even tried to copy his fake English accent. O'Brien reached out to Chi-Ling, pulling her to him in a tight embrace. Their lips met in a slobering open-mouthed kiss that was enough to make anyone in the room a little embarrassed. Enough to cause the revelers to stop their chanting and stare at the loving couple as they slowly separated and walked hand-in-hand into the President's office.

O'Brien was about the slam the door shut behind him when he saw his secretary still curled up in a little ball, sobbing.

"Everything is OK, my dear," O'Brien purred, "you may leave now and go home to your family. And take tomorrow off as a reward for your wonderful bravery."

Chi-Ling turned to her husband and gave him another sloppy kiss, then drew back and said, "my Sir Lancelot!"

The secretary scurried out the door and fled past the raucous bunch who took absolutely no notice of her.

O'Brien banged the office door shut with his walking stick.

***

It is with great difficulty that I describe the events that followed. I am bedeviled by thoughts that I do not want. I should have run after Colmes and walked with him. I should have shouted out loudly that Colmes was nothing of the scoundrel his accusers claimed. I should have told them to their faces that it was they who were the haters, not Colmes. But of course, this is all very well in hindsight. How was I to know that Colmes would simply disappear, and I mean completely disappear from our lives, 'our' being Rose the younger and myself?

Instead, I found myself first rushing to Colmes's office, but he was nowhere to be seen. I called out for Rose, but no answer. She too, had gone off. His office desk was exactly as it always was. Nothing had been touched. I ran down the corridors and through all the tunnels, even looking behind some of the huge pipes that populated the tunnels in most places. I ran down to the hairdresser, but he had not seen Colmes. Where could he be? I ran back to his office and looked more closely at his desk and searched its drawers. Everything was perfectly arranged according to his particular manner. The crossword puzzle remained exactly square with the desktop, unfinished. Actually, it was always unfinished. Nothing had been touched. He most definitely had not been back to his office. He had gone away, who knows where.

I stood at the door to his office as it slowly dawned on me that I was alone. That my life was suddenly changed forever, it was a turning point. Yet I refused to acknowledge this obvious, and looking back, inevitable outcome. Colmes was quite a bit older than me, and some day it had to happen. But not like this. Not so sudden, without a chance to say good-bye. I thought we were such great friends and colleagues. Had he no thoughts for me? Was I merely one of his accruements, like his *Times* crossword puzzle, or his walking stick?

I returned to my little office, it seemed so tiny now, and took to my bed. I was in a kind of delirium. My thoughts jumped from all of the encounters and problems that Colmes and I had solved, our happy banter, his silly Victorian ways, so rigid yet so open to, not surprisingly, Rose the younger. I loved her presence so much. I don't think I actually loved her, nor she me. It was more like a respectful and very close friendship. But now I yearned for her, and wondered where on earth she could be? Was she not concerned that Colmes had disappeared? Perhaps she had gone with him? No. Surely not. She was his daughter after all.

She would not want to live her life cooped up with an old man set in his ways. She had a life of her own to think about.

And so I tossed and turned on my bed, perhaps sleeping, sometimes dreaming crazy dreams, sometimes imagining I heard Colmes's knock on my wall.

And then, to my astonishment I found myself sitting at my desk writing my dissertation proposal. You might say that I was delirious. I banged away at my old Olivetti typewriter for I don't know how long, returned to my bed and again wrestled with my horrible dreams.

***

The local papers next morning featured on the front page bottom right, the headline *"Renowned professor fired for hate speech."* Of course, he was not actually fired, he simply quit and walked away. Dolittle did not get the chance to tell him "you're fired." There followed a reasonably accurate recounting of Colmes's hate speech and his general reputation of being a know-all, a cunning and mysterious buddy of the President of Schumaker university. And sources also informed the writer of the article that in fact Colmes was an imposter who did not even have an undergraduate degree. Had not graduated from college! So it was only to be expected that he would indulge in such misogynous behavior.

The article continued for another couple of paragraphs to speculate whether or not President O'Brien would be able to withstand this scandal, and mildly suggested that perhaps the President should resign for the good of the university.

Indeed. It was not long until it was announced that President O'Brien had resigned in order to take up a new position as President of the all-male University of Szchinzen somewhere in China.

***

The Provost had played her cards very well. The board of Regents of Schumaker university appointed her as interim President while a search was mounted to find a replacement for O'Brien whose great achievements in the university were lauded to no end. She of course appointed Colmes' nemesis Toekiarty to the position of Provost and Vice President for DEI (Diversity, Equality and Inclusion). A new era in higher education had arrived, and Schumaker University would be its proud leader.

Although all this was totally predicable as far as I was concerned, I was, in my fragile delirium thoroughly overcome by these changes and continued to take to my bed, alternately jumping up and banging at my typewriter, and the more I wrote (if that is what it was) I slowly managed to calm down a little. It was at this point, satisfied that I had completed my first draft proposal, that I heard the familiar knock on my wall.

Colmes was back!

Just to make sure, I pressed my ear to the wall and sure enough it was Colmes' familiar knock, there was no doubt. It was Colmes. I rushed out of my little office into the tunnel and saw that Colmes's door was ajar. I pushed it open so hard it banged the wall behind it and bounced back at me, I pushed again and then found myself standing in front of Colmes' desk. He was sitting like always, doing his crossword puzzle.

Except that it wasn't him. It was Rose the younger, sitting upright, dressed in a navy blue striped double breasted Victorian suit, tightly buttoned, bright white shirt with a starched collar, and deep blue striped tie. Her hair was dyed a dark resplendent black, clipped short, combed with a part on the left side. Her reddish brown eyebrows once bushy like her mother's, were now carefully shaped and trimmed. Her eyes, most disappointing to me, remained the original pale grey with a touch of green, but seemed dull, lacking the sparkle of a countenance that I had long admired.

In my haste and shock, I ran into her desk and had to put out my hands to prevent from falling. I grabbed at the wicker chair but it tipped up and clattered to the floor.

"Hobson," she said, "we have a most interesting case."

She even spoke with a fake English accent. I at last steadied myself and stood as erect as I could. This was not Colmes. It was an abomination of Colmes. I did detect a slight twitch at the edge of her mouth. She had it all down pat. But it wasn't enough for me. I stood silently for some time and she nonchalantly returned to her crossword. I had an urge to go on as if nothing had happened, what was the case? And so on. But it was just not the same. So I slowly turned and walked out of the office and back to mine.

***

I began in a robotic fashion to tidy up my desk, stack my belongings as though ready to depart. That was when I discovered on my desk the proposal I had typed in my fit of madness. I sat down to read it, mesmerized. For it was not a dissertation proposal at all! I had written a lengthy and somewhat garbled description of my dream. I could not believe that it was I who wrote this. And to this day I do not remember having done so. There have been times, probably kind reader you have also experienced them, that I have awoken from a dream and tried to write down what it was about. But I could only manage to recall small parts of it, and could never make sense of what I had written. But this was different. I wrote the dream while I was experiencing it. I wrote it in my sleep! It has to have been me. Who else? I am alone in my office. Always alone. It would be a cruel trick if someone had sneaked in and written it.

In any case, being an honest and true academic, I am obliged to present for you the dream, mostly unedited, except here and there where my unconscious grammar departed from accepted rules. I have given it a name. It is called, *The University of the Chosen.*

21. Hobson's Dream:
The University of the Chosen

Grace, exhausted, sore and confused, was pushed into a holding cell whereupon she collapsed on the floor. The crowd of young people milled around her. They too were sore and hurt. They were her fellow protesters and they had just been deposited here after the violent confrontation they had against police in front of Washington's Capitol. Someone lifted her up and placed her on a bunk, where she lay, in a swoon, a dream emerging from her mouth as if she were a character in a comic book. She tried to sit up, but felt an unbearable weight on her shoulders, and fell back. And then, under the weight of many hands, strange cold hands, her dream took off, a journey, one full of hope, to who knows where it would take her. But the weight on her shoulders held her back.

She was accepted into the University of the Chosen and the day had come for her to leave her Celestial Suburb and say good-bye to her parents, Pride and Doting. They called to her in unison: "Take care our little white girl, take care! Drive carefully!" Grace opened the door of her new electric car that she had Christened "Savior," but the weight on her shoulders stopped her from entering. She brushed and slapped at her shoulders, but the more she did so the heavier the weight.

Suddenly, the weight on her shoulders revealed itself. It was a wizened little monkey-looking thing as fat as it was tall, skinny hairy legs which it tightened around Grace's neck.

"Let me in and I will show you the way," ordered the disgusting smelling monkey, a horrible grin on its face, a long tongue licking its lips like a hungry dog.

"Who, who are you?" cried Grace, shaking in fear.

"Just call me Luke," answered the monkey, with a devilish grin.

What a strange name! She had never heard it before. In any case, Grace complied without thinking any more about it. She just had to get to university, it was all she had thought about for the past year. She said the magic words, "Phi Beta Kappa," the car door opened, the weight on her shoulders lifted, and she slid into the seat, only to find Luke sitting at the steering wheel.

"I'll drive. I know where to go. University of the Chosen, wasn't it?" Luke growled.

What else could Grace do but sit back and accept? But no sooner had she done so than they turned a corner and were suddenly in a the suburb of economic deprivation. Or that was what she guessed, never having been in one before.

"Don't worry. These are all my friends," said Luke.

"All of them?" Grace wished she had as many friends.

"All of them."

The car stopped at a corner where Grace pointed to a group of young African Americans chatting and laughing.

"You shouldn't use that word, you know," said Luke.

"What word?" asked Grace, feeling a massive weight return to her shoulders.

"You called them niggers."

"I said no such thing. I didn't utter a word!"

"They don't call me Devil for nothing, you know. Now apologize."

"I thought your name was Luke?"

"It is. Short for Lucifer, don't you like it?"

"Oh No! You're the Devil that Proud and Doting warned me about!"

"At your service."

Devil lowered the passenger side window where Grace could lean out to say her apology. "Now apologize! Go on then, say it!" he ordered.

Grace had always done what she was told. This was no exception.

"Guys, I mean you people, I'm sorry!" called Grace in a weak voice.

The group turned to her, made cat calls, called her white bitch and invited her to sleep with them.

Devil intervened. "You can't sleep with them. They're black and you're a white supremacist."

"What? I don't want to..."

"Yes you do. You're disgusting. Imagine what Pride and Doting would say if they knew that's what you want at the University of the Chosen."

"But we're not at the University of the Chosen yet, are we?"

"Not quite. But you see that guy standing on his own, all dressed so nice and his hair combed flat with a perfect part?"

"He's one of the Chosen?" asked Grace, wide-eyed.

"Now you're getting it." Devil called out. "Hey you there, blackie, get in."

The well-dressed boy or girl of the ghetto came over, as if called like a dog. Grace opened the door. "Climb in. We can all fit in the front," she said in her most friendly voice.

"Hello," he or she said. "Before I get in, you should know that I'm not what you think I am."

"She knows that," grinned Devil, as they sped off and out of the suburb of economic deprivation.

"I don't know," said Grace once again feeling that weight on her shoulders.

"Yes. I'm not a full African American. I'm a half-caste," said the boy or girl or whatever.

"So what?" said Grace, feeling confident, "that means nothing to me."

Devil intervened. "Careful, Grace. Careful what you say."

"My name is Algy," said the half African American with a grin.

"That's a nice name," said Grace, entranced and puzzled. "Is that what makes you so different?"

"Yes, you could say that. It stands for LG. Get it?"

Devil nudged Grace in the ribs. "Come on, say it, you know what it stands for."

"You mean LGBTQIA?" she asked nervously.

"That's about right," answered Algy with a smile that displayed his sparkling white teeth. His hand was already on her thigh.

"That's amazing. You're the first!" exclaimed Grace.

"Okay, you two. That's enough," ordered Devil. "We're there anyway. Where all the white girls are, is your door, Grace. The rest go in the other door."

Grace thanked Devil and offered to pay for the ride. "No need," said the Devil. "I'll keep an account. You'll pay soon enough."

"But my car?"

"Don't worry. It will be in the Chosen carpark waiting for you."

Grace turned to look for the campus, its beautiful old porticos, carved wooden doors. But she could see hardly any of this, just the tall spires peeping out above the haze. And there before her, was a large oily looking lake that lay between her and the entrance, her door, to the University of the Chosen. She looked for Algy who had quickly left her and disappeared into the haze. Maybe he knew of a secret way into the University. She stood there, puzzled. Between her and the dim outlines of the Chosen lay an uninviting lake, dark in color, almost as thick as black mud. The weight on her shoulders had returned, though it had slipped on to her back, like a knapsack full of stones.

She had come so far, the university almost in reach. Yet, there was no way she could get there. She dipped her toes in the lake, but pulled them out quickly. It was like a bog. She could not swim in it. The weight of Despair descended upon her, forcing her to drop down on her haunches. She wept. And in between the sobs, she looked up hoping that the haze would recede and the lake go away. Then she prayed, she knew not to whom or what. She had heard about people praying, but knew nothing of it. She had seen movies in which Muslims prayed and Buddhists chanted. Perhaps that was what she should do?

Now she lay down on the muddy grass, its coolness helping calm her small bosom. But under the weight, she heaved and sobbed, cried herself into a disturbed sleep. At which point help arrived.

Out of the gloom appeared a boatman, whistling joyfully as he rowed his kayak with rhythmic gusto. "Hey, you over there, are you one of the Chosen?"

Grace awoke. Was she having a dream within a dream? She stood and waved. The boatman was maybe an answer to her prayers? She had not asked for it. Had not asked for anything specifically. Only crying out for her wish to be granted. To get to the University of the Chosen where she knew she belonged. She waved and called out in her weak thin little girl's voice, "I'm here! I'm Grace, I want to go to Chosen University, but can't cross this awful lake! Is this the only way in?"

"My dear, this is the Slough of Decency. It is not a lake, per se. It's a bog, which the Board of the University of the Chosen refuses to drain. They say it would disturb the natural environment. There are some ways around it. But those are reserved for the special few as part of the University reparations agreement." The boatman put out his hand. "Come, I will row you across, though you will have to take up an oar as well. It's a two person boat."

"Oh, thank you kind sir!" cried Grace, full of joy.

"It's what I'm here for, my dearest."

As soon as Grace climbed into the boat, the weight of Despair fell right off and into the Slough of Decency, which bubbled and gurgled in response.

"Hang on!" Cried the boatman. "It may be a rough crossing!"

"And what is your name, good person?" asked Grace, putting on the best air of Decency that she could.

"They all call me Morality because without it, there could be no Decency, so they say."

"Then Mister Morality, why are you in the Slough of Decency? I thought all moral people would always be Decent."

"Well, that's the trouble. It's why there is such a bog of Decency."

"I don't understand."

"Too many people claim morality, see it in everything and everyone, especially words," said the boatman. "You have to be really careful in what you say, and even if you are, there's always someone who can denounce you as immoral. So everyone's scared to say or do anything. There's an excess of Decency, that's what."

"An excess of Decency? What's that?"

"It's this bog. That's what it is. Each and every day the claims of Decency grow and grow and the Slough gets bigger and bigger."

"That's terrible, Mister Morality!"

"Shhhh! Careful what you say, someone may hear you," whispered Morality, "you can't say Mister."

Grace fell silent, thinking. Then the outlines of the spires and stone porticos became much clearer, and so did her mind. "Mr. Morality, or is it Miss, Ms. or Mrs?" she asked a little cheekily.

"I'm a lady, if that's what you're asking," answered Morality with a straight face. "There are no moral men, even at your young age, you should know that."

Grace put her hand to her mouth. "What a truly horrible lady," she thought to herself. And at that moment, there was a sudden jolt of the boat and the boat-lady changed into the ugly monkey she recognized as Luke, the Devil. "You're not a lady, she cried, you're Devil!" She felt the weight once more on her shoulders.

"We're here," cackled Devil.

With great difficulty, Grace struggled out of the kayak. "You horrible man," she said, "all those nasty words you used. You should be ashamed of yourself!" She threw the oar that she had never used right at Devil's snarling face. He ducked, and it flew into the bog which gurgled and bubbled. And Grace felt the oily mud rising up to her knees."

"You better hurry if you want to make it to orientation!" cackled Devil.

Grace struggled, her feet feeling like stones. But she was determined. Nobody, nothing, would stop her from getting into the University of the Chosen. The weight on her shoulders pressed down, but she would not sink, not here. And with an Herculean effort she pulled her feet out of her Nikes and made one unholy leap to the shore and landed with such a thump.

***

When Grace awoke she found herself in a large hall, surrounded by empty mahogany chairs. The weight was no longer on her shoulders. She looked around but saw no one. Yet she felt that she was not alone. She brushed at her shoulders, afraid that Devil was sitting there once more. But it was not. She looked up and was dazzled by the high ceiling that seemed to reach to the heavens, decorated in gold leaf. And there were flying humans, they had wings, painted, or were they moving? She shook her head and cried, "where am I?"

One of the flying humans descended from the ceiling, her, or its, massive butterfly wings fluttering, causing Grace's hair to waver in the cold breeze. "Who are you?" asked Grace, frightened that it would be Devil yet again.

"I am your Archangel," sang the flying human or whatever it was. "I am here to guide you on your journey."

"But I thought my journey was over. Have I not arrived at the University of the Chosen?" asked Grace in her quivering little voice, feeling a little like Alice in Wonderland.

"You are almost there, my dearest. But you must, before entering, wash your feet clean of the mud you have brought with you from the Slough of Decency."

"Oh dear, I'm so sorry. I apologize for all the bad words I have said," cried Grace putting her hand to her mouth.

"And what of those you have not spoken?" asked the Archangel with a frown.

"But, but I can't stop words coming into my head," pleaded Grace. They're not bad unless I say them, are they?"

"Bad thoughts are evil thoughts just the same, when you are at the University of the Chosen. Surely you knew that before coming here? It was written very clearly in the brochure for new students, it's right there in the mission statement. Let me show you."

Archangel fluttered her wings and pulled out from under her, or its, flowing white silky robes a scroll that said:

"The University of the Chosen is dedicated to excellence in education and considers free speech that expresses the mission of the university to be the right and duty of every Chosen student. Excellence is demanded at all times and in all things, and our diversity-inspired curriculum reflects that dedication."

"It doesn't say anything about bad thoughts," said Grace nervously.

"You have not read the footnote," replied Archangel.

Grace strained to read the footnote. It stated: "Speech is defined as any word spoken or not verbalized, hinted at, or conveyed by any sign or action, or kept secret and not shared with others."

"Do you see, my dear?" asked the Archangel with an exaggerated, loving smile.

"Oh dear! I didn't read the footnote. Doting and Pride I am sure did not either."

"Never mind, Grace. We can fix that up easily. After all, that is why the University of the Chosen has a crash orientation course for every new student. Follow me through the wicket gate at the end of this room, this is called the mahogany room by the way, and the orientation room is called the blue and gold room."

"Those are the colors of the University!" observed Grace with a smile that glowed like a halo around her face.

"That's right," beamed Archangel, "and soon you will be wearing them!"

"I am so happy!" chirped Grace, feeling like Dorothy in the Wizard of Oz. She felt herself scooped up in Archangel's arms, transported aloft, then swooped down straight through the wicket gate. And there, resplendent in the room of blue and gold she found herself standing before a crowd of Chosen students all talking excitedly.

***

Grace stirred on her bunk. Her eyes fluttered a little and she saw through the blur the rest of her fellow demonstrators milling about in the holding cell. Some banged on the bars, chanting "Free-dom! Free-dom!" But Grace was too overcome by exhaustion and confusion, it was easier to close her eyes and return to her dream, if that is what it was.

The crowd of Chosen students gathered around her. Archangel had departed to the heavens. She found herself kneeling, hands clasped together, head bowed. The Chosen began to chant.

"Inno-*cent* or ignor-*ant*?! Inno-*cent* or ignor-*ant*?!"

Was she on trial? But this was a university. Was it not the haven of freedom?

The Dean of Freshly Chosen stepped forward and signaled for the chanting to stop. "Silence please, fellow, I mean…"

She was interrupted with boos and hisses.

"Silence please, chosen ones!" she cried. "We have before us our newest and freshest student. She, I mean who, has overcome many challenges on the journey to this, the Chosen University, the sanctuary of excellence and freedom!"

"Inno-*cent* or ignor-*ant*?! Inno-*cent* or ignor-*ant*?!" chanted the Chosen.

The Dean raised a hand signaling silence, and the chants gradually died away. "Let me say this. You know the old saying, though nobody knows where it came from, 'Forgive them Lord for they know not what they do?' "

The student response was a buzz of muttering and joking. The Dean was of course a person of authority and so should be treated as such. Her head held high, she pronounced:

"I am sure, in fact I know, that every Chosen one in this room has acted out of ignorance, especially before you were bathed in excellence at this grand institution of highest education."

Applause and cheers filled the splendid room of blue and gold, and on cue, the Chosen chanted, "Blue and gold! Blue and gold!"

The Dean looked down on Grace, still kneeling, her bare knees stinging with pain. She looked up, as though pleading. In fact she was pleading, pleading for admission.

The Dean raised her arms signaling another silence. The Chosen complied. It then placed its hand on Grace's head and said, "do you,

Grace Dolly solemnly swear allegiance to the University of the Chosen, so help you?"

"I do!" whispered Grace.

"Speak out, Grace. We didn't hear you," said the Dean in its strong voice.

"I DO!" cried Grace. "I do, I do, I do!"

The Dean then announced, with one hand still on Grace's head, the other raised aloft in a Nazi-like salute. "I hereby proclaim you innocent, and may your ignorance be left behind from whence you came!"

Deafening cries and cheers filled the great blue and gold room. The Dean continued. "Rise Grace Dolly, once of the Celestial Suburb! Rise and become one of the Chosen!"

Grace rose, all weight was lifted from her, so much so that she floated up above the crowd of Chosen, like Saint Catherine floating above the stairs.

***

As they say, what goes up must come down. And so it was with Grace. For that splendid moment of ecstasy, acceptance into the Chosen, wafting above the crowd of Chosen, she looked down upon them——and here's the ironic part—it caused her to feel superior. She had been Chosen. She was one them, no longer one of the deplorables of the Celestial Suburb. They were not chosen. And she heard Pride and Doting Dolly, her mom and dad, calling out to her, their voices so distant. She called out to them, "Mom! Dad!" and then regretted it so much. But it was too late. The crowd of Chosen had heard that plaintive cry, and they yelled out as one, "She's guilty! She's guilty!"

And suddenly all the lightness that had held her aloft disappeared, her balloon had popped and she fell to earth with a terrible plop.

She awoke to see the blur of faces staring down at her. Her fellow protesters had taken a moment to ask if she was all right. She had fallen off her bunk.

Anyone here called Grace? Your father has bailed you out!" called the jailer.

Other Fiction by Colin Heston

*Available from all bookstores around the world and digital platforms everywhere. **FREE on Read-Me.Org***

9/11 Two.

It's politics as usual when criminologist Maciver tries to thwart a terrorist drone tack on New York City Iranian terrorist Shalah Muhammad and his neurotic Russian American apprentice, Sarah Kohmsky, hire a Russian mafia boss, Uncle Sergey, and his evil nuclear scientist, Turgo, to hit Ground Zero on the anniversary of 9/11. Hearing of the plan from the CIA New York Mayor Ruth Newberg enlists Professor Larry Maciver, world renowned criminologist to thwart the attack. While the terrorists quietly orchestrate their attack, the drama unfolds as a battle between MacIver the careful scientist, and the impatient Buck Buick, Newark cop and former Marine bomb squad specialist. Will it be a drone, a missile, or a repeat of the 9/11 bombings? Das, Maciver's geeky assistant, thinks he has the answer. Can they save NYC or must it save itself?

The Tommie Felon Show and Other Outrageous Stories.

A collection of stories ranging from the absurd to the improbable, with a cynical twist. These stories will keep you guessing, their deeper meaning will haunt you forever. "...engaging, hilarious, unique... a commentary on human desires, shortcomings and the society we live in...vivid and real...some of the stories jump out pf the pages." "Almost as sarcastic and cynical as Kurt Vonnegut, Colin Heston is an author to watch out for, now and in the future. —*Readers' Favorite*).

Miscarriages

Teen Chooka grows up in the weird world of 1950s Aussie pub life. When his alcoholic dad dies, he searches for his identity, and that of his shadowy underage girlfriend, Iris. Captivated by the pub's many crazy customers and their raucous stories, Chooka becomes a boozer just like them. But Iris, after a miscarriage, disappears and Chooka sets out on a search that takes him to foreign places including Melbourne university and Vietnam. The search ends in a Melbourne pub, where they start over, but this time there's a different ending. "…a brilliant, unforgettable book about real people…a sensitive, touching and poignant story." —*Reader's Favorite.*

Ferry to Williamstown

In this raucous Aussie story, corpses pop up in the Yarra river while Lizzie entertains her powerful and kinky clients in her Winnebago, parked on the ferry to Williamstown. Tightly bound Detective Striker, confronted by the mob of Catholics, wharfies and communists who rule Williamstown, struggles to solve the mystery. Lizzie gets engaged to her uncle Bobby, the lame ferry driver, and her mum, Babs, spellbound by the strange Father Zappia, tries to solve her own mystery of St. Robert's toe. She throws a raucous send-off party for Lizzie, and out of the chaos emerge many truths. "…a gritty but comedic family drama …with many threads to unravel, Ferry To Williamstown will reward those who can untie its hilarious Gordian knot." —*Reader's Favorite.*

MONA and Other Twisted Stories

The opening story of MONA, inspired by the Museum of Old and New Art located in Hobart, Tasmania, sets the stage for this collection of short stories that adds an Australian flavor to Colin Heston's acclaimed *The Tommie Felon Show*. The stories range across many styles, prose poems, jottings that are almost aphorisms, classic stories of human emotion and the contradictions of human existence, dystopian themes and settings, all engaging, never dull. "Many of the stories appear straightforward, but their simplicity brilliantly reveals many truths about modern society—so-called—and the impossibility of human ambitions reflected in the societies they have created... one has to look beyond the words and the events in these stories to really appreciate them." —*Reader's Favorite.*

Fault Lines

A series of 29 short stories inspired by the vicissitudes of punishment in all its forms, its deliverers and recipients. Its universality across cultures and at every level of social life from the kitchen to the battlefield never ceases to amaze. The stories unveil the diverse motives and excuses for punishment that paradoxically form the foundation of that great shibboleth of humanity: justice. The stories range through childhood spats to military encounters, , family discourse and dysfunction, to the puzzle of how criminal justice manages to match a punishment to its respective crime (it can't). Taken together, the stories ask one seemingly silly question of human history: which came first, the crime or the punishment?

The Spy that Wasn't

In this collection of short stories, follow the exploits of supreme psychiatrist and criminologist Franco Ferrapotti as he weaves a web of intrigue in the labyrinths of the United Nations and the surreal world of Italian politics, big money, and of course, the Vatican. Other stories of high achievement explore the ancient origin of the animal species and gendered humans, the exciting zoo of enlightenment installed on the island that once housed Alcatraz, making it into the dream University of the Chosen, or if you prefer, getting elected the new Secretary General of the United Nations. But that's not all. Get a brief glimpse of the future where precision doctors edit who you are or who you want to be.

About the Author

Colin Heston is the pen name of a criminologist of international repute. His previous fiction includes *9/11 Two* (2016), *The Tommie Felon Show* (2017), *Miscarriages* (2018, 2019 Australian edition), F*erry to William-stown* (2020), and *Holy Water* (2022). His collections of short stories include *MONA* (2021), *Fault Lines* (2023) and *The Spy that Wasn't* (2023). Since 2021, he has published a new story every other Friday on the free library of open access publisher Read-Me.Org web site. In 2022 he also published a work of nonfiction, *The Art of Punishment,* in two volumes.

www.ingramcontent.com/pod-product-compliance
Lightning Source LLC
Chambersburg PA
CBHW021846010726
47493CB00005B/1582